Wonder Land

Volume 1: Black Ice

by Cain S. Latrani

Emery Press, LLC
Fort Lauderdale, FL
www.emerypressbooks.com

First Edition – March 2020
Copyright 2020 – Cain S. Latrani

ISBN (Trade): 978-0-9600505-2-9
ISBN (eBook): 978-0-9600505-3-6

Editing by Grammar Goddess Editing
Cover Design by Sweet 15 Designs

For Patricia

Contents

Chapter One: For Those About To Rock

TOWNGLEN. What a completely crap name for a place.

That was what Rick thought, anyway. It was what he had thought of his home town in general for a pretty long time. That it was a completely crap place. The sort of place where pretty much everyone knew everyone else, and had their heads shoved so far up each other's asses it was a wonder farts didn't pass through the whole community.

Actually, when he thought about it, he wasn't sure they didn't. It would explain a lot. Especially about old man Sarker. Odds were, the bastard was the tail end of the fart line. It was probably why he always had such a sour look on his face. Well, that, and he was an asshole.

Rick sighed, and watched the clouds pass by, reclining in the shade of a cherry tree, the only thing atop Wonder Hill. From there, he could see the entire stretch of Townglen, what there was of it. Most of the nearly three hundred people who lived there did so on farms that covered dozens, or hundreds, of acres.

Surprising how people so spread out could pass a fart along so efficiently. Not that he was surprised. Efficiency was the watchword of the town. If they had a flag, it would just have that word on it, and they would probably be efficient about making it.

A scowl found his face, rather against its own will, as he turned his eyes down to look across the rolling farmland. Cabbage and okra, as far as the eye could see. Those were the staples of Townglen, and the folk around there were damn proud of it. The annual Cabbage Festival in the summer was only matched by the annual Okra Festival in the winter, when pickled okra was traded, for reasons no one cared to remember.

Their parents, and grandparents, and great-grandparents had done it, so they did it, too. A complete lack of imagination, if you asked Rick, which no one ever did. Mostly because they didn't care. He was the odd lad, or so the rumors went. Too much like his father, with eyes always fixed on the horizon instead of on the cabbage patch at his feet.

Rick often wondered if that was true. *Was* he like his father? He could only take the rumors as his guide on that one. Max Wonder had died before Rick was born. The folk of Townglen had named a hill after him and planted a cherry tree, but past that, it was almost as if they would rather forget him. Why, Rick had never known.

According to his mom and Uncle Castor, Max Wonder had been a hero to the entire country of Liaob, of which Townglen was a tiny part. The stories Caster told him of their days as adventurers and the many times they had saved the entire nation had long fired Rick's imagination and stirred something in his soul.

His mother all but refused to speak of it, unless she had downed more than a few mugs of Granny Hen's so-called ale. More like kerosene if anyone wanted Rick's opinion, which has been established, no one did. He was a bit of an odd lad, after all.

Still, any time Delilah Wonder got a bit of that moonshine in her, even she would tell stories of the old days, when she, Max, and Castor had battled demons, dragons, and even more otherworldly monsters bent on domination and destruction. Tales of glory, honor, and justice. Tales of virtue.

Tales of his heroic father, who had fallen to a Lich while saving the world from an undead scourge. It had been Castor who had admitted that Max sacrificed himself to push the undead wizard into a portal beyond the realm of the world, giving his own life to save his unborn son.

Most people blew these stores off as too fantastical, but Rick knew they were true. He had seen the box of medals his mother kept on the top shelf of her closet. Awards from the Parliament of Liaob, for valor, heroism, and more. Nor was it just Liaob. Other nations had decorated his parents and uncle for their selfless service to the good of all.

Rick knew all the tales were true. Just as he knew that there, beyond the horizon, waited his own chance to walk in the footsteps of his father. To be the same kind of hero. To carry the name Wonder forward into the annals of history, as a champion of all that was right.

He just needed to get the hell out of farting Townglen long enough to do it.

Not that his mom would ever allow it. No child of Delilah Wonder was going to go running off to find adventure, heroism, and glory. Not while she was breathing. Given her current state, Rick could assume that by the time that stopped happening, he'd already be too old to even think of it. Delilah Wonder was nothing if not exceptionally healthy.

A little too much so for a woman in her mid-fifties, Rick thought. Not that anyone had asked, because, yes, no one cared. Especially not the various widowers around town. They just wanted Rick to shut up so they could court his mother.

Good luck with that. She was still capable enough with a dagger to send them all running for the hills, screaming for their own mothers. Something Rick himself was painfully aware of, after his last attempt to suggest he could just go look into one small adventure, then come right back home.

The knife Delilah had been peeling a potato with had found itself buried in the table in front of Rick in the blink of an eye, cutting his spoon in half before he even got the bite of cabbage stew to his mouth. He had never asked about it again after that, and had no plans to.

His mother was terrifying. In more ways than one.

So, Rick would find his way to Wonder Hill in the afternoon, once his chores were done, and daydream of things that would never be. Adventure, glory, fame, and immortality in the chronicles of heroism. The sort of stuff nobody cared about in a place like Townglen, his eternal prison.

Lost in thought, and a good bit of self-pity, Rick didn't even notice the shadow that fell over him, much less the boot that swung for his head. Even if he had, it was doubtful he could have evaded it. Not that boot, anyway. There was no one in Townglen capable of dodging an attack from *that* boot.

And so, *thunk*, into his head, went the boot.

"Lazy ass!"

Rick rolled in the grass, groaning in agony for a full minute, before the stars went away enough that he could sit up and throw a glare at Maari. Naturally, she deflected it with a wide grin, sending it off to parts unknown.

"Why the hell do you always gotta kick me in the damn head?" Rick yelled.

Maari leaned down, her grin getting wider. "Cause that's the one part of you that even you got no use for."

Rick flushed as her generous cleavage came into full view, then turned away quickly. "Whatever. Asshole."

Standing up again, Maari frowned, crossing her arms over her chest. "Is that any way to talk to your very best friend in the whole of the world, Richard William Wonder?"

"It's a way to talk to the girl who's been kicking me in the head for the last fifteen years," he snorted, still staring at anything but her.

"It's been more than fifteen," she snickered. "Pretty sure I kicked you in the head right after we were born."

Rick cut a dark glare over his shoulder. Maari lived to remind him they were born on the same day, and that she was out a full five minutes before him, making her older. He didn't know why that mattered, but apparently it did, at least to her.

"Whatever," he sulked, crossing his legs, and propping his chin in a palm to glare at the endless sea of okra and cabbage that lay in every farting direction.

Five minutes older that she was, Maari had always been the less mature of the two. Despite being now nineteen years old, the tall, curvy redhead with the sun-dappled freckles was as much a kid as she ever had been. First to climb a tree, first to dive into a pond, and first to throw a snowball in the winter. Maari Chambers was, and always had been, the living epitome of a tomboy.

A really hot tomboy, Rick's inner mom voice pointed out. He ignored that quickly. He hated his inner mom voice. It always said what his mom would say. Sometimes as she said it. It was like being embarrassed in stereo.

"You were thinking about that again, huh?"

Rick didn't have to look at her to know. The sound of her voice was enough. That tint of sadness that, as much as he tried not to, made him feel guilty. Like he was betraying some kind of promise to her.

"So what if I was," he pouted instead, like a totally mature man would.

Maari eased down into the grass by his side, folding her knees to her chest, and stared off at the horizon. The smile that always seemed to tease the edge of her lips was nowhere to be seen, making him feel even worse.

"I don't get it," she said after a long silence, resting her chin on her knees. "What's so great about out there, anyway?"

Rick knew he should try to explain it to her. He knew he should assure her that even if he left, he would always come home. He knew a thousand things he should do in that moment, all of them good and kind and wise.

Instead, he acted like a dick.

"You really *don't* get it," he said. "Out there is where I'm supposed to be. Like Dad. That's not something you could ever get."

Maari's eyes dipped, making Rick feel like the dick he - in all reality - was. "I guess it's not something somebody like me would understand, huh?"

While it seemed obvious that the correct course of action was to change tactics, Rick instead doubled down on dickishness. "Honestly, it just isn't. You belong in a backwoods place like this. I just don't."

Doubled down like a boss.

Maari's eyes, so vibrant and green, glimmered for a moment with tears she held back, making him realize that being a dick had been completely the wrong call to make. Before he could say anything, she punched him in the face, sending him sprawling in the grass. With that, she stood, and stalked away, leaving him alone to think on his poor life choices, and obvious inability to not be a dick.

"Crap," Rick sighed from the grass.

* * *

Twilight was descending by the time he got home, having stopped at the local healer to see if he could get something done about the black eye Maari had left him with. As usual, Kalie Henge had been too busy laughing at him to do much. Not that he was surprised. She'd known right away that he'd gotten the shiner from Maari, and as the two were cousins, he kind of hadn't been expecting much in the way of sympathy.

Some healing, maybe, but not sympathy. He'd left with neither, which he had to admit, was only fair. He had been a major dick to Maari, after all.

Regardless, he wasn't looking forward to his mom giving him shit about yet another black eye from his quote best friend unquote. Just because they'd been born on the same day, grown up essentially next door to each other, played together every day for the entire nineteen years of their lives, and had shared almost everything...

Rick stopped to thump his head against the front door of his house. There were idiots, and then there was Richard William Wonder. They'd need to invent a whole new word for him, as idiot didn't really cover it.

That said, he knew if he apologized, and really meant it, Maari would break out her trademark ear to ear grin, blow the whole thing off, and everything would go back to how it had always been. Mostly. For her, at least. He doubted he'd be able to forgive himself for talking to her like that. Not when she deserved so much better.

He thumped his head against the door again. It hurt a little this time. He figured he deserved that, so he did it a third time, just to try and drive the idea into his head that he should treat his friends better.

He only had the one, after all.

Rickwit. That was a good word for it. He was a total Rickwit.

He thumped his head against the door again, and sighed. Yeah, tomorrow he'd apologize. At the very least, it'd make Maari smile again, and that was more than worth it. Maybe, even, if she leaned over, he wouldn't look away so quickly. After all, it was pretty obvious she was trying to let him see. Maari was a lot of things, but stupid wasn't one of them. She knew just what she was doing, and he knew exactly why.

The door opened, sending him tumbling face first to the living room floor. Delilah, as agile as she had been in her adventuring days, sidestepped her falling son, and just watched as he face-planted into the hardwood. She could have caught him, something even he knew, but odds were, she'd already heard, and felt he deserved it.

"You had that coming," Delilah commented dryly as she stepped over him, confirming his theory.

He gave her a thumbs up. "Yup. Sure did. Thanks, Mom. You're the best."

"Making Maari cry like that," she harrumphed as she flopped back down on the couch and took a long drag off her cigar. "When you shoulda been banging the shit out of her. What the hell is wrong with you?"

Rick groaned. "Ya know, I think I'm just gonna stay here. Call me the new rug. Can't be a worse life than hearing you say shit like that."

"Language," Delilah chastised. "And no, you can't be a rug. You'll block the door too much. Now get your ass up and shut the fucking door."

"And here you are, criticizing my language," he muttered, pushing to his feet.

"I'm old, you're young, get over it," Delilah snorted as she dropped her feet on the coffee table and gave him a scathing look, followed by another snort. "Pansy."

Rick swung the door shut without looking at it. "As ever, you are a font of esteem building wisdom."

She arched an eyebrow, jabbing a finger towards his black eye. "Seriously, Rick. What the hell?"

"I don't know," he admitted as he moved to collapse into an easy chair. "I was just feeling kinda blue, and she said stuff that irritated me. It was dumb, and I'm going to apologize first thing tomorrow."

"Might wanna just fuck her instead," Delilah pointed out, jabbing her cigar at him. "I think that'd carry more weight than an 'I'm sorry'."

Rick tried to find something to say to that, and couldn't. Instead, he just sank deeper into the chair, offering up a humiliated sigh of, "Geeze, Mom."

"When I was your age," she started, prompting Rick to jump up quickly, waving her to stop.

"Please, don't tell me – Again! - about how much dick you got," he blurted.

Delilah blinked a few times in surprise. "You got some weird hang-ups, you know that? Most kids would die to have a parent who was so open and honest with them."

"They would die if they got it, that's for sure," he muttered as he slid past her and headed into the kitchen. "Not to obviously change the subject, but what's for dinner?"

"Ask Castor," she shrugged, sliding back into a more comfortable position. "He said he was gonna pick up some ribs from Portson and treat us."

"Think I'd rather go hungry," Rick gagged.

"Portson's ribs do suck some donkey dick, yeah," Delilah agreed, blowing out a trail of smoke. "Speaking of which, Maari's got great lips for giving blow jobs, ya know?"

Rick wondered how hard he'd have to bang his head against the cabinet to pass out. Pretty hard, he figured. At least enough to knock the door off the hinge. Maybe to break it in half. A small price to pay to no longer be part of this conversation.

"You pop a boner in there, son?"

"My apologies, cabinet-san," Rick whispered. "Even you cannot save me now."

Delilah leaned up, giving him a curious look. "You praying to the furniture again?"

"No," he told her with a pained smile. "Apologizing to it."

"Why?"

"I can't imagine."

"You're weird, you know that?"

"So I've been told."

Delilah settled back with a grunt, enjoying her cigar. Rick shook his head and crossed the kitchen to the cold keeper, knocked on it once, and opened the door. Inside, several shelves held the various staples any home needed, such as milk, eggs, bacon, ham, and a recliner with an ice pixie, who fluttered his wings to light them up, before turning the page on his newspaper.

Rick nodded a greeting. "Evening, Tuck," he added, grabbing the milk.

The pixie nodded a greeting of his own. "Heya, Rick," he replied. "Yer mom tryin' to talk ya into givin' Maari the old bedroom tango again?"

Rick took a moment. He needed more, but instead nodded. "Yeah. Pretty much."

"I feel for ya, kiddo, I really do," Tuck grunted. "No shame in bein' gay, ya know?"

"I'm not... why would you think that?"

Tuck gave him a hairy eyeball around the paper. "I've seen Maari."

"Great talking to you, Tuck," Rick said quickly. "Have a nice night."

The pixie ruffled the paper. "Don't go slammin' the door. Wife an' kids are asleep upstairs, ya know."

Rick eased the door shut without another word. Even the cold keeper pixie thought he should take advantage of his friendship with Maari to get in her pants. It was enough to make him wonder if treating her with respect was such an outlandish thing, after all.

The irony of that thought did not escape the rest of his thoughts.

"Hello again, cabinet-san," he muttered as he grabbed a glass and poured some milk. "I may be in need of your services after all."

"Stop talking to cabinets," Delilah called from the living room. "They ain't gonna wax your pole, kiddo."

"Mom, what the hell?" Rick all but begged.

Delilah burst into raucous laughter at his tone. Rick groaned, already knowing what had happened. Shaking his head in dismay, he headed back into the living room, where his mother was having some trouble with not falling off the couch. He waited.

And waited.

"You done?" he asked as she regained her composure.

"For now, yeah," she snickered, wiping tears from her eyes. "Damn, but you are easy. I never get tired of it, either."

"Real funny," he grumbled as he sat down in a chair. "Shouldn't you be imparting important life lessons to me or something, instead of pranking me?"

"Dunno," she shrugged. "You're the only kid I got. Figured I should practice parenting on you, so I can do a proper job with the next one."

Rick almost choked on his milk. "Next one?"

Delilah lost it again. Rick kind of hated his mother for a moment, but as he didn't want to spend any part of his life on a therapist's couch, decided not to dwell on that emotion too much. Emphasis on *too*. He would dwell on it a little, later on, when she was asleep, and couldn't hear him thinking it.

He was pretty sure she could do that.

"You're an asshole, mother dear," he snarled as he wiped milk off his shirt.

Delilah just grinned at him, cigar hanging out of her teeth. "It's called training, kiddo. Figure if I get you use to the real world, you'll be able to handle yourself after I kick the bucket."

"Like that's ever gonna happen," he deadpanned.

Delilah's smile turned bittersweet. "It happens to everybody, Rick."

And just like that, his dick counter went to two.

"Mom, I didn't mean..."

She waved it off, her smile turning softer. "I know. It's all good, kiddo. Forget about it."

The cold keeper door opened a crack, allowing Tuck's voice to drift into the living room. "Yer battin' a thousand out there, pal!"

Rick buried his face in his hands, and wondered if a person could actually die of shame. Sadly, it turned out that no, it was not possible. He kind of wanted to at that moment.

"He's got a point," Delilah agreed, nodding.

"Oh, for fuck's sake," Rick groaned.

"Hey, watch your language," Delilah admonished. "I didn't raise you to have no fucking gutter mouth, shithead."

"Perish the very thought," Rick whimpered.

* * *

An eternally long hour later, Castor shoved through the front door carting three boxes emblazoned with Portson's logo. Why Portson thought he needed brand management in an out of the way place like Townglen was anyone's guess. Regardless of that, the big red stamp of a pig eating ribs was pretty disturbing, if one considered it for very long.

Cannibalism. It's just wrong.

"Hey guys," Castor called as he kicked the door shut. "Who's ready to pig out?"

Rick groaned. Delilah rolled her eyes. Tuck shoved the door open to chime in that he was. Castor took all this with a shrug as he carted the boxes into the kitchen and set them on the table, then fell into a conversation with Tuck while Rick and Delilah pulled themselves up and wandered in to join them.

"Oh, hey, by the by, there, Castor," Tuck said with a snicker as Rick was pulling out a chair. "Ricky boy there done hurt both Maari and Dee-Dee's feelings today."

"What?" Castor exclaimed, giving his nephew an almost convincing look of shock.

"Told ya the kid was gay," the pixie said. "Save me some of them there ribs for the wife and kids, will ya, pal?"

"Yeah, sure," Castor replied absently, giving Rick a wounded look as he shook his head. "What'd you do to Maari this time?"

"Nothing, forget it," Rick tried to beg off.

"Musta been something for her to give you a shiner like that," his uncle pressed.

"Probably 'cause he didn't try to dick her," Delilah offered.

"Mom!"

"What?"

Castor sighed heavily. "Dee-dee, leave the kid alone, will you? Everyone is ready for sex in their own time. He just hasn't gotten to that point yet."

"Thank you!" Rick gave his uncle a look full of fervent praise as he grabbed a box.

"You know how much time he use to spend in the bathroom," Delilah snorted. "And how much toilet paper he ran me through, too. Don't gimme that 'not ready' shit."

"I think I'm gonna go eat in my room," Rick groaned.

Delilah gave him a withering glare. Rick sat back down. Castor ran a hand through his snow-white hair, scratched at his still black beard, then threw both hands up in the air as if to surrender to the insanity that was his family.

"Can we not talk about Maari for a bit," Rick pleaded. "I already said I'd make things right with her tomorrow."

Delilah started to say something, but paused, considered the pained look on her son's face, and relented. "Fine. But try not to fuck it up, okay? You know she's got it bad for you. Always has. I get that you aren't sure yet yourself, but at the very least, don't shit on her feelings, okay?"

"I won't," he agreed quickly. "I shouldn't have today. That was dumb, and wrong. I'm an idiot, and an ass. Don't worry, though. I got this. I know how to make her happy."

"Don't say dick, Dee-Dee," Castor warned as he fetched a beer from the cold keeper, passing a chunk of rib over to Tuck.

"I wasn't!" Delilah cried. "That's not the only thing I think about, you know."

Castor harrumphed at that. "Since when?"

"Watch it," she warned. "I can still kick your ass, old man."

"Old man?" he laughed. "I'm two years younger than you, big sister."

"Yeah, but my tits are still perky, while your dick barely works, so old man you are," she shot back.

"Oh, for the love of..." Rick whimpered.

"Only 'cause you got to the damn Jinn before I did," her brother grumbled as he eased down into a chair.

Delilah shrugged. "Not my fault he thought my tits should be perky till I die."

"Is so," Castor argued. "Cause you damn well flashed him."

"Worked," she pointed out with a great deal of smugness.

"Bah," Castor dismissed, waving the whole thing off. "Shut the hell up and eat your damn dinner. You're making Ricky blush again."

"Please, for the love of Imonya, leave me out of this," Rick pleaded.

"Whatever," Delilah muttered, snagging a box and pulling it over. "If Portson over-salted these again, I'm gonna kick your ass so hard, he'll feel it."

Castor shrugged. "Won't be getting' no cherry."

Several minutes passed in silence as they tried to figure out how to eat a meal as a family, something none of them had ever been overly good at. For that brief span of time, Rick thought he might get a reprieve from this day of terrible ideas biting him in the ass. Thankfully, Castor had him covered.

"So, Ricky boy, you talk to your mom here about what we discussed?"

Rick thumped his head against the table. This was it. This was how he would die. Murdered by his own mother as he tried to shield his Rickwit uncle from her unbridled wrath. He'd had a good run, though. Mostly. Sorta. Not really.

"Talk to me about what?" Delilah asked, looking from one to the other with considerable suspicion.

"Nothing," Rick tried to offer from his new place of refuge, face down on the table. "Ignore him. He's senile."

Seeing her son was going to keep his secrets, Delilah turned her attention on Castor. "Talk to me about what?"

Castor shoved a chunk of rib in his mouth and shrugged. This didn't seem to placate her. He'd kind of known it wouldn't, but had felt the attempt was worth trying. One could never know when they might get lucky, after all, and have an enraged demon lord attack or something.

Castor rethought that as he remembered Max and Delilah's wedding dinner, when an enraged demon lord had, in fact, attacked. It had not gone well for said demon lord, and somehow, he doubted he was going to fare much better now, considering the vein he saw starting to pulse in her forehead.

"Sorry, Ricky," Castor finally said. "I thought you'd already talked to her."

"Why would you think that?" Rick exclaimed, finally rising from the table to give his chastised uncle an incredulous glare. "I said I'd talk to her about when I felt it was a good time! Did you see my eye? Today was obviously not a good time!"

"Starting to get pissed over here," Delilah growled.

Castor gave a helpless shrug, and motioned for Rick to go ahead. Rick considered running for it, but knew that would be foolish. He wouldn't even make it to the front door before she'd bring him down. With a resigned sigh, he nodded, and accepted that the time had come.

It was time to break his mother's heart.

"Uncle Castor has been teaching me how to use Dad's swords."

Delilah said nothing. This went on for a very long time. Way longer than Rick had expected it to. Way, way longer. Long enough he was actively becoming afraid, as she just sat there, staring at him in anger and disappointment.

"Why?" she finally asked.

"Because," Castor started, only to be silenced as she raised a hand.

"Richard," she intoned, making a chill go down her son's spine. "Why would you do such a thing? I've made myself clear on a number of occasions. I do not want you to become an adventurer. I've already lost your father, and I am not about to lose you, as well. So, tell me, right now, why you would go behind my back on this."

From somewhere, Rick wasn't sure where, he found the courage to look her in the eye. It wasn't easy. When Delilah Wonder was angry, she had a very scary face. The kind of scary face that people only saw when it was the last thing they would ever see.

"Because I asked him to, so after my birthday next week I can go to Riscadil and become an adventurer, like Dad."

"Motherfucker!" Delilah exploded, shoving her chair back to stand so quickly, it clattered across the floor as her hands slammed on the table. "What the ever loving hell is wrong with you, Rick? What part of this is not clear? I said no, and that's how it's going to be. So long as you live under my roof..."

"But I won't be living under your roof if I go there," Rick snapped back. "I'll be twenty in five days, Mom. Twenty. Old enough to decide what I want to do with my own life. If you aren't okay with it, then I'm sorry, but this is what I want, and I'm doing it with or without your permission."

"So, what? Were you just gonna sneak off and leave me to wonder what had happened to you?" she bellowed.

Rick shook his head. "No, of course not. I was going to tell you before I left. I had wanted to today, but everything kind of went wrong, and I didn't think it was a good time..."

"Congratulations, shit for brains, you have managed to figure out that this was not a good fucking time," she roared. "Guess when else would be a bad time? Any fucking time!"

"Pretty sure you're gonna wake up Tuck's kids at this rate, Dee-dee," Castor put in, hoping to at least get her to lower her voice a little.

"Nah, it's good," Tuck offered. "They need to hear what happens when ya piss off the lady of the house."

"Thanks for that, Tuck," Castor groaned. "Super helpful."

"Mom," Rick said, as calmly as possible. "I get that you don't approve. I do. This is what I want, though. I had hoped you'd at least support me in that, if nothing else."

Delilah's jaw worked in outrage. "Castor, we need to talk, outside. Rick, stay your ass there, or so help me, your legs will be too broken to even think of going anywhere for the rest of your very short life."

"Yup, not a problem," he agreed as Castor withered and stood, already accepting his fate.

A moment later, the back door slammed. Not that it was going to help. Rick could hear every word of their very heated exchange. He felt a little bad for dragging his uncle into this, but not enough to get between them. He did value his life, after all.

"Your mom is super pissed," Tuck put in.

"Noticed, thanks," Rick moaned.

"She's kinda hot right now," the pixie added.

"Kill me," Rick begged, returning to his happy place, face down on the table.

* * *

"I know you're mad," Castor said as soon as the door slammed, hard enough, he noted, to shake the frame.

Delilah held up a finger, and wisely Castor stopped talking. "It's bad enough you went behind my back, but with Max's swords? Really, Castor? What the hell were you even thinking?"

"I was thinking that Ricky was bound and determined to do this," Castor replied, his tone dead serious, so much so Delilah took note and really listened. "Since he was a kid, all he wanted was to follow in his dad's footsteps. To be just like him, no matter what. He was always going to do this, Delilah, and nothing you or I said was ever going to stop him."

"Not training him would have stopped him," she argued.

Castor shook his head emphatically at that. "The hell it would. Just 'cause you blinded yourself to that, doesn't mean I didn't see it. Without any training, he'd have run off one day and gotten himself killed. With it, he stands some chance of living long enough to find out the truth about all that adventuring business."

As much as she hated it, Delilah could see his point. She did hate it, too. With every fiber of her being. Castor was right, though, and she could not deny that, which just pissed her off even more.

"So what then? I'm just supposed to sit here and let him go out there, face that shit, and do nothing?"

"Yeah, Delilah," Castor stated firmly, taking her by the shoulders. "That's what parents do when their kids grow up."

"Why the fuck do you gotta be so damn wise all the sudden," she grumbled.

"One of us had to be here, sis," he chuckled.

She shook her head, trying to find a way around it, and just couldn't. Castor was right. Rick was always going to go do this. No matter how hard she tried, she couldn't stop him. Everything in her screamed that she should. That she should do whatever it took, even if he hated her for it.

But...

"I wonder if this is how mom and dad felt," she sniffed, no longer able to hold back the tears.

"Probably," he admitted, a note of sorrow in his voice. "But we can do better than they did. Make sure Ricky always has a home to come back to. Pissed as you are, don't do what our folks did. Don't disown him for chasing what his heart tells him is right."

"Like I would ever," she blurted. "He's my son. He's my..."

Castor pulled her into a hug as she began to sob, already knowing what Rick was walking into, the world of horrors he would face. The walking nightmares, impossible choices, and soul-crushing despair that awaited him.

"He's your world," he whispered. "I know. He's mine, too."

"Damn you," she barked, wiping her eyes and shoving him away. "Damn you for all of this."

"Delilah, I had no other choice."

"Did you have to give him Max's swords?" she choked. "Those are all I have left of him, you bastard."

"Nah, they aren't," he pointed out with a soft smile. "You got Ricky. That's way better."

"Until he leaves, you mean, and takes everything Max left me," she whimpered.

Castor sighed. He'd known this was going to be hard for her. Just, maybe, not this hard. Delilah didn't like to show it, but she'd always had a soft side, buried under the foul language and crappy attitude. That was his favorite part of her, actually. How fiercely she would cling to the people she loved.

"You need to have more faith in him," he offered. "He's good, Delilah. As good as Max was at this age. He'll be okay. He'll see, and he'll come home."

"You think so?"

"I really do."

"If you're wrong," she said, rubbing her eyes with her sleeve. "I'm going to kill you."

Castor nodded. "Yeah, I figure."

"I could still break his legs."

Castor hung his head. "Please, don't do that."

"Fine," she sulked. "I was just saying. I could."

* * *

Rick still sat at the dining table when they returned, idly playing with his food. The ribs had gone cold, of course, not that anyone cared about that right now. They hadn't been very good to start with, so playing with them seemed the logical thing to do as he waited to find out just how dead he was.

He heard the cold keeper door close as his mother passed by, and silently cursed Tuck for the traitor he was. The little bastard had helped create this situation. The least he could do was stay for moral support or something. Probably too much to ask. Tuck liked having a home, after all.

He could see she'd been crying, too. Chalk up strike three for the Rickwit. He'd made his mom cry. Nothing else could possibly make him feel worse than that. Nothing she could say or do would make him feel smaller than he did in that moment, seeing that.

"Rick," Delilah said as she sat, folding her hands in front of her. "Your uncle and I have discussed this, and come to a decision."

He took note of how white her knuckles were, and kind of admired her ability to restrain herself. He could well imagine it wasn't easy. She had never been one for restraint. Of any kind. Especially verbal. Or physical. That he wasn't already unconscious was pretty amazing, really.

Seeing he wasn't going to say anything, Delilah continued begrudgingly. "Castor tells me that you've gotten pretty good with your father's dual sword technique. Of course, I want to see that for myself, but provided I'm satisfied, after your birthday I'll allow you to go."

Rick blinked, shook himself, and blinked again. "Wait. Seriously? You'll really let me?"

"*If* I think you can hold your own, yes," she said with a nod. "Which is a pretty big *if*, in my mind still. Otherwise, forget it, until you've had more training, and I think you can actually defend yourself."

Rick was already on his feet. "Yes! Yes! Yes! Thank you, Mom!"

The scowl that crawled across her face calmed him instantly, as she all but snarled, "Make no mistake, Richard, if I don't think you can take care of yourself, you aren't going anywhere until you can. I'm not going to go as easy on you as Castor, either."

It took him a moment to really process that, his mind and heart too overjoyed. When it did sink in, he felt the bottom drop out of his stomach. "Wait. Hold on. You mean, I have to defend myself against... you?"

Delilah nodded, very slowly, a nightmarish smile already in place.

"I'm so dead," he whimpered, slumping back down into his chair.

"Go easy on the kid, now, Dee-dee," Castor chastised. "He ain't got the whole lifetime of experience you do."

"Adventuring doesn't care about experience level," she snapped, sending Castor retreating almost under the table. "You never know what might happen during a mission. You could be dealing with a rebel Goblin faction one moment, then suddenly have a dragon descending on your head. What would you do if that happened?"

"Run like hell," Rick admitted. "Mom, I get it. There's a lot I'm not ready for. I'm not stupid. I've thought this through. I've got a plan."

"Really," she laughed, with no actual humor. "Tell me this plan, then."

"I'm gonna join up with the League," he said.

Delilah arched an eyebrow. "The Adventurers League?"

"Well, yeah," he offered cautiously. "I've read up on them, and they match adventurers to jobs that they can handle, as well as pair them with more skilled adventurers. It'll be perfectly safe, until I get some experience under my belt and I'm ready to take on stuff that's actually dangerous."

She chewed her lip for a moment. He had actually thought this out. Damn it. When did she raise a smart kid? She didn't remember raising a smart kid. She remembered raising a kid who thought if he jumped off the roof with a blanket tied around his neck, he could fly.

Okay, he'd been four, but still.

"All right," she agreed, nodding. "How much of your father's technique do you have down?"

Rick blew out a heavy breath as he thought about how to answer that. "I'm not very good with the whipping style yet, but as far as close quarters combat, I've beaten Castor in every practice session for the last year."

"I can beat Castor, so that doesn't impress me," she snorted.

"I'm right here, Dee-dee," her brother mumbled.

"Don't fucking care," she shot back. "This is my kid's life we're talking about here. Beating you isn't enough. You were great with a bow, but up close, you sucked."

"I didn't suck," he grumbled. "I was just in a party with you and Max. Anybody would look like they sucked with that standing next to them."

"He's got a point," Rick offered.

"You, shut up," she barked.

Rick sat back down instantly, and tried to be invisible.

"Okay, fine, here's what's gonna happen," she said after spending some time thinking on it, leaving the other two in a tense silence. "I'm gonna give you a crash course over the next week. Then, as I said, if I'm satisfied, you can go, on one condition."

"Which is?" Rick asked nervously.

"You get in over your head, you reach out to Neba and ask for her help."

Rick thought about that for a moment. It'd been a while since Neba had been around to visit, but he did remember her, more or less. Tall, Elf, haughty as shit, and one hell of a wizard. He'd always called her Aunt Neba, though, and she didn't seem to mind, so he guessed she'd be okay with him showing up on her doorstep begging for help.

Rick was an idiot, sometimes, but even he knew if he went asking for help, it'd be done in the form of begging.

"You got it," he agreed.

Delilah stared at him for a long time, her jaw working, but finally she held out a hand. Rick hesitated a moment then accepted it. He knew what she was doing, and how hard it was for her.

"We have a deal then," Delilah said, and with those words, Rick knew, she had given her most solemn word.

He couldn't help but smile.

* * *

The next morning, Rick woke in a great mood even though he'd barely slept. Not even in his wildest dreams had he imagined his mother would agree to let him go do the only thing he'd ever wanted. That she had still felt like a dream, enough so he had to pinch himself several times just to make sure he was really awake.

Thus, did Rick discover that pinching oneself kind of hurts and that he shouldn't do that. He decided someone should really put a stop to the rampage of the Rickwit before he actually did hurt himself.

Shaking that off, Rick got his head together and remembered that his crash course training with his mom started that afternoon, once his chores were done. First, however, was a more important matter. One he had already promised to take care of and now, more than ever, he wanted to tackle the right way.

He had to apologize to Maari and tell her the news. The second part of that put a real damper on his mood. She wasn't going to be okay with it, he knew. Like Delilah had said, Maari had been crushing on him for as long as he could remember. Him telling her he was going away wasn't the sort of thing she was going to be happy about.

He paused to stare at himself in the mirror, wondering why he'd kept his heart so closed off to her all these years. Sure, there was the whole thing about him going off to become an adventurer and everything, but there had to be more to it than that. Maari was amazing, after all, and any guy would be happy to have her as their girlfriend.

So, what was the deal, really?

When he thought about it honestly, Rick found it wasn't that difficult to understand. He guessed he'd always known, really. He just hadn't ever considered it because he'd always thought there'd be plenty of time to deal with it. Now, though, there was a week, and he'd be off to Riscadil. That changed everything.

It wasn't that he didn't care for her. In every way that counted, he loved her. It was that he didn't feel worthy of her. Maari was more than amazing. She was as close to perfect as a person could get. He needed to feel like he was good enough for her, and until he had at least tried to chase his dream, he knew he really didn't.

Anything they had would always be tinged with that regret he would hold if he didn't do this. She didn't deserve that. She deserved someone who was completely there for her. It really wasn't that hard to understand at all when he let himself be honest with himself.

"So I guess I should tell her that, too," he said to the mirror, and immediately began looking for reasons to avoid her for the next week so he didn't have to. Cause that's what a Rickwit would do, dammit.

"No," he told his reflection. "From here on, we're doing everything the right way and that's that. First, apologize to Maari. Second, tell her the news. Third, tell her she's beautiful, amazing, perfect, and that I lurv..."

Okay. This was gonna be hard. Yup.

Shaking his head, Rick headed downstairs, grabbed some breakfast under his mother's scathing eye, and hurried out to catch Maari before she headed out to work. Some things, he suddenly found, really just couldn't wait.

Maari. Just thinking of her made him feel stupid. Besides being the living definition of a tomboy, and thus, way hotter than any girl had a right to be, was the fact that her quarter Orc blood made her taller, stronger, and faster than even Rick could hope to be as an average human. Topping out at six foot two barefoot, Maari had gotten all the benefits of Hondo, her Half Orc father, with none of the drawbacks, like tusks. She'd also gotten her mom's looks, and except for Delilah, Tabitha was widely considered to be the most beautiful woman in Townglen.

At least until Maari had turned sixteen. After that, even Tabitha would readily admit her daughter outshone her in the looks department. Not that looks were all that mattered. Of course they didn't. It just... didn't hurt any, right?

Stop being a Rickwit, he chastised himself as he darted down the narrow foot path between his house, and Maari's, a quarter mile away. Maari was smart, talented, funny, capable, strong, and best of all, fun to be around. Despite her avid dislike of Rick's own desire to be an adventurer, she had always been up for having adventures of her own, be it skinny dipping in Cathman's pond in broad daylight, or chasing off a pack of wolves from Widow Humber's sheep, armed with nothing but a few rocks and her nerve.

She just happened to be insanely hot as well. Who was he to complain that she was the total package? Nobody, that's who.

It occurred to Rick he'd just considered himself a nobody, but he was comfortable enough with himself to set that aside and focus on the task at hand. Very mature of him, if he said so himself.

Best not to dwell on it. That way lay madness.

As it turned out, ahead lay madness as well. Madness was just lying about everywhere, it seemed.

It was typical, during all but winter, for Maari to bound about town in a pair of shorts, heavy boots, and some variety of low cut or otherwise almost revealing top. Peasant blouses, tank tops, and camisoles seemed to dominate her wardrobe. While anyone who didn't know her might be given pause to stare at the tall, voluptuous woman and the generous amount of skin she was showing, those who had known her all her life were just so use to it, they didn't tend to bat an eye.

It was just Maari, being Maari, after all. Not something worth noticing.

Spotting the young woman in a dress was as rare as snow in summer. It just didn't happen. There were too many things you couldn't do in a dress that Maari was going to do, no matter what she was wearing. Very early on, Tabitha and Hondo had gotten use to the idea that their daughter wasn't going to be the dress wearing kind of girl, and had stopped buying them for her. Enough of them had ended up as rags to make them give up on that idea.

As she had gotten older, her own taste had drawn her into the current fashion choice she sported, if it could be called fashion. Rick kind of didn't think it could, but honestly had never spent much time pondering it. It was, again, just Maari being Maari.

As he pushed past the last of the low-hanging tree branches that would put him in the front yard of her family home, however, he pulled up short, his breath caught in his throat, as he felt his resolve pretty much vanish. Solely because standing there on the front steps of her house, was Maari, in a dress.

A pale blue number with thin shoulder straps, it draped her body in a way so familiar it would have made a normal man jealous of it. Stopping short a good two inches above her knee, the flowing skirt billowed in the morning breeze as she pushed her hair back out of her eyes, looking at Rick in surprise.

For his part, he was suddenly light-headed due to all his blood going elsewhere.

"Uh... Maari..." he started, taking a step forward.

A smile broke across her face. "Heya, Rick."

"That's a nice... uh... I mean... you look... different... in a good way... I think... no... yeah... that's pretty... on you..."

"Sweep me off my feet, why don't you," she deadpanned.

Rick slumped. "You look really great."

"Gettin' there, ace," she retorted, looking almost slightly impressed.

Shaking his head, Rick laughed, at himself mostly, but also at the sarcastic tone of her voice. "Cut me some slack, will you. It's not every day I see you in a dress. You really do make it look great."

Maari's smile softened as her cheeks flushed. "Much better."

"I'm slow, you know that," he admitted as he walked over to her while she clutched her hands behind her back, looking somewhat nervous for reasons he couldn't even begin to wonder about. "Sometimes, I'm stupid, too."

She gave a slight shrug. "It makes you kind of adorable, so I'm okay with it."

Rick paused, giving her a wary look. "Not sure if that was a compliment or not."

"Something to wonder about, Mr. Wonder" she breezed.

Another laugh escaped him. Yeah. She really was perfect.

"Hey, so, if you have a minute or two, I was hoping I could talk to you."

Maari started a bit at the sudden turn of his tone to serious. It wasn't just that, either, it was everything. The way he looked at her, she could tell he had something big to say, and for a minute, her heart all but stopped.

"Sure," she managed, barely daring to hope that he was finally ready to say what they both knew. "We were just heading to temple for some stuff, but I got a bit."

"Richard," Hondo rumbled.

"Crap," Rick whimpered as the Half-Orc grabbed him by the shoulder and lifted him off the ground.

"Care to explain why my daughter came home yesterday crying?" the over-protective-father-of-the-year award winner for nineteen years straight growled.

"Oh, for Imonya's sake," Maari sighed.

"Uh, hi there, sir. You look super fit today. Been working out?" Rick didn't bother to squirm. It would do no good. Hondo was a beast of a man.

"Every day." The Half-Orc flexed very impressively. "Don't try to change the subject."

Rick wilted. "Sorry."

"Daddy, put him down," Maari demanded.

"In a minute, cupcake," Hondo told her with an overly sweet smile that just looked wrong around his tusks, then gave Rick a slight shake. "We need to have some man talk right now, okay?"

"Man talk?" Rick and Maari both echoed in confusion.

"Why did you make my princess cry, Richard?" Hondo all but sobbed, flailing Rick around like a rag doll. "How could you ever want to see tears in those beautiful eyes? What's wrong with you, boy? Women are to be treated as valuable treasures, protected and kept safe! Why can't you be more of a man?"

"Honey, stop that," Tabitha said as she exited the house.

Rick bounced off the yard to a sharp, "Yes, dear!"

"I think I may be dead," Rick whimpered.

"Not yet," Tabitha chuckled, then turned a dark glare on him. "Make Maari cry again, though..."

"Dead might be better," he sobbed.

"Both of you, knock it the hell off," Maari shouted, stomping a foot.

"But, cupcake," Hondo started, only to get a hand to his face from his daughter.

"Stop it, right now," she snarled. "I will deal with Rick. You two go ahead. I'll be there after he and I are done talking. Got it?"

Her parents sagged, but nodded all the same. "Yes, sweetheart."

"Love you, Daddy," Maari said with a grin. "Love you, Mommy."

With that, Maari snatched Rick up, threw him over her shoulder, and fled her parents so she could have what she hoped was the most important conversation of her life with him.

The irony of his current situation was not lost on Rick, but the view of Maari's butt was worth it, so he just went along with it.

Not that he actually had a choice.

* * *

Ten minutes later, Rick was sitting on a rock by Cathman's pond, the morning sun glittering off the water as Maari took a couple steps back, seeming to be aware rather suddenly of how she had carried him. Flustered by it, she fidgeted for a moment, pushed a lock of hair from eyes that had grown timid, and folded her hands behind her back, watching him in uncertainty.

"That was... uh..." he stammered.

Maari flinched. "Embarrassing, I know. I'm sorry."

"Oh, uh, no, I was gonna say awesome," Rick laughed. "That was awesome. You're awesome. Seriously."

Maari blushed, a soft smile touching her lips. "You don't have to say that. You can tell me the truth, Rick. I do get it. I'm not very feminine most of the time. I'm sorry about that. I try, but..."

Rick jumped to his feet. "What are you talking about? I mean, seriously, look at yourself! You're gorgeous! The most beautiful woman in the whole town. Probably the whole world!"

"Rick," she started, thrown by the sudden declaration.

"No, I mean it, Maari," he shouted. "Right now, really look at yourself! You are so beautiful, it makes me feel like I don't have a right to even look at you! Like I'm not worthy of you! Because I'm not! I'm not good enough for you. I know that. I've always known that. You were always there, right by my side while I was always looking off at the horizon, wanting to be anywhere else. That wasn't because *you* aren't good enough. It's because *I'm* not."

"I... don't..." she stammered, unprepared for the things he was saying. Things she had always wanted to hear, but now felt so sudden. Her heart ached, even as her stomach tied itself in a knot, filling her with terrible hope.

"Maari, the truth is, I do love you. I've always loved you. There's no other girl in the world I could ever want, because you're right there. My best friend. How could you not be good enough for someone like me? If anything, you're too good for me, and I know it. That's why I never said it. Why I always acted like I didn't know, and didn't feel the same. Because I'm not good enough for you, and I never will be as long as I have my eye on that horizon."

Having started, Rick found he couldn't stop. Almost twenty years of keeping it inside was too much. The words needed out. Staring into her shock-widened eyes, every bit it of came gushing forth.

"I thought, if I went, and if I did it, then maybe I'd feel different. If I could just go, and be like my Dad, even a little bit, then that feeling might go away. Maybe if I proved myself good enough for you, then I'd actually feel like I was. If I didn't, though, I was afraid that would always be there, between us. That regret that I didn't. You don't deserve that. I can't make you carry that. It's not right."

Maari blinked several times as Rick trailed off, keeping her tears in check, and smiled at him. Finally. He had finally said it. She had waited so long to hear him admit it all. She'd known, of course. It wasn't like he was deep. Still, finally, he'd said all the things she had always wanted to hear.

"You are such a fucking idiot," she groaned.

Rick gaped. "That's not... exactly..."

"I mean, give me a break here, will you?" she shouted. "I'm not perfect, you know. I snore. Really loud. So loud, I wake myself up sometimes. That's not all, either! My farts can clear a room! Ask my dad! Even he can't take them! I'm not some damn doll, Rick! I don't need you to be good enough for me. I just need you to want to be with me, dammit!"

They stared at each other for a long moment, Rick in surprise, Maari in anger. Rick's expression slowly shifted to humor, as hers slowly turned to embarrassment.

"Farts, huh?" Rick snickered.

"Shut the hell up, dipshit," she roared, turning her back to him to hide how red her face had turned. She hadn't meant to say all that. She'd had in mind, for years, what to say when he finally told her all those things. Instead, she'd bragged about her farts. What the hell?

Rick collapsed back down on the rock, laughing. "Snores and farts. So that's what you've been hiding from me. Oh, man, that's great!"

"Better than you wanting to run off and fight monsters," she snorted. "I mean, honestly. Trying to leave me behind, without ever even asking if I'd go with you. How big of an idiot can you be, Rick? You want to have adventures? Fine! I'm fine with that! I just want to go with you, you giant, colossal, impossible idiot!"

"But, Maari," he said with a grin, not even knowing he needed to hear her say that until she had. "You'd get your pretty dress all dirty if you did that."

Maari spun back around. "Yeah, well, idiot isn't a good enough word for you!"

"I know," he said, smiling up at her. "I tend to go with Rickwit."

Maari's anger faded in an instant. "Rickwit? Oh, hey, I like that. That's good. You *are* a Rickwit, too!"

Both of them burst into laughter, and after a few moments, when it had passed, Rick stood, and took her by the hands, looking up into her eyes, not even caring she was five inches taller than him. Nothing else mattered, but that smile on her face.

The most beautiful smile in the world.

"Maari, you look so beautiful right now. It's not even the dress. It's just you. When you smile, the whole world lights up, and so does my heart. I love you."

Maari struggled for words. None came.

"Uncle Castor convinced Mom to let me go to Riscadil, and apply for the League. I leave right after my birthday. Knowing you'd go with me, it makes me so happy, but please, let me do this on my own. Not to prove myself to you. I see now that was dumb. That I'm dumb. I need to do this for myself."

Her smile faded, like the sun dipping below the horizon at twilight. "You don't want me to go with you?"

He shook his head. "It's not that. Nothing would make me happier. It's something else, that's probably stupid, too, but I hope you'll understand."

"What?"

"I've never had to stand on my own two feet, Maari. I've always had Mom, and Uncle Castor, and you there to hold me up. I want to know I can take care of myself. Once I know that, I'll come back, and we can take care of each other, be it here or out there in the world. I get that's kind of dumb, but I hope you can understand it."

Maari sniffed, and wrapped him in a hug. "Yeah, I get it. You really are a Rickwit, though. Why wait for us to take care of each other?"

"Cause, you're stronger than me," he reminded her, folding his arms around her waist, and savoring the feel of her against him. So warm, so perfect. "I just want to be strong enough for you, too."

"That is dumb," she agreed. "But I get it. I don't like it, but I guess I get it."

"Really?"

Maari laughed. "Not at all. That really is just stupid."

"Yeah, I know," he said, holding her tighter. "I'm sorry."

"Forget it. Just come back soon, okay? I'll wait for you. I promise I will. Come back the man you want to be, okay?"

"I swear it."

They stayed like that for some time, just holding each other, believing that, finally, their paths were coming together. Both knew joy and hope at that thought. Nothing could possibly fulfill either of them more than believing they would be together.

"I'm sorry I made you cry yesterday," Rick added.

"You should be," Maari accepted.

"I did all that backwards from how I planned."

"You're such a Rickwit."

"Yeah, I know."

"Wanna see what I'm wearing under this dress?"

"Uh... I mean... kinda... yes... hell, yes."

"Good," Maari whispered as she shoved him down into the grass.

* * *

The next few days flew by for Rick. Mornings spent doing his chores, followed by afternoons training with his mother, and evenings with Maari, as she nursed his bruised body and ego. One of those things was way better than the others, and there were fleeting moments Rick wondered if giving up on this dream would be worth it.

Except, things were different now. When he looked to the horizon, Maari looked there with him. For so long he had thought she wouldn't understand. So much time wasted. Of course she understood. He'd been a fool to think otherwise. It should have been obvious from the very beginning that she would get it.

She was Maari after all. No one understood him better.

At last, their shared birthday arrived, and as always, Delilah and Tabitha busied themselves with preparations while Castor and Hondo tried very hard to help without getting in the way. They failed at this on an annual basis, but it was always amusing to watch.

Unlike his previous birthdays, this time Rick had a knot in his gut. Delilah had told him a couple days prior that she would let him know on his birthday if she felt he was able to take care of himself. If she gave him a gift, he wasn't. If she didn't, then letting him go would be her gift that year. It was enough to drive Rick mad as the morning turned to afternoon, and the actual party was still hours away.

It didn't help that Delilah had a great poker face. Whatever she was thinking, he couldn't make heads or tails of it. As the living room was transformed into birthday central, Rick would wander through and try to read her mood, but always left with nothing, her ability to be inscrutable dialed to about a million.

He tried prodding Castor, but his uncle was no fool and fled anytime Rick got too close.

Maari knew about as much as Rick and was in no hurry to help, somewhat enjoying his sense of torment. He found that made her really hot, which also made him wonder what that said about him.

Either something terrible or something awesome. He decided to go with awesome. After getting his ass kicked for four days straight by his borderline senior citizen mother, he needed the ego boost.

He felt that only fair. She'd thrown a dagger at his face. As in, an actual dagger, at his actual face. Testing his reflexes, she had called it. His ability to deflect an incoming ranged attack. He'd called it terrifying. He had deflected it, of course, as Castor had taught him, but still. An actual dagger, at his actual face.

There was tough love, then there was whatever Delilah Wonder practiced. He'd settled on Wonderlove, because it made him wonder if she loved him.

That aside, he felt good about things. His training with Delilah had gone better than he'd expected. Castor had done a far more solid job of preparing him than he imagined his mother would ever admit, and for the most part he found he was able to defend himself from lethal blows. His arms and legs had taken a pounding from the heavy wooden practice sword she'd used, but none of his vital parts had ever been hit.

Of course, that was when she'd decided to go with the actual dagger to the actual face part of training, so doing well under Delilah's tutelage came at a price, it would seem. Maari had rewarded him for not getting stabbed in the face though, so he was going to call that one even when he thought about it.

Still, even with that, he found himself wondering if he was as ready as he hoped. While he'd gotten pretty good with his father's twin scimitar style, there was one part of it he was still struggling with. A part that he knew he would need to master if he was going to ever really live up to the legend of Max Wonder.

The blades themselves were only mildly enchanted to make them far more durable and sharper than any ordinary swords would be. Not really anything that special, or unusual, Castor had assured him. The two main points that the blades had in their favor was the secondary enchantment that made it unnecessary to ever have them sharpened. No matter what happened, or what they struck up against, the business end of them would stay razor sharp, forever.

Again, not uncommon, but extremely useful. It was the other thing they could do that Rick was having a hard time with. The whip aspect, from which the scimitars drew their name. The Whip Blades.

Not overly original, but whatever.

With a thought, the blades could segment, joined together by a microfiber as durable as the swords themselves, allowing him, or rather, his dad, to use them as whips, which the name sort of implied. It gave more reach, and according to Castor, came in pretty damn handy for all sorts of situations.

Naturally, Rick couldn't get them to segment. He knew the command, but they just didn't respond. Why, he didn't know. On a really rare occasions, one would start to, then collapse back into sword form. No matter how much he focused, that aspect of the Whip Blades eluded him. Which, he already knew, his mother had noticed and no doubt held as a mark against him.

All of that aside, the fact he had managed to more or less hold his own against her made him think he was going to get a pass. If he didn't, he knew he'd just have to train harder, master the Whip Blades, and prove himself. Once Delilah made a deal, she kept it, and if not today, then one day very soon Rick was going to be ready to strike out, find adventure, and follow in the footsteps of his father.

He just had to not get a dagger to the face first. No problem.

If he was to admit to a doubt, which he was loathe to do, it would be how far from home he was actually going to be. As his birthday had drawn ever closer, he found, somewhat suddenly, that there was comfort in the sleepy little town he had always known. As much as everything about it irritated him, there was familiarity to it all.

He knew every step, and every stone. He knew exactly how long it took him to go anywhere. He knew every person, every house, and every animal, be it pet or livestock. He knew where he was going to eat, and where he was going to sleep. He knew everything about it, and in that knowing, there was a sense of safety he realized he had always taken for granted.

Riscadil was no tiny farming community. It was one of the biggest cities in the entire country of Liaob. Situated where the Keening Straight met with the Kienrin Sea, it was the center for trade and commerce on the west coast of Liaob. Ships, both by water and air, came and went from all over the world, and the culture of Riscadil was a melting pot of races, religions, and attitudes.

It was a little daunting to think about. To be lost in the bustle of such a place, knowing nothing and no one. As much as it thrilled him, it also frightened him. He really, truly was giving up everything he knew for this and that, above all, was a sobering thought.

Before he knew it, lost to his thoughts as he was, Castor was calling him. It was time. He and Maari's party was ready to start, and with it, his future would be decided.

* * *

Rick sat on the couch, thoughts of adventure, home, family, and everything else that had plagued him far from his mind. It was a bit surprising how little it took to make that happen. Or, it would have been, had he been able to think about it. He wasn't. All he could think about was how badly he didn't want to stare at Maari's chest in front of his family, her family, and everyone else who was there.

All because Tuck and his family just had to sit on the back of the couch. Stupid ice pixies.

There was cake – chocolate, Rick's favorite, with Maari's favorite butter cream frosting. There were balloons. There were streamers. The radio was tuned to that station that played all the modern music, even though Delilah hated it. Half the town was either there, had already stopped by, or was on their way. There were two piles of presents, several of them rather large.

Rick saw none of it. All he saw, all he knew, was that Maari was sitting next to him in that blue dress and wasn't wearing a bra. Or anything else under it. Her gift, to be unwrapped later, she had said.

Of course Tuck's whole family had to sit on the back of the couch. Why wouldn't they?

Rick found he kind of hated ice pixies. They were dicks.

Birthday wishes flowed like water before the cake was finally served along with ice cream, which was Tuck and his family's gift. It was painfully good, so Rick somewhat forgave them for sitting on the back of the couch. Not entirely, but a little.

Then came the giving of gifts. From the members of the small community who weren't terribly close to them, they got the traditional gifts of pickled okra and cabbage, and as they did every year, smiled and thanked them for it. With that out of the way, the presents from the folks who were closer started coming, and Rick was finally able to focus on something other than Maari's chest.

Granny Hen gifted Maari with a set of pink hair clips, each sporting a different flower, despite Maari having never used hair clips in her life. For Rick, a pair of work gloves that were durable, but still allowed him good movement. Both smiled and thanked her before she tottered off, already half-drunk from her own moonshine.

Cathman, not as drunk or disconnected, gave Rick a good pair of boots, sturdy and built to last for a good few years. For Maari, a pair of pants, the meaning of which was lost on no one except Maari. Good old Cathman. Still a fair bit disconnected, but at least better than Granny Hen.

Portson, thankfully, did not give them ribs, for which they were eternally grateful. To Maari, he gave a new outfit, mail ordered from a shop in Riscadil that consisted of a tank top and denim shorts. To Rick, he just gave money, a good hundred lita. Rick re-gifted him with a fair amount of side eye over Maari's gift, but said nothing.

From Widow Humber, Maari got a giant ass war-hammer. Rick wasn't sure what to make of that, but according to the kind old lady, it was for fending off wolves from the local livestock. Maari was beyond thrilled, which was great. Rick got a pair of pants made of heavy leather. He felt Widow Humber may have gotten the two of them confused at some point.

More gifts followed from other close friends of the family. Clothes, money, and other items were showered on the two, and generous thanks were returned. Eventually, the guests began to filter out, leaving the two families to give their gifts privately, for which both Rick and Maari were grateful. As much as they appreciated the well wishes and presents, the quiet that followed, alone with their parents, put them more at ease.

Well, Maari anyway. Rick's nerves cranked up as the last of the guests departed. Thankfully, Tuck sent the kids to bed, raising the temperature in the room considerably. It wasn't much, but he appreciated it. He doubted he could take much more tension than he already felt.

Naturally, Delilah decided to draw things out by giving Maari her presents first. Rick shot her an annoyed look, but she was too busy fussing over Maari to pay him any mind. For a moment, he was torn between being irritated and being jealous. He kind of wanted to fuss over Maari himself, but also wanted to know what his mother had decided.

In the end, it was too much trouble to stress over and he settled back to wait. She was five minutes older, and this was how it had always gone. Gifts from Delilah, Castor, Hondo, and Tabitha were given, mostly new clothes, but Castor had been thoughtful enough to give her a nice necklace, which Maari made a big deal about, leaving Castor with a wide grin.

With Maari's moment in the spotlight over, they turned to Rick, who calmed himself the best he could. To his surprise, however, only a single present was placed on the coffee table. A large box, well-wrapped, set before him by them all, as a single gift. He hesitated at this, unsure what to make of it.

Exhausted from playing hostess all night, Delilah collapsed into an easy chair, waving at him. "Ain't nobody here getting any younger, dipshit. Open the damn thing so we can go to bed, and you can do Maari."

"Delilah," Tabitha chastised, giving Hondo a quick look.

"What?" the Half Orc asked, glancing about, perplexed by the snickers that floated from the adults, and the looks of embarrassment shared by the kids.

"Ignore her, bud," Castor offered quickly. "She's an asshole. Always has been."

"Bite me," Delilah shot back.

"I think the quicker you open it, the quicker they'll stop talking," Maari suggested, nudging Rick to hurry the hell up, before her dad figured anything out.

Rick nodded and grabbed the gift, not wanting Hondo to pick up on the fact his daughter wasn't as pure and innocent as he thought. Odds were, Rick wouldn't survive the realization. As he lifted the box, it hit him. He was probably going to be around to face that, as his mother had given him a present.

A surge of disappointment ran through him as he set the gift in his lap, staring at it. So, she didn't think he was ready. That was that, then. His dream would have to be put on hold, possibly for some time. It stung, more than a little, to come so close and still have it all be so far away.

Still, he smiled as he untied the bow. They had gone through a lot of trouble, and as much as his heart ached at the moment, he wasn't about to show it. Not today. Not when they were all smiling at him as he lifted the lid and looked down at what they had, as a family, given him.

What he found sent him into a spiral of confusion.

A soft, studded leather tunic with a high collar and a hardened chest cover rested within. Nestled behind it, two scabbards and a belt, designed to allow easy access from the hips. He stared at it for a full minute, trying to process it, before glancing over at the leather pants Widow Humber had given him, and noting they were of the same style and color. As were the gloves from Granny Hen, and the boots from Cathman.

"I don't..." he tried to say, shaking his head in confusion.

"You pass," Delilah said, all humor gone from her eyes. Instead, there was only sadness, but pride as well. "There's a train ticket to Riscadil under the armor, and the money from Portson and the rest will keep you fed and in a bed until you get there. A bit longer if you aren't stupid with it."

Rick looked around at them. Hondo and Tabitha watched him, she with a hint of tears in her eyes, and he with a soft smile that failed to hide his concern. Castor simply sat, looking so much older than he should, but also very proud. Maari smiled, but there was fear in her eyes as well.

"I passed?"

"You did, kiddo," Delilah said in a pained tone. "I hate it, I won't lie. I didn't want you to. I wanted you to suck. You don't. Castor was right, and that hurts me to say more than anything. You are as good as your dad was at this age."

"Wait," Rick said slowly, looking at them each again. "I actually passed?"

"Geeze, you're dense," Maari groaned.

With that, it all hit him. He had passed. His mother thought he was capable. He was going to Riscadil. It was all really happening. Everything he had dreamed of, all of it, was within his grasp.

Rick shot to his feet, fists in the air, sending his gift tumbling out onto the floor, shouting, "I passed!"

"Good for you, numbnuts, now go try the damn armor on so I can see if it needs any adjustments," Delilah snorted. "I'm not about to send my idiot brat off to Riscadil looking like the complete shithead he is."

"Oh, right," Rick goobered, before gathering the whole thing up and running to his room.

"How long do you think it'll be before he realizes he's gonna need help," Maari wondered.

"Give it a minute," Delilah chuckled. "He ain't real bright."

Rick ran back in, grabbed Maari by the hand, and hauled her back to his room.

"Getting smarter, though," Castor commented.

"Both of them are," Tabitha agreed, looking rather pleased.

"Why's he need her help?" Hondo asked.

No one thought it wise to answer that question.

* * *

It took a few days after his birthday, as the armor needed some adjustment and Delilah refused to allow him to leave until he could pull the Whip Blades from their new scabbards in a single, fluid motion, but Rick was fine with that. The ticket to Riscadil sat on his dresser waiting for him, and any delay now was just a triviality.

Between practice and waiting for his mother to make the needed adjustments, he spent time with Maari, the two discussing the future they hoped to share. It was more daydreams than anything, but it made them feel better about being apart. As if it wasn't going to be that far or that much time, when they both feared it would be.

Finally the day came. Rick woke early and shared a last breakfast with Castor and his mother before meeting up with Maari, and the group began the two-hour trip to Nathan's Hollow, another small town on the trade road heading north, where the only local train station was to be found.

Tabitha and Hondo, as well as many of the townsfolk Rick had known his whole life, gathered to wish him well, though he could tell they were worried for him. He tried to assure them he'd be fine, but all knew the stories of young adventures left in unmarked graves. All he could do, in the end, was smile, and promise to see them all again soon.

The trip to Nathan's Hollow was filled with advice from his mother and uncle, much of it centering around letting the people with the proper skill sets do their job, and not to touch any strangely placed treasure chests he might find. Something about shapeshifting monsters that could look like furniture. He filed that away, but still found it pretty far-fetched.

Rick knew his place in things. He was a fighter. His job was to take down enemies, and protect his party members. Just like his dad had done. It was a pretty straight forward job, no matter how you looked at it. All that was left, in his mind, was to register with the League, meet his new party members, and kick some ass.

With his gear stowed in a duffel bag over his shoulder, he smiled the whole way there, oblivious to the growing looks of fear and doubt on the faces of his mother and uncle, and the steadily increasing sense of sadness that settled over Maari like a cloud. All he could see was the bright future that awaited him.

After arriving at the small station, they headed over to the wide wooden platform to await the train. It was the longest thirty minutes of his life, spent sitting on the bench, his leg twitching, as Maari extracted promise after promise from him to write often and come home whenever he had the time.

At one point, as he sat, staring down the tracks, too nervous to even really notice how low cut Maari's top was, Castor wandered over with two cups of tea, obtained from the station master, and kicked him in the shin. Rick yelped, finally looking at something besides the stretch of rails.

"What the hell?"

"Scoot over, so an old man can sit," Castor grinned.

Rick turned to take in the plethora of benches, and the scant few people lounging about. "Why?"

"Shit, you're dumb," his uncle sighed, then nodded over to where Delilah stood, on the edge of the platform, watching for the train, her body tense. "Go talk to your mom, dipshit."

"Rickwit," Maari offered as she accepted a cup of tea from Castor.

"Now there's a word we didn't know we needed," he laughed.

Rick sulked a moment, then nodded. "Fine. I get it. I'm going. Just don't try anything funny with Maari. You already know I can kick your ass."

"Now why would I try anything," Castor mused with a grin as he settled next her and draped an arm around her shoulders. "She's already going to be my wife before you even hit Riscadil, you know."

"Funny," Rick groused. "A million comedians out of work, and you've got jokes."

Maari rested her head on his shoulder and batted her eyes. "Who says he's joking?"

"You're both assholes," Rick snorted and walked away.

In spite of his own anxiety, by the time he reached his mother, it was obvious even to him that she was far more nervous than he was. He paused a moment, thinking about that. It only took him that one moment to get why, and when he did, he felt bad about everything. Bad was the wrong word, he knew. It was worse than that.

He felt guilty. He knew he was breaking his mother's heart, and he was doing it anyway. Chasing the line of work that had claimed the one great love of her life, and left her to raise a son without a father. When he was honest with himself, he couldn't imagine what she was going through, or how hard this was for her.

"How you doing, Mom?" he asked, stepping up next to her.

"Well, they haven't announced a derailment, so I'm pretty shit, kiddo," she growled. "Thanks for asking."

Rick suppressed a grin and gave a nod. "I'm sorry. I really am. I never wanted to hurt you. I hope you know that. I just..."

"You want to know what it was like," she said after he trailed off. "Your father's life. You want to know what he was like. Who he was. The things he saw and did. You want to feel close to him in some small way."

Startled that she knew, he looked at anything but her. "Yeah. I guess that's about right."

"That what you told Maari, or did you give her some shit about wanting to be good enough for her?" Delilah asked.

Rick flinched. "I gave her the shit version. I don't think she'd understand the real reason I want to do this."

"Hell, I don't get the real reason you want to do this," she snorted. "This business, it killed him, Ricky. It killed your dad. He was good, too. One of the best in the world. You have no idea what you're in for. All the things Castor never told you. All the shit he left out of those stories he filled your head with when you were little. Sometimes, being one of the best isn't good enough."

Rick finally looked her in the eye. "I know that."

Delilah took a moment to understand what he was saying, then shook her head. "You think you do. You really don't. So many things I wish I'd told you, and now it's too late. You'd just think I was trying to scare you into staying home. You have no idea the world you are walking into, kiddo. None at all."

"It's going to be hard," he said quietly. "And painful. I'm going to get hurt for real. I'm going to see people die. I know all that. I'm not a complete idiot, Mom. I know it's not all glory, gold, and babes. I get that."

"Then why, Ricky?" she all but begged. "Why do this to yourself to chase his ghost?"

"Because, Mom, for all of that, he made the world a better place," Rick insisted. "Not just for others, but for you and me. Yeah, he died, but he died giving me a world I could live in, happily and safe. If I can do that for my kids, then why wouldn't I?"

Delilah tried to think of something, anything, to say. She couldn't. Instead, she simply looked down the tracks, where a distant plume of smoke was just becoming visible, as the faint echo of a steam whistle reached them.

"I really am sorry I hurt you," Rick said.

"I know," she admitted. "Just come home to me, Ricky. Come home safe. Don't try to be a hero. Don't take unnecessary risks. Do your job and come home safe."

"I can't promise that," he admitted.

"I know," she said, looking sad, and Rick saw, old. So much older than he had ever seen her. "But at least don't be reckless. That was always Max's biggest problem. He had to show off. Always so damn reckless. Be smarter than that, kiddo. Please."

"That I can do," he agreed. "I think we both know that when I try to show off, I just end up hurting myself."

She didn't want to, but Delilah laughed at that. "You really do."

The whistle came louder as the train became visible. Around them, passengers began to rise and gather their luggage. Rick moved to do the same, only to be stopped as Delilah grabbed him, wrapped him in her arms, and held him tight. He felt her tears on his neck, and did the only thing he could. He held her back.

"I love you, Ricky," she whispered, voice thick with grief, fear, and doubt. "So much. I love you so much, I can't stand it."

"I love you, too, Mom," he assured her. "More than anything."

She pushed him back, patted his cheek, and nodded, then sent him over to grab his duffel as the train slowed, almost to them.

"More than anything, except your father's legacy."

A moment later and the train had stopped, the locomotive belching steam as the conductor stepped out and people began forming a line. Tickets were torn, and the small gathering diminished quickly, as Rick faced the people he loved most in the world and found it was far harder to say goodbye than he had ever imagined.

"Be safe," Castor said, ruffling his hair, then clapping his shoulder. "I'm proud of you, Ricky."

"I love you," Rick replied, holding out a hand. Castor took a moment, then shook it, accepting his nephew was now a fully grown man, even if he still saw him as baby boy.

"Remember what I said," Delilah tried not to plead, thought it still came out that way.

"I promise I will, and Mom, thank you. I love you."

She nodded and stepped back, not wanting him to see her cry. Not now. That would be cruel, and the memory of her own mother's tears as she had left home, Castor at her side, still haunted her. She didn't want that for him. Not for her boy.

Maari moved to hide her from his view, a wide smile on her face as she held out her arms. Rick stepped into them, the feel of her so good he wanted to linger for days. Behind him, the conductor tugged his cap down and gave them a moment, having seen this many times, and knowing how few times that embrace would ever be shared again.

"I love you, Rick," she told him. "More than anything, I love you. Come back to me. I'll be waiting."

"I promise I will," he answered. "You won't have to wait long. Next time you see me, you'll never have to say goodbye again."

She kissed him, and then let him go. It was time. Stepping back, she felt Delilah and Castor's arms around her, holding her up, and was grateful. She held them back, and together, they watched Rick board the train, and hoped against hope that one day soon he would return.

Nodding to the conductor, Rick handed over his ticket, got half of it back, and headed into the passenger car to find a seat that let him see them one more time. Moments later, the whistle blew and the first jerk of the train ricocheted down the cars as the locomotive began to move.

He waved and they waved back as the station drew away, quickly little more than a speck in the distance, and then gone from sight. Rick watched it the whole time. His past fading from view as his future approached.

"This is gonna rock," he assured himself as he settled into his seat.

Richard William Wonder was on his way.

Chapter Two: Are You Ready?

RISCADIL. What a completely amazing name for a place.

Granted, that was just what Rick thought, and so far he'd only seen the train station, but still, even that was amazing. Domed ceilings rose high in the air between elaborately decorated arches, and even between those, there were sprawling murals that depicted key moments in Liaob's history that dazzled the eye.

The platform was so crowded he had trouble getting through, the sea of people far beyond the entire population of Townglen, all in a hurry to get where they were going, many reading the evening paper as they walked, somehow avoiding each other as if it were second nature.

Pressing through the crowd, he broke free into the central concourse, dominated by a massive fountain around which an even greater sea of people hustled to and fro or simply sat on the benches, awaiting the arrival of trains. Above the ticket counter, a massive ticker board showed times, locations and delays, the information changing almost too fast to keep up with as trains came and went.

Rick slowed and spun in a circle as he walked, trying to take it all in. If the station alone was this incredible, he could barely wait to see the rest of the city. Provided, of course, he could figure out how to get out of the station in the first place, which he quickly realized, he couldn't. Stairs went everywhere and they all seemed to lead back to the main concourse.

Eventually, he got the gist of it and found his way out onto the street. All the trains entered the station through tunnels so he hadn't even gotten a decent look at Riscadil on the way in, coming in over the Keening Straight and almost immediately into the pitch black of the passage beneath the sprawling metropolis.

As soon as he stepped through the revolving door, he was assaulted by a thousand sights, sounds and smells. That last one he could have done without. Mostly because it smelled of horse shit. He blinked a few times as the setting sun washed straight down Station Street and into his eyes, but as his vision adjusted he beheld the city of Riscadil in all its glory.

It was a good bit uglier than he had expected.

The wide sprawl of Station Street was filled with carriages, wagons, carts, and cabs, the plethora of horses creating a horrid smell he found gagged in his throat. Between the two sets of four lanes down which they traveled stretched a wide swath of greenery, boasting wrought iron lamp posts that overhung the street. Past them, the rise of towering buildings of bleak brown stone dominated his view. Impersonal and imposing, they stretched dozens of stories high, their purpose impossible to guess at due to their uniform facade.

Between them, weaving through the street, were thousands of people. They walked briskly but didn't run for the most part. Here and there children sprinted back and forth, in general there was a sense of being in a hurry, but not that big of a one. He stood, marveling at how easily they navigated the seemingly endlessly movement of the traffic, as if all of life here was a ballet.

A really smelly ballet.

"Pardon, sir?"

Rick jumped half out of his skin as a hand touched his elbow, spinning to find a man in a porter's uniform by his side. His hand went to his chest unconsciously as he offered the fellow a nervous smile.

"Sorry to startle," the porter said, tipping his cap. "You looked a bit lost. Thought I might could be of help."

Rick relaxed. "Uh, yeah, I think so. This is my first time here."

The man's face lit up. "Come from down south, have you?"

"How could you tell?"

He shrugged slightly, looking pleased with himself. "Accent gives it away. Me grandparents are from Nathan's Hollow."

"Oh, hey, that's right up the road from Townglen," Rick blurted.

"Oi, Townglen, is it?" the porter asked with a smile. "Small world, this, ain't it?"

"You know it?" he returned with a great deal of surprise.

"Aye, that I should, sir," the porter nodded with a good bit of smugness. "Me uncle lives there. Rotund fellow, by the name of Portson."

Rick gaped. "Portson's your uncle?"

"Oh, aye," Porter Portson assured him. "Bit of a daft fellow, really. Makes terribly over-salted ribs. Trying to brand them, or some such."

Rick shook his head, trying to wrap his mind around the likelihood of this encounter. "Sorry, I'm just... wow... yeah, that's Portson."

"You must be Ricky Wonder, then, 'eh?"

Rick's astonishment vanished. "He told you I was coming, didn't he?"

Porter Portson's smile widened. "Aye, sir, that he did. Asked me to catch you on the way outta the station. Lend a hand if I might. Leopold Portson, at your service. Friends call me Leo, sir."

Laughter, slightly cynical, escaped Rick at that. "How typical. Even this far from home, and everyone has their head up my ass."

The younger Portson shrugged. "Small town folk be like that. Not such a bad thing. Course, you'll learn that after being here for a time, sir."

"If you say so," Rick doubted. "Still, I guess I should be thankful. I don't have the first idea where to go."

Leo tipped his cap again. "Then it's a good thing I be here, ain't it, sir?"

"That it is, Leo," Rick agreed. "So, first order of business is to find the Adventurers League headquarters, and get myself squared away with them."

"Ah, about that, sir," Leo said with a grimace. "Be a bit late in the day for doing that. They close up shop around five come these days. Won't be able to get in and see them till morning. Doors open about nine. After that, I'm sure they'll be happy to have a fellow of your lineage walking through their doors."

"Oh," Rick deflated. "I didn't know they had regular hours."

"Didn't use to," Leo admitted. "Course, that was then, and this be now. Adventuring ain't what it used to be. All punch the clock sort of thing these days. So I hear anyway."

"Really," Rick deflated further. "That's not exactly in the brochure."

"Brochure is meant to get you here, sir," Leo pointed out. "Sign you up, collect the dues. Not likely they'd put the less glamorous stuff about it all in there."

Rick supposed that made sense. "Well, okay. That's all well and good. I can deal with it. If that's the case, then I guess I'll be needing a place to stay for the night."

Leo nodded enthusiastically. "Plenty of those round about here, and more besides, depending on your means and desires."

"I've got means," Rick assured. He'd been very careful with the money he'd gotten for his birthday, and still had a good amount to his name. Enough, he figured, to get him a decent room, and a hot meal with breakfast to go with it.

"Ah, course you do," Leo grinned. "No wonder with a Wonder, 'eh, sir?"

Rick had no idea what that meant. "I guess not?"

Leo chuckled at his modesty. "Well then, if it be a decent stay you be looking for, head on down to Clover Lane, 'bout six blocks or so straight on from here, hang a left, and go another three. Put you right on the doorstep of the Cantasol Hotel. Finer place you aren't likely to find so close by. Not without crossing over to Longmire Town, at any rate."

"Longmire Town?"

"One of the boroughs, you know."

"Oh, right, of course."

Leo rocked on his heels for a moment. "There be six, sir."

"And this one is?"

"Aven, sir, the heart of Riscadil."

"Right, of course," Rick agreed quickly. "I knew that."

"Course you did, sir," Leo replied, either believing him, or too polite to let it show he didn't.

"So, six blocks down, turn left, then three, to the Cantasol Hotel."

"Dead on, sir."

"Cool," Rick said, nodding. "Thank you. And tell your uncle thank you, too. I appreciate it."

"Been my pleasure, sir," Leo answered, with a tip of his cap once more. "Good to have a Wonder back in town."

"Good to be here," Rick agreed, feeling like maybe this wasn't so different from Townglen after all. "And, thanks again."

"Be here most evenings, sir, if you ever got a need again," he replied with a wide smile. "Don't hesitate to look me up. Always happy to be of help to a Wonder. Scouts honor on that."

With a nod and smile, Rick waved and headed off, feeling pretty good. The sheer size and bustle of the city had thrown him at first, but it seemed even here there were those ready to be of help. Honestly, it was still a pretty friendly place, just like back home when he thought about it. Bigger, but not so different.

A spring in his step, Rick trotted down the sidewalk. Yeah. This was just a bigger version of Townglen. A little less personal maybe, but the same community spirit wasn't so hard to find. Knowing that, it made him feel good. Relaxed.

He had no idea.

* * *

Two hours to walk nine blocks seemed a bit absurd.

Try as he might, Rick couldn't get into the flow of foot traffic versus the horse drawn variety. He tried waiting for an opening, but he was certain he'd die of old age before one actually presented itself. He had tried moving with the crowd, but he couldn't predict their path and always ended up being out of step, and in the way of some wagon or cab.

The cabs were the worst. Wagon drivers would just give him an irritated wave. Cab drivers would give him a tongue lashing that made him feel an inch tall. He wasn't entirely sure what they were saying, but it felt really insulting. Their accent was similar to Leo's, but the words seemed either entirely made up or just random gibberish with a few actual words woven in.

Then there were the Dwarven cabbies. After two, if he saw one coming, he just waited on the sidewalk and didn't even try to cross the street. Between the sputtering nonsense language they all used and the borderline Dwarven rage they all seemed to share, he felt it best to just avoid them entirely.

Eventually he made his way to the Cantasol Hotel, long after the sun had set. Back home, as the saying went, they rolled up the sidewalks come sun down. In Riscadil, it seemed a whole new sort of life started. Where before he had mostly seen men in suits and bowlers mixed with women in sharp business dress and fedoras, all keeping their eyes on where they were going, now he was seeing an entirely different sort of crowd.

The men seemed much younger, more around his age, and were decked out in brightly colored shirts, left unbuttoned to show off their chests, and wore no sort of headgear at all. The women on the other hand, wore mostly very short dresses with tassels and fringe, and bonnets of some kind. Like their companions, they were young, and all of them were raucous, running around in the streets shouting to each other, and on occasion, waving bottles of booze in the air as they dashed to wherever they were going.

The whole city seemed to turn into Rickwits as soon as the sun went down. As bizarre as their behavior was, he was kind of glad to see it. At least he wouldn't be the dumbest person in this town. They already had those by the bushel.

It occurred to him he sounded like a bumpkin or an old man. He wasn't sure what to think of that. Probably best if he didn't think at all. That had occasionally worked out for him in the past.

Shaking his head at the strangeness of it all, he pushed his way through one of the four revolving doors that lead into the lobby of the Cantasol, and instantly felt more out of place than he ever had in his entire life. Partly it was the string quarter in the corner playing some slow waltz piece. A fair bit of it was the massive, shimmering chandeliers that dominated the ceiling.

The majority of it, however, was just the fine dress of the people moving through the lobby. Men in tuxedos, with women in elegant gowns, sporting jewelry Rick felt certain was worth the GDP of Liaob were everywhere, moving with a leisurely pace that spoke volumes of the fact they believed the world would wait for them.

Red carpets caressed a black and white tiled floor, laid out like diamonds with golden gilt edges that glittered in the light from the chandeliers, greeting him as he eased his way forward, feeling fairly certain Leo didn't quite grasp what Rick had meant by means. Certainly he had a bit of money on him, but he seriously doubted it was enough to even breathe the air in this place.

He got no more than three steps before an attendant seemed to magically appear by his side, a serving tray holding fluted glasses of champagne balanced perfectly on his fingertips. Rick stared at him in awe, not just for how deftly he moved, but for his complete lack of expression. If he thought the man before him unworthy of being here, he held no hint of it anywhere in his eyes or any other part of his face.

Cautiously, Rick took a glass, and the attendant vanished just as swiftly as he had appeared. Unsure what else to do, Rick eased his way towards the front desk, trying not to draw too much attention to himself with his farmer clothing and the giant duffel slung over his shoulder. This proved pointless, as he didn't make it halfway before people were staring at him, mostly in curiosity, but many in barely concealed disgust.

Okay, so, not that much like Townglen, then. Right. Not a problem. Even a place like this probably had cheap rooms for merchants passing through. He'd nab one, vanish from sight, and stay that way until morning when he could maybe use a back exit or something.

"Excuse me, sir, may I help you?"

Rick managed not to spill the glass of champagne somehow. What was with all the sneaking up on people anyway? Was that a Riscadil hobby or something?

Looking over his shoulder, he found a finely dressed man of Half-Elven stock with a thick shock of curly black hair and well-trimmed mustache watching him with a bit of bemusement. His hands clasped behind his back, he didn't seem to show the disgust others held or even the slightly mocking humor. Just... curiosity and a bit of a smile.

"Yeah, hi, sorry, I think I may not have been supposed to come in the front door or something," Rick all but whispered as he slid over to the gentleman.

"We only have the front doors, sir," the other said with a bit of a twinkle in his eyes. "The back entrance is for staff, and I am fairly certain you are not among that number."

Rick nodded slowly. "Of course. This is going super great."

"Perhaps if you tell me what it is you're looking for, I can help you," the gentleman offered, his slight smile still in place, his eyes never breaking contact with Rick's own.

Clearing his throat nervously, Rick nodded again. "Sure, yeah. I was looking for a room for the night, dinner, and maybe breakfast in the morning."

"We do offer all of those services here, of course, to any customer who can afford our rates," the gentleman replied, his voice oddly soothing as more of the well-dressed patrons wandered by, staring at Rick oddly.

"Okay, yeah, sure," Rick said nervously, trying to manage his duffel, the glass of champagne, all while reaching for his wallet. "I've got about eighty lita still, so I guess, whatever that'll get me."

"Eighty, you say?" the gentleman asked, cocking his head slightly to the side. "Please forgive my impertinence, sir, but that wouldn't even get you our cluttered broom closet. This is the Cantasol, after all."

Rick stopped trying to reach his wallet. "So, pretty upscale sort of place is what you're saying?"

"Indeed, sir, that is what I'm saying, yes," the gentleman agreed, his expression never wavering from his mildly amused smile.

"Of course," Rick muttered, feeling foolish. "I'm so sorry. I was given the wrong impression. This is not a place I should be. I get that now. I'll just go find somewhere else that's not here."

The gentleman nodded slightly. "I regret that we are unable to meet your needs, sir, but if I may ask, are you new in town?"

"Yeah, very," Rick admitted, trying to figure out what to do with the clearly expensive glass he was still holding. "Got off the train about two hours ago. Met a guy who's a relative of a guy I know back home. He sent me here. I don't think his idea of means is the same as mine."

"Clearly," the gentleman agreed, snapping his fingers. An attendant appeared from nowhere as the well-dressed man with the bemused smile took the glass from Rick and deposited it on the tray with an extremely graceful move.

"And where might you have arrived from, if I may be so bold, sir?"

"Townglen," Rick replied, watching in awe as the attendant floated away. "I doubt you've heard of it."

"Do not underestimate me, sir," the gentleman said with a trace of mirth. "I am the concierge to the Cantasol. Knowledge of geography is a must."

Rick stared at him in confusion. "Does that mean you have?"

"Of course, sir," the gentleman replied with a slight nod. "Townglen is a small farming community of three hundred people, approximately two weeks away by train. It is known for its cabbage and okra crops, as well as being the birthplace of Max Wonder."

"I had no idea Townglen was so well known," Rick mused.

"It's more Mr. Wonder than anything," the concierge admitted. "However, as you are quite far from home, and in need of a place to stay, I am obligated, by duty and Scout's Honor, to render aide, sir. May I ask your name?"

"Rick," he said. "Rick Wonder."

"Mastoval," the gentleman answered with a slight bow. "Would you be a relative then?"

"He was my dad, so yeah," Rick told him.

"Of course he was," Mastoval agreed.

Rick stared at him for a moment in beleaguered agony. "You don't believe me, do you?"

The other man gave a slight shrug. "Such things are not for me to believe or disbelieve, sir. I am simply here to facilitate whatever our guests may need."

Rick gave a slow nod. "So, that's a no, then."

"It hardly matters," Mastoval countered. "Now, why don't we step outside, sir, so I can help you find a place to stay for the night that is more in line with your budget. It would be a shame if you were unable to conduct your business in our fair city properly."

"Now you're just trying to get the grubby looking farm kid out of sight," Rick muttered as he accepted the sweeping gesture Mastoval made towards the front doors. He hadn't missed the whispers running through the well-dressed clients, and had no doubt that part of Mastoval's job was keeping the common riffraff out of sight of the elites who glided about within the fine hotel.

Back on the street, Rick was slightly surprised when Mastoval didn't abandon him. He had half expected the concierge to disappear as soon as he was out of the hotel. Instead, he joined Rick and walked him a few steps from the front doors where more finely dressed people were arriving in cabs.

"Pardon me, sir, please, if I seemed rude," Mastoval said. "Such was not my intent. However, our clientele is rather accustomed to a certain level of attire, and I felt they were beginning to make you uncomfortable."

"More like I was making them uncomfortable," Rick grumbled.

Mastoval's smile widened by a centimeter. "They live to be uncomfortable with something, sir. Think nothing of it. At the moment, my only concern is seeing to it your stay in Riscadil does not include a night spent trying to sleep in alley."

Frustrated, Rick waved a hand at him. "Why do you even care?"

"You entered the Cantasol, sir," he replied with another bow. "It is my duty to care."

The Rickwit strikes again!

"That was rude of me," Rick said. "I'm very sorry, Mr. Mastoval. Please, forgive me, and thank you for your help."

Mastoval's eyebrow quirked up as his smile grew deeper. "That is the other reason, sir. Our clientele may be privileged, but they lack manners. One such as yourself does not. On occasion, even I enjoy being spoken to with respect."

"I can imagine it," Rick chuckled.

"I certainly hope not, sir." The concierge grinned back. "But let us not dwell on such things. A young man, fresh to the city, and no doubt planning to knock on the League's door first thing in the morning will need a night's rest and a proper meal. I believe I know just the place."

"I certainly hope so, 'cause past this, I've got no idea where to go."

Mastoval smiled as he rested a hand on Rick's elbow and turned him towards the street, his other hand rising, a single finger extended. "Leave that to me, sir. A concierge is but a servant, and my goal is to meet the needs of those who enter my domain."

A cab pulled to a stop as a surly looking Dwarf leaned down. "Watcha be needin', then?"

"If you would be so kind, sir, please escort this gentleman to 3812 Hasburn Lane, on the double. Send the bill to me."

"Whoa, now," Rick balked. "That's too much. I can pay my own fare."

"Don't much care who's payin', long as money trades to me hand," the Dwarf snarled.

"Mr. Wonder, please," Mastoval insisted as he opened the cab's door. "It is but a small thing, and the very least I can do to maintain my good standing and Scout's Honor. Simply tell the woman you will soon meet that I sent you, and she will take proper care of you, rest assured."

Rick hesitated a moment more, but found the kind smile on the concierge's face was something he could not defeat. "I guess. But I'll pay you back for this one day. I promise that."

"I have no doubt of it," Mastoval agreed as he watched Rick climb into the cab.

With a crack of the reigns, he was off, leaving the concierge standing on the sidewalk, his hands folded behind his back, a smile on his face.

"Not everyone has forgotten the debt this city owes to your father, sir," he mused as he turned back to the hotel. "Some few of us still believe a great deal remains before that is repaid properly."

* * *

Thirty-eight twelve Hasburn Lane, located in the old quarter on the north side of the Aven borough of Riscadil, was not even remotely what Rick had been expecting during his cab ride there. Thoughts of everything from a flop house, of which he'd heard terrible tales, to a hostel, of which he'd heard even more terrible tales, had all floated through his mind. What he found was a brownstone.

It wasn't even a remarkable one, at that.

After a few more barely legible words from the cabbie, which Rick was fairly certain meant he'd be back if Mastoval failed to pay, he found himself standing alone, late in the evening, in front of a house and with no idea what he was doing there. Things were not going the way he had thought they would.

Still, Mastoval had seemed a decent enough sort, so while he had a bit of trepidation about the situation, Rick hefted his duffel over his shoulder and mounted the steps to the brownstone. All he could hope for now was to wake up not missing his liver or any other body part he probably needed in order to live. Like his eyes.

Glancing about, he took a deep breath and knocked. Several moments passed in silence. He was beginning to think Mastoval had sent him on a wild goose chase. About to knock one more time just to be sure, he heard locks being undone and stepped back as the door swung open, revealing the occupant of the house.

Again, not what he had been expecting. It seemed the day for that.

Staring down at him was a full-blooded Orc. With hair rollers. And a night gown. And face cream. Rick had a hard time forming words as he stared up at the behemoth of a woman before him as she glared down with extreme annoyance.

"Well, what you be doing knocking at me door this late at night, boy?" she finally asked.

Rick swallowed hard. "My apologies, ma'am. I didn't mean to disturb you."

"Except you done gone and have," she huffed. "If you be selling something, I no be interested in it, just so you know already. Other than that, you got no good reason to be round and about this time of night, so shove off with you before I call the police."

"No, wait," he blurted as she began to swing the door shut. "I'm Rick Wonder."

"Good for you, boy," she snorted. "I no be interested."

"Mastoval sent me!" he yelped as the door swung towards his face.

The door stopped an inch from being shut, and eased back open, the Orc staring down at him intently. "That be true? If it not, I'll be having your head, boy."

"I assure you, ma'am, it is absolutely true," Rick bleated as quickly as he could. "It's a confusing story, really, but I just got to Riscadil, and I was directed to the Cantasol by a porter who's the nephew of a friend from back home, but that hotel was crazy expensive, and then the concierge took pity on me and sent me to you, and I'm not really sure why, but I need a place to sleep for the night."

The Orc sighed heavily at that. "That Masty. Always be picking up strays and sending them me way. All right, then, boy. I believe you. Come on in, but don't be tracking no mud on me carpet."

"No, ma'am," Rick replied, both relieved and somewhat terrified as he eased past her when she stepped back to make room for him. He paused to wipe his boots, overly aware of her watchful gaze, and when she nodded, he breathed a sigh of relief.

"I be Charlotte Goodkin," the Orc said as she swung the door closed and locked it. "I suppose you be me guest for a time, then. There be rules, though, so don't you be thinking this is gonna be some free ride, boy."

"No, ma'am, I would never ask for something like that," Rick agreed as he trailed after her down the narrow hall and past a flight of stairs heading up. Atop them, Rick caught the briefest flicker of movement, but Charlotte was rolling on so he trailed her and hoped it wasn't something that was going to eat him in his sleep.

A moment later, he found himself in the kitchen where he was waved to take a seat at her table. Easing down, he watched a moment as the towering Orc set about reheating a pot of something, and fetching a bowl and some glasses from the cabinet. Nervous, he waited as she worked, trying not to be a racist, but still unsure just what Orcs ate.

He'd heard stories. Mostly from Hondo, who probably wasn't the best source of information, but still.

Several minutes later, a glass of iced tea and a bowl of warm stew was placed in front of him as Charlotte eased down holding a cup of black coffee. Timidly, Rick took a bite and found the stew incredibly good.

"Wow," he said, somewhat relieved. "Thank you."

Charlotte nodded. "Eat up now, boy. Be showing you to your room once you be done. Wake up is at six sharp, and breakfast is something you be helping make. Cleaning up after, too. Then you be free to go and do whatever you wish, but if you be staying a second night, be back by seven, or be finding somewhere else to sleep. Understand?"

Rick nodded vigorously. "Yes, ma'am! Six sharp, help with breakfast and cleanup, be back by seven."

She nodded with a soft grunt. "Good, then. You not be my only guest, either. Don't be a bother to the other. Shy thing, she be. Keep your hands to yourself and your tongue civil, you be hearing me?"

"Absolutely," Rick agreed between big bites of stew. He hadn't realized how hungry he'd gotten until he'd started eating, and it really was incredibly good.

She sat watching him eat, and when he was done, waved a hand at the sink. Getting it clearly enough, Rick cleaned up after himself, leaving the dishes to drain, and looked to her. She gave another soft grunt and waved him to follow her upstairs, where she showed him to a simple, but comfortably appointed room.

"You be sleeping here tonight," she informed. "Don't be making no messes you don't want to be cleaning. If you be needing anything besides what's here, best tell me now. Once I be asleep, waking me be dangerous to your health."

"Actually," Rick said after a moment's thought. "I'd like to write a letter to my girlfriend, and one to my mom back home. Let them know I made it here and that I'm okay."

Charlotte softened by a tiny amount. "Everything you be needing be in the desk there. Be sure you tell that mama of yours that you be eating well."

"Yes, ma'am," he responded with a smile. "And thank you."

Charlotte gave a slight nod and walked away, leaving Rick alone in the room. He closed the door, set his duffel to the side, and gave a deep sigh of relief. He'd been worried for a while there that he'd end up sleeping on the street or worse, but this felt a little like home, and despite Charlotte being mildly terrifying, he felt a bit more at ease.

She was almost as scary as his mother. Not quite, but close.

He took some time to write a proper letter to Maari, as well as one to his mother and uncle then turned in for the night, making sure to set the alarm clock by the bed. Tomorrow was going to be a big day, after all. The day he joined the League and started his journey to becoming a great hero and a legendary adventurer. He could barely wait.

Exhaustion claimed him quickly, but his dreams were as epic then as when he was awake.

* * *

The alarm roused him from a peaceful sleep, the best he'd had in two weeks. Sleeping on a train or in various stations along the way didn't make for the most comfortable rest, so the bed Charlotte had lent him had been almost like dying and going to heaven.

Checking out a secondary door, he found a washroom and cleaned himself up a bit before dressing and heading down to find Charlotte already awake, and her other guest as well. She was a young Elven woman in simple traveling clothes with an unruly mane of chestnut hair, sporting large glasses over bright blue eyes that looked rather startled. He smiled, and she hid behind her cup, so he ended up just sighing to himself and giving the Orc an apologetic look.

"He be safe enough, me think, Emi," Charlotte rumbled.

The Elf nodded, and stammered out a good morning, before again retreating behind her cup of coffee. Rick supposed that was good enough and returned the greeting before looking about, prepared to make breakfast.

"Since this be your first day, and Emi here can't cook to save her soul, go ahead and have you a seat. Be me treat today," Charlotte told him, levering herself up as she waved at a chair on the opposite side of the table from Emi.

"Thank you, ma'am, but I really don't mind helping," he told her.

"All well and good, boy, but take the generosity and be having you a cup of coffee," she replied with a slight smirk. "You can be doing the dishes after, though, if you be that eager to help."

"Yes, ma'am," Rick agreed quickly and dropped his butt in the chair, not wanting to get on her bad side.

Emi squeaked and sank deeper into her seat. Rick tried to appear non-threatening. Considering the way her face reddened, he wasn't sure if he was succeeding or not, but drank his coffee and minded his manners all the same.

He wasn't sure what he'd been expecting, but bacon and eggs were served shortly with some fried potatoes and toast. Just like back home. He supposed that somewhere in his head he'd always seen Riscadil as a strange land where people ate exotic things. Seeing the simple meal placed before him, he actually found it rather comforting.

With breakfast done, he washed the dishes as he'd been instructed with Emi helping to dry them, though the poor mousey young woman jumped and squeaked each time he handed her something. As soon as they were done she fled the room, leaving him feeling somewhat baffled. Rick had always considered himself the friendly sort.

"How about that," Charlotte chortled. "I think she done be taking a liking to you, boy."

Rick gave her a very doubtful look. "How can you tell?"

"She actually stayed till all the dishes was done," the Orc replied, smiling at him over her coffee.

He guessed that was as good as it was going to get. Taking a moment to have another cup of coffee, he asked directions to the nearest post office, which Charlotte was happy enough to provide. Thanking her once more, he returned to his room, gathered his things and headed out.

He was ready.

* * *

After a stop to mail his letters, Rick discovered something about life in Riscadil he hadn't been prepared for. Honestly, he had to admit it was two things, and not the first two. One came on the heels of another, as seemed to be the case. Since he had arrived, he'd learned a lot of things. Some people were very kind, for example, while others were not.

In this instance, what he discovered was that getting a cab was a lot harder than it looked. No matter how much he waved, they passed him right by, picking up other people. He tried to study what they were doing differently to get the cabbie's attention, but couldn't find anything special. They just raised a hand, same as he was doing.

After more time than he cared to consider being wasted, he gave up and started walking. The League headquarters was in midtown and he was on the north end, so he was aware it was going to be a trek, especially after his attempt to just walk a few blocks last evening had taken so long.

That had been in the evening, however. This was the morning. Hard as he found it to accept, traffic was worse. Not just the actual traffic, either, but also the foot traffic. The press of the crowd was impossible to escape, and often as not, he found himself trapped in the flow, unable to tell if he was even going in the right direction.

By late morning, he was completely lost, and even attempts to ask for directions seemed to get him ignored or not politely told to get lost. Which he already was. Whatever kindness he had found seemed to be all the city of Riscadil had to offer for newcomers, lulling them into a false sense of security then slapping them around with a big reality stick.

It was around that time he learned the second thing. It was really hot in Riscadil. All the concrete and steel reflected the oncoming afternoon sun, driving the temperature through the roof. Add in the heavy duffel he was lugging, and as noon set in, he felt like he was drowning in his own sweat.

Not to mention, breakfast was already a thing of the distant past and he was starving. He didn't know where to go to deal with either thing, and wasn't entirely sure where he was. It was enough to finally drive him to finding a bench, heavily painted with graffiti, and just sit for a bit to gather his nerves.

"What you doing," a husky voice asked in his ear, hot breath washing over his neck, sending chills down his spine.

Jerking around, he found a Goblin leaning over, glaring at him. This quickly became the third thing Rick learned. Riscadil had a real gang problem with the various monstrous races, especially Goblins. Distantly, he recalled Castor mentioning something about that, but looking at the dark-green-skinned creature with bright red eyes watching him, he became acutely aware of just how little he really knew.

"I'm just sitting," he said after a tense moment.

"On my bench, hucko," the Goblin snarled. "Don't see you paying no rent for this squat, either. Owe me coin for it now, you do."

"Pretty sure it's a public bench," Rick offered, trying to be reasonable.

The Goblin leaned in closer. "Don't be seeing no tag that says that. Do be seeing my tag on it. Pay up, hucko, or be getting bled. You feel my wind?"

Rick tried very hard to understand any of that, but really didn't. "Okay, look. I'm sorry. I wasn't aware this was your bench. I don't read Goblin. How about I just go and we don't get violent?"

"Violent, 'eh?" the Goblin sneered. "Hucko don't wanna get bled, and don't wanna coin up. Be a real problem for me. Got my cred to stay established with, yes?"

Growing irritated, Rick pushed to his feet. "Look, pal, I'm trying to be nice here. You want a fight, trust me, you will be sorry."

"Big words," the Goblin snorted, tugging a dagger out from behind his back and hopping up to perch on the back of the bench. "Not be seeing no steel to back them up with."

Rick dropped the duffel onto the bench and pulled out one of the Whip Blades. "See my steel now, pal?"

The Goblin looked at the scimitar, then at his dagger and back. "Big hucko, got some big steel. Gambling he can't use it. Maybe just for show. Can squat on a bench and not coin up anytime he wants. Good odds for me, still."

"Come find out," Rick snapped.

"Ahem," a new voice intruded. "Sir, I'm going to have to ask you to put the sword away."

Glancing back, Rick found himself faced with a Half-Elf in a police officer's uniform. Wondering just when all his luck abandoned him, he hesitated, looking back to the Goblin, who was suddenly sitting on the bench looking afraid, the dagger nowhere to be seen.

"Thank goodness, officer," he whimpered. "This man just came out of nowhere and began brandishing this awful weapon at me. I was afraid for my life!"

Rick's jaw almost hit the sidewalk.

"Yeah, whatever, Enzo," the officer grumbled. "That might carry a little more weight if I didn't know you, and you weren't sitting on a bench tagged with your name."

Enzo glanced at the paint. "I have no idea who did this, officer. Tarnishing my good reputation is simply unforgivable."

The officer scowled. "Enzo. Take a hike. Now."

The Goblin hopped to his feet, giving the policeman a dark scowl. "It'd be nice once in a while, Anton, if you'd play along. Just for the damn tourists, you know?"

"Yeah, whatever," Anton deadpanned, waving at him to get lost. "Don't let me catch you playing with your mother's kitchen knife, again either, or I'll tell her what you've been doing."

"Killjoy," Enzo grumbled, stuffing his hands in his pockets, sulking all the way down the street.

Rick struggled with all of this. He was still struggling with it when the officer stepped closer, watching him curiously. A tap to his hand from the police baton the Half Elf carried brought him back.

"I really would like you to put that away, sir," Anton reminded.

"Huh? Oh. Right. Sorry." Rick scrambled, stuffing the blade back in the duffel. "I thought he was... I mean... before you showed up he was talking like..."

"Hucko gonna be bled if he don't coin up?" Anton chuckled.

Rick nodded. "Yeah. Like that."

"It's an affectation," Anton informed him with a wry grin. "For the tourists. Sounds scary, like they don't have a good grasp on Common. Gives the impression they might be almost feral. A lot of the time they get a good bit of money out of people with it."

Rick slumped. "I'm an idiot."

"Nah," Anton laughed. "Just obviously not from here. Don't worry about it. Enzo's all talk. If you'd actually gone at him with that sword, he'd have run screaming."

Exhausted, still hungry and hot, Rick collapsed back onto the bench. "It must be really obvious. I can't even get a cab."

"That's because you look poor," the officer pointed out with less than no tact. "Cabbies in this part of town won't stop for someone who doesn't look like they can pay."

"Oh, for..." Rick groaned. "And here I actually have money."

Anton chuckled at that. "Can't be helped. That's just how this town works, pal. Where were you trying to go, anyway?"

"The Adventurers League," Rick told him.

Anton nodded. "Go back up here to this intersection, and head about four blocks west. That'll put you right on the south end of Wonder Plaza."

Rick died. "Four blocks? Wonder Plaza? Are you messing with me?"

"Absolutely not, sir," Anton laughed. "It's just right over there. You can see it from the intersection.

"Of course you can," Rick moaned.

The officer gave another laugh. "Don't worry. If you stay long enough, navigating this place becomes second nature. It's not as impossible as it seems right now."

"I'm gonna take your word for that," Rick grumbled as he pulled himself to his feet. "But if I can bother you for just a moment more?"

"Sure," Anton said with a nod. "What's up?"

"You know anyplace around here that's cheap to eat?" Rick whimpered as his stomach growled.

Anton gave a hearty laugh at that. "There's some shops around Wonder Plaza, but they can be pretty pricey. Personally, I recommend heading about two blocks down, and three over, to Rumble Park. There's a really nice noodle stand to one side. Cheap, but damn good and stays with you for a while. The cook doesn't skimp on the ingredients."

Rick glowered. "Rumble Park, huh? First Wonder Plaza, now this. I can't get away from them no matter where I go."

Anton cocked an eyebrow at that. "It's not much of a surprise, really. I mean, Castor Rumble, and Max and Delilah Wonder saved this city several times. It's only natural they'd get memorialized."

"Yeah, I know," Rick groused. "Believe me, I know. Castor never shuts the hell up about it. Still, I guess I didn't expect I'd keep running into it. Honestly, I probably shouldn't complain, but living in that shadow, it's a lot deeper and darker than I thought it'd be."

Anton seemed honestly confused. "You talk like you know them personally."

"I do," Rick told him as he slung the duffel over his shoulder, got his bearings and headed out to find the noddle stand. "Castor's my Uncle."

Officer Anton Strakinsy watched the young man head down the street, processing that bit of information. He'd heard rumors, of course, that Delilah and Max had been expecting a child when Max died, but to think he'd randomly run into the second generation Wonder on the street seemed pretty far-fetched.

"Nah," he finally said to himself. "Couldn't be. That's just too crazy."

* * *

Finding Rumble Park turned out to be as easy as Anton had said, and the noodle stand was just as obvious, set up on one side. As he approached, the scents wafting from it made Rick's stomach go crazy, though he managed to restrain himself from diving into the place while drooling. He was somewhat proud of that fact.

Thus did Rick receive yet another lesson on how different Riscadil was, as he met Sunny, the transgender Bugbear who ran the place. He'd never seen a Bugbear in person before. Much less one in a dress, cooking noodles. He was feeling somewhat jaded at this point, however, and just took a seat at the bench that ran along the front of the small stand.

Sunny was an excellent cook, as it happened, and the meal was not only filling, but as Anton had said, affordable. After some time in the shade and a cold drink, Rick was feeling a good bit better and thanked Sunny with a nice tip, which got him a wink, a smile, and a suggestive comment he knew he was not going to be considering later on. Eight feet of fur and muscle, no matter how you dressed it up, was too intimidating for him, and he had a thing going on with Maari.

She covered his intimidating quota nicely, thanks.

Feeling more optimistic, he headed back up, and after only a few close calls with horses and wagons, found himself standing before Wonder Plaza where a forty-foot tall statue of Max Wonder, arms spread out as if to embrace the entire city, stared down at him. Rick wasn't sure how he felt about that.

Awkward came to mind.

Moving through the flower bed and fountain decorated plaza lined with expensive looking restaurants, gift shops, and clothing outlets, Rick began to have the first tingling of an existential crisis as the Wonder brand assaulted him from every direction. He knew his father from the stories he'd been told growing up, but somehow it seemed as if the entire city of Riscadil knew him better.

Or at least how to cash in on his memory better. He couldn't help but wonder where all the residuals his mother was owed were going. Then again, she'd never held a job as long as he could remember, so maybe she was getting them after all.

He did, however, feel a bit cheated by all the High Winter presents she'd said were too expensive to buy.

Rick decided to put his existential crisis and pending therapy needs on hold for now as the glass and steel tower of the Adventurers League rose up before him, a monolithic three-sided spire design that glittered in the afternoon sun. He paused before it, staring up at the massive golden sun-shaped crest that adorned the side of the building somewhere around the fiftieth floor.

He'd made it. He was here. Yes, he assured himself, he truly was ready for this.

He wasn't ready for this.

It occurred to him that this may be the case shortly after entering the lobby. To the left, a reception desk hunkered, a sullen-looking Marilith busy filing paperwork with all six arms while glaring out across the lobby, as if daring anyone to step near her. Opposite her, a large waiting area filled with chairs held a good six dozen people, all in various states of adventure dress, from fighters, to clerics, to what Rick assumed was meant to be a barbarian, in his hot pink loincloth.

Past them, a series of twelve teller windows could be seen, all but two holding signs that declared the next window should be used. Above each, a ticker counter showed a number with a sign above it stating what number was being served. Between the waiting area and the reception desk, a bank of elevators, each holding a Kobold in a uniform of red jacket and hat, ferried people up and down.

Rick pursed his lips and tried to figure out what the hell he was supposed to do. In the brochures he'd read, one of the first big selling points of the League was a promise of personalized service to all those who sought the life of adventure, fame, and glory. Somehow he hadn't been expecting whatever this was. He couldn't guess why.

Finally deciding to try what appeared to be the quickest method, he turned to the receptionist, but as he approached he found her sullen glare only deepening. Steeling his resolve he approached anyway, set his duffel down, and after looking at the small placard that declared the receptionists name to be Marilyn Urkenveknotch, dove in head first.

"Um... hi," he started.

She paused in her paperwork filing, glaring up at him with barely concealed rage. "What can I do ya for, toots?"

"Um... yes... hi... my name is Rick Wonder..." he stammered, unable to reconcile the sugary sweet tone with the seething desire to disembowel him he saw in her eyes.

"Uh huh," she drawled. "Whatever ya say, sweetheart. Whatcha be needing?"

"Oh... right," he managed, distantly wondering how a demon ended up working reception in the first place. "I wanted to sign up for the League."

"Course ya do," she replied, making it sound as if it was the least exciting prospect a sentient creature could aspire to. "Go take ya a number, and wait to be seen by an evolutionist."

"Ah... yeah," Rick hesitated. "I was hoping there might be a slightly faster way. Max Wonder was my dad, you know, so I..."

Marilyn swept up, the snake-like lower part of her body coiling, scales rasping as she leaned over, her forehead almost touching his. "I don't give a donkey's shit if your pops was the King of Tiama, toots. Go take ya an accursed number and wait yer stinking turn, or so help me, I'll devour the souls of yer kids before they scream their first breath into this world. Ya got me, darling?"

Rick stared wide-eyed into her purely hate driven gaze and felt his soul shrink. "Yes, ma'am. Sorry, ma'am. I apologize for bothering you. I'll just go take a number and wait my turn. Thank you, ma'am."

Marilyn settled back down, resuming her filing. "Thank ya for choosing the Adventurers League, where fame and glory await yer hard work, or some shit."

Rick backed away quickly, dragging his duffel with him, before he might anger her more. Turning, he found the roller that dispensed numbers and tugged it, getting one that said, in an overdone gothic font, four-eight-ten. He stared at that for a long time then at the overcrowded waiting area, and sighed heavily, as the current number being served was eighty-three.

This had not been in the brochure.

He couldn't help but wonder if this was actually worth it. As he stood there holding the scrap of paper that determined his future, he watched as dejected individuals drifted away from the teller windows, their eyes holding only their broken dreams and crushed hopes. One after another, they were rejected and drifted, like ghosts, back into the world, bereft of purpose.

But this was why he'd come all this way. It was why he'd trained for years, risking his mother's wrath every step of the way. This was not just his passion, it was his purpose, and he wasn't going to let some stupid system like this stand in his way.

Tossing the ticket aside, he turned, marched back to the reception desk, and slammed his duffel down onto it, saying, "Listen up, Marilyn. I'm Richard William Wonder, the son of Max and Delilah Wonder, and nephew of Castor Rumble. I'm not just some random kid who wandered in off the street. Being an adventurer is in my blood. It's my legacy. Now, you get someone down here to talk to me, or I'm going to show you just why there's a giant-ass statue of my dad outside the front doors of this place. You hear me?"

Marilyn turned eyes filled with the heat death of the universe up to him. "Since ya insisted so strongly, kid, then sure. I'll just call somebody down to have a word with your great and mighty self. Stay right there."

"Thank you," he sniffed.

Five minutes later, two security guards were dragging him towards the front door while Marilyn waved goodbye. Rick realized he probably should have seen that coming. Hindsight, ever 20/20, made him think that waiting in line wasn't such a bad idea after all.

Almost to the door, the two Ogre guards carrying him between them like he was a sack of potatoes, Rick saw his dreams, his goals, his purpose, fading away, when someone called to them to stop. The guards immediately did, and turned around, allowing him to see an Elf in sharp business suit sporting a neatly trimmed goatee waving them back over.

The two lumbering Ogres carted him back, but did not set him down. He felt that was a bit overkill. It wasn't like he'd actually pulled a sword out and started waving it around. He'd just kind of threatened to. Sort of.

"What seems to be the problem here?" the Elf asked.

"Marilyn called us," the Ogre on the left said.

"Troublemaker at the front desk," the one on the right added.

They both nodded and looked to Marilyn, who glared back with a promised passion for blood, death, and torment.

"A troublemaker, you say," the Elf mused. "What sort of trouble?"

The two Ogres looked at each other nervously, with the one on the left admitting, "Uh... we didn't ask."

"Security manual says to keep troublemakers out," the one on the right added with a shrug, making Rick bob up and down.

The Elf nodded. "That's true. Okay. So, hey, Marilyn, honey, what's going on here?"

She sighed so heavily several universes grew deeply depressed. "Says he's Max Wonder's kid and wants to be given special treatment."

"Max Wonder's son?" the Elf echoed thoughtfully, looking Rick over. "Well, then. Set him down, boys. Off you go. I'll handle this."

The Ogres shrugged, making Rick dizzy, but put him on his feet and rumbled off, leaving him feeling very disconcerted and certain he should never again try the intimidation route. It really wasn't his thing.

"Hi, there, pal," the Elf said with a grin. "I'm Jacan Glass, head of project development here at A.L. So Max was your father, huh?"

"Huh?" Rick flailed mentally. "Oh. Uh. Yeah. I'm Rick Wonder."

The Elf shoved a hand out. "Nice to meet you, Rick. Welcome to the League."

Rick shook his hand, very confused. "Wait. You mean welcome as in I'm in, or welcome as in I'm in the building?"

"In the building," Glass chuckled, giving Rick's hand exactly two shakes before letting go, producing a handkerchief, and wiping his own hand. "We have a pretty stringent code for new employees, so I'm sure you can understand that we don't just accept anyone who walks in, right?"

"Well, I mean, yeah," Rick floundered.

"Good, good," Glass agreed, waving Rick to walk with him towards the waiting area. "We are the largest private security firm in Riscadil, after all. That comes with a certain level of expectation from our clientele. We need to know that everyone we bring in is more than capable of handling themselves when things get dicey. It isn't a personal issue, but a PR one, you know?"

"I... guess?" Rick said, not entirely sure what the Elf was even saying at this point.

"Awesome," Glass stated, pausing near the rows of chairs, and steepling his fingers before his chin. "What I'm trying to say here, Rick, is that anybody can walk in off the street, claiming to be anything. If we took that as law, we'd be putting our reputation and our clients' lives at risk on a daily basis, based on nothing more than the good word of strangers. Not a sound business plan, am I right?"

Rick boggled a bit. "Well, I mean, no, not really."

"Great, great," Glass replied, nodding. "So, here's my thing, and it is my thing, not your thing, okay?"

"Your thing," Rick echoed in confusion.

Glass looked over the sea of would be adventurers. "If you are Max Wonder's child, please stand up!"

Fourteen people stood. One of them was a Half-Orc. Rick gaped at that more than he did the Halfling who had to stand on the chair just to be seen. It took a minute, mostly due to the shock, but it did sink in, as they fell into a heated argument over which of them actually was Max Wonder's offspring.

Glass saw it happen, and gave a soft smile. "Now you get it."

"I really am, though," Rick said quietly.

Glass nodded, waving Rick to join him as he walked towards the front doors. "Maybe you are, Rick. I've heard Max had a kid. So it's not impossible. The thing is, how am I supposed to know? You see that, don't you? The position it would put me in, to take someone at their word and cut them loose with the corporate reputation on the line? It's just not a smart business decision, that's all."

"Yeah... no... I mean..." Rick stammered.

"Hey, look, Rick," Glass said as he opened the door. "Maybe you go out there and prove yourself and come back here and make me eat my words. That'd be awesome. I'd be the first to apologize and hand you a contract. Cross my heart on that, and let you take it to the bank. For now, though, we just can't have people walking in, making big claims, and upsetting our staff. So, give it a few weeks and maybe try your luck again, okay?"

"I... uh..." Rick felt dizzy from the speed of the Elf's speech, and wasn't entirely sure he understood everything the man was saying.

"Great, thanks for your interest, have yourself a nice day," Glass said with a smile, waving Rick to leave.

Slowly, confused, disappointed, and with his existential crisis threatening to explode back into full force, Rick nodded and stepped out the door. He heard it swing shut behind him, and simply stood there, staring up at the towering statue of his father and desperately trying to grasp what had just happened.

Looking back over his shoulder, he saw Glass already striding across the lobby, while Marilyn wished him well with six middle fingers. Slumping, he realized he really had no choice and walked away, utterly defeated.

There was no adventure in the future for Rick Wonder.

* * *

After wandering around Wonder Plaza for a while, marveling at how his family name was being exploited while he couldn't even get in the front door of the League at this point, Rick retreated away from the mockery that was beginning to dawn on him. Distraught and depressed, he soon found himself settling onto a bench, his duffel between his feet, trying to figure out what to do now.

"Hucko comes crawling back," Enzo hissed in his ear. "Owes some coin, yeah?"

"Shut the fuck up, Enzo," Rick muttered, leaning back to stare at the sky.

Enzo scowled, and clamored over the back of the bench to sit next to him, sulking as he gave a morose, "Fucking Anton."

"Whatever," Rick grumbled, ignoring the Goblin as he tried to figure out a path forward.

Enzo watched him for several minutes then rubbed his eyes and sighed heavily. "Got turned down by the League, didn't you?"

Rick shot him a baleful glare. "How the hell would you know that?"

Enzo shrugged. "I've seen that look a few million times, pal. Kids walk in, all bright-eyed at the prospect of fame, fortune, and glory. Walk out a couple hours later looking like a Lizardman just ate their pet gerbil right in front of them."

Rick shook his head and tried to ignore the Goblin again. "Not my fault."

"It's never anybody's fault," Enzo agreed, sort of. "People think, cause of that statue, that they're gonna walk in and become the next Max Wonder. Then they hit the big brick wall of reality. Ain't nobody ever gonna be Max Wonder, except Max Wonder, and he's dead."

"I could be," Rick snapped, sitting up and jabbing a finger at the Goblin. "I actually, really could be! I know I could!"

"Whatever," Enzo scoffed. "What makes you so special?"

"Because he was my dad, dammit!" Rick shouted. "I'm his son, Rick Wonder! Not some pretender! Not some groupie! I really *am* his son!"

Enzo gave him a dour look. "Sure you are, pal. And I'm the long lost chieftain of the Murdu Clan, just biding my time to lead Goblin kind to a new era of prosperity in our own nation."

Frustrated and angry, Rick reached down and yanked one of the scimitars from his duffel. "Oh, yeah, smart ass? Then what about this?"

The Whip Blade vibrated in his hand for a moment, began to segment, and then snapped back. Rick groaned and slumped over, beyond tired of the constant humiliation he had endured since he'd arrived in Riscadil. Nobody believed him, and after what Glass had shown him, he couldn't even argue it. When every Tom, Dick, and Sally claimed to be the child of Max Wonder, how was anyone to know the real deal when they saw it?

"Is... is that... really... a Whip Blade?' Enzo gasped from beside him.

Glancing over, Rick saw the Goblin had a look of shock, reverence, and awe on his face as he held a trembling finger out, pointing at the scimitar.

Startled, he spent a full minute trying to process what was happening, but got only static back from his brain. It was, it seemed, done indulging him for the day.

"Yeah," Rick admitted apathetically. "It's the real thing. It was my dad's."

"He had two," Enzo prodded.

Rick pulled the other, held them up for a moment, and then stuck one away. "Uncle Castor told me that when they fought the Arch Lich, Obedell, Dad used these to keep from being pulled through the interdimensional portal, but ended up letting go to push Obedell the rest of the way through. That's why they were left behind."

"Murdu's nutsack," Enzo whispered, tapping the sword gently with his finger. "You really *are* Wonder's kid!"

For a moment, Rick felt elated, but it faded quickly. "Great. The only person who believes me is a Goblin street punk. Naturally."

"Low level entrepreneur," Enzo snorted. "And hey, at least I believe you."

Rick admitted that was a mild improvement. "Yeah, okay. Sorry. I'm just having a really bad day."

"I can imagine," Enzo agreed, settling back, still eying the sword with adoration. "You know, my pops always said Max Wonder was one of the first to stand up for Goblin rights in this town. Pushed back against a slums resettlement project that would have shoved us all off to Old Town on the north side of Copper's Bay. According to him, Wonder was the first hucko who ever sat down in a Goblin house for dinner and treated us like real folk. Called him a hero, cause he was just a decent person."

"Dad did that?" Rick asked, taken aback by this.

Enzo gave a slight shrug. "Pops says so. He's a lot of things, but my pops ain't no liar, so I figure it must be at least sort of true, you know?"

Rick stared at the sword for a minute. "Nobody ever told me about that."

"Probably a lot of things nobody ever told you about him," Enzo said. "That's how people get when somebody dies. They only wanna remember certain things, you know?"

"Yeah. I guess that's true."

"So how come you didn't just show them League bigshots the Whip Blade?" Enzo asked after a few minutes.

Rick held it out again, and despite straining as hard as he could, the blade didn't show a single crack. Slumping again, he admitted, "I can't get it to work most of the time. Even when it does, it only does what you saw. I don't know why. I guess, maybe, I can't be like my Dad after all."

Enzo felt kind of bad, and rubbed his head, looking at anything else. "Or, maybe, ya know, you're trying too hard."

"Huh?"

"Like, when you gotta take a shit real bad, but no matter how much you strain, nothing comes out until you relax a little," Enzo explained, then looked embarrassed and lowered his head. "Not that using your dad's swords is like taking a shit, or anything. I'm just saying."

Rick shook his head. "No, I get it. Maybe. I hadn't thought of it that way before. I always assumed it was a force of will. Uncle Castor just said I had to will them to work, so maybe I took it wrong or something. I don't know."

Enzo gave him a nervous smile. "You ain't so bad, for a hucko."

"What does that even mean?" Rick asked.

Enzo fiddled with his fingers. "It's just Goblin for human."

Rick stared at him for a moment in surprise, then burst into laughter. "That's pretty good! I thought it was an insult or something. I really am a hucko, though."

Relieved, Enzo chuckled with him, "It sounds scary, 'cause it's Goblin, you know? We just use it to try to hustle folks who don't know the language."

"It does sound bad, I gotta admit, especially when you hiss it," Rick agreed, then laughed again and put the scimitar away. "I guess things aren't always what they seem, huh?"

Enzo fidgeted for a minute, then looked at him with a bit of shame. "I'm sorry, Rick. You really are a pretty okay guy."

"Forget it," he told him with a wave. "I thought I was going to come here and be an adventurer. Guess I really did end up just being a tourist. Still, at least I tried. That counts for something."

"So, that's it?" Enzo asked, surprised by Rick's sudden turn to morose. "You're just gonna give up?"

"Not much else I can do," he grumbled. "The League won't even let me in the door now. All that's left is to give up on it and go home."

Enzo snorted at that. "Man, fuck the League. They ain't nothing but a security company anymore, anyway."

Rick pondered that for a moment. "That's what that Glass guy called it, too. What's that mean?"

"Security means security," Enzo told him, tapping the bench between them for emphasis. "They hire out their employees as bodyguards, and to protect buildings and stuff. They don't do no real adventuring anyway. Closest they get is when the cops need a few extra bodies for crowd control during parades and stuff, and even then only if there's been a lot of heavy drinking."

Rick shook his head slowly, taking it all in. "Are you serious?"

"As a dead man in pajamas," the Goblin returned. "The League is risk adverse these days. All that adventure stuff, it came with too many insurance claims from would-be heroes getting killed in action. So they changed direction and became a security company, but built the whole thing on this adventurer concept. Signing up with them is abandoning the idea of being an adventurer as sure as going home would be."

Seeing the final nail in the coffin of his dreams, Rick slumped back across the bench, staring at the sky again. "So, that's it, huh? There never was any chance I was going to be able to be like my Dad. That's just great."

"Says who?" Enzo asked with a wide grin.

"Uh, apparently everybody," Rick pointed out.

"Just cause the League got all scared, doesn't mean there's no adventure to be had, pal," the Goblin countered with an even wider grin. "This here is your lucky day, actually. You dodged that dead end career, and ran into me, and I know just where you gotta go if you really want to have adventures."

Rick doubted that strongly. "Oh, yeah? And where's that?"

"The Shy Market," Enzo intoned in a voice hushed with awe.

"That sounds really made up," Rick said.

Enzo blinked and then scowled. "Well, it ain't. Trust me, Rick. I get the word on the street, and the Shy Market is a for real deal. Folks who need actual help, with actual troubles, go there to hire actual adventurers to fight monsters, counter curses, and recover all kinds of magic items every day."

"Uh huh," Rick droned, not buying this for a minute. "And let me guess, you'll tell me how to find it for a bit of money?"

"What do you take me for?" Enzo exclaimed, his outrage very real. "Here we was, getting to be friends, and you gotta impugn my reputation like that? I'm just trying to help you out, ya dumb hucko!"

"Okay, okay, sorry," Rick said quickly, giving a slight bow, his hands clasped in front of him. "Please accept my apologies. I didn't mean to tarnish your good reputation."

Enzo scowled for a moment, then snickered. "Not like it's that good to start with, 'eh?"

Rick gave him a wink around his clasped hands. "Dunno what you mean, buddy."

"Whatever," Enzo laughed. "You really are a big, dumb hucko, but I guess you're pretty okay, too. Only reason I'm even telling you this is 'cause you wanna be like your old man, and like I said, my pops really respected him. Who knows, maybe you'll turn out to be half the guy he was, ya know?"

Rick lowered his hands. "I can only try, with everything I have."

Seeing the sincere look on his face, Enzo's laughter faded, replaced with a tinge of actual respect. "Well, okay then. Gimme a sec. I'll write down the directions to the place, and the password you'll need to get in. After that, it'll all be up to you."

Rick watched as he dug a notepad and pencil out of his back pocket and began scribbling down the information. He recognized a few street names from his earlier lamentable attempt to navigate Riscadil traffic, and realized that Enzo was actually being completely sincere. So when the Goblin tore the page out and handed it to him, Rick took it and smiled.

"Thank you, Enzo. I really appreciate you looking out for me and believing me."

Taken aback for a moment by the respect in Rick's voice, Enzo slowly began to smile. "Go show them League assholes what a Wonder can do, yeah?"

"Count on it."

* * *

Rick walked through the door of Charlotte's brownstone to find her standing in the hallway, arms crossed over her chest, staring up at the clock that read one minute to seven. Giving her a nervous smile he wiped his feet, closed the door, and locked it behind him as she eyed him some expression he couldn't make out. It seemed like a mix of annoyance and mirth.

"I'm back," he offered timidly.

"You like to be living dangerously," she rumbled.

Rick nodded. "I'm very sorry for being so late, ma'am. I had trouble getting a cab, and had to walk most of the way back from mid-town."

Charlotte cocked an eyebrow. "What you be doing in mid-town, then?"

Rick sagged a bit as he set his duffel down. "I went to try and join the League."

Charlotte burst into laughter. "How that go for you, then? Everything you dreamed it be, I bet."

Shaking his head, Rick admitted, "Not even close. About as far from what I thought as is possible."

She gave a grunt and relaxed, waving towards the kitchen. "Left you some dinner in the cold keeper. Pixie's name be June. Be polite or she'll freeze your eyes closed. Got a nasty disposition, that one."

"Got it," he said and walked past her, heading for the kitchen. At least he knew dinner would be good. Just as he knew he'd have a decent night's sleep. Tomorrow he'd check out this Shy Market and see if it was everything Enzo claimed.

"Something else done happened, though, now didn't it?" Charlotte asked as he reached the kitchen door.

He glanced back at her. "What makes you ask?"

She shook her head and moved to join him. "You got that set to you, of a man who done had his dreams all ground up and spit out, but you don't got that look of one what has given up. Makes me think you got something else planned then."

Rick had to admit her instincts were pretty damn good. Offering her a shrug, he stepped into the kitchen to retrieve his dinner, wondering how much he should tell her. Enzo made the Shy Market sound a bit shady, so it might be best if she not know.

"Hi there, June," he said to the pixie lifting weights to one side of the box.

"What's up, Wonderbread," she shot back.

Rick nodded. "Okay, then."

"So?" Charlotte pressed.

Rick bobbled his head. "Yeah, I admit, the thing with the League had me down a lot. I was ready to give up. Throw in the towel and head back home, admit my defeat, and let it go. Then I heard a rumor about someplace else I could go. Someplace I might could find real adventure."

"The Shy Market," she said, her tone thick with disapproval.

Rick didn't even try to face her. "Yeah."

"You best be watching your step now, boy. That place, it does what you probably heard, but it do more besides," she told him. "They got all kinds of jobs for people what be desperate for the life you looking for, but they got other ones. Darker ones. Lots of bad things happen in that place. Not the kind of thing a young man, fresh to the city and alone wants to be getting involved with while he got nobody to be watching his back."

Rick shook his head in frustration. "What other choice do I have now? The League is a joke. Everywhere I look, people are holding up my Dad, making money off his sacrifice without even caring about what it cost him, or my mom, or me. This isn't even about me wanting to be a hero like him anymore. It's about standing up for my family name. Making people remember that Wonder is about more than just making money on a dead man's memory."

"That's all well and good," Charlotte retorted. "But is it what your daddy would be wanting you to do, or what you be doing for yourself."

Rick cast a glance over his shoulder. "It's what I want, to honor his memory."

She sighed. "Then I guess there no be stopping you from doing this. All right, then. What I said about going alone, though, still hold true. You be needing a proper party to be going with you."

"Not a lot of chance of that," Rick muttered as he finished reheating the grilled chicken and noodle dinner then joined her at the table.

"There always be ways, boy," she winked.

Rick sat for a moment, confused. "Like... what?"

"You be wanting to go to the Slaughterhouse," she said, looking rather smug.

He had no idea what that even meant. "Am I getting a ham?"

"Not that kinda slaughterhouse, boy," she chortled. "It be a bar on the south side of town in the Weeds District. Called the Slaughterhouse. It be a gathering place for others what the League didn't find good enough. Plenty of young ones like you looking for adventure, and be needing a leader to help them. Somebody like you, what got that Wonder name."

"Oh," Rick said, still not getting it. After a moment, it sank in what she was actually telling him. "So, wait. You mean, I can go there, recruit a party, and then go to the Shy Market?"

"You not be the brightest boy," she snorted. "That's just what I be saying."

Rick started eating, thinking about it. "That's... really good to know. Yeah. That's exactly what I needed to know. Thanks, Charlotte!"

"Thank me when you not be dead," she grunted. "All this adventure business. Lot of foolishness. Best thing for you would be to go home, marry that girlfriend you got and have some babies. All you doing, in my mind, is rushing off to be dead."

"Maybe," Rick admitted. "But better to die chasing your dream than to live without ever having tried."

Charlotte shoved up from the table. "Now you do sound like your daddy. He was as dumb as you be."

She was gone a full five minutes before Rick realized it. "She knew. She knew he was my Dad."

He wasn't sure how to feel about that.

As he grappled with that, Charlotte stopped outside Emi's room and gave a light knock. A moment later, the skittish young Elf cracked the door open, looked at her, and then swung it wider, her expression one of curiosity.

"He be going to the Slaughterhouse tomorrow," Charlotte informed her. "This be your chance, girl. Don't be wasting it. That boy is the son of Max Wonder. If you gonna find what you seek, he be the one you need standing at your side."

Emi considered this for a moment then nodded, her face set with as much determination as she could muster. "Thank you, Charlotte."

"Kids today," the Orc muttered as she waved it off. "All in such a big damn hurry to end up dead. What a shame."

Emi closed her door, and leaned against it, hand to her chest, clutching her night gown. "Rick Wonder, huh? Okay. Time to be brave."

Chapter Three: Guns for Hire

DESPITE HIS ASSERTIONS to Charlotte the night before, the next day found Rick full of misgivings about his current plan, and his situation as a whole. So far, his well-laid plan for becoming a famous adventurer had gone completely off the rails. Winging it had never exactly been his style, so it was understandable that he was feeling somewhat unsure about recruiting complete strangers to take on who knew what kind of mission.

Still, as Castor had always said, nothing risked, nothing rewarded. The situation might not be ideal, but it was, in Rick's mind at least, still better than tucking his tail and going home to admit defeat after only a single day in Riscadil. For one thing, his mother would never let him live it down. For another, he felt certain he wouldn't be able to face Maari.

Mostly though, he just couldn't bring himself to throw in the towel without having tried every possible avenue. Max Wonder wouldn't have given in so easily, and Rick was determined to at least measure up to his own father, even if no one else thought him capable.

Which wasn't exactly true, he knew, but it certainly felt that way. He kind of wanted to blame the giant statue of Max in Wonder Plaza for that, but he knew it was just his own self-doubt rearing up. Considering how well things had gone thus far, he figured it was okay to be having a bit of that.

Not that he was going to wallow in it. Of course he wasn't. He was Richard William Wonder, after all. The son of the greatest adventurer to ever live. The son of two of them, and the nephew of a third! He had no time to wallow in anything, be it self-pity or melancholy.

He was pretty sure those weren't the same thing. Pretty sure.

So, with his head up and what he hoped was a determined look in his eye, he faced the new day and this second chance to prove himself. Right after breakfast.

Which Emi was not there for. That was weird.

Charlotte assured him it was because the Elf had urgent business very early that morning, but Rick couldn't help wonder if he'd somehow offended the young lady. Of course, he had time to mull it over as he made breakfast for himself, Charlotte, and June as well for some reason.

Charlotte called it fair as he'd been expecting to cook for Emi, but as she was already gone, she hated to see him be disappointed. He wasn't entirely sure about the logic of that, but shrugged and set to work anyway. His Orcish landlady must have been decently impressed with his cooking skills, as she thanked him with a tip on how to catch a cab so he wouldn't waste the whole day wandering the streets.

Hit one up off the main thoroughfare. They were more likely to pick up less obviously well-off people. Seemed rational when he really thought about it for a moment. So much so, he kind of felt stupid for not thinking of it earlier. Then again, he was new to town and a notorious Rickwit, so with a sigh and some thanks, he gathered his things and headed out.

He'd considered going to the Slaughterhouse first, but as he struggled to find sleep the night before, he had realized it would be better to check out this so-called Shy Market instead. Just in case it was another dead end. There was no sense gathering a party if he was going to be leading them to nowhere. Idiot that he was, on occasion even he had a bright idea.

Before he knew it, he'd managed to secure a handsome driven by a positively delightful Halfling gent, and was on his way to the address Enzo had given him. Besides his single smart idea, Rick had also spent a good deal of time trying to envision just what he was going to find at his destination. Thoughts of a boarded up old manor had clashed with an expansive underground market, staffed by shady people in masks.

Twenty minutes later he was standing outside a barber shop. Riscadil continued to baffle him.

It took him another ten to realize that the address Enzo had given him was for a set of stairs nestled between the barber shop and the antique store next to it. This made him feel slightly better, as at least it descended into darkness and possible mystery.

Or a well-lit, large steel door.

So much for mystery.

Rick spent a few more minutes staring at the door in slight disappointment, then gave up and knocked. He was pretty sure Enzo had either decided to give him the runaround or had fallen victim to some urban legend. Granted, Charlotte had confirmed the Shy Market was a real place, but he was having a hard time believing that this was it.

A slide on the door banged open, revealing only two large, dark eyes set into blue-hued skin. Rick tried very hard to look as non-threatening as possible. Which, even he had to admit, wasn't very hard.

"What?" the creature on the other side demanded.

"I... oh... right," Rick stammered. "Space dolphin."

The creature sighed wearily, rolled their eyes, and the slide banged shut. Rick had a moment to wonder if he'd messed something up before the heavy sound of a massive bolt being drawn echoed to him and the door swung open. With more than a little reservation at this point, he pushed it wider and stepped into the Shy Market.

It was very red.

This gave him pause. Obviously.

Before him lay a hallway, a good ten feet wide that extended a good ten yards, before ending at a large set of plain wooden doors. On either side, the walls were draped in curtains of a deep, blood red. He wasn't sure if this was meant to be opulent, intimidating, or just plain garish.

"In or out, kid," the creature behind the door barked.

With a slight jump, Rick stepped forward and pushed the door behind him, only to find it swinging away on its own. Or rather, the guard, which he assumed it to be, had pushed it closed and slid the large bolt back into place, locking him in.

Looking up and over his shoulder, Rick had to take another moment. He'd never seen a Hobgoblin in the flesh before. Of course, until extremely recently, he'd never seen an Orc in person before either. This morning he'd made breakfast for one.

"You gonna stare all day, or what?" the Hobgoblin asked as it... or rather she, moved to sit on a stool nestled in the corner next to the door.

"I... uh... sorry," he mumbled.

A good six and a half feet tall, the blue-skinned monster of a woman, who seemed to be made entirely of muscles and cleavage, flopped back onto the seat, brushed her ponytail of dreadlocks off her shoulder, stared at him in annoyance for a moment then gave a slight groan and picked up a book.

Riscadil was a very strange place.

"Uh... so..."

"I answer the door," the Hobgoblin cut in before he could finish. "I don't answer questions and I don't give guided tours."

Rick swallowed hard. "Right. Of course. I just..."

She held up a hand. "Don't. Answer. Questions."

Rick chewed his lip. He'd stood up to a Marilith yesterday. That was an actual, honest-to-goodness demon. This was just a Hobgoblin. With a book. No way it could be worse.

"I get that and I'm not trying to be a pest," he pressed.

"Yet you're succeeding," she pointed out as she opened the book to the tasseled marker and began reading, ignoring him as fully as possible.

Rick looked down the hall, drummed his fingers on his thigh then turned back to the reading Hobgoblin.

"Is this the Shy Market?" he blurted.

She slumped on her stool, put the marker back in the book and closed it before giving him a withering glare. "No. This is the happy sunshine palace of fun. Open to kids of all ages. Please, see a clown for a balloon animal."

Rick glanced down the hall where she gestured and then felt really stupid.

"A simple yes would have sufficed," he grumbled. "There was no need for sarcasm."

The Hobgoblin quirked an eyebrow above her bored glare. "There's always a need for sarcasm."

"Right," Rick muttered, adjusting the duffel over his shoulder. "So this is actually the Shy Market."

"Please be sure to visit the petting zoo," the Hobgoblin deadpanned, then gave the most condescending "go-away" wave Rick had ever seen.

He took all of one step before turning back around, to find she had already returned to her book. "Can I ask your name?"

"You can ask," she replied. "Don't mean I'm gonna answer, on account of I don't answer questions. In case you were wondering. Or have a short attention span."

Frustrated for no reason he could name, Rick turned and got another step before spinning back around. "I just wanted to know who exactly I would be complaining to management about."

With a weary groan, the Hobgoblin closed the book, yet again. "Okay look, kid. If I answer the questions you are so obviously desperate to ask, will you please go away?"

Rick wasn't sure how to react to that. "Probably."

"Fine," she grumbled, and waved him on.

"So this Shy Market, they have jobs for adventurers?"

"Yu-huh," she replied in complete boredom.

"For real adventuring jobs?"

"Seems like that was answered with the first question, but what the hell. Yes."

Rick glanced down the hall. "And I can just, like, check it out, without having to take one or lose a body part or anything?"

The Hobgoblin actually blinked several times in shock at that. "What the hell kinda place do you think this is, kid?"

Rick deflated visibly. "I really have no idea."

"Oh, for the love of Juzba," she groaned, rubbing her eyes. "Look, it's just a place where people who want help from folks braver or stupider than them can post a request and maybe get it answered. That's it. No weird bodily sacrifices or anything."

Rick pondered that a moment. "Sounds kinda... normal."

"Imagine that," she muttered.

"So... um... hi. I'm Rick."

She stared at the hand he stuck out, then let him know in a really exasperated tone, "I don't care."

"Right," he mumbled. "I just thought, you know, if I was going to be doing real adventuring, I might be here a lot, and it seemed, you know, like maybe I should get to know the staff or something."

With a look of supreme irritation, she relented, saying, through gritted teeth, "Fine. Hi. I'm Tunya."

Rick stared at her.

"Don't say it, kid."

"I wasn't gonna say anything," he bleated.

"Sure."

He stared at her.

"For the love of..." she groaned.

"Sounds like tuna."

"Please," she begged. "Go away."

"Sorry," he pleaded. "I'm so sorry. I don't know why I said that. I wasn't trying to be rude. I'm just kinda nervous and this isn't what I was expected, but nothing in this city has been what I was expecting, and I'm really sorry, please don't hit me."

Tunya threw her book at him. She hit him square in the face.

"I deserved that," Rick admitted.

"Yu-huh," she agreed.

"Sometimes I'm a Rickwit," he explained.

"Noticed," she drawled.

"I'll just... give you this back... and go away," he whimpered.

"That would be glorious," Tunya told him with a tired smile.

Rick bent to gather the heavy hardcover book she'd thrown at him, and then paused, staring at the title. He stayed that way long enough that Tunya was beginning to fear he was having a seizure or worse, had thought of another question to ask.

"*I, Wonder*," Rick said, picking the book up slowly. "*The Autobiography of Max Wonder*."

"Yeah," Tunya told him with a shrug. "Apparently he was a big deal around here. I'm kind of new to the city myself, so I figured I should catch up on the history and stuff."

"I didn't know this existed," he told her, staring at the large, heroically posed image of his father below the title. "How could I not know about this? Why wouldn't Mom have told me he wrote this?"

"Uh, I really don't know, but if you don't mind, I was kind of getting to a good part," Tunya replied, making a grasping motion for the book.

Rick didn't notice, too transfixed with this newest piece of his own past he'd been ignorant of his entire life. "I just... I don't get it."

"They're like, twenty lita down in Wonder Plaza, kid," she snorted. "So maybe get your own?"

Rick shook himself out of it. "Yeah. Thanks. I will. Sorry about that."

"No big deal," she said, taking the book back and against her better judgment, asking, "You okay there? Looked kinda like you saw a ghost."

"I kinda did," he said with a wan smile. "He was my dad."

"Spoilers," Tunya chastised.

"What?"

"Spoilers!" she barked. "Don't ruin the ending."

"Sure," Rick managed, somehow. "I'm gonna go away now."

"Good," she all but gushed.

Rick walked away, more confused than he'd ever been in his entire life.

* * *

There had been a plan, at the beginning. Go to Riscadil. Join the League. Become famous. It had seemed almost foolproof. Not because it was grand or elaborate, but because it was simple. The simple things were, supposedly, the hardest to mess up. That's what made them simple, really.

Yet, as Rick walked down the red curtain lined hallway, he couldn't help but think that he had overlooked one tiny detail in his extremely simple plan. Not that he could even blame himself for it, though in a way, it was glaringly obvious now he should have at least considered it. After all, the only way to screw up a foolproof plan was to be a big enough fool.

Riscadil was nothing like what he had imagined. The League had not been at all like he'd imagined. Hell, even the alternative, the Shy Market, was turning out to be nothing like he'd imagined. Even Charlotte's house was wildly different than anything he'd imagined.

It occurred to him as he reached the doors, the problem here seemed to lie with his imagination. It was terribly unreliable. Which is why he'd missed that one tiny detail. He'd failed to take into account that his extremely simple plain was not prepared for reality being completely different than he had imagined.

Opening the doors, Rick stepped into the heart of the Shy Market, the only road left open to those who sought a life of adventure, fame, and glory.

It was covered in corkboard. Because of course it was.

He stood for a moment in the doorway, glancing around at the moderate-sized room before him. The walls were covered, from waist high to the low ceiling, in corkboard tacked with thousands of simple sheets of paper. Four other individuals were already present, examining the various offerings, and didn't even bother to give him a cursory glance.

Feeling betrayed by the blandness of reality, he stepped in and closed the door behind him. Several lights flickered overhead, casting the entire room in a stuttering wash of false daylight, slightly green in hue. It reminded him of a bathroom at a train stop on his way to Riscadil.

"Adventure awaits," he sighed softly, giving the other people present a quick look.

A Chthonian, with pitch-black skin and a pair of horns curling from the back of his skull, one broken off halfway, wearing soft leathers and a range of daggers at his back stood next to a Dwarf in plate mail, the two quietly debating a pair of requests. Across the room, a human woman wearing leather clothing stitched with arcane sigils stared upward, while the Halfling at her side, adorned in clerical vestments, studied the lower half of the wall.

Part of him wanted to introduce himself, but he refrained, bearing in mind that none of them had so much as looked his way when he entered. Moving further into the room, he spotted a second door on the same wall as the one he'd come in through, though a sign upon it declared it to be by invitation only. Outside of that, there was nothing remarkable or noteworthy about the Shy Market.

Further disappointed by the stubbornness of reality to be so average and unexciting, Rick turned to give the requests a look, figuring he may as well familiarize himself with them before returning with a party in tow. Even here he found reality to be obnoxiously dull.

Typed pages with a line for the date the request was made, followed by the name of the person making the request, as well as contact information and an address, preceded a brief description of the need of the potential client, with the reward offering listed last. The sheet held no sign of character or flavor, and bore no special designs or markings. Not even a logo or mysterious sigil. Just the facts and nothing more.

Rick spent a few minutes looking over the walls and found that the requests were sorted after a fashion. The oldest were at eye-level for the average humanoid, and ranged from locating missing persons, to protecting merchandise, to recovering rare items, with the rewards increasing the farther he moved down along each of these various unlabeled categories.

Even the requests were organized in a dull, dreary, efficient manner. It made him want to thump his head against the wall, which he did, finally drawing the attention of the Halfling Cleric, who only gave him a slightly pitying look and resumed ignoring him completely.

Living a life of adventure was beginning to look a lot like work.

Still, at least he had verified the actual existence of the Shy Market. All he had to do now was head over to the Slaughterhouse and hopefully recruit a party that wasn't as disappointing as everything else had been since he'd gotten to Riscadil.

Apparently, Rick liked to tempt fate with thoughts such as those.

* * *

As Rick was discovering the depressing normalcy of the Shy Market, Corporal Anton Strakinsy of the Riscadil Police Department was wandering the labyrinthine shelves of the Precinct Archive. However frustrated Rick was by the dull efficiency of his location, Anton was equally irritated by the complete lack of any at his.

Whatever attempt had been made at organization had, he felt, been utterly lost along the way. Boxes stuffed to overflowing were shoved onto the towering shelves any way they would fit, or simply left to sit on the floor in piles that often made getting past them more hazardous than walking a beat could ever hope to be. All of it beneath light fixtures hanging high above, a good third of which were out.

Fortunately, Anton wasn't looking for a what so much as a who, if Sensor could properly be called that. Anton had his doubts, but felt that might sound a bit racist if he spoke it aloud, so had always refrained. Riscadil was a powder keg already. No sense throwing a match at it.

The keeper of the archive, Sensor was the only one capable of locating anything in the place. This made him exceedingly necessary, a fact that Sensor himself didn't seem overly fond of, but was quite happy to maintain. It beat being deported back to his plane of origin apparently. Hence, the chaotic mess that was the Precinct Archive, or as Sensor called it, a filing system.

Anton had long had doubts about that, but couldn't argue the giant floating eye creature always knew not only where something was, but the exact details of whatever it was an individual might be seeking. Call it an exceedingly good memory or a quality of his species, the Riscadil Police Department had long ago decided to keep the strange creature on staff for just this reason, provided he didn't try to enslave the world again.

That one time didn't count apparently. Accidentally turning a quarter of the Police Department into zombies, however terrible it had been, had done wonders for the city budget. They were all dirty cops, too, which was the only reason Sensor still had a job.

The mayor had given him a commendation for it, at the insistence of Max Wonder, they said. Now and again, even Anton found Riscadil to be a strange place.

Hailing from some far away and utterly alien dimension in the greater multiverse, Sensor's species had once been a terrible scourge upon the whole of the world. Despite their many defeats, and the eventual loss of interest in invading this plane of existence, they still cropped up from time to time with some bizarre plot of conquest.

The true name of their home plane, and of their species as a whole, was as impossible to understand as their native language. The creatures were simply too alien. More than demons, devils, or anything from the high planes, Sensor's race had long remained truly enigmatic and completely dangerous. No one really understood what they wanted, how they thought, or what they even were.

Known by many names over the generations, from The Outer Lords, to Eye Tyrants, to The Elder Gods, these days they were simply called Olders, and most of them still on this plane had given up plans for world conquest and instead settled into civil service work. Which was kind of the same thing when one thought about it sideways.

Enormous creatures, Olders looked like giant balls with a single great eye dominating their features. A mouth filled with terrifying fangs didn't help, no more than the upwards of a dozen tentacles they sported, each ending in an eye of some strange color. Powerful, ancient, and utterly alien in every way, they made great civil servants.

Anton wasn't sure how he felt about that. It all seemed wrong somehow.

It wasn't just the Olders, either. A lesser version of their species, commonly called Puffers, had settled into working city surveillance for the RPD. The telepathic link they shared, some kind of individualistic hive mind, which made no sense at all, allowed them to relay vast amounts of information very quickly between themselves and their larger cousins the Olders.

Naturally, the Riscadil Police Department found that quite handy and had offered them a deal a very long time ago, leading to their current state as an ancillary aspect of law enforcement. Creatures of pure chaos working for order. If there was anything else in the world that could capture the sheer strangeness that was Riscadil, Anton had never come across it.

Well, maybe his ex-wife.

Turning a corner, Anton spotted Sensor and gave him a wave. The giant, hovering Older instantly made a deep, prolonged groaning noise that Anton knew meant he was happy to have company. Sensor loved company the way most people loved having poison ivy.

"Hey, pal," Anton called as he approached. "How you been?"

"Solitary," Sensor rumbled, turning away from the officer as he magically manipulated various boxes into whatever passed for his filing system. "Beautifully, wonderfully, gloriously solitary. Thanks for ruining it."

"Yeah, well, that's what us little meat sacks do, you know," Anton replied with a warm smile, which always annoyed Sensor even more. "Ruin everything."

One of the eye tipped tentacles whipped around and managed a glare with its sickly gray-green gaze, which Anton thought was quite impressive, as it had no actual brow to furrow. It was one of Sensor's special talents. He could glare at someone with a tentacle. Anton patted it above the eye, his smile growing even more warm and friendly.

The tentacle withdrew quickly as the Older swung around, grumbling, "I really hate you, you know that, right?"

"Aww, c'mon, Sensor," Anton chuckled. "Hate's such a strong word. I like to think we have a begrudging respect for one another. Sort of an antagonistic friendship."

The massive creature managed a bored look of supreme hatred. "No, it's hate, Anton. There's no respect. No friendship. Just pure, delicious hate."

"I'm feeling a little unloved," Anton replied with a look of mock sadness as he took one of Sensor's tentacles in his hands and began stroking it.

The Older recoiled instantly. "There was a time I would have boiled your brain in your skull, very slowly, just to listen to you scream."

"Aww, your sweet nothings are my favorite, sunshine," the officer returned with a wink, then blew the giant creature a kiss just because he could.

Sensor shuddered and floated a few feet away. "There's something wrong with you, man. Like, really wrong."

"Relax, big guy," Anton chuckled as he leaned against a shelf. "I'm just messing with you a little. Truth is, I've got a question only you can answer. I was hoping you'd help me out, then I'll be out of your personal space."

"Forget it," the Older grumbled, levitating to the top of the shelves, taking the items he'd been cataloging with him. "Last time I helped you out, I got reprimanded by the Chief. My visa renewal is coming up, and I do not need more black marks on my record because you can't keep your nose out of things that don't concern you."

"That was one time, and it was a misunderstanding," Anton argued. "Didn't I stand up for you and tell the Chief it wasn't your fault?"

"Didn't make the reprimand go away," Sensor shot back, managing a close approximation of a shrug with his tentacles.

Anton's smile faded slightly, mostly because the Older had a point. "I don't need to take anything out of the archive, if that helps."

"It doesn't," Sensor told him.

"Okay, look, can I be straight with you?"

"That'd be a first," the giant creature laughed.

"I just need you to do a records search. Hospitals, midwives, and birth certificates. I'm looking for somebody, and I don't really know for sure whether or not they were born in the city. You've got access to the national archives, so I figured you could probably find it, if it exists."

Sensor floated back down, his main giant eye hovering less than a foot from Anton's face. "What part of 'forget it' did you have trouble understanding? Those sorts of searches are logged by the Elder Older you know. If this isn't actually related to anything you're doing paperwork on, I could get in a lot of trouble, so again, forget it."

He jabbed Anton in the chest with one of his tentacles as he said it, making the eye at the end look a little dizzy. Anton glanced at that, as did Sensor. The former smiled, while the later scowled and hovered back, spinning away, a clear signal the matter was settled.

"Even if I brought a honey-bun?" Anton offered sweetly.

Sensor's entire body language stiffed, one eye tentacle peeking around. "That's bribery, man."

"Oh, gimme a break, Sensor," Anton shot back, pulling the wrapped sweet from his satchel. "It's just me, offering my good friend a little treat, while he checks to see if someone actually exists. That's not even remotely bribery."

"That's the literal definition of bribery," Sensor snarled, spinning back around, trying to look disinterested, though his eye tentacles were all fixed on the honey-bun. "Unless, I mean, for example, you were looking for an old friend, or something."

"That's close enough to true, sure," Anton agreed, wiggling the honey bun around as he watched the eye tentacles trace it like a hawk. "Won't take you five minutes, then you get this and I get lost."

Sensor struggled with it for about a half a minute, before rolling his main eye dramatically and slumping, his tentacles drooping, but still remaining fixed on the honey-bun. "Fine! Okay! Just gimme that and I'll do the search."

Anton started to hold it out, then hesitated, made a show of thinking about it, then tossed it in the air. "Okay, but I don't want this little show of trust from me to you to be forgotten."

"Whatever," Sensor muttered, catching the honey-bun and holding it in the air magically. "Asshole. Never should have let you know I had a sweet tooth."

"Life is full of comprises, big guy," Anton soothed, watching as the honey-bun was carefully unwrapped and floated into the Older's oversized mouth.

"Oh, that's just... yeah... mmmm..." the creature moaned in what was nigh on ecstasy. "You get this from Plimpard's Bakery?"

"Dude, don't talk with stuff in your mouth," Anton replied, looking anywhere but at the creature. "And yeah, I did. I know that's your favorite."

"Yeah, yeah, oh mama," the Older sighed, allowing the bun to dissolve. "That's the stuff. Now, who you looking for?"

Anton actually hesitated this time. "You aren't gonna be happy with me."

"I never am," Sensor retorted, still too lost to his sugar orgasm to really notice Anton's change in demeanor.

"I need you to search for any record of Delilah Wonder having a son."

Sensor stopped, his big central eye slowly rolling back down to Anton as his brow furrowed. "You want me to what?"

Anton smiled at him.

The Older hung there for a long moment, the last of the delightful taste of the honey-bun fading. Finally, he sagged and rubbed his forehead with two tentacles.

"For the love of everything unholy, Anton," he groaned.

"Five minutes," the officer reminded, holding up a hand. "That's all it'll take you. Then you can curse me from the glory of your solitude. I promise."

"What is it with you people and Wonder," Sensor grumbled. "I just don't get it. The guy was a total tool. Cocky, arrogant, rude, and not half as interesting as he found himself to be."

"Somebody dislikes competition," Anton muttered.

"What was that?"

"Nothing, forget it," he said quickly. "Look, I ran into this kid yesterday who was getting hassled by Enzo. He said he was Castor Rumble's nephew. It put this itch in my brain, like it was something I should look into. Just in case. So, here I am."

Sensor glared at him. "I could remove that itch along with your brain."

"Let it go, will you," Anton groaned, rubbing his eyes. "The guys been dead for almost twenty damn years, Sensor.

Besides, don't you want to know if his kid has suddenly turned up in the city looking to follow in his daddy's footsteps?"

The Older struggled with that one. "It's Wonder's fault I can't go home without being sent to prison on my native plane, so no, I won't let it go. Still, you do have a point about his kid. That could be valuable in the right circles."

"The right circles?" Anton asked pointedly.

Sensor frowned. "Not that I have anything to do with those kinds of circles. I'm a good, law-abiding, tax-paying citizen. I'm just saying... "

"Can you do the search, or not?" Anton asked, feeling slightly pained at the creature's attempts to look innocent.

Everyone in the RPD knew different. Sensor ran his own bookie business on the side. The only reason he never got in trouble for it was because he never did anything blatantly illegal that would reflect badly on the department. That, and he wasn't very good at it.

"Fine," he finally groaned. "Gimme a minute. And don't move anything!"

Anton settled back as Sensor set about establishing a telepathic link with the wide network of Olders scattered across Liaob, searching for any information about Delilah Wonder having a son. As always, it was kind of a creepy thing to watch. Mostly because all the eyes on the tentacles would glow, while the central eye rolled up until it was almost impossible to see.

Anton took the opportunity to put a box of reports on the wrong shelf.

A few minutes passed before the Older settled and shook himself slightly, saying, "Well, I got good news, and I got bad news."

"Let's have the bad news first, then."

"Nah, the good news," Sensor replied. "The bad news makes no sense otherwise."

Anton shrugged. "Whatever, man."

"Good news is, Delilah does have a son. Name's Richard William Wonder. He was born just a little over twenty years ago. Not long after Max died, actually. So, odds are, Richard really is his son. Unless Delilah had a piece on the side, that is."

"Dude, don't be like that," Anton groaned.

The Older looked confused for a moment. "What? You meat sacks are always doing stuff like that. I'm just saying."

"What's the bad news?"

"Oh, right," the creature sniffed. "He was born in some little out of the way place called Townglen. School records were the last thing I could find on him, but it seems like he was still there. At least, a couple years ago. After that, nothing."

Anton thought that over for a moment. "Townglen, huh? That's where Max was born. Makes sense Delilah and Castor would go there after he died. From what I've heard, they weren't close to their own family."

"I got a picture of him, if you wanna see it," Sensor offered.

"Baby picture, or recent picture?" Anton asked, not sure if the Older was messing with him.

"High school graduation. So kinda recent."

"Let's see it."

Extending one tentacle, the Older projected an image of a late-teens male, human. Anton stared at it for a long time, then nodded, waving for Sensor that he could stop.

"No mistake," he said. "That's the guy I met yesterday."

The Older shifted slightly, looking down at the officer from the corner of his eye. "Then, what you're saying is..."

"We got a Wonder back in Riscadil, and he's looking to become an adventurer. Hell, he told me he was looking to join the League, but with how things are there these days, he's not going to find what he wants with them. Which means..."

"He's gonna end up eye-balling the Shy Market, sooner or later," Sensor groaned. "Great. That's gonna make a ton of work for me somewhere down the road."

Anton mulled this over, then waved to the Older. "Thanks, big guy. I'm gonna go see if I can catch this kid before he does something stupid."

"Whatever," Sensor muttered as Anton hurried away. "Ought to just let him get himself get killed. Put an end to all this hero worship nonsense this city has going on once and for all."

Anton was already gone, though, leaving the Older alone. He hovered for a moment, disconcerted for no reason he could name, then sighed and set back to work, whistling to himself.

Anton was almost to the stairs when he heard the scream of outrage as Sensor realized something was out of place. Despite his mounting concern, that was enough to make him smile.

* * *

After departing the Shy Market with one last look of annoyance from Tunya, Rick managed to catch a cab and headed across town to the Slaughterhouse. The look of concern the driver gave him was enough to make him wonder what sort of place he was going to, but he set that aside, preferring to spend his worry over his dwindling funds.

He needed work and quickly if he was going to keep surviving in Riscadil.

As much as his previous experiences had taught him the dangers of an overactive imagination, he still found himself trying to picture what sort of a place the Slaughterhouse would be. Images of an actual slaughterhouse rebuilt into a tavern, as well as an arena overflowing with fistfights as the cast-offs of the League fought for the right to lead a party of their peers began to drift through his mind.

He tried to shut that down, well aware now that it was likely going to be some sort of normal, average, and completely unassuming place. Still, as the streets turned from well-manicured to overgrown and the cobblestones became more broken, he couldn't help but imagine a worn down building with women of ill-repute waving to passersby from the shattered windows. Or more likely, he realized, some kind of opium den with the thin veneer of acceptability plastered over it by playing host to heartbroken would-be adventurers.

He just hoped nobody offered him the chance to run any drugs. That wasn't the sort of adventure he was looking for.

Finally, after some thirty minutes of navigating the streets of Riscadil, the cab came to a stop, the driver calling down to him that they had arrived. Pushing his expectations out of his head, Rick stepped out and found himself faced with, as he had feared, a perfectly ordinary tavern, a faded old placard squeaking in the breeze proclaiming it to be the Slaughterhouse.

It wasn't even a two-story building. That felt like the real rip-off for some reason.

After paying the driver, Rick hefted his duffel over his shoulder, sighed heavily and walked towards the front door. Another heavy steel affair, this one wasn't locked and required no secret words to enter but did groan loudly as he pushed it open, the rusted hinges making it a bit harder than he'd expected.

Inside, the tavern was fairly well lit with a bar stretching across most of the back wall, shelves of bottles dominating the backdrop against which the heavy-set barkeep worked. A dozen or so tables filled the main room, most of which were little more than scrap wood laid atop barrels, the rest being actual tables that somehow looked even less stable. Stools were mixed with chairs and a low haze of smoke hung in the air, though it smelled only of tobacco and nothing more exotic.

Two waitresses in rather short skirts and low cut tops wandered about looking bored, as a healthy collection of would-be adventurers huddled over their drinks. Makeshift armor, cheap weapons, and holy symbols to deities Rick had never seen before dotted the entire sea of forlorn-looking individuals, only a few of whom glanced up at his entrance before returning to drowning their sorrows as cheaply as they could.

This didn't look terribly promising, he had to admit.

Forcing himself forward, even less certain about this than he had already been, Rick made his way to the bar, his duffel making a heavy thud in the low, murmuring silence of the bar. A few people glanced his way then returned to ignoring him as he leaned across the counter and motioned to the barkeep.

In for a penny, in for a pound, he figured.

"What you be having, lad?" the old man asked, giving Rick a look that spoke volumes of how many like him he'd seen come through.

"I guess... a beer, maybe?"

The barkeep managed to look only slightly annoyed. "Any particular brand you looking for?"

"Whatever you have on tap?"

The old man gave him a withering look.

"Just... surprise me... with something cheap."

"That I can do," the old man snorted as he turned to pull a less than clean glass from under the counter and fetched a pale-colored beer, which he handed over with a nod as he turned away.

Rick fumbled for a moment, then called to him, as quietly as he could, "Excuse me?"

"Yeah?"

"Are you the owner here?"

The old man slumped slightly then returned to lean on the counter, staring at Rick in something akin to mild irritation tinged with humor. "I am. What can I do for you? Got a complaint about the service?"

Swallowing slightly, Rick shook his head. "No, not that. I just had a few questions."

"Get a tour guide then," the other man scoffed.

"About the bar," Rick added firmly, growing very tired of how rude people in Riscadil seemed to be.

Straightening, the old man gave him an appraising look. "Let me guess. League wouldn't have you. You heard about this place. Figured you could find some other folk who wanna make a mark on the world and drug yourself down here, even though you actually think this joint and most of these poor sods are beneath you. That about right?"

Rick blinked. "Well, that's about half right. I don't think anyone is beneath me."

"Sure you don't," the barkeep replied with a humorless smile. "So what is it you want to know? How to get their attention or something?"

Rick fiddled with the glass of beer in front of him. "If there's some sort of process or something I'm supposed to do. Someone I need to speak with, maybe. I just want to know how this works so I don't step on any toes, you know?"

The old man crossed his arms over his broad chest. "Well, that's a step in the right direction. At least you got some consideration to you. Better than most who wander in here. Not that it'll get you far with this lot."

"Thanks," Rick replied, feeling very lost and uncertain. "I think."

"Um... excuse me... um..." a timid, small voice interceded, dragging both men to look to Rick's left.

"Emi?" Rick bleated.

"You know this one, darling?" the barkeep asked.

Emi it was too. Decked out in a deep purple dress that was way shorter than it had any right to be and bore arcane stitching, the timid Elf plucked at his sleeve as she peered up at him from under the wide brim of a tall hat that came to a point, though it was flopped over and looked far from new. Nor did the cloak she wore brushed back from her shoulders. The black knee boots seemed to be little used, but overall, it was not a look Rick ever would have expected from the shy, nervous young woman.

"I was... um... waiting... for you," she stammered, her face coloring as she jerked her hand back from him.

The old barkeep looked somewhat surprised. "Emi, sweetheart, you gotta be kidding me. This guy is who you were waiting for?"

"What do you mean, this guy?" Rick asked with some annoyance. "And, Emi, how do you know this guy?"

"Melvin," the barkeep offered.

"Oh, sorry, hi, I'm Rick" Rick offered quickly. "How do you know Melvin?"

Emi fidgeted nervously. "Um... well... that's a long... uh... story, really... and... um..."

Rick waited, but Emi seemed to have developed a bit of difficulty with words. And breathing. Melvin sighed and rubbed his face as the Elf steadily grew more nervous. Rick was still trying to figure out what she was even doing in a dive like this in the first place.

"Okay, darling," Melvin finally said. "Have a seat, catch your breath, and then, like we talked about, just express yourself, okay?"

Emi nodded vigorously as she clambered onto a stool, looking red-faced and dizzy. Taking pity on her, Melvin poured her a drink, then looked at Rick and shrugged as if to say, you know how she gets.

Rick really didn't think he had any idea anymore.

It took a few minutes and more than a few shots of whiskey, which left Rick even more surprised than he had been, but Emi finally got a grip on herself and nodded her thanks to Melvin before waving for Rick to join her at a table in the corner. Not quite certain at this point what was going on, he followed, beginning to wonder if he was having some kind of weird dream.

Hopefully it wasn't going to turn into one of those where he was wearing no pants.

"Okay... so... um..." Emi started, eyes darting about nervously as she fiddled with the drink in front of her. "I guess... um... you wanna know why I'm here... and stuff..."

"That would be a good place to start, yeah," he agreed. "But truth is, you don't have to tell me if you don't want to."

She shook her head, eyes going wide. "I don't mind... I'm just... um..."

"Nervous?" Rick offered.

"Yeah," she whined, sagging in her chair. "That's kind of why I'm here, actually."

Rick waited for a full minute, but Emi couldn't seem to find the courage to speak, instead just turning her glass in her hands, which were obviously shaking, and looking anywhere but at him. Seeing it, he nodded and decided to get the ball rolling.

"Well, why don't I start," he offered. "My name is Rick Wonder, I'm from the village of Townglen, and my parents are Max and Delilah Wonder. Obviously my dad died before I was born, so I only really know him from the stories I've heard. I came to Riscadil to become an adventurer and try to understand him a little better by being like him."

"Oh," Emi squeaked.

"I know, it's kinda dumb," he admitted. "I guess that's just one reason I'm here. I really want to do this, be an adventurer. I want to live that life, do good things, and be someone who makes the world a better place. I want to live up to Dad's legacy and do the kinds of things he did for the reasons he did them."

Emi was shaking her head before he even finished. "That's not dumb. Not at all! I think it's really admirable!"

Realizing she had almost shouted it, she instantly turned a deep red and sank into her chair.

"Thank you," Rick said. "How about you, then?"

"Um... okay... right," she whimpered. "I'm Emeri Landari, but everybody calls me Emi. I'm a Wizard with a specialty in Evocation magic. I trained at The Solarium in Shindalel, but I'm from the city of Morininsta in the northern reaches of Gulinlan."

"Wow, the Elven nation," he replied, rather impressed. "You've come a long way to be here then. All the way across the Kienrin Sea."

Emi sank deeper into her chair. "It's not that impressive, really. I kind of flunked out at The Solarium, because... um... I got too nervous, and couldn't do any spells in front of the assessment administrators."

"Oh," Rick said slowly. He tried to think of something else to say that wouldn't be insulting or disparaging. Nothing came to mind, so he ended up just adding a second, "Oh."

"I've never done anything outside a controlled environment with only my tutor watching," she added. "I'm kind of a terrible wizard."

"Come on now," Rick countered. "You can actually work magic. That's pretty amazing, right?"

Emi sank a little deeper. "I only really mastered one cantrip. I know a couple of low tier spells, but I always end up stammering over the words and they fail."

Rick stared at her for a long moment. "Oh. Okay. You know, I'm really trying to be supportive here, but you're making it kind of hard."

"I know," she moaned, sinking almost under the table before suddenly shooting back up and grabbing his hands. "Charlotte told me who you are, though, and that you would be coming here, and I thought if I could get in a party with you, you being who you are, then maybe I could get some actual experience with adventuring and get better at spellcasting, and even if you don't want me to be part of the party, I can do other things, like carry your stuff or something, by which I mean I'll do anything, or well, not anything, I can't cook, or clean, and I don't think I can do sex stuff either, cause I've always been too scared to try it, but I can at least carry things or something, and maybe some sex stuff if you don't ask me to look..."

"Emi, please stop talking!" Rick cried, horrified at the barrage of words erupting from the woman and the direction those words were taking.

Maari would squish her like a bug if she knew.

"Sorry," Emi squeaked, recoiling back, turning a violent shade of red.

Rick held a hand up. "No, it's okay, it's just, that was a lot very suddenly."

She nodded vigorously, sending her hat flopping over. She pushed it back with way more chagrin than Rick felt was warranted.

"Okay, so, let's sum up, okay?" he offered, giving her a warm smile. "You want to prove yourself as a wizard, is that about right?"

She nodded slowly. "I... um... want to go home one day and make them admit they were wrong. That I'm not useless."

Rick's eyebrows shot up. "They called you useless?"

She nodded again, tears brimming in her eyes. "When they kicked me out."

Chiding himself for being a soft touch, Rick smiled at her and nodded. "Well, everybody told me I was stupid for wanting to be an adventurer, so we've got that in common. How about you and I show everyone they were wrong about us?"

Emi's eyes slowly widened. "You mean...."

"Let's you and me be the first members of our new adventuring party."

Emi threw herself across the table, hugging him frantically. "Thank you, thank you, thank you! I promise you won't be sorry, unless I have to cook or do something with sex or...."

"No sex stuff," Rick put in quickly, pushing her back into her seat. "I've got a girlfriend back home who's bigger than you *and* me. So there will be no sex stuff. Now please stop bringing that up. You're making me nervous with it."

Nodding so vigorously her hat almost flew off her head, Emi whimpered, "Thank you for this, Rick. I'm probably just going to let you down, but I will try my hardest to be brave."

Reaching over to push her hat back atop her head, Rick grinned at her. "No worries, okay? My job is to protect you. You may only know one cantrip, but as long as it's a good one, we'll do fine."

"Firebolt," she said, the first glimmer of a smile starting to show.

"That's a good one, all right," he agreed. "So, now all we need is a few more people and we can get started. You know how to get these people's attention?"

Breaking out in a bright smile, Emi nodded. "I do!"

* * *

After taking a moment to talk to Melvin, Emi ushered Rick into a back room that had been set aside for prospective party leaders to interview individuals in a more private setting than the main bar area would allow. No sooner were they inside than Rick noted it didn't look as if it had been used in a while. A layer of dust had settled over everything, and much of the room was being used for storage.

Melvin admitted somewhat sheepishly that it had been some time since anyone had wanted to step up and take the reins of actually leading a party. Most of the people out drowning their sorrows were waiting for someone else to do it, though even then many of them had long since given up and simply came to bemoan dashed dreams.

Shaking his head, Rick set aside his duffel, rolled up his sleeves, and with Emi's help, set about making the so-called interview room somewhat presentable. Or at the very least, less dusty. Some three hours later, he felt it was something he could work with.

A long table, formerly for larger gatherings out in the common room, had been moved to the middle with a chair for himself and another for Emi, who Rick insisted was to be his equal partner and co-leader, no matter how much she argued she didn't deserve it. A third chair was set on the other side so they could conduct a proper interview, though by the time they had finished moving most of the stored crates, furniture and booze to a corner, Rick realized they had no idea what to even ask.

Another two hours was spent sorting that out over lunch, which Melvin was nice enough to give them for free as they'd done a lot of cleaning he couldn't seem to find the time for.

At least they'd gotten that out of it.

Finally, with their list of questions decided and the room in decent enough shape, Rick took the last step, according to Emi. Directly outside the room hung a large bell. When someone wanted to signal they were interested in forming a party, they simply rang the bell and then awaited the petitioners' arrival.

Taking a few minutes to don his armor and swords, feeling it was best to present himself professionally, Rick stepped out, took a deep breath, and rang the bell as hard as he could.

Everyone looked up, and then went right back to their drinks.

Of course.

Not about to be deterred at this point, he nodded to himself and stepped back into the interview room, took a seat beside Emi, and waited.

For another hour.

It was almost enough to make him give in. Just sitting there making idle chit-chat with Emi so as to avoid sending her into another full meltdown, while nothing happened made him think that perhaps this was the universe giving him a sign. He really wasn't suited to a life of adventure and should turn back now.

When the door finally creaked open, admitting a tall, willowy, red-haired Half-Elf in green dyed leathers, Rick was at the brink of telling Emi it just wasn't meant to be. Instead, he held his tongue and stared in surprise as the woman looked around the room and sort of wandered her way over.

"Uh, hi," Rick finally managed.

"Heya," the woman said. "Wow. This room has some really great vibes. Nice bit of an echo, too. I like it. Feels good here."

Rick exchanged a befuddled look with Emi. "Okay. I guess. That's good. Probably."

"Oh, yeah," the Half-Elf said as she settled in the chair. "Means things are gonna go really great. Totally a sign that we're, like, supposed to meet and stuff."

Rick blinked a few times then gave a sort of nod. "That's... good to hear. I'm Rick Wonder, and this is Emi Landari. We're recruiting a party with the goal of securing work through the Shy Market and building our fortunes as adventurers."

"Wow," the woman said. "That was so authoritative. I'm feeling very drawn to you right now. You've got this strong aura. Just makes me want to kind of like, fall into it, you know?"

"Uh... okay... thanks, I guess?" Rick stammered.

The Half-Elf went wide-eyed for a moment then mimed her head exploding. "Man, I am so sorry! I just got so caught up in your intensity I totally forgot for a second, you know? I'm Mimi Avaman from the Knot Hill Druid Clan. It's so totally awesome to meet you, you know?"

"Back at you," Rick stumbled, giving Emi a curious look, but getting only a blank stare in return.

Thanks, Emi. Super helpful.

"So, tell me, Miss Avaman..."

"Mimi," she cut in. "You can call me Mimi. There's no reason for us to be so, like, formal and stuff, right? We're gonna be saving the world together and stuff, you know? Let's just put all that stuffy stuff to the side and roll with each other like the wind, yeah?"

Rick had no idea what she was talking about. "Okay... uh... Mimi."

"Yeah," she intoned, smiling. "Mimi. I like the way you say it, makes it sound like a name."

Rick fiddled with his list of questions. "It is your name, isn't it?"

"Well, yeah, I mean, sure, but the way you say it makes it sound like a capitol N name, you know?" she responded.

"Sure," Rick said slowly, having no idea what she meant. "Anyway, tell me, Mimi, why do you want to be an adventurer?"

She nodded several times, smiling at him. "That's a great question, Rick. You are so strong. I can feel it. You bring out my inner hero already."

Rick was having serious second thoughts as she thumped her fist over her breast and then pointed at him.

"I... uh..." he flailed.

"I guess, you know, I wanna be an adventurer because I look around and I see the world, and it's, like, sick, right? It needs to be healed of violence and sadness and loneliness. It just makes me cry in my soul, you know? So, yeah, I wanna heal the world and turn tears into smiles," she told him, nodding and smiling the whole time.

It occurred to Rick that she was high as a kite. He wasn't sure how he hadn't noticed that right away, but she was most definitely incredibly high.

"So... um... do you have any special skills that would be helpful?" he asked.

"Yeah, totally," she said with a wide grin. "I can, like, turn into birds and small woodland animals."

"Wow," Rick managed.

"Oh, and I know some healing magic and stuff like that. I'm pretty versatile really. I'm also really great at getting drum circles going and helping build the energy, you know?"

"Uh... huh..."

"Oh, and my bead craft skills, not to brag, but they are seriously amazing," Mimi added, looking as smug as she was capable. Which, wasn't very.

"You don't say?" Rick stumbled. "Well, okay, I think that about covers it. We'd like to interview a couple more people before we officially form a party, of course, but we'll certainly keep you on the short list."

"Awesome." Mimi nodded, and then made no move to get up.

Rick stared at her as she smiled, still nodding.

"You can go."

"Oh cool, like, thanks, Rick." Mimi beamed as she stood and wandered her way back to the door before thankfully vanishing.

"I liked her," Emi said, the only thing she had said the entire time.

Rick face-planted onto the table.

* * *

Another half an hour passed before the door eased open, admitting a young man with tousled brown hair and a somewhat befuddled look on his face. Wearing simple armor adored with some symbol Rick didn't recognize, the man looked around the room then pointed at the chair as if to ask if he could sit. Offering him a warm smile, Rick waved to it.

It took the fellow another minute or two to make his way there as he got momentarily distracted, it seemed, by the pile of crates and furniture in the corner. He made it eventually, however, and sat, still staring at the corner with something akin to awe.

"Hello," Rick started. "I'm Rick, and this is Emi. We'll be leading this party, should it ever get formed, and would like to ask a few quick questions if you don't mind."

"Hi," the man said, waving at each of them.

Rick waited a moment, but he didn't seem interested in saying anything else, too fixated on a dust mote floating by, caught in the afternoon light coming through the windows.

"So, what's your name?"

"Toddson," he replied, fixing his gaze back on Rick then suddenly standing and extending a hand. "What's yours?"

Rick felt all the wind go out of his sails. "Rick. I just told you that."

"You did?" Toddson asked as he sat back down. "Wow. Hey, you did. I'm sorry. Totally blanked out there."

"I can imagine you're a bit nervous," Rick tried to rationalize.

"About what?" Toddson inquired, looking honestly confused by Rick's statement.

Rick circled a finger in the air. "All of this?"

"Nah, this seems like a cool room," Toddson told him, "Nice pile in the corner. Very... pile like."

"Okay," Rick struggled in vain. "So, Mr. Toddson..."

"Oscar," Toddson... maybe... interjected.

Rick blinked, looked at Emi, got nothing helpful from her, then back at the man who was maybe Toddson, but maybe Oscar.

"Sorry, I thought you said your name was Toddson," Rick said slowly.

"It is," the man nodded.

"I'm sorry, I'm a bit confused now," Rick told him.

Toddson, or Oscar, looked at him in awe. "Man, I know just what you mean. I'm confused all the time."

Rick ran a hand over his face and pressed on for reasons he wasn't sure of anymore. "So... um... Oscar Toddson?"

"Who?"

"You!"

"Oh, no, it's Toddson Oscar."

Rick could find no way to grasp that. "Sorry. I didn't mean to be rude. Is that a cultural habit?"

"What?" Toddson asked, looking very confused by the question.

"Having the last name first," Rick suggested.

Toddson stared at him, cocking his head to the side a little. "Toddson is my first name. I think it's just a family thing. I never really thought to ask my parents about it, though. Why? Is it important?"

"Nope," Rick said quickly. "So, Toddson, can I ask, why do you want to be an adventurer?"

"I have no idea," Toddson said with a nonchalant shrug. "Just sorta seems like the thing I should be doing."

"Uh-huh," Rick intoned very slowly. "And what do you do?"

"I'm a good juggler."

Rick really wanted to go back to his safe place, face down on the table. "As an adventurer, I mean. What do you offer to a party? What role would you play?"

"Oh," Toddson exclaimed, smacking himself in the forehead. "That makes way more sense. Yeah, I'm a Cleric."

"I see," Rick nodded. "Of what deity?"

Toddson stared at him for a very long time. "I forget."

"You... what?" Rick stammered, utterly lost and confused now. "How can you forget what deity you serve as a Cleric?"

"Well, probably because it's the Forgotten One," Toddson replied. "Past that, I don't really remember much about them, though."

"Yeah, I've never heard of that god," Rick pointed out.

Toddson snapped his fingers and pointed at him. "Cause he's forgotten. Get it?"

Rick slumped. "But you do know healing magic, right? At least tell me you know healing magic."

"Pretty sure, yeah," Toddson replied with a grin.

Rick fell back in his seat, exasperated. "Pretty sure?"

"Yeah, my spells sorta just come to me," Toddson admitted. "Whatever what's his face thinks I need to cast, when I need to cast it. I think that's how it works, anyway. Can't quite seem to remember that, either."

"Okay, well, I think that'll do," Rick said quickly. "We'll be making our final decisions later today and we'll let you know."

"Cool," Toddson said, then sat there for a minute more.

"You can go," Rick stated.

"Right, yeah, duh," Toddson laughed.

As soon as he was out the door, Rick face-planted back onto the table.

"I liked him," Emi offered.

Rick rolled his head around to glare at her and got a nervous smile in return. Beyond disappointed, and mostly angry that Jacan Glass at the League really did have a legitimate point, Rick rolled back to be face down on the table.

At least it couldn't get any worse.

* * *

Twenty minutes later, it got much, much worse.

Having barely recovered from the high-as-hell Druid, and the Cleric of... whatever he was a Cleric of, Rick was, yet again, ready to call it a wash. Obviously the only people here were all lunatics, and he wasn't about to put his life in the hands of a pothead and a guy who couldn't even remember the name of his own god.

He was desperate, but not that desperate.

As he turned to tell Emi that maybe this wasn't going to work, the door all but exploded off its hinges, admitting a tall, lanky human dressed entirely in white. Okay, not entirely, Rick realized as the dazzle faded slightly. There was also a lot of gold.

A good six feet tall with a well-coiffed pompadour and an even more well-maintained chevron mustache, the man who sauntered into the room wore a billowing white silk shirt left open almost to his navel. Around his neck danced several gold chains, one of which bore a medallion of some sort. Bracelets of gold jangled on his wrists and dazzling rings dotted most all of his fingers.

It was the pants that Rick really had a hard time with. They were excessively tight, of a soft, brushed leather, and absurdly white. As were the knee boots he wore, that also bore gold chains dangling around them. It was like being in the presence of a really glittery...

Rick wasn't sure what, actually. Just something really glittery and white.

"Congratulations!" the man cried as she swaggered across the room. "Today is your lucky day. I have decided that you are accepted as members of my party. You may now feel thrilled beyond words."

"Uh..." Rick gaped.

"Lancaster White at your service, my poor slobbering man, though really, it's fairer to say that you will be at my service, obviously," the fellow declared, then laughed uproariously.

"Whaaa...." Rick continued to gape.

Lancaster shimmied his way over to the table. "Naturally, good lad, you'll be a junior member. An apprentice, if you will. Only the loveliest of women are allowed to stride in my considerable wake, such as this vision of beauty before me. Hello, gorgeous!"

He leaned across the table, taking Emi's hand and kissing the back of it with a wink that wasn't so much sensual as it was not fit for viewing by anyone under the age of eighteen. Probably not them, either. Rick was pretty sure it constituted sexual harassment, actually.

"Abba phu bubla!" Emi blathered.

"Of course," Lancaster cooed, pulling back to strike a pose that put his... uh... manhood on display.

"I'm very confused right now," Rick muttered.

Lancaster cast a gaze his way and ran a hand down his bare chest. "Of course you are. Why wouldn't you be? How can someone so you be so lucky to as to be in the presence of someone so me? I feel your pain, my young apprentice, and I'm here to assure you that all will be well. Just follow me and you will know the glory of my castoffs! A veritable rain of secondhand babes and small change. How fortunate can you possibly be?"

"Gurba phub mammma!" Emi continued to blather.

Rick gave her an annoyed look, then sighed heavily. "Honestly, I think I may be cursed."

Lancaster swept over to him and patted him on the head. "Come now, boy! Buck up! Looks aren't everything, unless you're me!"

Emi made a long spluttering sound, which was at least better than the random nonsense she had been rambling. Rick rubbed his eyes and accepted that he should stop assuming things couldn't get worse. Reality apparently took that as a challenge.

"Mr. White!" Rick snapped, standing up and leaning over to be as close to the walking caricature as he could. "I am the one organizing this party, and I will decide if you get to be a member. Now please sit down, shut up, and when asked a question, answer it like a sane human being!"

Lancaster blew him a kiss. "I like it when young men are forceful, so you know."

"Oh, for the love of..." Rick cried.

Lancaster gave his boisterous laugh again and fell into an exotic lounge across the chair. "I'll humor you, lad, but only because you have a sharp tongue and I admire that in a man. Not as much as I do in a woman, but close. After all, there's enough Lancaster to go around."

Emi gave a long squee. Rick made a point of ignoring that.

Settling back into his chair, Rick tried very hard not to look directly at the absurd thing happening in front of him.

"Now then, Mr. White..."

"Call me Lancaster," Lancaster insisted. "But say it slow, and roll the 'r'."

"No," Rick said flatly.

Lancaster gyrated in the chair a little and purred. Rick wasn't sure how to react to that.

"So, tell me what qualities you bring to party," he inquired instead.

"Mostly, all of this," Lancaster replied, stroking his chest.

"Yeah, no," Rick retorted.

Emi lost the ability to breathe. That was probably for the best.

"If you must know, my young and almost attractive friend, I am a member of the Night Brand, the world's largest Thieves Guild," Lancaster stated with a pompous chuckle. "I am a man of many talents, most of which involve entering and leaving places without the permission of the owners, as well as the expert handling of all manner of devices, mechanical and sexual."

Rick stared at him in disbelief. "You're a Rogue?"

Lancaster sniffed at that in disdain. A very sensual disdain. "I am an artist, sir. A veritable celebration of the art form of roguish behavior. I am, in every way, the living epitome of swash and buckle."

Rick couldn't figure out how to wrap his head around any of that. "Yeah, those things have nothing to do with being a Rogue."

"They do when I do them," Lancaster purred, then licked two fingers and stroked them across his mustache.

"Did my mom put you up to this?" Rick asked, without even meaning to.

"Maybe," Lancaster cooed mischievously. "What's her name? She might have begged me to do it last night in the throes of passion."

Rick really thought about punching him. Instead, he answered the man's question. "Delilah Wonder."

The gaudy thing in front of him laughed outrageously at that. "Ahhh, that was funny, my little friend! For a moment there, I almost wanted to believe you! However, I..."

Lancaster trailed off, Emi having caught his eye as she nodded at him. The oversized smile that had been fixed on the Rogue's face since the moment he walked in the door began to fade as he turned back to Rick, his brain clearly churning.

"Wait, seriously?"

"My name is Richard William Wonder," Rick stated, barely holding his annoyance with this buffoon in check. "My mother is Delilah Wonder. My father was Max Wonder. My uncle is Castor Rumble. If you call me your little friend, or anything other than Rick even one more time, I am going to kick your ass. Understand?"

Lancaster gaped at him for a full minute, before managing to say, "Holy shit."

"Now then," Rick said slowly.

"I've got the son of a Wonder for a protégé!" Lancaster exploded, leaping up and thrusting his hips out dramatically. "I'm even better than I already knew I was!"

Rick crumpled up the paper he'd had his questions written on and threw it over his shoulder. Emi passed out on the table next to him. Lancaster thrust his hips a few more times in joy.

"Thank you, that will be all," Rick snapped.

"Come now, son," Lancaster pressed, sliding into a sit on the table in front of Rick. "Show me your... swords."

"Get out!" Rick bellowed.

Slipping back, Lancaster sniffed indignantly. "Fine. I'll play your game. When you come to your senses, you may beg my forgiveness outside. Ta!"

With that, he swaggered his way out the door, his tightly clad buttocks wiggling all the way, leaving Rick seething, his knuckles turning white as he fought the urge to beat the fool senseless. After a moment, he collapsed back into his chair and forced himself to take several calming breaths. No matter how he looked at it, this was just not going to work.

"I liked him," Emi whimpered.

Rick gave up.

* * *

"No, Emi," Rick stated emphatically. "Forget it. Those people are not what we want. They're not what anybody wants."

"Rick," she whimpered, fidgeting in her seat. "We have to be realistic about this, I think. It's been two hours and nobody else has shown up. If we don't make a decision soon and head back, we won't have any place to sleep tonight. Charlotte really will lock us out."

Rick paced the room for a moment, trying to decide if it was even worth it. "But they're all so... insane!"

"I'm sorry," Emi wilted.

"I mean, I think that Druid was more than a little high. The Cleric can't even remember what god he serves, and don't even get me started on that idiot in white! A Rogue, my ass!" he shouted, storming back and forth. "No wonder the League turned them down! Anyone with a brain in their head can see none of those people aren't fit to be anywhere near anything like a real adventurer!"

"I'm sorry," Emi sniffed.

"By all the gods of this world and every other, if my Dad had seen any of those people, he'd have laughed them right out of the business entirely!" Rick raged. "And let me tell you, I grew up around real adventurers! They don't act anything like that! They have class! Dignity! Self-respect! And more importantly, a sense of honor!"

"I'm sorry," Emi sobbed.

"My mother is a gods-damned paragon of... uh..." Rick slowed, then stopped, his brain grinding to a halt as he realized what he'd been about to say.

Delilah Wonder was a lot of things, but she was certainly no saint. Nor was she exactly normal. Neither was Castor, when he really thought about it. Actually, they were both really weird. Like, crazy weird.

Ah, hell.

Rick slumped. "Gods damn it. Why the hell is everything so fucked up?"

"I'm sorry!" Emi wailed.

Starting, Rick turned and really noticed that the Elf was sobbing her eyes out. "Emi, no, wait, please stop. It's not your fault those people are crazy. Or my family, now that I really think about it."

"B-b-but I made you do this!" she blubbered.

Great. Way to go, Rickwit.

Collecting himself, he moved to pull his chair over beside her and patted her on the shoulder as comfortingly as he could. "No, I was going to do this before I even knew you'd be here. It's my fault."

"No," she bawled. "You're trying to help me, and I'm not worth it!"

Oh, come on!

"That's not true, Emi. You are absolutely worth it. I just came in here with the wrong expectations. It really is on me."

"But they're the same as me!" she slobbered, then collapsed into incoherent wailing.

Okay, that was kind of true, but he wasn't about to tell her that. "No, they aren't. You're cool, and awesome, and brave. Those guys, they're not good enough for you. I just want to be sure that anyone we let join us is going to be as serious about this as you and I are. That's all."

"Really?" she whimpered, snot dripping out of her nose.

"Really," he assured her.

Sniffing back her tears, she nodded slowly. "I don't think we're gonna do any better, though."

"Yeah, I kind of agree with you there," he lamented, rubbing his eyes. "And, Emi, I know you want to get out there and prove yourself. So do I. It's just, I dunno about these people. They seem kind of unstable. And not in the capable way my mom and uncle are. Really badly unstable."

"Are we giving up, then?" she asked, before snorting back more snot.

Rick was really missing Maari after that. "No. We aren't. I'm not sure about them, but if you want them, then okay. We'll... try and make it work."

She nodded, her hat flopping over her face. "I wanna go and get brave, Rick. I don't think waiting is going to help. We can't do much worse, after all."

"Yeah, let's not put that to the test," he said quickly, giving her shoulder a squeeze. "Life has a way of making you regret saying stuff like that."

A barbarian in a hot-pink loincloth burst through the door. "Are you guys still hiring?"

Rick and Emi both stared at him for a long moment, before shouting over each other, "No!"

* * *

Having given Emi time to clean up and make herself presentable, Rick led the way back out into the bar proper, easily spotting the trio of weirdos they had, for lack of a better word, interviewed earlier. Most of the patrons had gone, with the day turning to early evening, but those three still remained, scattered about with a few other customers who had long since passed out on their tables.

Giving Emi one last look that begged to know if she was sure about this and getting a timid smile in return, Rick sighed heavily and faced the music. For better or worse, he had gathered a party. He just hoped they didn't get him or Emi killed at some point.

"Mimi, Toddson, and Lancaster, if you could join us, please," he called.

Glancing around, the three rose and walked or swaggered over, joining them by the doorway to the interview room. The Druid was clearly still high. The Cleric got lost at least twice walking across the room. The Rogue managed to perch seductively on the edge of the bar, despite Melvin's outrage.

"Okay, so, after talking it over, we've decided," Rick said, then paused, hoping for a last minute miracle to save him from this disaster. When one didn't present itself, he finished, "To have the three of you as members of our party."

"Sweet," Mimi drawled with a smile.

"Naturally," Lancaster cooed, running a hand up his leg in very improper ways.

"What party?" Toddson asked.

Rick face-palmed, took a deep breath and looked them over. "We'll meet here tomorrow around ten in the morning. From here, we'll go to the Shy Market, secure a job, and get to work. Everybody got that?"

"Yup," Mimi nodded, swaying more than a little.

"Can it be a sexy job?" Lancaster asked, throwing Emi a wink that almost undid her.

"Wait, what's going on?" Toddson begged.

Rick shook his head slowly. "Okay, so, you're gonna be a problem."

"Fear not, my young fan," Lancaster pronounced, sliding off the bar to wrap an arm around the befuddled Cleric. "This devote man of the cloth and I are boarders at the same establishment. We're veritably old friends! I'll ensure his prompt arrival personally!"

"Who are you?" Toddson asked in dismay.

"Lancaster," said Lancaster. "I live next door to you."

Toddson thought really hard about it. "The gigolo?"

Mimi coughed up smoke and laughed. Rick liked her slightly more after that.

"No, I am a member of the Night Brand, the world's most exclusive Thieves Guild. Remember?" Lancaster urged.

"Nope," Toddson admitted with a shrug. "Sorry."

"Never mind," the Rogue muttered. "I really do live right next door to him. He'll be here. Fear not. We will sally forth as a complete party, or my name isn't Lancaster White!"

"Yeah, but I mean, is that really your name?" Mimi asked.

"It is!"

"But, like, are you sure?"

"As sure as I have it tattooed above my perfect ass," Lancaster shared with a wink.

Mimi nodded at that, looking impressed. "I kinda wanna see that."

"Follow me, and I assure you, you shall," he promised.

"This is making me uncomfortable," Toddson whined.

"What is?" Lancaster asked, looking innocent.

Toddson wavered a moment. "I forget."

"Yup," Rick lamented with a nod. "We're so gonna die horribly."

Chapter Four: Dirty Deeds Done Dirt Cheap

DESPITE THEIR LUCK in finding a cab, Rick and Emi still made it back to Charlotte's with only minutes to spare before the Orcish landlady's curfew. As she had before, Charlotte was waiting in the hallway when they entered, a less than pleased look on her face.

Before Rick could even say anything, Emi began gushing about their good fortune at the Slaughterhouse, taking Charlotte completely off guard. When the Elf's babbling turned to fawning praise towards Charlotte herself for directing Rick to the tavern, the hulking woman's dour expression softened considerably.

Rick decided to put out of mind that particular weakness of Charlotte's. Somehow, he doubted he'd be able to get the same reaction from their landlady.

Over dinner, Emi continued rambling, telling Charlotte all about their new companions, which sent the Orc into an obvious state of deep concern. While Emi herself was oblivious to Charlotte's mounting worry as the details of their new party were laid out, Rick noticed it plainly enough. Already concerned himself, seeing an Orc get fretful did little for his state of mind.

Only once did Charlotte turn that worried gaze to him, however. Catching it, he gave her one in return, letting her know he was already aware of the possible problems, and with a brief glance towards the overexcited Elf, hoped he reassured Charlotte that he would take care of Emi.

She seemed to pick up on his intent and turned back to Emi without a word, allowing the young woman to revel in her glee. For himself, Rick nodded, smiled, and agreed when he knew he was supposed to, but silently hoped they weren't making a terrible mistake entrusting their lives to these people.

By morning that concern had only deepened. Much of his night had been spent tossing and turning, trying to figure out how he was supposed to spin such bad cards into a winning hand, before sheer exhaustion had finally claimed him. With the alarm, he found his peace of mind was still as far from reach as it had been the night before.

Recalling his conversation with Jacan Glass, Rick found he was agreeing with the man even more, having now seen for himself just how unsuitable some people actually could be for the line of work they were wanting to enter. As much as it pained him to agree with the smug-looking Elf on anything, there was no escaping the fact that the party he had gathered were all very likely terrible at their jobs.

Resolving himself to ask Charlotte if she knew anything of the connections his new party had claimed to have, Rick decided to try and make the best of the situation. Because that always went so well for him.

As if to emphasize that thought, he never got a chance to ask Charlotte anything. As much as his concern had deepened, Emi's enthusiasm had heightened. Over breakfast, her tendency to babble had apparently been dialed to a thousand, after which, the knob was clearly broken off. Neither he nor Charlotte could get a word in edgewise as the young Elf gushed over everything from how exciting it was to be heading out for a real adventure to how pretty Mimi's hair had been to several points in between those two very distant destinations.

Before Rick knew what was happening, he and Emi were dressed, geared up, and in a cab heading back to the Slaughterhouse for their morning meeting with their party. He had really wanted to get some information from Charlotte, but as her brownstone and any sanity it provided receded into the distance, he accepted his apparent fate and made peace with the fact he was going to die among idiots.

Somehow, it seemed the right way for a Rickwit to go.

As much as he wanted to put that out of his mind and hope for the best, reality once again had its way with him and didn't even leave any money on the dresser. He was kind of getting use to that. His entire three days in Riscadil so far had sort of made him feel like a cheap date in general, at least as far as his relationship with reality was concerned.

Upon entering the Slaughterhouse at ten minutes to ten in the morning, he found Lancaster, Mimi, and Toddson already present, sitting around a table in the half-full establishment, the Rogue and Druid passing a blunt between them, while the Cleric stared at the ceiling in what Rick quickly decided to call fascination.

It was the least disturbing possibility.

"Well, this is off to a great start," he muttered as he led Emi to join them, the Elf practically bouncing out of her skin in excitement. Enough so, he was starting to wonder if he was going to need a leash for her. The kind parents got for hyperactive children.

"Ah, good morning, friends," Lancaster called, exhaling a plume of smoke as he motioned them to sit. "We were just talking about you. In good ways, of course. Not as good as ways people talk about me, but still, good ones."

Rick rolled his eyes as he fell into a chair. "Do you ever turn it down a little?"

"Turn what down?" the Rogue asked as Mimi offered Emi the joint.

Rick was thankful that she refused, not ready to deal with a high version of the Elf. It left him free to wave at Lancaster, saying, "All of this. You. In general."

Laughing heartily at that, the other man lounged in his seat and stroked his chest, which looked to have been waxed, possibly recently. "You can't turn this down, Rick, my boy. One cannot be a star if they do not shine."

"Whoa," Mimi hiccupped past a thick cloud of smoke. "That's, like, super deep."

"You know how deep I can get, darling," the Rogue winked, violating at least a dozen sexual harassment laws in the process.

"Wow," Rick exclaimed. "So do not need to know that."

"Relax, my lucky protégé," Lancaster chuckled. "If anything, you should be taking notes."

"Not gonna happen."

Toddson seemed to realize people had joined the table at that point and smiled, offering Rick his hand. "Oh, hey there. I'm Toddson."

Not since his mother had stormed out of the kitchen had Rick so wanted to go to his happy place, face down on the table. Instead he sighed, shook the Cleric's hand and said, "I know. We met yesterday. Somehow, you are hard to forget."

"Ah, that's a nice thing to say," Toddson said blithely. "Thanks... um... Grant?"

"Rick."

"Right!"

"Imonya save me," he groaned.

Mimi offered Toddson the joint, which he took and stared at a moment before offering it back to her. She accepted it with a smile. Emi smiled like a lunatic and fidgeted in her chair. Lancaster kept stroking his chest. Rick rubbed his eyes and wondered if his mother holding him coming home so soon over his head could possibly be worse than this.

Only barely, he decided. Only so very barely.

"Okay, so," he finally said. "Before I came here yesterday, I stopped off at the Shy Market to get some sense of it, so if you guys have already had breakfast and are ready to go, we can head out, decide on a job and get to work."

They all stared at him blankly. It was awkward.

"I'm sorry, but what's the Shy Market?" Lancaster finally asked. "I mean, I know you mentioned it last night, but I assumed you were talking about the lovely Elf's bedroom and was kind of distracted by that thought."

"It's a place adventurers can get work outside the League," Toddson offered.

Everyone took a turn staring at him blankly. It wasn't awkward as much as baffling.

"What?" he asked nervously. "Did I forget my pants again?"

"No, and please never do," Rick cut in quickly. "Basically, exactly what he said. A place we can secure work as an adventuring party. So, if there's nothing else?"

"Lanny, tell him the else," Mimi coughed, finishing the blunt.

"Lanny?" Rick struggled.

"Ah, yes, the else," the Rogue intoned playfully. "I almost forget. We had a few things we wanted to sort out before we joined you on this escapade towards my greatness and your joyous new lives in my venerable shadow. A few minor quibbles, really, but as I'm allowing you to play the brave leader of this lovely band, we thought it best to discuss it, so I can shoot down your terrible ideas and we can go with my brilliant ones."

Rick blinked a few times, assuming some of that had made sense in some other plane of existence. Giving Emi a brief look, he got only her overactive smile in return, sighed heavily, and waved Lancaster to go ahead. He felt certain it was going to be more stupidity, but what the hell? It wasn't as if things could get worse.

One day, he knew, he'd have to stop thinking that.

"All right, then," Lancaster exclaimed. "So, we're a party now, but the delegation of duties remains rather unclear. You are the figurehead, of course, but what role does everyone else play in your imaginary little world, Rick, my sweet?"

"Uh... what?" Rick stumbled.

"He means, outside our duties, what can we do to help the party as a whole," Mimi translated, by some form of obscure magic, obviously. "Like, when we make it big and stuff, you know? Who's responsible for what?"

"You mean like a treasurer or something?" Rick asked, not entirely sure he was following them.

"Yeah, like that," Mimi gushed, pointing somewhere near him. "Treasurer. Man, that's such a cool word, you know? It just has this whole vibe of responsibility to it."

"Okay," Rick said slowly. "Well, if I'm the leader, then I guess Emi would be the treasurer. She's really responsible, I think, and has a lot of solid education at her back, being a Wizard. So, if that's okay, I guess that can be her role."

"Are you sure?" Emi asked nervously. "I mean, maybe somebody else wanted that job."

Rick looked them over then nodded to her emphatically. "I'm sure."

"Sounds good to me," Lancaster agreed. "I feel safe putting my jewels in her hands, after all."

"Yeah," Mimi said, smiling broadly. "You got that whole good with money aura to you. I can just feel that you'd be great at it."

"Hi, I'm Toddson," Toddson said, holding his hand out to Rick.

"We're past that," Mimi whispered to him, very loudly.

"Ah," Toddson said, and resumed staring at the ceiling.

Lancaster gave the Cleric a somewhat concerned stare, then turned back to Rick. "We can figure out the rest as we go along, I think. Mostly, we just wanted to know that you were capable of making a snap decision and had faith enough in the people around you to entrust them with duties, rather than assuming all responsibility yourself."

Rick was no longer sure what was going on, mostly because that actually made sense. A lot of sense. It had been a test. A clever test. As much as he was entrusting his life to them, he realized in a flash, they were entrusting theirs to him. Not just their lives, either, but their livelihoods and very possibly, their futures. That such a thoughtful, intelligent, and well-planned question could be posited by them staggered him.

"I see," he said at length. "I think I may have misjudged you guys."

"Happens all the time," Mimi told him with a laugh. "But, you know, you gotta be careful who you trust. People can promise anything then bail with all the money. I wanna do good in the world, but weed isn't free, right? Well, I mean, if you grow your own then I guess it is, but Knot Hill's a long ways off, and man, I've really gone through my stash since I moved here, you know?"

"Uh... huh," Rick decided to agree.

Lancaster shook his head, reached out, took Rick by the chin, turning his attention bodily back to himself. "What she means to say is, we were a little afraid that you might welsh on us. It's possible you and the lovely Elf there with the perky bosom might still, but at the moment, your answers satisfy us and we're willing to give you a shot to earn our trust. Which brings us to the second matter."

Rick glanced at Emi again, but she was still no help so he nodded, saying, "Which is?"

"What's the name of our party?"

Rick could only stare at him in confusion. "I'm sorry, what?"

"All great parties have a name, muffin," Lancaster pointed out. "I mean, if Max and Delilah Wonder really are your parents, then you know that much, right?"

"I don't recall my mom ever mentioning anything about their party having a name, actually," Rick admitted. "Granted, she didn't really like to talk about it, but I figure Uncle Castor would have said something at the very least."

"Pretty sure they were just called Team Wonder, unofficially," Toddson offered, surprising everyone yet again.

Lancaster shrugged. "That actually makes sense, when I think about it. The point remains, however, that we need to have some means of identifying ourselves to clients and other adventurers. Something that people can use when they want to request us specifically after our undoubted fame explodes across the city, country, continent, and world. Something that will be good for branding, marketing, and merchandising purposes in our retirement years."

Rick lost the ability to understand people. "You have put a lot of thought into this, haven't you?"

"Been to Wonder Plaza recently?" Lancaster retorted.

Rick had to give him that one. Begrudgingly, but he still did.

"Okay well, I admit, I haven't really thought about that," he said. "So I guess the table is open to suggestions."

"Lancaster and the Wannabes, obviously," the Rogue smirked.

"No," Rick stated flatly, waving off the other man's pout.

"Speed Weed," Mimi giggled.

"No," Rick groaned.

"Oh... um... maybe... no... wait... I think... um..." Emi stammered, then flushed and sank in her chair. "Never mind. I dunno."

Rick slumped. "Maybe this is something else we can figure out later?"

"Powerage," Toddson said.

Everyone took yet another turn staring at him in surprise. He smiled and waved.

"That's... actually good," Rick admitted.

"Not as good as mine, but not bad, I admit," Lancaster agreed, sort of. "It does have a nice ring to it."

"Like, an authoritative ring, yeah," Mimi added eagerly. "Like, the sort of thing that makes you think of people with a strong sense of duty and other stuff like that, you know?"

"I like it," Emi squeaked. "It sounds... brave."

Rick couldn't help but smile. "Okay. That's it then. That's who we are. Nice one, Toddson."

"Thanks, Mike," the Cleric said. "What did I do?"

"On that note," Rick groused as he pushed to his feet. "Let's get going. I'd like to have some time for us to look at what the Shy Market has to offer, and for us all to agree on the job we're going to take. Everyone ready?"

With smiles they all stood and looked to Rick in excitement. Despite his misgivings, he found himself feeling that maybe, just maybe, this might work out after all. They weren't so bad, really. Not as inept as he had thought. Not really. Mostly. Hopefully.

"Powerage, let's move out."

* * *

Nobody had any money. That put a damper on the idea of getting a cab. Rick really wanted to be surprised by that, but couldn't bring himself to be. Lancaster, of course, had a few lita, but nowhere near enough, and Rick's own finances were in little better shape. Toddson wasn't sure what money was, and all Mimi had was a half-full bag of weed.

Accepting that they were going to have to walk, Rick shrugged and had waved everyone to follow him when Emi managed to squeak out a sound moments before producing a wad of cash from her satchel.

While everyone else reveled in their now firmly established treasurer's competence, Rick just smiled and hailed a cab. He'd have to ask her later how she had so much money on her, but knew she may well refuse to answer, or worse, explain it all in gibberish. For now, he felt it best to simply keep up with how much it cost her and make sure she was reimbursed later.

With that small hiccup out of the way, the newly formed adventuring party of Powerage was on their way to the Shy Market. Everything was going great, oh yes, it was.

One phrase of Space Dolphin later, and Rick found himself once more in the company of the door guard, Tunya, who looked thrilled to see him. Even more so that he had brought friends. If she could be any happier, he was sure she might actually smile. Slightly.

"This is Tunya," he waved. "She doesn't answer questions, so let's not bother her, okay? We're here to get a job, not be annoying."

"Kinda past that, aren't you?" the Hobgoblin grumbled.

He shot her a pained look. She didn't seem to care.

"Greetings, my blue-hued lovely, I am Lancaster," the Rogue drooled at her chest. "Feel free to scream it all night."

Tunya sighed heavily. "Seriously?"

"Lancaster, what did I just say?" Rick whined.

The other man tossed a smirk his way. "I asked no questions, did I?"

Rick face-palmed.

"So, tell me, Lancaster," Tunya intoned heavily, glaring down at him. "You ever wanted to find out what the inside of your own colon feels like?"

"On occasion," he shot back with a smirk.

Tunya clearly had no idea what to do with that, so instead looked at Rick and motioned for him to take the obnoxious Rogue elsewhere. From the sharpness of her indication, Rick assumed she meant in a hurry.

"Let's go, guys, before she kills Lancaster," he begged, waving them all down the hall.

"Later," Lancaster offered with a wink as he blew her a kiss.

"You are so sexy," Mimi added. "Like, wow."

"C'mon," Rick groaned.

"Excuse me," Emi meeped out as she hurried to all but hide behind Rick, which he took as a great sign of their future.

"Hi, I'm Toddson," Toddson offered, holding his hand out to Tunya.

"I don't care," she barked.

"Oh, cool," he accepted, then kept smiled and nodding until Rick grabbed him by the collar and drug him away.

His momentary faith in them fading quickly, he turned slightly to mouth an apology at Tunya, who just kept glaring. Making friends everywhere he went, that was good old Ricky Wonder all right. Awesome.

Moments later, Rick was herding his new cats into the main room of the Shy Market, where hopefully, they wouldn't be able to break anything, annoy anyone, or do any other kind of unspecified damage to his sense of sanity. That last one was what worried him most of all.

They all paused a moment, glancing about at the paper-covered corkboard, each of them looking as disappointed as Rick had felt when he'd first visited, what felt like forever ago, even though it was only yesterday. Before he could say anything, they spread out, looking over the various requests, Lancaster managing to bump into the same Chthonian Rick had seen there the day before.

"I'd say I'm sorry, but I can tell you liked it," the Rogue suggested, making the tall, lanky half-devil lean away from him in considerable dismay.

"Sorry," Rick offered quickly, yanking Lancaster back. "So, so sorry. Please don't mind us. We're all idiots."

"Uh... sure," the man replied, dismay surrendering to abject confusion.

Shaking his head, Rick hauled the protesting Rogue back, waving for the rest to gather round. Thankfully, Mimi thought to bring Toddson, as Rick began berating Lancaster. "What is wrong with you? Seriously. Can you act like a sane human being for five minutes?"

"Stars gotta shine," Lancaster pouted.

"Stop talking," Rick insisted. "Now, all of you pay attention. From my earlier visit, I'm pretty sure these requests are laid out by difficulty and age. The harder the job, the bigger the payout, but the more dangerous as well."

"So let's just go to the end, grab the biggest, and hit the streets," Lancaster smirked.

Rick could no longer hold back the urge to slap the moron upside the head. "That is what we will *not* be doing."

"Why not?" the Rogue argued, smoothing his hair back into place. "The sooner we make a name for ourselves, the sooner we're rolling in dough and babes. We grab a hard job, kick some ass and instant fame is ours."

Giving him a glare, Rick jabbed a finger at him. "Listen, jackass. We have no idea what we're doing. We can't even work effectively as a team yet. We need to start with something simple so we can get a feel for each other's abilities, strengths, and weaknesses. We need time to develop teamwork before we go diving into something genuinely dangerous, so we're going to stick to the easy section of the wall for now. Got it?"

Lancaster rolled his eyes at that. "Look, kid, just because you have the balls of a scared squirrel doesn't mean the rest of us do. We can handle it. I mean, you've got me here, right? Just let me do the job selection and you can play leader man later."

"Lanny, wait," Mimi cut in, grabbing him by the arm before he could walk away. "I think Rick has a point."

"Just 'cause he's got the last name Wonder, doesn't mean he knows anything," Lancaster protested.

"And how many jobs have you been on, huh?" Rick snapped.

"Well," the Rogue hesitated. "Not many, I admit. Just south of one, maybe. That doesn't matter, though. I've got skills."

"I've never taken a job like this at all," Mimi said.

"Me either," Emi managed.

"Sup, Mick," Toddson waved.

"Gonna take that as a no, too," Rick muttered.

Lancaster began to argue the matter further, but Mimi squeezed his arm, silencing him as she said, "Look. I don't know how to coordinate my magic with either Todd or Emi yet. Rick's got no magic, same as you, and you guys need to be able to work together. Like he said, we need time to develop some teamwork. It's not gonna hurt to start slow and build our skills, ya know?"

Glancing to each of them, Lancaster finally groaned and threw his hands up. "Fine. Whatever. We'll do it the slow way."

"Thank you," Rick said, breathing a sigh of relief. "Now, the easier jobs seem to be in this area, so why don't you guys look them over, find some that look good, and we'll discuss them, okay?"

With silent agreement, they all turned to the task, leaving Rick to gather himself. He'd come closer than he liked to losing his temper with Lancaster, and while it was obvious to him now the Rogue could really push his buttons, he also knew he needed to keep a cool head. He would have to figure out how to deal with him.

A hand fell on his shoulder, making him jump half out of his skin. Glancing back, he found the Chthonian smiling at him, and slumped. Just what he needed. He already looked like a fool in front of other professional adventurers.

"First time out with a new party, huh?" the Chthonian asked.

"That obvious?"

"Yeah, kinda," he said with a slight grin. "I'm Hasim, by the way."

"Rick," he replied, taking the offered hand and shaking it.

"Wonder, yeah, I caught that," Hasim chuckled. "Might not want to shout that so much, though. That name has a way of making other people feel a bit competitive. Some might try to sabotage you, just because."

"Fantastic," Rick groaned.

Hasim chuckled again, patting his shoulder. "I'm just saying, you're right to take it slow. Build your reputation a little at a time and let that speak for you more than a name does, yeah? You wouldn't be the first to come in here shouting the Wonder name, after all."

Rick gave a bitter laugh. "Why am I not surprised to learn that?"

"Probably has something to do with that giant statue in Wonder Plaza," Hasim replied. "Has a way of making people act stupid for the sake of fame."

"Right now, all I want to do is secure an easy job, get these guys to develop some team skills, and get paid," Rick admitted. "I haven't had time to think about fame for at least a couple days."

Hasim grinned at that. "Best you don't start any time soon either. The League likes to keep the work we do hush-hush, anyway. They don't like having their marketing infringed on."

"Yeah, that doesn't surprise me either," Rick said, rubbing his eyes and feeling very tired for some reason. "Well, like I said, for now I just want to get these guys into something like a cohesive team. We can worry about everything else later."

The Chthonian nodded, watching the four with a doubtful look. "Where did you find them, anyway? The Slaughterhouse?"

"Yeah, that'd be where," Rick admitted in pain.

"Should have asked me about that yesterday," Hasim chuckled. "I'd have directed you to where serious adventurers gather."

"Wait, what?" Rick gaped. "So, is it too late to tell me now or something?"

"A little too late, yeah," the other man answered. "Mark of a good adventurer is that they stand by the party they have."

"Even if they're... them?" Rick whimpered.

"Even then, pal," Hasim laughed. "Don't worry, though. You're being smart about this. Give them time. They might just surprise you."

"I can hope," Rick moaned.

"When you guys settle on a job, show it to Tunya on the way out," Hasim told him. "She'll make a note of it for the guys who run this place so they can contact the client and let them know you'll be stopping by for any particulars not in the request."

Rick nodded. "Got it. Though Tunya doesn't seem to like me much."

Hasim shrugged. "She doesn't like anybody."

"That seems likely," Rick mused. "Thanks, Hasim."

"No worries, Rick," the Chthonian replied warmly. "Be careful out there, yeah?"

"I'm gonna try," Rick agreed. "Gods help me, I'm gonna try."

The lanky half-devil patted him on the shoulder once more, and with a soft laugh, excused himself. Watching him go, Rick wondered if maybe he should have followed his instinct yesterday after all and tried to introduce himself. Not that it mattered now, of course. Hasim had made one point Rick couldn't ignore.

These idiots were his party and he would stand by them. It might just kill him, but he'd do it. Somehow.

* * *

Thirty minutes later, the four horsemen of the Rickpocalypse returned with four wildly different versions of easy. Part of him really wanted to be surprised, but at this point, he took it more as a sign of their personalities, and having had a bit of time to think on it, had come to believe that perhaps that might even be a good thing.

Why have only one kind of cheese when four created a unique flavor? He admitted that was a terrible analogy, but so far it was the best he'd managed to come up with. It made the knot in his gut slightly less tense.

Emi was the first to offer a request for consideration. Locating a missing cat for a two hundred and fifty lita reward. Despite the rest of the party treating it with all due seriousness, for which Rick was very grateful, ultimately they all decided that between the sheer size of the city of Riscadil and the small reward, it was probably best to hold that one as a backup.

Mimi, on the other hand, had turned up a request to act as bodyguards for a team of archeologists looking to set out in search of a mythical lost island said to hold many advanced technologies, somewhere in the south Kienrin Sea.

The trip was expected to last up to six months and the reward was a cut of any profits gained. Rick somehow doubted she quite grasped the concept of easy, but considering the island in question was mythical, it could well be a six-month cruise for no pay.

The missing cat moved up in the ranks.

Lancaster produced, with great flourish, a request to eliminate an elder demon lord from an old manor a few weeks north of Riscadil. Rick didn't need to hear anything else about that one. There was no way this team was ready to face something that powerful, so there was no point in hearing what the reward was.

All that left was Toddson, which meant Rick was ready to start scouring the city for a cat. To his surprise, however, the Cleric held out a missing person's request. A young woman had vanished a few weeks back and the client was offering a one thousand lita reward for information on her whereabouts. After a bit of deliberation, everyone else agreed that the risk to reward factor present made this the obvious choice.

Toddson then promptly forgot what they were even doing, so Rick decided to chalk this one up to a fluke. A lucky fluke, sure, but still. When he got no real argument from even Lancaster, that pretty well sealed the deal.

The others quickly fell into a conversation about what they were going to do with their reward money while Rick headed back down the hall to report they were taking the job to Tunya. To his surprise, Toddson followed him, closing the door behind him softly and waving Rick to wait.

"Hey, Ron, are you sure this is the job you want to take?" the Cleric asked. "I mean, you guys said I picked it, and I'm... well... me, so if you have any second thoughts, I get it."

Rick gave him a quizzical look, but shook his head anyway. "No, I think this is exactly what we need right now. It's a pretty simple, straightforward job with a solid reward. Don't worry about it, you did good."

Toddson nodded, but still looked troubled, prompting Rick to hesitate. Most of the time the Cleric seemed pretty relaxed, even happy, so seeing him any other way was strange. Or, maybe it wasn't. Rick accepted he didn't really know the guy.

"Toddson, if there's something..." Rick started.

"I don't remember picking it," the other man explained. "I mean, I know I forget a lot of stuff, but I really don't remember picking that one. I was looking at something else completely, and then next thing I know, I'm holding this one. I think..."

Rick waited a moment as Toddson seemed to struggle with what he wanted to say. After a moment, he calmed, nodded to himself and looked Rick in the eye, appearing more focused than Rick had seen him before.

"I think my god wants us to do this one," he said. "Which means it must be important. So, you know, let's just be careful, okay?"

"Your god?" Rick replied slowly. "The Forgotten One?"

"Yeah, him," Toddson said. "Sometimes I do things and I don't know why, but they always work out for the best. I know that doesn't make sense, but every now and then he guides me like this. I just, I dunno, felt like I should tell you that. Like it's important I tell you that."

Rick considered it for a moment, then reached out and squeezed his shoulder. "Well, if a god thinks we should do this, then we don't really have any room to argue, do we?"

Toddson visibly relaxed at that. "Yeah. I guess you're right. Thanks, Ben."

Rick nodded, hoping his look of consternation didn't show too clearly. If it did, Toddson didn't seem to see it as he turned to rejoin the others, leaving Rick to handle the official filing on his own. Not sure what to make of it all, he headed down the hall shaking his head.

Toddson's weird, possibly imaginary deity may or may not have compelled him to accept a request for some reason. Sure. Why not? At this point, all Rick could really hope for was that Toddson himself was actually a Cleric and not just a deeply disturbed individual. Otherwise things were going to get problematic, very quickly.

Not that it mattered. It really was a good job. Exactly the job they needed.

That thought made him falter in his steps a little. It was a little too perfect for them, really. Pausing, he glanced back, wondering for the first time if maybe Toddson wasn't so crazy after all.

"You settle on something?" Tunya asked, making him start.

He ignored the amused look she gave him and held it out, saying, "Yeah. We're gonna take this one."

The Hobgoblin took it and glanced over it. "Cool. I'll make a note in the log book and have the boss let the client know you're coming. You heading straight there, or what?"

Rick thought that over for a minute. "I think I'm gonna take these guys and get them fed first. Then, yeah, straight there. So, mid- to late-afternoon, I guess?"

Tunya nodded, and pulled a large book out from under her stool, flipped through it for a moment then grabbed a pencil and began making notes. "Okay. Got it. Request from Carto Manascetti accepted. Party will meet him at his residence in the late-afternoon. Who should I note is coming by?"

"Um... us?" Rick fumbled.

Tunya furrowed her brow in a way that made him feel an inch tall. "And who is us, exactly? You want we should give them all your names, just yours, the team identifier or what?"

"Ah," Rick groaned, realizing what she was asking. "Best to go with the team name, I think. My name may cause more problems than it solves."

She actually laughed at that, surprising him. "Oh, right. Wonder. I get it. So what's the team name, then?"

"Tell him Powerage will be by to handle his request."

Tunya grinned slightly. "Powerage it is, then. Welcome to the world of adventuring, Wonder man."

* * *

Rounding everyone up, Rick managed to get them outside with minimal fuss, which felt like a small miracle in and of itself. Once there, he suggested grabbing lunch and everyone jumped at the idea for which he was grateful. He needed time to form a plan, mostly on how to deal with Lancaster when they met with the client. The last thing he needed was the egocentric Rogue trying to take charge of that conversation.

Noting they were only a few blocks from Rumble Park and aware that while Emi had money, she didn't have an infinite amount, he suggested they walk and spend some time getting to know each other. Once again, Lancaster was the only one who seemed to have any issue with this, which was not even remotely shocking.

Falling back a couple of steps, Rick decided to simply listen and try to learn a few things about them. Lancaster quickly fell into a vain attempt to hold a conversation with Toddson, which only served to frustrate the Rogue. Rick wasn't sure why, as he did most of the actual talking.

However, it did give him a few insights into Toddson. While the supposed Cleric was absent-minded in the extreme, he did seem oddly well-versed in the local history and geography of Riscadil, as well as many other bits of trivia. He was also incredibly good-natured. His memory issues aside, Rick found himself warming to the man somewhat, as his amiable attitude engendered a certain sense of calm in others. Even Lancaster, who despite his growing frustration with Toddson being unable to keep up his end of the conversation, never seemed to become openly angry with him.

Then there were Mimi and Emi. While the young Elf was hopelessly frazzled and shy, Mimi somehow managed to pull her into a conversation and after only a couple of blocks, the two were chatting away as if they were lifelong friends. As they spoke, Rick learned that Knot Hill was clear on the other side of Liaob, little more than a small farming community largely populated by a clan of Druids. Sort of a commune, actually, from how it sounded. Lots of free love and pot. This was not overly surprising.

What was, however, seemed to be Mimi herself. Apparently, she had broken with her clan traditions to come to Riscadil and pursue a life as an adventurer. She claimed it was because their earth goddess had come to her in a dream, having grown sickly from the advancements made in technology and culture. According to the Druid, this goddess beseeched her to help heal the world, and without any hesitation she had set out to do just that.

Rick had to admit, her goals were somewhat more noble than his own.

As they reached Rumble Park, Emi finally confided to Mimi her own reasons for seeking adventure. Rather than laugh, Mimi just smiled, hugged the young Elf, and told her that the bravery she sought she had already gained, just by being there. The look on Emi's face was pure joy, and in that moment, Rick knew, despite how she seemed, Mimi was a good soul and he was glad he had met her.

Waving the party towards Sunny's noodle stand, Rick tapped the Half-Elf on the shoulder, asking her to hold up as the rest gravitated towards the sumptuous smells wafting their way. Mimi hesitated, looking nervous, but did as he asked.

"Am I in trouble?" she asked as soon as the others were out of earshot.

"What? No!" Rick exclaimed. "Why would you think that?"

She smiled slightly, and shrugged. "I got accepted into a party once before, but got kicked out on the way to our first job together."

Rick had no idea how to take that. "Did they say why?"

"Well, the leader of the party was this Cleric of Frun, if you know who that is," she replied.

"I really don't," he admitted.

Mimi glanced after the rest. "I don't wanna be rude, ya know?"

"You aren't," Rick assured her.

She nodded slowly, steadied herself, and explained, "Frun is the main deity of the country of Tervil, to the north. Apparently, he's a very strict god and doesn't allow any kind of... well... recreation, ya know?"

Rick was pretty sure he got that part. "No drinking, swearing and so on."

"Or smoking anything, much less unmarried sex, yeah," Mimi laughed slightly. "So I didn't really fit in and stuff."

Rick offered her a kind smile. "How you live your life is none of my business, Mimi, not so long as I can count on you to do your job. So, no worries. It's not like I've ever... uh... refrained from partaking in a little recreation myself."

The Half-Elf visibly relaxed at that. "See? I knew you were cool. I just felt it all in your aura and stuff."

"I appreciate that," Rick chuckled. "No, I just wanted to thank you for what you did back at the Shy Market. Lancaster was getting under my skin, and I didn't handle myself well. You really helped defuse the situation, and I wanted you to know how much I appreciate that. So, thank you."

Clearly surprised, Mimi actually flushed a little and waved him off. "Oh, forget it. You really were right. I wanna do some good in the world and everything, but I don't wanna die. Your idea sounded way smarter. Besides, you're the party leader, Rick. I gotta have your back."

Startled, Rick found himself smiling warmly. "I... wow. I was really wrong about you. I am so sorry for that."

She shrugged, and out of nowhere hugged him. "I get that a lot. Not many people apologize for it. Thanks. You're really awesome and I'm so happy to have met you."

Painfully aware of just how tightly she was pressing him against him, Rick patted her back, saying, "Me, too. So, you know, maybe let's go eat."

She pushed back and nodded, smiling brightly. "Hell, yeah. Let's do some bonding and adventuring and let's just make this crazy bunch a family, you know?"

Rick laughed. "I absolutely do."

* * *

"Did you have to flirt with the Bugbear?"

Lancaster threw Rick a dazzling smile. "When you have this much love to give, everyone deserves a chance to experience it."

"That's deep," Mimi agreed.

Rick gave her a look that begged her to not encourage, but all he got back was a helpless shrug and smile. Shaking his head, he decided to turn his attention back to the Rogue. "All I'm saying is, sometimes hitting on people isn't the best way to introduce yourself."

"Don't clip my wings, man," Lancaster snorted. "How else am I to fly?"

"You can fly?" Toddson asked in surprise.

"He doesn't mean that literally," Rick pointed out.

"Mean what?" the Cleric asked in confusion.

Rick decided to let that go as well. "Look, Lancaster, you can do whatever you want when we aren't on the clock. When we are, just please reign it in a little, okay? We want to present ourselves as professionals."

"I am a professional!" the Rogue argued.

"Professional what, though?" Toddson snickered.

That was a good one, Rick admitted.

"Professional everything," Lancaster claimed, gyrating his hips suggestively. "A man has to have many talents to get by in this life, after all."

"You live in a flophouse," Mimi giggled.

"Who's side are you on?" the Rogue demanded.

"We're all on the same side," Rick put in, trying to get them to settle.

"Doesn't seem that way," Lancaster grumbled, then suddenly swept Emi into his arms and dipped her. "Thus far, only my beautiful Elf has refrained from mocking the obvious greatness that is me."

Emi made some noises Rick was pretty sure only dolphins would understand. Thankfully, Mimi rescued her and steadied her to her feet before waving a finger at Lancaster, chastising him for disturbing such a pure flower.

Rick thought it best not get involved with that.

With lunch behind them, the party was heading out of Rumble Park and looking to catch a cab across town to meet with their first client. Rick had already asked Emi if she would mind paying, promising to refund her the expense once they collected their reward. With a nervous titter, she'd agreed quickly enough, apparently just happy to be of use.

As Rick cast about for a cab, he felt a strangely familiar tap on his shoulder, and with a glance, found a police officer looking him over. Not just any police officer either, but the same one he'd encountered when Enzo had tried to shake him down.

"Hello again," the officer smiled. "Mr. Wonder."

Rick did not like the way he had said that, but nodded anyway. "Officer. Can I help you?"

Anton bobbled his head a little. "Probably not, but I might be able to help you. Take a little walk with me, will you?"

Looking over at his party, Rick hesitated. "Actually, we're kind of busy at the moment. Can this wait?"

"It's not anything official," Anton told him. "It's just a friendly conversation. Won't take but a couple minutes, then you and your... uh... friends here can be on your way."

"Rick?" Emi asked, eyes jumping from him to the police officer nervously. "Are we okay?"

Forcing a smile, he nodded. "Yeah. We're fine. I know him. He just wants to talk to me for a second, then we'll be going. You guys just wait there, yeah?"

Glancing at each other in apprehension, they all nodded. Rick hoped they would actually do it. Mostly just Lancaster, really. Toddson had probably already forgotten what was happening, while he doubted Mimi would do anything too reckless. Nor Emi, for that matter.

Actually, he couldn't imagine Emi doing anything that had ever brushed up against reckless.

"Okay, you got me for a couple minutes," Rick said. "Let's take that walk."

Anton cocked an eyebrow. "You act like I'm arresting you or something."

"Cop says let's talk a walk, that sounds kind of shady," Rick explained.

Anton thought about that for a second, then laughed. "I guess it really does, huh? Wow. Not at all how I meant it to come across. Guess my people skills are getting rusty. Probably ought to socialize outside work more."

"So, this isn't anything..." Rick trailed off, walking a few yards away from his party.

Anton waved a hand at him. "Gods, no. I really did just want to talk to you for a minute. I've been looking all over the place for you for almost two days. Ever since I found out who you really are."

Rick crossed his arms over his chest. "Who I really am?"

"Max Wonder's son," Anton said pointedly. "Yeah. I know. I looked into you after you mentioned Castor Rumble was your uncle. Sounded kind of far-fetched, but it stuck in my head, so I dug into it a little. Found out it was true, and figured I should talk you out of doing what you are obviously about to go do."

Rick was shaking his head before Anton even finished. "Don't bother. This is what I came here for. My mom and my uncle both tried to talk me out of it, and here I am. Sorry, but I have no reason to listen to you."

"At least let me make my case before you shut me down," Anton grumbled. "I've had two days to think about how to do this, you know?"

Rolling his eyes, Rick accepted the police officer wasn't going to let him be until he had his say. "Okay, fine. Just, don't get your hopes up."

"Noticed that, thanks," the other man muttered, then gave him a stern look. "Okay, so, what I wanted to say was, I get it. I get all of it. Really, I do. Max Wonder was... amazing. All the things he did, the stuff he accomplished, it wasn't just heroic. It was almost super heroic. I can see how you might feel like you have a lot to live up to."

"I really don't," Rick grunted.

Anton hesitated. "Oh. Uh. Wasn't expecting that."

Rick chuckled at the befuddled expression on the officer's face. "I can see how you'd think that. That's not why I'm here or why I'm doing this, though. Nobody ever made me feel like I had to continue Dad's legacy or anything like that. Pretty much the opposite, really. Mom hated the idea of me doing this, and Uncle Castor only agreed to train me with the swords because he was scared I'd run off and get myself killed if he didn't."

Scowling, Anton rolled his hat around on his head, trying to figure that out. "So then why the hell are you doing this?"

With a shrug and a laugh Rick told him, "'Cause I can. Cause I want to. This isn't about living up to him, but in a way, it is about me respecting what he did, I guess. I dunno how to explain it in a way that makes sense, but if I was going to try, I guess I'd have to say it's because this is the world he made and I want to safeguard that."

"I certainly can't argue that this is the world Max Wonder made," Anton agreed, more or less getting what he was saying. "But, Richard, the world has changed since then. There aren't any big, terrible things happening anymore. If you want to do what you say, there's a better way."

"Such as?" Rick asked, doubting very strongly what the officer was saying.

Anton tapped the badge on his chest. "Join the Riscadil Police Department. Become an officer. Serve and protect, that's what we do. You can put your skills to use in a much safer way while still protecting the world your father made."

Rick gave a slight snort at that. "Bound by the law, you mean?"

"Since when has that been a bad thing?" Anton argued, feeling slightly offended.

Seeing he had stepped wrong, Rick held his hands up quickly. "It isn't. Sorry. I didn't mean to say that it was. What you and every other officer in the city do is one of the noblest callings there is. It just... it isn't for me."

"Give me one good reason why," Anton insisted.

Rick took a moment to really think about that, then nodded. "Because it isn't just protecting my dad's legacy I'm after. I want to have adventurers. I want to risk my life, save not just this city, but the world. I want that life. That's not something being a police offer can give me. If it was, then that's what I'd do."

"It's incredibly dangerous, Richard," the other man pressed, his eyes filled with concern. "You don't know that you can count on those people to have your back when things go wrong. At least with us, you would know your back was covered."

"Really?" Rick questioned. "Do you know that your fellow officers will have your back? 'Cause I read the news, man. I know how bad the corruption is in your agency."

Anton sighed, shaking his head. "Yeah, okay. It's got crap pay, and you never really know who you can trust. I wish I could argue that, but I can't. Still..."

Rick held a hand up. "I get it. I could do a lot of good, doing things your way."

"You really could," Anton urged. "Having someone like you, a Wonder, would be the best thing that ever happened to this department. You could be an icon."

"A tool," Rick countered. "A public relations puppet. If I wanted that, I'd have had my mom come speak for me at the League."

"It wouldn't have to be that way," Anton tried to insist, but he knew Rick was right. He hated it, but he knew.

"But it would," Rick told him. "You think I never considered this? I did. This is the only way that I can do what I feel is right and still be in control of my own fate. This is all I've got. Anything else, and I may as well have stayed in Townglen, hidden from the world, turning a blind eye and a deaf ear to every wrong that came along. At least this way, I can really do something or die trying. That's worth any amount of risk."

Defeated, Anton held his hands up in surrender. "Okay, I get it. I can't change your mind. I see that. Still, I had to try. If for no other reason than because I feel I owe it to your family for all they did for us."

"My mom would really appreciate that," Rick laughed. "And thanks. I appreciate that you tried."

Anton gave him a look that said he doubted that. "So, what are you guys heading out to do? I assume you've already secured a job from the Shy Market?"

"We have," he admitted, a little surprised a police officer was so aware of a place Rick had thought to be clandestine. "We're just looking into a missing person's request, though. Nothing crazy or shady."

"Oh," Anton said slowly, looking relieved. "That's actually... good. We're stretched kind of thin these days, so that would really be helpful. We don't have the resources to devote to looking for every runaway who comes up as missing."

"Gee, it's almost like I'm helping you guys do your job," Rick replied with a sly grin.

"Yeah, yeah," Anton snorted back. "Who is it you're looking for?"

"Don't know," Rick admitted. "We're on our way to meet the client. We don't have all the details yet."

Nodding at that, Anton chewed his lip for a moment. "Tell you what. Once you have all the information, hit me up. I'll see what I can do to help you out."

Rick blinked. "Seriously? You were just trying to talk me out of being an adventurer and now you want to help me?"

Anton waved that off quickly. "I'm not going to talk you out of it, so I may as well take advantage of it. Besides, like I said, we don't have the resources we need to hunt down every person who gets reported missing. As long as you're doing something like this, it benefits everyone."

"Okay, then," Rick agreed hesitantly. "You got a deal."

"Great," Anton said with a smirk. "So I guess I should let you get back to work, then, huh?"

"Yeah," Rick agreed, still eyeing him somewhat suspiciously.

"Don't give me that look," Anton fussed, walking back to the party with him. "In a way, I kind of won this debate of ours."

"How do you figure that?" Rick balked.

"Well, you are kind of doing police work," the officer told him, returning the sly smile Rick had given him a moment ago.

"Whatever," Rick groaned as they approached the others.

Mimi tried to hide the joint she'd been smoking. She failed.

Rick face-palmed as Anton quirked an eyebrow.

"Seriously, Mimi," Rick groaned.

"I get nervous around the fuzz!" she wailed.

Anton clapped Rick on the shoulder. "Good luck, Richard. You're gonna need it."

"Thanks," Rick drawled, shoving him away before waving his team together. "Mimi, put that out, will you? Come on. We got work to do."

* * *

An hour and one overly apologetic Druid later, the team of Powerage found themselves outside the grounds of an old Colonial-style home surrounded entirely by a high brick wall the same shade of red as the house. Guards patrolled the yard, watching them exit the cab with more than a bit of an unnecessary aggression.

This was Rick's first hint that things were not as they seemed. He kind of missed it, though.

Scanning the stately house for a moment and nodding to the guard at the gate, Rick decided it was time to deal with the one major problem he did see and turned to Lancaster. Naturally, the Rogue smiled at him broadly. This did not make Rick feel better.

"Lancaster, I think we need to deal with something before we go in there."

"Such as?" the other man asked, taking a moment to comb his absurd pompadour.

"Let me do all the talking," Rick instructed. "I don't want you to say anything. At all. Do not hit on anyone. Do not make suggestive comments to anyone. Do not do anything but stand there looking important."

Lancaster gave him a dour look. "May I ask why you feel the need to express all of this?"

"Because you're you," Mimi pointed out with less than no tact. "And Rick wants to make a good impression."

"But also because I think that if you really want to be in charge of the team later on, you shouldn't put yourself out there, in case things go wrong," Rick added quickly. "I don't expect anything to go wrong, but if it does, it'll fall on me and not you, right?"

Having been glaring at Mimi, Lancaster still seemed to pick up on what Rick was selling and after a moment of thought, nodded. "That does seem a wise approach, I'll grant you that. As I said before, you are the figurehead my friend. I'll allow you to take the responsibility, and the blame, should it come to that. Just don't forget to share the credit equally when things go well."

"Wouldn't dream of it," Rick agreed quickly.

Sparing a glance to the others, Rick gave one last nod, turned and waved them forward. It was time, finally, to go to work.

That lasted right up to gate guard, who tossed them a snarl and waved them to keep moving. This would have been the second hint, and like the first, it went right over Rick's head.

"Yeah, hi," he pressed instead. "The Shy Market should have informed you we were coming. We're Powerage."

The guard scowled then rolled his eyes and waved to someone else. A moment later he was joined by another man, a Half-Orc actually, who looked terribly imposing in his suit and tie. They whispered to each other for a moment, throwing glares at the team as they did. After a bit of that, the first guard nodded and unlocked the gate.

"Seems you are expected, after all. Just be on your good behavior or we'll make sure you never have any kind of behavior ever again. Got that?"

Rick smiled. "Of course. We're all on the same team here. Your boss is now our boss and all that."

"Whatever," the man growled, waving them to follow the Half-Orc.

Inside, the team was greeted by staggering finery, the likes of which Rick had seen at the Cantasol. The vast foyer was dominated by a glittering chandelier, while richly textured rugs swept up stairways to the second floor and the balcony that dominated their view. Portraits of dignified looking men and women adored the walls, all of them depicting Dwarves, Rick noted.

They were ushered on too quickly for him to really take it all in, and soon found themselves in a small room lined with bookshelves, each covered by a frosted glass door. A billiard table took up one end of the chamber, the felt a deep, vibrant purple that somewhat clashed with the red drapes hanging over the windows. The tinge of cigar smoke loitered in the air, especially by the bar where liquors of obvious expense snuggled each other.

"This is a bit more than I was expecting," Rick murmured.

"Tell me about it," Mimi agreed, pausing to run her hand over a large globe hunkering in one corner. "Looks like our client won't have any problem with payment."

"At least we can be sure of that," he agreed, waving Lancaster away from the bar as the Rogue sniffed the various bottles.

"I was just seeing what they are," the Rogue complained.

"Don't care," Rick shot back. "Do not touch anything. This is our client. We show them the utmost respect, okay?"

"Fine, fine," Lancaster grumbled.

"Good to hear that," another voice boomed across the room as the door swung open, admitting a stout Dwarf in a red velvet smoking jacket. A cigar dangled from his mouth as he sauntered in, eyeing them all carefully, the lights glowing off his balding head. The larger thing, in Rick's mind, was that he bore no beard, sporting only a thin mustache. That was definitely weird.

"Mr. Manascetti, I presume?" Rick posited, falling into what he hoped was a confident looking stance with his hands folded behind his back.

"One and the same, yeah," the Dwarf nodded. "You must be the adventurers the guys over at the Shy Market told me would be coming. What was it you called yourselves? Powerhouse?"

"Powerage, sir," Rick corrected with a smile. "I'm Rick, this is Mimi, Toddson, Lancaster, and Emi."

Manascetti nodded to each before offering a thick hand to Rick. "Call me Carto, son. You ain't like these gombas I got around here. We got a more professional-like relationship and I prefer to be on a first name basis with people I work with."

Rick accepted his hand and found his grip vice-like and a bit damp as the Dwarf pumped his arm furiously for a moment before releasing his hand. Then he hit the bar, pouring himself a drink. He paused, offering one to Rick, who politely refused.

"We'd like to get right to business, sir, if that's okay," he explained.

Manascetti seemed to accept that well enough and put the liquor away. "A real go-getter, are ya, son? I like that. All right, let's talk business. Have a seat."

Taking a chair opposite the other man, Rick again hoped he presented a polished, professional look, crossing his legs and folding his hands in his lap. "First of all, we'd like to know everything you can tell us about the missing individual."

"Of course," Manascetti sighed heavily. "Her name is Lucinia Avalinion and yeah, that's an Elf name. She's from Gulinlan, originally. Her father was an old friend of mine who died about six months back, very unexpectedly. Out of respect for her, as her ma had passed long ago, I brought her here to raise as if she was my own."

"I see," Rick responded. "That's very selfless of you, sir."

"Ain't it?" Manascetti laughed. "Thing is, Lucinia wasn't so appreciative. I set her up with the finest schooling and everything. Instead of being happy, she started cutting classes and running with a bad crowd. I tried my best, but I've got no kids, so I guess I did a piss-poor job of being fatherly."

Rick figured that seemed about right. "So she's not very old then, I take it?"

"Eh, about early twenties," the Dwarf replied, shrugging. "Her dad had fallen on hard times, so she hadn't gotten a chance to further her education any. I made some arrangements for her to attend Riscadil University."

"I see," Rick said slowly. "Well, it may have just been culture shock."

"That's what I said," Manascetti declared. "But still, we ended up fighting all the time. Then one day about a month ago, she just up and vanishes. I don't see nothing or hear nothing from her for about a week, when I get word the cops have pulled a girl from the bay, what fits her description."

"Wait, what?" Rick fumbled.

"Yeah, that's not the weird part," the Dwarf said quickly. "Get this. When I go to see for myself, all prepared for it to be true, what with that bunch she was running with, they tell me the body has gone missing. How do you like them apples?"

"Missing?" Rick stammered. "Okay, that is weird."

"Nah, that's not what's weird," the other man insisted. "Well, okay, kinda weird, but it's the Riscadil police. They lose shit all the time. No, what's weird, is that she shows up here, very much alive, a couple days after that. Tells me she's come to get her things. That she's moving out and is gonna do her own thing. Thanks me real polite and proper and everything."

Rick thought that over a moment. "Sir, if I may, it would seem that whoever the police pulled from the bay was not her. If anything it appears she simply wished to do something else with her life."

"Does seem that way, don't it?" Manascetti asked, before leaning in closer. "Except she was different, Rick. Like, not herself. All the stuff what she'd been through, with losing her parents, and coming here and the people she fell in with, it gave her this attitude, you know? Like she had this huge chip on her shoulder. That girl that came to collect her stuff, she was soft spoken, polite, warm and like a completely different person."

"Maybe she just wanted to make a clean break with no hard feelings?" Rick offered.

"Maybe," Manascetti replied with obvious doubt. "I told myself that at first, but I couldn't get those eyes out of my head. It was like there was someone else inside her body. It was damn creepy. So, I got to talking with a friend of mine what works for the cops. Got some photos of the girl they pulled from the bay."

Rick waited a moment as Manascetti seemed to struggle with the matter. "And?"

"It was her, Rick," the Dwarf said at last, looking as if a ghost had just crossed his grave. "It was Lucinia they pulled out of the bay that day. Who went missing from the morgue. Then turned up on my doorstep, alive and well, but acting like a completely different person. It was absolutely her."

Rick settled back, digesting that for a moment. "And now you want us to locate her? Why?"

"I wanna know what happened to her," Manascetti said slowly, caught between dread and anger. "I wanna know who did this to her and why. I need to know. Like I said, her father, he was a good friend to me. I owe him this much. To know what the hell happened to his daughter."

"Sir, if I may, this is a bit different than what the notice in the Shy Market indicated."

Manascetti was already nodding. "I know, I know. I was afraid if I put all this in there, nobody would help me, you see. I mean, it's like I'm talking about the undead or something, right? Ain't none of that no more, not since old Max Wonder sent Obedell packing. I admit, this has even me spooked, so I figure most adventurers would steer well clear of it."

Rick tried very hard not to flinch at the mention of his father or Obedell. He completely missed Emi obviously flinching at the mention of the famed Arch Lich.

"So, now that you're here," Manascetti continued, noticing neither of their reactions. "I'm willing to offer double what the notice said I'd pay. I just need to know what happened."

"Sir, we would have done the job for the original offer," Rick told him. "That's our job."

Manascetti smiled at him then laughed. "I love this guy. So honest. Tell you what, Rick. 'Cause you're such a straight shooter, forget the notice. Two thousand is what I'm paying you kids, if you bring me information about Lucinia, what happened to her and where she is now. Deal?"

The Dwarf leaned forward, shoving a hand out. Rick considered it for a moment then nodded and took his hand. "You have a deal, sir."

"Fantastic," Manascetti laughed. "Ah, this puts my old heart at ease, knowing folks like you are on the job. I gotta say, I had my doubts about this Shy Market business, but here you are. Just fantastic."

"We're happy that you're happy, sir, but I would rather hold any celebration until we complete the job," Rick cautioned. "Speaking of which, it would help us immensely if you could provide us with a photo. Even better if you have five, should we need to split up in the course of our search."

"Consider it done," Manascetti stated before fumbling around for a bell, which upon being rung, brought forth one of his heavies. "Get these kids some pictures of Lucinia. Enough for everybody, and don't dawdle, dammit. They're hard-working kids."

The guard nodded and vanished, leaving Rick free to ask, "About this crowd she fell in with, sir?"

Manascetti stopped just shy of spitting. "Political science brats. You can find them hanging out around the University, talking about revolution and getting high. Gods know what else they were into."

"That's a good place to start, regardless," Rick admitted, as the flunky returned with the requested photos and began handing then out. Instantly, Rick was taken with the woman he saw.

Slender of features, with wide blue eyes and thick golden curls that tumbled down her shoulder, Lucinia was every inch the sort of beauty one would expect a privileged Elven lady to be. Except, of course, that according to Manascetti, she wasn't. Something in this story seemed off and for once, Rick noticed it.

He just wasn't sure what to make of it.

Folding the picture, he stood, offering Manascetti his hand. "Thank you, sir. We'll get right on it and be in touch as soon as we know something."

"Man, you kids are something," the Dwarf said in awe, pumping Rick's hand again. "You don't even ask for an advance or nothing."

Rick smiled at that. "People get paid for work done, sir, not work they have yet to do. That's how I was raised, anyway."

Manascetti exploded into laughter at that. "I like you, Rick, do I ever. My kinda guy. You do good here, I may have more work for you and your crew in the future, yeah?"

"That would be great, sir," Rick agreed. "But first things first."

"Yeah, yeah," the Dwarf groused, collapsing back into his chair. "Go on, son. Do your thing. I'll be waiting to hear from you."

"Of course, sir," Rick said with a smile. "Powerage, let's go. We got one hell of a mystery to solve here. Time to get to work."

* * *

After leaving Manascetti's stately home, the team found no cabs anywhere in sight. Considering they were in a largely affluent, residential area, Rick couldn't say he was surprised. Still, it left them with a short walk if they were going to find a ride anywhere.

Make it big and hire a driver. Yes, that was certainly a plan.

After about ten minutes of walking and listening to the team chatter excitedly about their now two thousand lita reward, however, Rick noticed one voice that was strangely absent from the din. Lancaster's. Usually he had found the pompous Rogue preferred to be in the midst of whatever was going on, and upon glancing over his shoulder, found him trailing the party, a troubled look on his face.

Falling back, Rick joined him, giving him a gentle elbow to the side. "What's up, man? I figured you'd be thrilled over the doubling of the payout for this."

"Hmm?" Lancaster returned, only just appearing to notice Rick had joined him. "Oh. Yes. That is great. Good job, Rick. Couldn't have done better myself."

Rick slowed to a stop, pulling Lancaster with him, suddenly very troubled by the man's mild-mannered response. "Hey, seriously, what's going on? You don't seem like yourself at all here."

Sparing a look towards the rest as they continued on, Lancaster waited a moment then turned to Rick, a troubled expression in his eyes. "I recognized that name."

"Who's? Manascetti's?"

"No, the girl," Lancaster told him quickly. "Avalinion. I know I've heard that name somewhere before. I just can't quite seem to bring it to mind. Must be spending too much time with Todd."

Rick chewed that over for a moment, his own sense that something was amiss rearing its head again. "Maybe you heard it on the news or read about her in the papers?"

Lancaster waved that off. "No, that's not it. Even Manascetti said her body vanished from the morgue before he could get there to identify her. I've heard that name somewhere, though. I'm sure of it, and Rick, I got a cold chill when I heard it back there. Something... I don't know. Something bad, I think."

Looking back up the street, Rick nodded slowly. "Yeah, something about that story didn't sit right with me, either."

"How so?" Lancaster asked, watching him carefully.

"Manascetti said he set her up with the best education then mentioned Riscadil University," Rick replied. "Which is hardly the best. Hell, I almost went there after high school. It's basically a public university, little different from a community college. Not to mention that picture of her he gave us. She looks accustomed to having the best in life. Doesn't sit with his story of her growing up on hard times."

Lancaster pondered that a moment, rubbing his chin absently. "So why would he tell us such an obvious lie, then?"

"I'm not sure," Rick admitted. "Either he thinks we wouldn't know or he himself is unaware of the fact that the good days of that particular school are well behind it. There was a time it was a high-end university, but places like East Liaob have overtaken it. Even with my family connections, I couldn't get an interview there."

"Hard to imagine you living a happy college life," the Rogue snorted. "This is definitely the life you were meant for."

"I think that was a compliment," Rick retorted.

"It was," Lancaster declared, slapping him on the shoulder. "We both picked up on something back there that felt off. Now we just need to figure out what it was and if it's bad news for us. If this girl is in trouble with Manascetti or is running from him, I do not want to be any part of her getting hurt."

"I was thinking the same, but it's still good to know we're on the same page," Rick agreed. "Maybe once you recall where you know her name from, that'll help."

Shaking his head, Lancaster seemed somewhat frustrated with his own inability in that regard. "Maybe I heard it during my training. I know another member of the Night Brand in Riscadil. He might be able to shed some light on this, if that's the case."

"Okay, good," Rick said. "I think we've got a good few leads to chase down here, so odds are, we're gonna have to split up. I think tomorrow, though. It's getting late and those political science kids Manascetti mentioned probably won't be around."

"That cop friend of yours is likely gone home for the day, too," Lancaster said. "I'd rather like to know if that girl from the bay really was our target or not."

"You and me both," Rick snorted.

"Guess we'll find out tomorrow," Lancaster said, waving at the rest of the team as they finally stopping, noticing the two weren't with them.

"Yeah, just not sure I'm gonna like where it's taking us," Rick admitted. "Still, I'm glad we're on the same page, Lancaster. Really."

The Rogue laughed at that and ruffled his hair playfully. "Of course we are. You are our leader, aren't you? It's only natural you'd be on the same footing with the guy who let you be in charge."

Rick had to laugh at that, as well. "Yeah. I guess it is."

With that, Powerage joined back up and prepared to head home, ready to face their big day the following morning.

They had no idea.

Chapter Five: Who Made Who?

RETURNING TO CHARLOTTE'S well ahead of the curfew, Rick had settled back, allowing Emi to fill their landlady in on the details of their adventures that day. Or rather, he'd let the over-excitable Elf babble incoherently about the whole thing. For himself, he was still too preoccupied with his earlier conversation with Lancaster.

While he could only barely tolerate the man, Rick had to admit, Lancaster had good instincts. Something with Manascetti's story was very off, though for the life of him, Rick couldn't figure out just what it was. Either his idea of good education was outdated, or he was deliberately trying to mislead the team. While Rick kind of hoped it was the former, he couldn't ignore the possibility of the latter.

One thing he was certain of, however. The fear in Manascetti's eyes when talking about the apparent resurrection of Lucinia Avalinion had been very real. Whatever had happened, something about the young woman had changed, enough so that Manascetti was now sincerely afraid of her.

While his claim of just wanting to know what had become of her seemed sincere enough, Rick still found himself troubled. Manascetti clearly had resources at his disposal, so why hire an adventuring party by way of the Shy Market to look into this?

Something about all of this just didn't feel right.

After dinner, Emi continued to ramble for a while, until the excitement of the day finally got the best of her and yawning began to punctuate her endless recounting of every detail she could remember. With a patient smile, Charlotte shooed the girl off to bed, for which Rick was somewhat thankful. While Emi was a sweet person, she was also a bit hard to manage in large doses.

Charlotte returned as Rick was finishing cleaning up from dinner, the dishes all washed and the table wiped down. She paused a moment, casting an appraising eye over it then nodded, seeming satisfied by his work. For no reason he could name, that made him feel good.

"Well, I think I may have a busy day tomorrow, so I'll be off to bed myself," he said as he hung the hand towel up to dry.

"Be waiting a moment," Charlotte replied, waving at him to sit as she poured them both more coffee. "We got something to talk about first."

Unsure how to take that, he eased down. "Okay. Hopefully, I haven't done anything wrong."

Charlotte snorted a laugh at that. "Not yet, but I be patient. Be thinking you will, sooner or later."

"Gee, thanks," Rick drawled. "Making me feel right at home here."

She gave a soft chuckle at that. "That be more true than you know, but never mind it for now. We got more important things to be talking about."

"Every time you say something like that, it makes me want to ask a million questions," he groaned.

"Put them aside, boy," Charlotte told him, tapping the table between them. "That be a tale what will be told in good time. For now, I need to be knowing if you trust this bunch you gathered up with your life and with Emi's."

Rick leaned back, taking that question seriously. "Well, they are strange, that's for sure. I'm not entirely certain Toddson's deity is even real, and Lancaster spends more time on his hair than I think any sentient being would find sane. Mimi's got a somewhat chronic habit with the chronic, too. Still, all of that said, after today I have a good feeling about them. I think they'll have our back."

"What's your gut saying?" she pressed, eyeing him carefully.

"I trust them," he replied without a second thought. "I can't really explain why, but I do. I guess the best way to say it is that I've seen no real reason not to."

Settling back, Charlotte considered all that for a long moment then sighed softly. "I guess that be all can be asked, then."

"I appreciate your concern, Charlotte," Rick said slowly. "But I promise you, I'll look out for Emi no matter what. I can assume you sent me to the Slaughterhouse specifically because she was going there already, so I can surmise from that, you want me to protect her."

She nodded, offering him a weary smile. "She no be cut out for this adventurer business, boy. Me thinks even you be knowing that. She be headstrong and refuses to see it. Got too much to prove, to people what won't ever be satisfied, no matter what she do. Somebody got to keep her from getting herself killed. You being who you be, me thinks you the one to trust with that."

"You know a lot about that," he replied with some measure of concern. "Me being who I am, and all."

"Done said it be a story for another time," she answered, waving the matter off. "You not be ready for it now."

Staring into his mug, Rick accepted that pushing likely wasn't going to get him anywhere, and after a moment nodded. "Okay, then. I'll be patient and wait for you to decide when the time is right. You're trusting me, so the least I can do is return that trust."

Surprised, a slow smile spread across Charlotte's face as she reached into her breast pocket and produced a key, which she slid across the table. "That be the right answer, me boy. You got more of your daddy in you than you be knowing about."

Rick had no idea how to take that, so decided to avoid it entirely as he picked up the key, asking, "And this is?"

"What be opening the front door," she said. "You be a working man now. Can't be worrying about curfews and all that. You and Emi need to be coming and going as the need come up."

Rick smiled at that. "I see. Thank you, Charlotte. This'll be a huge weight off Emi's mind and mine. I appreciate your trust."

She shrugged. "Just don't go and be losing it, boy. That's all me ask. Now, get off with you to bed. Got a mountain of work to do come morning, if any of that girl's babbling be even half true."

Nodding, Rick pushed to his feet. "It was, more or less. At least she got the big details right. We went in looking to find a missing person and got something a whole lot more complex. I don't think anything dangerous, but still, a good night's sleep would be smart."

"Enjoy them while you can get them," she called after him as he headed for the stairs, then murmured to herself after he was gone, "You do well, you not be getting a whole lot of them in the future. No more than your mama and daddy did."

* * *

The following morning brought Rick and Emi back to the Slaughterhouse once more, the entire party having agreed it was the best place to meet up. Mostly because it was a place they all knew, but also because it was close to where the other three lived. Enough so, they could walk, while Emi could easily pay the cab fare for she and Rick to get there.

While he didn't like the idea of Emi constantly footing the bill, Rick had to admit it was the most logical solution. For now, at least. If things went well, they could eventually invest in a proper meeting place, but that was somewhere in the future. Like getting a personal driver or reliable income.

Farming okra didn't seem so bad these days for some reason.

Rick put that out of his mind quickly. He'd chosen his path and no matter how many strange twists and turns things had taken since then, he was determined to see it through. The future would take care of itself. All he had to worry over was the present.

With the other three already present, Rick and Emi joined them, making casual conversation as they finished up breakfast. Rick hadn't known the Slaughterhouse even had a kitchen, though he realized that did explain how Melvin had provided lunch so readily the other day. Of course, he also hadn't known Melvin had been running a tab for his three new friends.

He found out when Lancaster was quick to point him out as the party leader and Emi as the treasurer, making that tab their problem all of the sudden. While Emi fretted and stammered at Melvin, making the older man look at her in a sad, patient and paternal way, Rick just went to his happy place, face down on the table and wondered if there were any cabinets he could bang his head against until this all went away.

Melvin agreed to keep the tab open until they got paid, to everyone's relief. No cabinets appeared to save Rick, however, so he considered this matter a draw.

"Okay," he groaned once Melvin had departed. "If we're done spending our first reward before we even get it, let's lay out our game plan for the day."

"We actually started spending it before we even met you," Mimi admitted sheepishly. "I think we've all been broke for a while."

"More or less," Lancaster agreed. "Melvin was kind enough to roll all our tabs into one after we became a party, however, no doubt due to my dazzling skills at persuasion."

"Who's Melvin?" Toddson asked.

Mimi patted him on the head. He smiled. Rick rubbed his eyes and counted to ten. They were all still there when he finished, so he heaved another sigh and decided to press on. There really wasn't any other choice, after all.

"Putting that aside," he said, feeling tired already, "Lancaster, you're going to go look into the Avalinion family name with your Night Brand contacts, right?"

The Rogue nodded, turning more serious than Rick had ever seen him. "I am, yes. I still can't remember where I heard it, but the more I've thought about it, the more certain I am that it's something important. I'm almost positive I heard it during my training, which means it likely has some connection to the Guild. A patron, maybe. I'm not sure. I should know more by this afternoon."

"Good," Rick replied, feeling slightly more confident in the flamboyant Rogue. "The more information we have, the better. If Manascetti is trying to snow job us, I want to know."

"I dunno, Rick," Mimi chimed in, voice full of hesitation. "He seemed genuinely concerned for Lucinia and really afraid of her, too. I didn't get the feeling he was lying about that."

"Neither did I," he agreed. "Which is why I want you to go to find those political science kids he said she was hanging around with. Odds are, they'll be at Riscadil University. Asking around with that picture of Lucinia should take you to them, and I think you might have more luck with them than any of the rest of us would."

Mimi made a doubtful face. "I don't really know anything about political science, you know."

"No, but you do you know a lot about the kind of culture they probably think would be better than our current representative monarchy. Not to mention, you've got weed to offer. I'm betting they'll open up to you."

"I guess you have a point there," she agreed, though the uncertain look remained on her face.

Rick reached across the table and squeezed her hand. "I trust you on this, Mimi. This is something only you can do."

The look faded instantly, replaced with pride and excitement. "Yeah. Only I can do this. Awesome. You can count on me."

He smiled, feeling like he was two for two so far. "I'm going to track down my officer friend and see what he can tell us, as well as another source of information I thought of last night. I think it'd be best if I took Emi with me, so all that's left to decide is who's taking care of Toddson."

"Hey, Steve," the Cleric waved.

"Why do you think it's best to take Emi with you?" Lancaster asked. "Do you not trust us to look after her?"

Rick smiled sardonically at that. "Emi, you want to go visit a Thieves Guild?"

The young Elf instantly flushed and began blathering incoherently. Rick was pretty sure he caught something about her doing it if he really wanted her to, as well as something else about hoping it didn't include doing any sex stuff, which she'd also do, if needed, so long as she didn't have to look. The rest was just noises.

"Point made," Lancaster admitted when she finally ran out of steam and tried to sink under the table. "I'm guessing this is why her going with Mimi is also out of the question?"

"Pretty much," Rick lamented, pulling the Elf back into her chair and fanning her. "Mimi needs to fit in naturally, which is going to be hard to do if Emi is having a meltdown."

"I could get her high first," the Druid offered with a helpful smile.

Rick smiled at her. Mimi looked at Emi, sighed and nodded that she got the picture. Normal Emi was already a handful. There was no telling what getting the Elf high would do. Considering the need to gather information, it was best not to risk it.

"As I said, point made," Lancaster continued. "It may just be me, but having a forgetful Cleric in tow might make Mimi's job more difficult as well. Best I take him with me, unless you want to keep him an eye on him, Rick."

"I can, if you need," Rick replied. "I admit, I don't know a lot about the Thieves Guilds, but if there's some level of secrecy involved, I wouldn't want you to compromise it."

Lancaster gave Toddson a doubtful look. "I'm pretty sure I could take him anyway, if that was the case."

"Where we going?" Toddson asked.

Rick suppressed a laugh. "Point made. Toddson, you're with Lancaster."

"Sure... wait... no..." the Cleric fumbled, then paused to rub his temple. "I can't go with him."

"Uh... why?" Rick asked, more than a little surprised.

"There's something else I need to do," Toddson told him, visibly trying to concentrate. "Just gimme a sec. It'll come to me. There was a thing... a thought... what was it?"

Glancing at the others and getting only shrugs in return, Rick tried to decide what to do. As he did, Toddson grew frustrated, dug a notebook out of his satchel, threw it down on the table in anger and started leafing through it. After a moment, he stopped, read whatever was written in it and snapped his fingers.

"The girl we're looking for might have died and come back," he said. "That isn't possible anymore, 'cause the last great undead, the Second Abomination, the Arch Lich Obedell, was banished from our world, taking with him the last remaining knowledge of necromancy."

"Yes?" Risk asked slowly after the Cleric looked around the table in triumph.

Toddson's smile faded when he saw nobody was following. "Well, necromancy isn't the only way to bring someone back, right? There used to be resurrection magic, known only to the most powerful of Clerics. Sure, it borders on necromancy, but it's divine. There may be some Clerics who know something about it still."

Rick blinked several times, trying to figure out if Toddson was a lunatic or a genius. "That's... a damn good point, actually. I take it you have some idea of where to start looking into this?"

Toddson nodded. "I think so. There's a temple here in the city that I go to when I need to mediate or do other priestly stuff. I usually just sort of get this urge to go and usually I can't remember what I was doing there later, cause, well, the Forgotten One and all. I'm sure you guys have noticed, I have some short-term memory issues."

"We can barely tell," Lancaster deadpanned, earning him a slap upside the head from Rick.

Toddson grinned at that. "Anyway, the head priest there, I can kind of remember him. He's a nice guy. An Elf. He's older, well, old. Has gray hair and everything. He may remember something about resurrection magic, how it works and if anyone still knows how to use it. I figured I should go and ask him."

Rick nodded, still shaken by Toddson's surprising insight, as he let all that sink in. "Okay, then. Can you get there okay?"

"Yeah," the other man assured him. "It's important and I think my god is guiding me to do this, so I should be okay."

Leaning back, Rick took a moment to think it over anyway. He would prefer to have someone accompany the Cleric to make sure he didn't wander off task. However, that he'd thought of it at all was pretty amazing and he appeared invested enough that he had even made certain to write it down. Finally, he nodded.

"All right, then. You go look into that. We'll meet back here by five in the afternoon and share what information we've gathered. Sound good?"

Everyone nodded, and after a bit of prodding to rouse Emi back to a functional status, Rick had her make certain they had cab fare, which she eagerly assured him they did. That done, he stood, gave another nod and waved them on.

"Let's get to work, then, Powerage."

* * *

Two hours later, Rick and Emi were sitting on a bench not far from Rumble Park, watching people go about their business, idling away the day. Where Rick was kicked back, relaxed and seemingly content to do nothing, Emi could barely sit still, constantly fidgeting, glancing about and checking the time. It was enough that he had begun to seriously wonder if letting Mimi get her high wouldn't have been better.

"What are we doing again?" she finally asked, unable to take sitting still any longer.

Rick sighed. "I told you. This is where I first met that cop, and we need to ask him for information about Avalinion. If she was the girl they found in the Bay, then she's come back from the dead somehow, which might be very bad."

Emi nodded, looked around and fiddled with the hem of her dress. "Why don't we just go to the local police station and ask for him?"

Rick tried very hard to keep his cool, but it was getting hard, as this was the fourth time she'd asked that. "I don't know his name. I think it's Anton or something, but I have no idea what his last name is. Besides, there's another guy who hangs out around here that may be able to help us out."

"I dunno," she said after a long pause. "It feels like we're doing nothing."

"We kind of are," he admitted. "But there's nothing for it. This is the only place I know for sure I'm likely to run into either of them."

Emi frowned. "Everyone else is doing something."

"Emi, for crying out loud," Rick groaned. "They're doing exactly what we're doing. Trying to gather information. This is part of the job. Sure, it isn't exciting, but you have to put in the legwork if you want to see results."

She sighed again, more heavily. "I guess so. I just thought adventuring would be more exciting."

"It likely will be," he told her. "Let's get our feet wet before we try to swim across Copper's Bay, though, okay?"

"Yeah," she mumbled, looking around in boredom.

Another thirty minutes of her sighing and fidgeting passed before Rick got lucky, feeling hot breath on his neck and the words he had been waiting to hear floated into his ear.

"Coin up, or get bled, hucko."

Rick laid his head back and smiled. "Heya, Enzo. How you been?"

The Goblin grinned back at him and flicked him on the forehead. "Getting by. What brings you back around? Need me to tell you how to do your thing again?"

"In a way," Rick chuckled, sliding over to make room for him. "You told me you got the word on the street and I kind of need that right now. Unless you were bullshitting me?"

Enzo clamored over the bench, shooting Emi a wink as he did, which sent her reeling back into babbling incoherency. "You tell me. Did you go check out the Shy Market or what?"

"I did actually," he admitted. "Wasn't exactly what I was expecting, but then again, what has been since I got to this nutty town?"

"Um... Rick..." Emi fluttered.

"Just so you know, information doesn't come for free," Enzo told him. "Depending on what you wanna know, that is."

"Yeah, yeah," Rick groaned. "I'm a little cash poor at the moment, so maybe you can do me a solid this one time?"

"Rick... um... that's..." Emi floundered.

"That'd be the second time I did you a solid," Enzo snorted. "What do I look like to you? A barkeep? I don't run no tabs, you know."

Rick rolled his eyes. "Cut the crap, Enzo. I took your advice, okay? I even gathered a party at the Slaughterhouse and we have a job. We do right by the client, we got two thousand lita coming our way."

"Rick... um... why..." Emi wobbled.

"Got you a party from the Slaughterhouse, you say?" Enzo laughed, before jabbing a thumb at Emi. "That where you picked up this nervous breakdown in action? Cause if so, I ain't ready to say you're good for it."

"Lay off," Rick told him. "She's a Wizard. She's supposed to be like that."

"Wait... um... what..." Emi squiggled.

"Your mama teach you to lie like that?" Enzo snickered. "I always heard she was actually good at it."

Rick glowered. "My Uncle Castor, actually."

"Are... uh... wait... I... Rick..." Emi melted.

"Yeah, it shows," the Goblin told him, with a jab to his arm. "Never learn to lie from a Ranger. Only thing they know how to fool is big dumb animals."

"Hey, now," Rick recoiled. "No need to be so insulting. Here I am asking you for your help and you start taking pot shots at my family? What's that about?"

"Why are we talking to a Goblin?" Emi shrieked, making several people passing on the street pause to stare. Emi deflated into a puddle of self-conscious trembling instantly.

"Way to be racist," Enzo drawled after a long moment of staring at her in surprise.

"Wow, Emi," Rick groaned.

Overcome with a look of horror, the Elf grabbed Enzo and began shaking him as she was overcome with verbal diarrhea. "I didn't mean it like that at all cause there's nothing wrong with being a Goblin and I'm sure you're a really nice person or you wouldn't be friends with Rick but I thought we were waiting for a police officer or somebody from the League cause Rick didn't tell me we were meeting a Goblin and I wasn't trying to be racist and I'm really sorry so please forgive me!"

Enzo stared at her in shock for a full minute. "Holy shit."

"Emi, take a breath," Rick told her. "This is Enzo. He's the one who told me about the Shy Market and the only reason we have a job to do as adventurers. He's my friend. Okay?"

The Elf squeaked something unintelligible, let go of Enzo quickly and then tried to straighten his shirt, only to recoil before finally slumping back on the bench in red-faced embarrassment. Through it all, Enzo simply stared in confusion.

"She's excitable," Rick offered.

"You think?" Enzo exclaimed.

"Give her a minute, she'll be fine," Rick deflected. "Now, about this other thing."

"Yeah, okay, sure," the Goblin said, scooting closer to Rick. "Just, you know, do something about this disaster here, will you? She's making me feel bad just looking at her."

"Emi, Enzo accepts your apology," Rick tried.

"He does?" she whimpered.

"I do?" he doubted.

"You do," Rick ordered.

"I do," Enzo confirmed.

"Thank you," she blathered. "I'm really sorry."

Enzo ran a hand over his face, and sighed. "Forget it. It's all good. I guess Rick wouldn't be hanging with you if you were really an asshole, so, you know, we're good."

Emi teared up and nodded vigorously, sending her oversized hat flopping over her face. Rick shook his head, reached over to adjust it and patted her on the shoulder. She tried to smile, or at least, that's what it looked like. Rick decided it was best not to ponder.

"Anyway," he suggested.

"Yeah," Enzo fumbled, grasping that lifeline quickly. "What is it you wanna know?"

"Just wondering if you've seen a woman around town," he replied, digging the picture of Lucinia Avalinion out of his pocket and offering it to the Goblin. "It's cool if you haven't, but I figured I'd ask, just in case."

Enzo took it and unfolded it, then let out a long whistle. "Now that's an upscale looking Elf, Rick. What you want with her, anyway?"

"She's considered a missing person," he said. "Our client is hoping we can locate at her and verify that she is safe and well. At the moment, that's about all I know for sure."

Enzo frowned, staring at the picture for a long moment, then offered it back. "Try the Cantasol. I may have seen a dame that looks like her coming and going from there on a few occasions. Not saying it is her, but it does kinda resemble her."

Rick tucked the picture away, eyeing the Goblin suspiciously. "Did you try to shake her down?"

Enzo flinched. "She looked like a tourist, okay? One with deep pockets. Turned out, she knew Goblin and said a few rather unpleasant things about my lineage."

Rick hesitated. "She knows Goblin, huh."

Enzo shot him a curious look. "Why? That important?"

"Depends on how hard it is to learn it," Rick admitted.

"Ain't like they teach it at school," Enzo replied, catching on to what Rick was thinking. "And it sure ain't the kind of thing you can pick up casually. No, as fluently as she spoke it, she had to have been taught it by a native speaker."

Rick pondered that for a moment, this new puzzle piece feeling important, but no matter how he tried, he couldn't get it to fit with what Manascetti had said. "I think I need to find that cop. Anton was his name, I think."

"Rick?" Enzo prodded. "What's going on, pal?"

He shook his head. "I'm not sure, but things just aren't adding up. Yesterday, Anton offered to help me out if I need, and I think I really do, more than I expected. You know where I can find him?"

Still looking worried, Enzo nodded. "He's usually having lunch over at Sunny's about now. You can probably catch him if you hurry."

"Thanks, Enzo," Rick said, pushing to his feet and grabbing Emi by the hand. "I owe you big time."

"Hey, be careful, will you?" the Goblin called as Rick hurried away, dragging the still-floundering Elf with him. "You big, dumb hucko. Don't go getting yourself killed or nothing."

* * *

Anton leaned back, patting his stomach as Sunny gathered up his bowl. "I tell ya, it's a total mystery to me why you keep this place running out of a dump stand like this. Food that good, you should be in the Plaza."

"Oh, stop," Sunny giggled. "And don't call my place a dump!"

"Sorry, sorry," Anton returned, tossing a few bills on the counter. "Anyway, thanks for the grub. See you tomorrow."

"Always," the hulking Bugbear promised with a wink. "Unless you want to see more of me sooner."

Anton snorted as he stood. "I've got one ex, Sunny. Last thing I need is a second."

Leaving Sunny howling with laughter, Anton stepped out into the park and paused to plop his hat back on his head. As he was buckling it in place, he heard his name being called, which was enough to make him hesitate. It was pretty rare in this part of town for anyone to call out to an officer, much less by their first name.

Turning, he saw Rick headed his way, a dizzy looking Elf trying to keep up. Everything became clear.

"Hey, Richard," he said with a nod. "Please tell me you aren't already in trouble."

"What?" Rick gasped, staggering to a stop in front of him, the Elf with him collapsing as she panted for breath. "Why would you even ask me that? You saw me yesterday. What kind of a person do you take me for?"

"Max Wonder's son," Anton pointed out.

Rick's face went through several attempts to find an argument to that, before succumbing to acceptance. "I'm not in trouble yet."

Anton grinned at that. "So, tomorrow, then?"

"Shut up," Rick groused. "I was actually looking to take you up on that offer to help out with this missing person."

"Lucky me," the officer deadpanned. "Only one day and you're already turning to the law-bound police for help."

Rick gave him an annoyed glare. "Only 'cause you offered."

"I'm kidding, relax," Anton chuckled. "I'm happy to help, if I can. Come on, let's get you and your friend a bench and you can tell me about it."

"Huh?" Rick puzzled, then glanced back at the pile of heaving exhaustion that was Emi. "Oh, come on. Adventuring is going to require running a lot, Emi!"

"I... know... I'm... working out... some..." she wheezed.

"Oh, this is already going way better than being a cop," Anton snickered.

Rick held a hand out, begging him not to start. Anton rocked on his heels, smiling, leaving Rick to help Emi to her feet and a moment later, plop her down on a bench. Which she promptly slid off of. Pointedly ignoring the Half-Elf officer, Rick gathered her up and lay her down. That ended better.

"Anyway," he said, turning back to Anton. "I was hoping you could look into some odd information the client gave me about this missing person."

"Who's the client?" Anton asked.

Rick hesitated. "I think there's some kind of privilege involved here, isn't there?"

Anton shook his head, giving him a tired look. "Sure. Why not? What's the odd information?"

"Namely, that she may have been dead then got over it," Rick replied digging out the picture and offering it. "The client believes this person was found dead in Copper's Bay then got better and paid him a visit."

"That's not horrifyingly creepy at all," Anton mused, giving the picture a look, then frowning. "And suddenly terrifyingly possible."

Rick's gave him a curious look. "Please don't tell me that it might be true."

"Okay, I won't," Anton smiled. "Have a nice day."

"Are you serious right now?" Rick gaped.

Anton shrugged. "She does look a lot like a young woman who was found in the Bay, Richard. I'd have to take the picture with me and check with some friends to be sure, but yeah, at the moment, I'm pretty serious."

Rick rubbed his chin, considering that. "Okay, so, let's say for a second that it is the same person."

"As I said, horrifyingly creepy," Anton put in.

Rick waved at him to hush. "Anything you know about what happened?"

"I wasn't working that scene, so no," Anton admitted. "The only reason I know her face is because of another murder scene I was at that ended with me escorting a body to the morgue. I'm pretty sure this was the girl they had brought in from the Bay scene, though."

"Well, that's certainly not what I was hoping for," Rick muttered.

"Could be a case of mistaken identity, you know," Anton offered. "Hell, might even be a sibling with a strong resemblance or something."

Rick was already shaking his head. "I'd sure like to believe that, but so far, everything is pointing to this woman coming back from the dead."

Anton glanced down at the picture again, a knot forming in his gut. "You know what? I think I'm going to go have a talk with some people. Find out what I can. Where can I reach you?"

"I'll be meeting back up with my team at the Slaughterhouse around five," Rick said, noting the sudden change in Anton's demeanor, and getting a knot of his own. "I've got another lead I want to chase down, just to see where it takes me, but you should be able to catch me there."

"Five o'clock," Anton confirmed. "Richard, be careful, okay? If this woman did come back from the dead then this is bad."

Rick gave him a dour look. "Gee, you think?"

"Bad enough that I may have to report it to the Royal Inspectors."

Rick rocked back a bit. "Oh. That kind of bad."

Anton gave a grim nod. "Don't go rushing into anything, okay?"

"Yeah, I think that's one thing we can agree on," Rick said slowly. "There is one other thing I should tell you, though."

"What's that?"

"The client said she came back different. Like there was someone else in her body."

Anton went stiff. "The Slaughterhouse, at five. You better damn well be there, Richard."

"Count on it."

Rick stood for several minutes as Anton rushed away, trying to make sense of all of this. He had a lot of pieces but nothing that formed a picture, or at least, not one he could see. No matter how he turned it around, Manascetti's story was becoming more and more plausible all the time.

Someone else was living in Lucinia Avalinion's body. That alone terrified him.

"Rick?" Emi asked.

"Come on, let's get a cab and head over to the Cantasol," he told her. "I know a guy there who might be able to fill in some of the blanks."

* * *

Despite feeling as if time was of the essence, Rick ended up sitting at Sunny's for another half an hour while Emi had lunch. Something about being hypoglycemic. He assumed that was an Elf thing. Apparently, a pork cutlet bowl took care of it, so he had one too, just in case.

Rick was not the brightest guy.

However, he was not a complete idiot, either. His gut feeling that something was off had been accurate. Whatever Manascetti's interest in Lucinia, Rick was now certain it had nothing to do with caring for her well-being. The Dwarf hadn't given them the whole story, he was sure. Something else had happened. Something Manascetti didn't want them to know about.

It was the only way any of this made any sense. Or rather, the only way that didn't involve necromancy. Considering that there hadn't been a single case of it anywhere in the world after the banishment of Obedell that seemed highly unlikely. Which only left Manascetti hiding the real reason he was looking for Lucinia and whatever event had actually led to the change in her personality.

Granted, that didn't explain the mystery of the young woman the police had pulled from the Bay, but Rick set that aside for the moment until he had some hard evidence that it really had been Lucinia. A resemblance wasn't enough to go on. The more he thought about it, the less likely it seemed.

No, he thought, the more likely scenario was that Manascetti had done something that had shaken Lucinia so deeply she must have changed her view of him. At least, that's kind of what he was hoping it had been. The alternative was very frightening.

By the time they reached the Cantasol, Rick had almost convinced himself that Manascetti had deceived them about the real reason behind Lucinia's change in behavior, as well as the true motives behind his desire to find her. The woman from the Bay was most likely a red herring, or a case of mistaken identity. That was, in his mind anyway, the far more realistic and believable probability.

Standing before the grand hotel once more, Rick put all that out of his mind for a moment and smiled. Things had certainly changed in the few days since he had last been there. It felt as if it had been far longer.

One look to his left as Emi got tangled up in her own cloak reminded him why.

Pausing to save her from her own questionable fashion choices, Rick forged ahead into the lobby of the Cantasol and was again overwhelmed by the sensation of being someplace he didn't belong. Even in the early afternoon, the wealthy patrons in their finery loitered and drifted, making him wonder just what the hell any of them actually did for a living.

Ignoring them, he scanned the room and quickly spotted Mastoval, who was just taking note of him as well. Offering the man a nod, Rick eased into the lobby and then eased back to fetch the awestruck Elf and pulled her off to a corner, where hopefully they wouldn't draw too much attention.

Mastoval joined them a moment later, his soft smile already in place as he gave Emi a bow, then threw a questioning look Rick's way. "I take it you have not suddenly come into an inheritance, sir?"

"Not exactly, no," Rick chuckled. "Though I have secured work, so that's something."

"Ah, yes," Mastoval replied with a slight nod. "I hope the League is agreeing with you."

"Oh, yeah, the League," Rick fluttered. "They were... less than impressed with me. I ended up securing work outside of them."

The Half-Elf's eyebrow raised very slightly. "I see. Well, no matter. As long as you are accomplishing your goals, that's all that matters."

"So I keep telling myself," Rick managed, giving Emi a pained look as she floundered into a potted plant, nearly overturning the thing. "Let's call it a work in progress."

"Indeed," Mastoval commented in a very neutral tone. "Then what brings you here today, sir?"

"That's kind of a long story, actually," Rick replied, offering a timid grin. "The short version is that I was hoping you could help me find someone. I was told they were seen coming and going from here."

Mastoval's smile softened. "If they are a client, then you must understand, I am not at liberty to discuss their personal matters, sir."

Rick shook his head quickly. "No, no. Nothing like that. I would never ask you to compromise your integrity. I was just hoping you could tell us if she is staying here and maybe, help me meet with her, so I clear up a few things."

Mastoval's smile faded. "I cannot make any promises, sir. The safety and privacy of our clients is my first and foremost concern."

"Of course," Rick agreed, digging out the picture of Lucinia. "It is kind of important though, as I have come to believe her life may be in danger, or at the very least, under some sort of threat. I just want to find out what's really going on, and if possible, help her."

"That is most noble of you, I admit," Mastoval said, his soft smile returning as he took the offered picture and began unfolding it. "If I can be of service, I of course will be, but should this individual be a client and have no desire to see you, then my hands will be..."

Rick hesitated as Mastoval trailed off, staring at the picture in open shock. "Oh, that's probably not a good thing, huh?"

The concierge recovered quickly, offering Rick the picture back. "My apologies, sir. I'm afraid this is not a matter I can help you with."

Rick groaned. "Look, I need to thank you for helping me out the other night. Charlotte has been amazing and I really appreciate all you did for me."

"It was my pleasure, truly, and the least my Scout's Honor would allow," the Half-Elf said, offering a slight bow. "But I still cannot help you with this."

Emi spun around, staring at the concierge curiously.

"Okay," Rick said, trying to figure out what to do now. "Just, you know, be on the lookout for some real brutish guys who might come looking for her, okay? Our client seems to be very intent on finding her and I'm starting to get a bad feeling about what he actually intends to do when he finds her."

Glancing over his shoulder for a moment, Mastoval leaned in, studying Rick carefully. "Might I ask the identity of your client?"

Rick smiled. "You know I can't tell you that."

Mastoval's smile broadened at that. "Of course not. I rather expected as much, but I am relieved to hear you say it. You understand my position clearly then."

That threw Rick more than a little. "I think I do, yes. Sorry to bother you, Mastoval, and thanks."

"Think nothing of it," the Half-Elf assured him. "Though, if I may make a small suggestion."

"Of course."

"I believe the lady you are looking for has an interest in trains," Mastoval told him with a wink.

"Now that is interesting," Rick murmured. "We'll get out of your hair now."

"Be safe, sir, and please, think of us when you are looking to upgrade your living accommodations. Our penthouse suites are very secure."

Smiling, Rick nodded and guided Emi out the door, having gotten entirely more than he had been expecting. He'd doubted from the start that he'd actually get to meet with Lucinia, but Mastoval had been far more forthcoming than he had anticipated.

For his part, Mastoval watched them go, his soft smile in place until they were out the door. It vanished as soon as they did, the Half-Elf turning on his heel and making his way to the elevators as quickly as decorum would allow. The concierge of the Cantasol did not hurry, after all, for it aroused worry in the hearts of the clientele that all was not well.

Reaching the far end of the hallway, he stepped into the lift, nodding to the Kobold who was stationed there. Without a word, the dragonkin cranked the handle, closing the doors and sending them up to the only other stop that particular elevator made.

"Something wrong, boss?" the operator asked after a moment.

"Not at all," Mastoval assured. "Why do you ask?"

"You're not smiling," the Kobold replied timidly, unable to recall ever seeing his superior without his trademark expression in place.

Catching himself, Mastoval gave the operator a soft smile. "All is well. Think nothing of it, lad."

The Kobold accepted that as the elevator reached the penthouse floor and the concierge quickly stepped out into the hall, waving for him to not go back down just yet. Whatever the boss said, something was definitely up.

At the end of the hall, Mastoval paused, collected himself and knocked on the door. A moment passed before Lucinia Avalinion opened it, giving the Half-Elf a worried look. Taking a moment to glance behind him and finding the rest of the corridor clear, she swung the door wider and leaned against the frame.

"You aren't smiling. What's wrong?"

Mastoval scowled. "We must talk."

"About?"

"Someone was just here looking for you. An adventurer. He was hired to find you."

Lucinia chewed her lip for a moment. "It's not like we didn't expect that. Manascetti's men aren't exactly world class detectives, you know. It was only a matter of time before he turned to either the League, The Shy Market or one of the other places."

"It's less that an adventurer showed up, than it is about his identity," Mastoval pressed.

"Okay," Lucinia said slowly. "So, who is he?"

"Richard William Wonder."

The Elf's eyes went wide. "Right. So. We need to talk. You might want to come in for this one, 'cause I think I'm gonna need a lot to drink."

"Imagine that," Mastoval growled, pushing into the penthouse, shoving Lucinia as he went, slamming the door behind him.

* * *

"Wait," Emi begged as Rick led her through the busy streets. "What just happened? Where are we going? He didn't tell us anything!"

"He did, actually," Rick assured her, pausing at the corner. "He told us a lot, really."

Emi frowned. "Like what?"

"He admitted she was a client, for starters, and that she was staying in one of their penthouse suites. He also told us she was looking to get out of town."

Emi blinked several times. "He didn't say anything like that!"

Grabbing her hand, Rick led her through the traffic, crossing the street as fast as he could. "Not in so many words, no, but he implied it all, which was as close as he could come to saying it."

"I don't get it," Emi grumbled.

Exasperated, Rick paused, wishing he had sent her with Mimi after all. "Okay. You know how he asked me who we were working for?"

She nodded slowly. "Yes, and you told him you couldn't say."

"Right," he said, then waited a moment to see if she picked up on it. When she didn't, he sighed and explained, "Then he said I could understand his position, which was him telling me Lucinia was a guest of the hotel."

Emi scrunched up her nose. "I still don't get it."

Rick slumped. "Because he is the concierge and his job is to protect the interest of his clients, just as ours is to protect the interests of our client."

"Oh." Emi blinked very slowly. Rick watched as the proverbial lightbulb finally switched to the on position. "Oh! I get it!"

"Good, let's go," Rick urged, grateful the Elf had finally understood.

"So, wait," Emi yelped, dragging him to a stop. "Then, that means when he said she was interested in trains, he meant she was looking to leave town?"

"Exactly," Rick exclaimed.

"And when he said their penthouse suites were very secure," she continued, puzzling it all out at last.

Rick nodded emphatically. "That she was staying in one and as such, was safe from any harm until such time as she could leave the city, yes."

"Okay, but," Emi cried, grabbing Rick before he could hurry along again. "How's she affording a penthouse at a place like that?"

Rick stopped dead. That was a good question. How was she affording a penthouse at the Cantasol? Manascetti said she'd cut ties with him. Without that, Lucinia basically had nothing. Didn't she?

"Oh, no," Rick whimpered. "I think I know why Manascetti wants to find her."

"Why?" Emi asked, not liking the look of dread that had crossed his face.

"I think she may have stolen a whole lot of money from him," he replied. "Enough to stay at someplace like the Cantasol, where she's safe from him, and to get very far away."

Emi's eyes grew very wide. "Then, what does that make us?"

"I'm not sure yet," he admitted. "But right now, I think our best bet is to find out as much as we can about where she might be looking to go. Fortunately, I know just who to ask."

"It's not another Goblin, is it?" Emi begged. "Cause, I didn't handle the last one very well."

"It's not," Rick promised. "Come on, we need to hurry, I think. This is all starting to feel very bad, and the sooner we get to the bottom of it, the better."

Emi nodded, holding out her hand. Grasping it, Rick hurried them along Station Street, the sprawling train station looming ahead, where hopefully Leo was already at work. If he wasn't, Rick had no actual idea what to do next.

Luck runs with the Wonders, his mother had once told him, and for the first time, he was beginning to believe it as he pushed through the station doors and spotted Leo heading up the steps, adjusting his jacket. Spotting Rick, the porter smiled broadly and waved, hurrying his step to join him.

"Hello again, sir," Leo laughed, shaking Rick's hand. "Good to be seeing you again, it is. What brings you around? Not leaving town already, are you?"

"Not even close," Rick told him, setting Emi down on a bench as she struggled to catch her breath from their run. "I was actually looking for you. Hopefully, you can help me out with a job I'm working."

Leo lit up. "A job, is it, sir? Blimey! To think a Wonder would come around asking me for help for something like that!"

Rick strained to keep smiling. "Yeah, well, you did kind of say I should look you up if I ever needed help."

"So I did," Leo chuckled. "Done forgot all about that. Course, I never really did expect you to take me up on it, either. I mean, what's a porter going to do to be helping out somebody like you, sir?"

Rick yanked the picture of Lucinia out of his pocket and all but shoved it in Leo's hand. "You can start by telling me if you've seen this woman around the station lately."

Leo's face fell as he realized that really was all Rick was going to ask of him, but unfolded the picture anyway and took a look, at which point his smile returned. "Sure enough have, sir. Can't say as I know her name, but I done seen her coming about every few days for a couple of weeks now."

Rick struggled for words at that. "Wait. Every few days for a couple of weeks?"

"Oh, aye, sir," Leo confirmed with a nod. "On my Scout's Honor, that be the truth."

Emi cocked her head, looking at Leo curiously.

"Hold on, that can't be right," Rick floundered. "What was she doing?"

Leo waved a hand back down towards the main concourse. "Studying the old rail line maps."

"What?" Rick gaped.

"Oh, for sure she was, sir," the porter insisted. "Spend a good hour or more each time, just looking them over. Can't say as to why, though. The lady never did have any luggage or such with her, so not much use for a porter, you see."

Rick slumped against the wall, his mind reeling. "Why would she care about old rail line maps?"

Leo shrugged. "I took it she had an interest in the historical value of them, to be honest. Most of those lines are long since dug up, now that all the trains went to underground tunnels."

"They used to run above ground?" Emi asked.

Leo nodded. "True enough, Miss. Most of them went to underground a good thirty years ago, and the last of the elevated lines got torn down twenty years back when Obedell tried to seize the city. Good old Max Wonder gave him what for, though, he did. Good bit of the city had to be rebuilt after that, mind, but it was worth it to see that monster sent packing."

"Great," Rick groused. "Here I thought she was trying to skip town, and she was actually looking to tour my Dad's old fight scenes. None of this makes any sense!"

Leo gave him a doubtful look. "Don't think that was her interest, to be fair, sir. Seemed she was more interested in figuring out where the lines use to run to. As I said, I don't know for certain, but I do know a bloke we could ask."

Rick shook his head, his entire theory shot. "Sure, let's see if we can make some of this add up."

Looking at him in concern for a moment, Leo turned and scanned the concourse, then waved. A moment later, a fellow porter came jogging up the steps, looking from Leo to the other two curiously.

"Able, got a question for you," Leo said, holding up the picture. "This young lady bent your ear for a good bit last week about the old rail lines, didn't she?"

The other man looked at the picture, then smiled, nodding. "That she did. Was real interested in them, she was."

"Why?" Rick begged.

Able shrugged. "Don't know for sure. She mumbled something about the old K Line, though. Said she couldn't remember where it ended."

Leo rocked back on his heels. "The old K Line, 'eh? That's proper strange. As I recall, the only place that went was out to the old rail yard near the processing plants in Auberdeen."

"Oh, hey, that's right," Abel laughed. "Least, that's what she was saying earlier today."

Rick's head snapped up. "Earlier today?"

"Yes, sir," the other porter nodded. "She was by a few hours ago. Heard her say something like that before she ran off out of here."

Settling back, Rick tried to clear his mind of confusion and focus on what he did know. He had been so sure she was running from Manascetti, but now that no longer seemed to be the case. So what was Lucinia doing staying at the Cantasol and looking into abandoned rail yards in an outer borough? Shaking his head, he found that none of this made any sense.

"Thanks, Abel," he finally said. "And Leo, thank you, too. I had hoped all of this would make more sense, not less, but at least it's something to look into."

"Not a bother," Abel said, nodding.

Leo, on the other hand, seemed more curious. "Make more sense of what, sir? If you don't mind me asking?"

"It's a long story," Rick assured him. "I'll tell you all about later. For now, it looks like we're going to be taking a trip out to Auberdeen."

"Isn't it getting late for that?" Emi asked.

Rick glanced up at the clock over the main concourse. "To go straight there, yeah. We need to meet up with the others. Maybe they've learned something that will shed some light on all this."

Clearly confused, Abel tipped his hat and headed away, leaving Leo loitering, watching Rick nervously. "You done gone and got yourself mixed up in some big adventure, have you, sir?"

"Looks like," Rick groaned. "It was supposed to be a simple missing persons search, though."

"No wonder with a Wonder, then, eh?" the porter chuckled.

"I'm starting to think that's something that's going to haunt me," Rick muttered, waving Emi to follow him. They'd gotten all they were going to here. It was time to find out what everyone else had learned.

* * *

An hour later, Rick was becoming somewhat bothered by the growing payback he owed Emi for her constant covering of cab fare as they arrived at the Slaughterhouse. That thought was put out of mind almost instantly upon stepping out of the cab, however, when he spotted Anton waiting for them.

"Well, this can't be good news," he grumbled.

Emi made a soft squeak before asking, "Why not?"

"He looks agitated," Rick pointed out, then waved to the officer as Emi paid the cabbie. Somehow, he just felt certain this already strange case was about to get even stranger.

As soon as the cab pulled away, Anton approached, nodding to Emi before saying, "Richard, I sure hope things have gone well on your end, cause if they haven't, then this is not going to be a fun conversation."

"Then it's not gonna be," he grunted, rubbing his head. "Every time I think we're close to understanding what's going on, each lead we follow makes it even less clear."

Anton gave him a look of sympathy before holding out a folder. "Then this is really going to make your day."

Hesitantly taking it, Rick flipped it open and immediately felt the bottom sink out of his world. "Fuck me sideways."

"Yeah, pretty much how I felt," the officer said. "That is a photo taken of the woman pulled from Copper's Bay, just before her autopsy was to be performed. As you can see, that is clearly the same woman you are looking for."

"Yes, it most certainly is," Rick said softly. "Who I know for a fact right now is very much alive."

Anton frowned at that. "You're sure of that?"

"Very," Rick admitted, flipping through the rest of the paperwork in the folder, then paused and went through it again. "Wait. There's no actual autopsy results here."

"No, there isn't," Anton agreed. "Seems that right after the photo was taken, the young woman sat up, apologized to the coroner for the inconvenience, and walked right the hell out of the morgue."

Rick blanched. "Seriously?"

"That can't be good," Emi whimpered.

"Got it straight from the doctor's mouth," Anton told them. "Jonas Burke. He was the head medical examiner for the city for twenty years. Until he retired a few weeks ago, right after accepting the blame for losing a body. That body, to be precise."

"Hold up," Rick struggled.

Anton waved him down quickly. "I went to see him after we talked and he told me the whole story. He even gave me a copy of the file he'd kept. Burke said he tried to report it and was asked to take early retirement. He wouldn't say by whom, but I get the feeling it was someone pretty high up the food chain..."

"That sounds ominous," Rick said slowly, looking at the picture of Lucinia again.

Anton looked around for a moment as Rick digested this newest bit of information. "You know I have to notify the Royal Inspectors about this, don't you?"

"Yeah," he said, closing the file and offering it back. "I'd appreciate it if you'd give me a couple of days to try and sort this out before you do, though."

Anton waved him to keep it. "Why, though? This is no small thing you've gotten yourself mixed up in here, Richard. This is the first case of necromancy we've seen in twenty years."

"I get that," Rick agreed. "But I started something and I'd like the chance to see it through to the end. I'm not asking you to keep them out of it entirely, just give me two days to try to figure this out on my own. If I haven't by then, I'll turn everything I've learned over to them myself."

Shaking his head, the officer was clearly torn between his sense of duty and his desire to help Rick. "Fine, okay. Two days. Don't make me regret this, though."

"Not planning to," Rick snorted. "This is why I came to Riscadil, Anton. If I drop everything at the first sign of trouble, then what am I even doing here?"

"This isn't trouble, Richard," Anton exclaimed. "This is world-ending levels of bad! Trouble would be getting caught trespassing while you tried to catch somebody's husband cheating on them. We're talking necromancy here!"

"I get the difference," Rick snapped back. "But this is my case. I accepted this job, and I owe it to myself and the rest of my team to at least try to see it through before we tuck our tails and run away!"

Anton held his hands up. "I get it. Okay. Sorry. I just... I don't want to see you get yourself hurt trying to chase after your dad's reputation."

Shaking his head, Rick handed the folder over to Emi who tried very hard to look anywhere but at the two men. "That's not it, Anton. This is, plain and simple, me trying to finish whatever I start. That's just how my mom raised me to be. It's got nothing to do with my dad at this point."

Anton scoffed at that. "Necromancy pops into the picture and you expect me to believe it has nothing to do with your dad? Really?"

Rick sighed, his shoulders sinking at that. "I guess that would make it hard to swallow, huh?"

"Just a little," Anton retorted, holding up two fingers that were touching. "About that much."

Rick nodded. "I've got one more lead to look into. Let me see what I find out and what the rest of my team has learned. If things get too dicey, I'll hand everything over to you, so you can turn it over to the Royal Inspectors immediately. How's that?"

"A little better," Anton sniffed. "I'm not trying to question your dedication, Richard. I really am just worried about you. I don't want to see you show up in an autopsy photo, okay?"

"Won't happen," Rick tried to assure him. "My mom would kick my ass back to life, just so she could kill me for dying."

"You know, I actually kind of believe that," the officer told him with a dour look.

"You ever met her?"

"No."

"Trust me," Rick told him, clapping him on the shoulder. "It would happen."

"You've got two days," Anton replied, not even cracking a smile.

"Then I best get to work," Rick stated with a grim look. "Thanks, Anton. I appreciate the help."

"Yeah, thank me by not getting killed," he answered, watching Rick and Emi head for the bar. "And don't be mad at me if I don't wait the full two days to call in backup for this."

Rick didn't hear the last part of his comment, but had he, he would have assured the officer he wouldn't have. No matter what he'd said, he was scared half out of his mind at the implications of what he'd found himself in the middle of.

Chapter Six: You Shook Me All Night Long

ON THE SHORT WALK to the front door of the Slaughterhouse, Rick ran through everything he knew one more time, but it still came up as a lot of contradictions and meaningless information. About the only thing he could be sure of at that point was that Manascetti had lied to Powerage about why he was really looking for Lucinia.

Though, to be fair, even that was something Rick could no longer be sure was entirely accurate. After all, he now knew that the Dwarf had told them the truth about her having died and come back. Odds were good at this point that whoever she had been before her death, she was someone else entirely now.

Which left him with a few million other questions he couldn't even begin to guess at the answers to. Whoever was walking around in Lucinia's body right now seemed to mostly be interested in abandoned train lines, which didn't exactly seem threatening.

Who was in Lucinia's body? How had they gotten there? What were they looking for? What had Manascetti not told them? How much did he really know about what was going on? Most importantly of all, who was the necromancer who had pulled this off, and what was *their* agenda?

Shaking his head to clear his thoughts, Rick swung open the door of the bar and waved Emi inside. Before it had even swung closed behind them, they spotted Lancaster on the far side of the main room waving at them. Just from the look on his face, Rick knew there was more bad news coming.

Crossing the room, Rick noted several of the patrons looking up from their drinks, watching him and Emi curiously, some of them casting hopeful glances. Word must have spread that regulars had secured actual adventuring work. Choosing to ignore that for now, Rick touched a hand to Emi's back, hurrying her along.

"I take it you've had about as much fun as we have," he said softly as they joined the Rogue.

Lancaster snorted at that. "You know how I was all gung-ho back at the Shy Market?"

"Yeah?"

"You were right about us getting in over our heads," the Rogue told him. "I think we're there now."

"Fantastic," Rick sighed. "So, what did you learn?"

"Trust me, you'll want to hear what the other guys have to say first," Lancaster replied, jerking a thumb at the door to the backroom Rick and Emi had used to interview them before. "It'll make more sense that way."

"And save the best for last?" Rick asked, half joking.

"Actually," Lancaster hesitated.

Rick slumped. "Take a simple job, and have everything go straight to hell. I hate when my mom is right about stuff."

"Good to know this is normal, at least," Lancaster scoffed. "That makes me feel a ton better. I'm guessing you guys learned something that's going to make all of this worse."

"So much worse," Emi peeped.

"Awesome," the Rogue groaned.

"Emi, go ahead and join the others," Rick suggested, waving at the door. "I want to talk to Lancaster for a second."

Both the Elf and the Rogue gave him curious looks at that, but thankfully she did as he asked. While he figured he'd have to tell her sooner or later, he kind of doubted she really needed to know what he was about to say just yet.

"This feels ominous," Lancaster commented as the door closed. "Or potentiality sexy."

Rick gave him a tired glare, but got only a cocky smile in return and decided to just get on with it. "Back at the Shy Market, after we settled on this job, Toddson said something strange to me in the hallway."

Lancaster leaned back against the wall, eyeing him nervously. "I already don't like where this is going."

"Short version, he thinks this deity of his compelled him to grab this particular request," Rick explained. "Now, I'm not entirely convinced the Forgotten One is even real, much less that Toddson is even a Cleric, but let's say for a minute both things are true."

"You're talking about divine intervention setting us on a path to be in the middle of all this," Lancaster said, looking more than a little unsettled by the implications.

"Yeah, and after what I've learned, I'm not sure I can argue it," Rick admitted. "But that's not really what I wanted to talk to you about."

Lancaster tossed him a dubious look. "That kind of seems like a big conversation to have right about now."

"Until you consider the alternative," Rick cut in. "What if Toddson is in on this?"

Lancaster started to reply to that then stopped, thinking about it seriously for a minute. Finally he shook his head. "No. I don't think so. I mean, I'm not best friends with the guy or anything, but I've kind of known him for a while, and I've never seen any reason to think he's anything other than he says."

Rick mulled that a moment, and then nodded. "Okay, then. I felt the same way, but I couldn't ignore the possibility. It made me want to get your take on it, since you somehow seem to be the most... well... intelligent person in this group, beside me."

Lancaster scowled. "I think there was a compliment in there somewhere."

"Somewhere," Rick said with a wry grin. "Point is, Mimi's too trusting, and Emi's too... Emi, to really weigh that sort of thing accurately. You've shown a knack for picking up on things, and after our conversation yesterday about Manascetti, I feel like I'd be smart to trust your instincts."

The Rogue smirked at that. "Now that sounded like it hurt."

"More than you'll ever know."

Lancaster laughed, but it faded quickly. "Still, this idea that some god is using us like pawns bothers me. Todd may be okay, but who knows what this deity of his is after, or if they can even be trusted."

"Not much for it now," Rick replied. "One thing my mother beat into my head was that you always finish what you start. However strange this has gotten, and however we got involved in it, we have an obligation to see it through."

"Let's just hope somebody is still willing to pay us when it's all said and done," the other man grumbled.

"Let's hope," Rick agreed, opening the door for him.

* * *

Beyond the door, Rick found the interview table still set up and loaded down with a wide selection of food, the other members of the team busy eating. Despite his frustration with how quickly they were burning through any reward they may or may not still get, he had to admit he was hungry.

After a moment of groaning and looking at them at all in annoyance, he gave in, pulled up a chair and grabbed some for himself. Across from him, Mimi was devouring a salad while Toddson appeared to be fascinated by a plate of chicken wings. Rick decided not to think about that and paid more attention to Emi as she minced her way through a steak.

"So, Lancaster tells me we all have news," Rick commented as they all begin to wind down. "Why don't we start with you, Todd?"

"Sup, Harry," Toddson said with a smile and nod. "What are we doing again?"

Rick sighed heavily. "So, Mimi, why don't we start with you?"

"Oh, sure," the Druid fumbled, shoving the last of her salad in her mouth and chewing quickly. "You aren't gonna believe what I learned."

"I have a feeling I just might," Rick told her with a tired smile.

She seemed confused by that then set it aside, saying, "So, after I got to the campus, I went around like you suggested, showing people Lucinia's picture and asking after her friends. Took me a bit, though, cause nobody seemed to know her, so I ended up giving up on that and just started asking where the political science kids hung out."

"Wait, nobody?" Rick asked. "That's a little odd."

Mimi snorted a laugh. "It gets weirder."

"Great," he groaned.

"I did end up finding those kids, though it feels a little weird calling them kids, cause I think a couple of them were older than me," she continued. "And when I showed them her picture, they said they didn't know her, either."

Rick did a double-take. "Please tell me you didn't just accept that?"

"Duh, of course not," she retorted. "I shared some weed with them, thinking they'd open up to me, but even then they were all like, nope, never even heard of her. So, while we're getting high, I had this great idea."

"Oh boy," Rick groused.

"No, really, it was a great idea," she insisted. "I went to see the political science professor. The students might be covering something up, but the teacher, she'd remember her for sure, right?"

Rick begrudgingly admitted that was a great idea. "And what did you learn from her?"

"She'd never seen or heard of her, either," Mimi said. "I felt like that was pretty crazy, so I spent a bit getting high with her while I tried to figure out what to do. Then I had another great idea. Which kind of sucked actually, because I think she was kind of into me. She was pretty hot for a middle-aged Elf, and I was getting a real vibe. If I hadn't had my idea, I'm pretty sure I would have gotten laid."

"You... wait... what?" Rick balked.

"Chill, Rick," the Druid snickered, amused by his baffled reaction. "Never mind that, 'cause this is where things get really strange."

Rick slumped in his chair. "I can't wait."

"I went to the faculty office and was all, like, hey, I'm with the League and I'm looking for this girl for her family, and stuff. Showed the picture, dropped the name, and guess what?" Mimi paused, staring at Rick in excitement.

He stared back her for a moment, then asked, dryly, "What?"

"They never heard of her either," Mimi told him in a hushed tone. "Like, they have no records of her ever attending the University. At all. Not by name, and no matching picture on file that they could find."

Rick sat up, realizing what she was saying. "She never attended that school? At all?"

"Looks like," Mimi said.

"Wait, that doesn't make sense," he boggled. "Why would Manascetti drop us a false lead like that? This doesn't add up."

Mimi was already nodding. "I know, right? He totally lied to us! Sent us out looking for fake ducks, or something!"

"A wild goose chase," Lancaster corrected. "Though I think I can shed some light on the why, as soon as Toddson tells you what he learned."

"Hey, man," the Cleric waved. "Long time, no see."

Rick rubbed his face. "Okay. So. Toddson, you went to check with a Priest you know about resurrection. Please tell me you wrote down what you leaned?"

"I did?" Toddson asked, surprised by this, and then lit up with a bright smile. "Oh, hey, I did, didn't I! Hang on a sec. I probably did make notes. That sounds pretty important."

Pushing down his urge to go to his happy place, Rick waited while Toddson dug out the notebook and began scanning through it. After a moment, he paused, read for a bit, and then nodded. Pointing at it, he declared he had, in fact written it all down. Then he sat there smiling.

"What does it say?" Rick begged.

Toddson blinked. "Wow. That'd be helpful, wouldn't it?"

"A little."

"Right, so," he said, clapping his hands together and scanning it again. "The old Priest guy told me that there use to be resurrection magic a long time ago. Very powerful Clerics and Paladins had access to it, to revive fallen allies in the fight against evil."

"Sounds useful," Rick admitted.

"No kidding," the Cleric chuckled. "It became much more widespread during the Abomination Wars about three hundred years ago, when the gods made it more available to lower ranking Clerics and stuff. I guess there was a lot of fighting, 'cause it was a war and all."

"The Abomination Wars was when Obedell first appeared," Lancaster added, throwing Rick a meaningful look. "He was turned into an Arch Lich by the First Abomination, the Quicksilver Witch, and together they created more Abominations."

Emi sank deeper into her chair, but nobody seemed to notice.

"I remember studying that in history," Rick said, trying not to think too hard about how many times the infamous necromancer's name kept cropping up today. "So what's all this got to do with now?"

Toddson shrugged. "Beats me."

"Notes, Todd," Mimi urged, tapping the book.

"Oh, hey," the Cleric gasped. "I forgot about that."

Rick sank closer to his happy place. Down at the other end of the table, Emi pulled her hat down and just listened, drawing Lancaster's eye for a moment. Watching her briefly, he filed her reaction away for later.

"Okay, so after the Abomination Wars, there was a big population boom as technology, medicine, and stuff advanced," Toddson continued. "Eventually, the gods revoked the ability to use resurrection magic at all, due to the large numbers of people spreading around the world. I guess they were afraid that eventually there would be a crisis or something, if people didn't die as much."

"Which means what?" Rick asked.

Toddson fiddled with the book a moment. "Nobody has been able to use resurrection magic for over a hundred years now. The gods don't allow it anymore. So... yeah."

"Got it," Rick groaned, rubbing his eyes. "Well, I was hoping that would end differently, but I can't say I'm surprised."

Toddson closed the notebook, looking at Rick uncomfortably. "Did I mess something up?"

Startled by that, Rick forced himself to smile. "No, not at all. You confirmed what I was already suspecting. Good work, Todd."

The Cleric visibly relaxed. "Thanks, Pete."

Rick rubbed his eyes again and counted to ten before turning to Lancaster. "That just leaves you."

"Actually, it leaves you as well," the Rogue countered. "I'm very curious as to what you learned."

"I'm not sure just what I've learned at this point," Rick admitted. "I was kind of hoping you'd be able to put some of it into focus."

Lancaster took a moment to think about that then nodded and straddled a chair. "Fair enough. I'll finish first, though I do hope you come to a fine climax on all this."

"Wow," Rick struggled. "Innuendo much?"

"Thank me later," the other man shot back with a wink. "So here's what I know. After meeting with my Night Brand contact, I now know where I remember the Avalinion family name from."

"The suspense is killing me," Mimi whispered to Toddson, who apparently had forgotten what was going on.

Rick really wanted to care about that, but just didn't have it in him.

"Have you ever heard of the Scarlet Ring?" Lancaster asked Rick, ignoring the two idiots.

"No, can't say as I have," he said, not liking the sound of it. "Why?"

"Elven crime syndicate," Lancaster explained. "Rumor has it they have their fingers deep in politics and corporate dealing all over Gulinlan, or at least they did. Nobody has heard much from them for a while now."

Rick settled back, crossing his arms. "What's this got to do with everything else?"

"The head of the syndicate was the Avalinion family," the other man said with a wicked smile. "About twenty some years back, they tried to move into Liaob, here in Riscadil, and ended up in a turf war with another crime syndicate called the Ironriggers."

"Hold up," Rick waved. "You're telling me that Lucinia is from a mafia family?"

"I am, yeah," Lancaster said. "That's not the good part, though."

"This gets better?" Rick gaped.

"The Ironriggers are run by none other than the Manascetti family," he stated. "As in, the guy we are working for right now."

Rick flopped back in his chair, too shocked to even think. While this certainly did put a lot of things in perspective, it also raised a whole slew of new questions, none of which he cared for. It had, however, solved at least one mystery, and that was what Manascetti had been keeping from them.

"Okay, so this Scarlet Ring and these Ironriggers get in a turf war," Rick said finally, his mind still reeling. "How'd that go down?"

Lancaster gave a slight shrug. "Apparently, the Ironriggers won and drove the Scarlet Ring out of Riscadil. From what I was told, it got pretty damn bloody. Especially out to the east side of the city where the Ring held most of their power."

Emi perked up at that. "In Auberdeen?"

Lancaster gave her a curious look. "Yeah, actually. They made a lot of inroads with the unions working the processing plants out there. How'd you know about that?"

"We didn't," Rick said. "But a whole lot of things just became a hell of a lot clearer."

"Such as?" the Rogue pressed.

Starting with learning that Lucinia was apparently a guest at the Cantasol, Rick related all he and Emi had learned, from the young woman's interest in the Auberdeen rail lines, to the fact she actually *had* come back from the dead. Rick was suddenly grateful Anton had left the file with him, as it made it a lot easier to convince the others when they saw it with their own eyes.

"Okay," Lancaster said slowly, dropping the file back on the table. "So, apparently we've stumbled into a hell of a mess here."

"Looks like," Rick agreed. "Though, at this point, a lot of it makes a hell of a lot more sense than it did earlier."

"How so?" Mimi asked, her brow wrinkled in confusion.

Rick chewed his lip a moment. "Well, as it stands now, I'm guessing Lucinia is a surviving heir from those turf wars and has come looking for something the Ring left behind in the processing plants. Probably some money or something. Manascetti doesn't like the idea of her being back in town and wants us to find her so he can deal with her, and probably nab whatever she's looking for, for himself."

"Makes sense," Lancaster agreed. "Though the part about her coming back from the dead is still pretty freaky."

"Unless she's working with a necromancer who's been laying low ever since Obedell got banished," Toddson said, drawing looks of surprise from everyone.

"He's got a point," Rick said slowly. "About twenty years ago was also when Obedell was banished, so the timeline fits. If the Ring had necromancers working with them, they may have pulled up stakes and left with them."

"Creepy," Mimi intoned with a shudder. "Necromancy just isn't cool."

"No, it's not," Lancaster said, rubbing his chin. "But it does make sense. Legend holds that the Quicksilver Witch was an Elf, so if that's true, then it isn't impossible that Obedell may have had ties to the Ring."

"She was," Emi peeped. "I mean the Quicksilver Witch. She was an Elf."

Lancaster shrugged. "I guess Emi would know. So all that's left to figure out is what Lucinia is looking for."

"And why Manascetti sent us on that wild goose chase with the University in the first place," Rick reminded him.

"For that matter, why he fed us that whole line of crap to start with. Adventurers are basically mercenaries, after all."

"Unless he knew," Toddson said softly. "Knew who you are."

Rick felt a cold chill run down his spine. "Okay. How would he know that?"

"Dunno," the Cleric answered with a smile. "Just had that thought pop in my head."

Rick stared at him for a long moment, trying to figure out if he was being honest or not. Finally he shook his head and decided it was best to just keep an eye on him. If he was playing them, sooner or later he'd slip up.

"Well, regardless, from what we've learned, Lucinia has apparently found what she was looking for, or at least the general vicinity of it. Odds are, she's going to make her move pretty quick. We might want to try and beat her to the punch."

"Uh, why?" Lancaster asked. "I mean, the client misled us and we're already sure she's involved with a necromancer. I hate to say it, Rick, but you really were right about us not getting in over our heads here."

Rick gave him an annoyed glare. "Oh, sure, now you want to listen to me."

"I was wondering the same thing, actually," Mimi put in softly. "I mean, this is starting to look pretty scary."

Rick nodded slowly. "I agree, it is. However, whatever Lucinia is looking for, Manascetti wants. At this point, it may be our only bargaining chip with him, 'cause I'm pretty sure he doesn't intend to pay us."

"Which is why he was so generous about doubling the reward," Lancaster groaned. "Okay, I am starting to not like this guy."

"Our best option right now may be to beat her to the punch, grab whatever it is she's looking for, and maybe her while we're at it, and hold them both over Manascetti's head," Rick suggested. "I can't guarantee we'll still get paid, but I am sure of one thing that will at least get us something in all this."

"Which is?" Mimi asked.

"A chance to bust two different crime syndicates, nab a necromancer, and recover a ton of likely stolen money," he replied with a smile. "That sort of thing tends to come with rewards as well, you know."

Lancaster smiled. "And fame."

"And more work," Toddson added.

"Basically, yeah," Rick said, pointing at Toddson as he nailed the most important aspect. "As well as the ability to set our own payout, because of the fame."

"Ooh," Mimi squealed. "We're gonna take down some bad guys, save the day, and be heroes!"

"I like this plan," Lancaster laughed. "Let's do it."

"When are we doing it?" Emi asked, looking at the clock on the wall nervously.

"Right now," Rick told her as he dug out the key Charlotte had given him and held it up for her to see. "And don't worry about the curfew. I've got a key to the front door and Charlotte's permission to be out as late as we need."

Emi scrunched up her face for a moment, thinking it over, then nodded. "Okay, then. We go now."

"Now it is," Lancaster agreed.

"Hell, yeah!" Mimi enthused.

"What's happening?" Toddson asked, confused.

Rick patted him on the shoulder. "Powerage, it's time to kick some ass."

* * *

Despite what he'd said to the others, Rick had only one real goal. Confronting Lucinia and getting some answers about the identity of the necromancer she was obviously working with. Everything else had been to get the others fired up to go, as he doubted he could face this situation alone.

He felt a little bad about it, though if all went well, they would still get all the things they were hoping for. Being able to hand over the name of a necromancer to the Royal Inspectors, as well as possibly two high ranking members of criminal syndicates would certainly land them a certain amount of notoriety, after all. Provided all went well.

The only real concern he had at the moment was the possibility that the necromancer in Lucinia's employ would be with her. He still wasn't clear on what level of spellcasting ability Toddson and Mimi had, but if Lucinia wasn't alone, he knew for a fact Emi would be badly outclassed. Not to mention himself and Lancaster.

All he could hope for now was that things went well, and they could catch Lucinia alone, and off guard. Failing that, perhaps they could locate whatever it was she was seeking and use that to get to her. The only problem there, of course, was that they had no idea what she was looking for, which just meant he was gambling on finding the woman herself.

Calling it a longshot was an understatement, but after hearing what the others had discovered, Rick couldn't see any other option. They had no cards to play, and he kind of doubted Anton was going to wait a full two days before reporting all of this to the Royal Inspectors. After that, any chance they had of coming out of this ahead, or even finding out why Manascetti had misled them, were going to be gone.

Still, as they made the long trip into Auberdeen and night fell, Rick began to have second thoughts about this course of action. It occurred to him that Lucinia need not be with a necromancer for her to not be alone. If what Lancaster had said was true and she was the heir to powerful crime family, there was a good chance she would have trained guards with her.

Facing any sort of force, in unknown territory, under the cloak of night, was a recipe for disaster. However, even in realizing this, he had only to look around the carriage they had hired, at their set and determined faces, to know it was too late to back out now. Each of them was looking beyond the possible danger and at the potential reward.

Except Emi. She looked terrified.

And Toddson. He just looked confused.

Mimi kind of looked high, actually.

Rick decided not to look at them anymore. His already waning resolve was only falling faster thanks to that. Best to keep his own wits about him and hope like hell Lancaster actually knew how to handle himself in a fight. The man's insistence on wearing white clothing and decking himself out in jewelry made him an easy target, after all. If he lacked significant skill, Rick had to worry about him more than the others.

It all came down to the one thing he could not ignore in the end, past his doubts and even his fears. Within a week of reaching Riscadil and becoming an adventurer, like his father, he was involved in a job that had led him to a necromancer. As much as he hated it, Anton had not been entirely wrong. This felt like his father's shadow falling over him, and as much as he wanted to avoid that, he couldn't help but wonder if this was somehow fate.

Or the working of a strange and forgotten god. That left him eyeing Toddson once more, and wondering just what was really going on with the Cleric. After all, Toddson had expressed concern over this job, due to his feeling certain his strange deity had manipulated them into taking it. In light of all that had transpired, Rick couldn't help but wonder himself if that was the case.

The time for pondering the strange workings of fate and gods soon passed, however, as the carriage drew to a stop, depositing them on the outskirts of the abandoned processing plants Lucinia had apparently been seeking. Watching their ride pull away, Rick took a moment to look up at the swath of stars overhead, then back towards the bright glow of Riscadil in the distance.

They were truly in unknown territory now, and it felt far more isolated and lonely than he had expected.

"All right, guys," he whispered, waving them together. "According to what Lancaster's contact said, the Scarlet Ring had their center of their power in the old hog processing plant on the south side of the yards. Let's start there and see what we can find. Spread out, but stay in eye contact."

Everyone nodded, save Toddson, who seemed troubled. Hesitating, Rick held the rest back, watching the odd Cleric for a moment as he nodded to himself a few times.

"That's cool," he finally muttered, before pulling his holy symbol from under his armor, a simple iron affair with an elaborate eye motif, and clasping it firmly. "I beseech thee, cast your divine grace upon mine eyes, and allow me see as thou sees. Show me the path unto she whom I seek."

"Toddson?" Rick started, reaching for him.

The Cleric raised his head, his eyes glowing brightly for a moment as he looked about, then pointed towards a plant on the north end of the yard. "She's there. I see her."

Rick followed the direction he pointed, then turned back to him as the glow faded from his eyes. "You sure?"

"About what?" Toddson asked.

"Locate Person," Lancaster said. "He cast a spell, Rick. If he says she's there, we'd be wise to listen."

"I agree," Emi offered. "The casting was different, but I recognize the structure of the magic."

Considering it for a moment, Rick looked to Mimi, who simply nodded her agreement. "Okay, then. Good work, Todd. Let's move out."

"Wait, what did I do?" the Cleric hissed. "Guys? Where are we going?"

Slipping across the yard towards the building Toddson had singled out, Rick gave it a quick look and figured it to be a central packing facility. Massive sliding doors stood half open, revealing a large open area and the remains of an old, and now rusted rail line running between two loading docks on either side.

Motioning to the others, Rick waved Mimi and Lancaster to the far side of the doors, then indicated Emi and Toddson should take the other side with him. Everyone stared at him in confusion.

With a soft sigh, he accepted that Castor had trained him far better than most people would be, and whispered as loud as he dared, "Lancaster, take Mimi and cover that side. You two, with me."

They all nodded and hurried into position. Deciding to train them on the basics of hand signals later, Rick glanced into the loading dock and found it empty and silent. Catching Lancaster's eye, he waved him forward. Thankfully, the Rogue picked up on the intent of the hand motions quickly and with a nod, eased inside, pulling two daggers from his back as he went.

Waving the others to hold position and hoping they got what he meant, Rick swung in as well and dropped to a knee, hands on the hilts of the Whip Blades. When nothing stirred, he nodded to Lancaster and they mounted the concrete steps onto the docks, moving quickly towards the back, where they paused again, listening.

Nothing stirred, but Rick held position anyway, looking around carefully. The east side of the dock, where Lancaster was, dead-ended against a cinderblock wall. Near Rick, however, a heavy steel door leading deeper into the facility stood open and a flight of rotten stairs went up to a manager's office. Doubting anyone could have navigated those without leaving considerable evidence, Rick waved Lancaster to come join him and the rest to move up.

Gathering them near the open door, Rick glanced down the hall, but saw nothing in the gloom. "Okay, guys. Toddson says she's in here already, so let's be quick and quiet about locating her. I'll take point with Lancaster at my back. Emi, you follow, then Toddson, with Mimi bringing up the rear."

"Why am I in back?" the Druid asked.

"How well can you see in the dark?" Rick returned.

Mimi nodded a little. "Pretty good."

"Then you watch our back," he said pointedly.

"Ooh," the Druid said, wiggling a finger at him. "I get it now."

"I'll remind you that neither of us can exactly see well in the dark," Lancaster said, glancing down the hall. "I'd be a bit more concerned about what lies in front of us over what may come from behind."

Rick shrugged. "I just don't want to get caught in a trap here. Anybody coming at us from this way, we're gonna run right into anyway. If they are aware of us and try to flank us, I want to see it coming."

The Rogue considered that for a moment, then nodded. "Can't argue that."

"Let's go."

Easing forward, Rick pulled both blades, spinning them to keep them tucked against his forearms as he hugged the left side of the wall. One step behind him, Lancaster hugged the right, both of his daggers tucked behind his back. Trailing them, Rick could hear Emi breathing heavily, and the soft scraping of metal as Toddson readied his mace.

After only a few feet, moonlight filtering in from holes in the sagging roof allowed their eyes to adjust enough they could more or less see, though Rick didn't like anything about this situation. They were basically walking blindly forward, with no idea of what dangers could be lurking around any of the corners.

Reaching a half closed door on the right, Rick paused, motioning for Lancaster to check it out. Nodding, the Rogue put his palm to it and gently swung it open, making barely a creak. Beyond lay what looked to be an old office of some type, molding furniture revealing little as to what purpose it had once played.

Moving on, they checked each door they came to for what felt an eternity, pausing at each creak of old wood or soft flutter of animal life that had taken up residence. Nearing the rear of the plant, they rounded a corner and found themselves faced with two swinging doors through which light shone, bringing the entire team to an instant stop.

Deciding Toddson may just be a Cleric of a real deity after all, Rick waved everyone to hold and eased forward, hoping to get at least some idea of what was happening on the other side of the doors. To his surprise, Lancaster paced him, taking up position on the other side. For a moment, Rick felt a bit ashamed of ever doubting the other man.

Nodding to each other, they palmed the doors and eased them open, leaning in to glance through. Beyond lay a large central packing facility with a long serpentine beltway of metal rollers gone to rust and collapse surrounded by heavy steel bins, most of which lay overturned. None of that was what held Rick's interest, however.

Standing towards the south end of the room, about halfway across, was Lucinia Avalinion, decked out in finely made leather pants that hugged her curves a little too tightly, a simple cotton shirt, and a long leather coat. Facing her were seven men in dark clothing and cloaks, all brandishing curved daggers, save one, who held a well-carved wooden stick of some kind.

"Get on with it, then," Lucinia was saying. "You didn't track me all the way here just to idly threaten me, I assume."

"Hardly, my dear," the man with the stick chuckled. "If, in fact, I can rightly call you that. I've no intent on killing you just yet, however. I'm much more interested in exactly who you are. I know it wasn't my master who ended up in that vessel, which begs the question, just who did."

"Don't get how that matters, to be honest with you," she replied with a smirk. "You're gonna kill me either way."

"Probably," the man admitted with a shrug. "That vessel is now useless to our purposes, so it depends on how useful you prove."

Lucinia laughed at that. "Trust me, pal, you won't have any use for me. I tend to just make trouble. It's about the only thing I really am good at."

"Pity," the man said with regret. "Still, I think it wise to keep you alive until such time as we can attempt the soul transfer again. Just to make sure you don't hijack it once more, obviously. Which means you'll be coming with us."

Glancing at Lancaster, Rick cocked an eyebrow. Getting his meaning, the Rogue considered it for a moment, then gave him a grim look. Whatever was going on, those men were about to get away with their prize. Getting it, Rick nodded and held up three fingers.

Lancaster grinned and waved everyone to be ready to run as Rick silently counted down, dropping one finger after another. When he closed his fist, he and Lancaster shoved forward, running into the room, weapons at the ready, the others following behind them.

"Hold it right there," Rick yelled.

The assorted men jerked towards them in surprise, as did Lucinia. Spotting their weapons, the dark clad men swung their own towards them, while the Elf just rolled her eyes and dropped her hands.

"Seriously," she cried. "I had them right where I wanted them!"

"Drop the daggers," Rick ordered. "We can make this real ugly for you guys. Nobody wants that."

The man with the stick snorted at that. "Manascetti's adventurers. I'm surprised you children aren't out chasing your tails. No matter. The lady, or whoever she is, is coming with us. We have plans for her."

"Great," Lucinia grumbled. "Now I've gotta do this shit the hard way. Thanks, Rick."

"I... what?" Rick gaped.

Darting forward, Lucinia grabbed one of the men, twisting his arm back, dragging a cry of pain out of him as he dropped his dagger into her waiting hand. Spinning him around with practiced ease, she shoved him back and sent herself into a twirl, delivering a sharp kick to his jaw that left him laid out on the floor, before she hopped back, brandishing the dagger.

"That was unexpected," the man with the stick commented in irritation.

"Then this will really make your day," Lucinia winked as she flipped the dagger around and stabbed herself in the chest.

Crumpling to the floor, blood spreading rapidly across the front of her shirt, the much sought after Lucinia left everyone else gawking in total confusion. Slowly, far too slowly, Rick began to realize just how bad this situation had just gotten.

"Dammit," the leader of the other band snarled. "You fools! I needed her alive! Only she can tell me what I want to know!"

"I think..." Rick began to say, but was cut off as Mimi shoved past him, holding out her hands to the other men. Rick tried to grasp for her, but with a sword in each hand, that proved futile.

"Hold on," the Druid cried. "Just, hold on. I know healing magic. I can still save her. There's no need for more bloodshed, okay? Just let me heal her and we can all figure this out without anyone else getting hurt."

"Mimi, fall back, dammit," Rick yelped.

She waved a hand at him without looking. "I can do this, Rick. Trust me."

Glancing to Lancaster, Rick got only a frightened look back, confirming his own sense of the situation. A quick look over his shoulder showed Toddson brandishing his mace but just as uncertain as everyone else, while Emi was on the verge of panic.

"I get it," Mimi said, easing closer to the bleeding woman. "You have a lot of questions for her. We do, too. Let's figure this out together. I can save her and we can all get the answers we want, okay?"

The leader of the other group shook his head and sighed. "I'm afraid that will not be possible, dear lady. While I did want to know who had taken up residence in that body, I have no need of your healing ability to still make some use of this vessel. This is but a minor setback, nothing more."

"That's not how you made it sound a second ago," Mimi suggested, giving him a nervous smile. "What do you really have to lose by letting me help her?"

"Nothing, I suppose," he admitted, leveling his stick on her as deep red orange energy began to gather around it. "But you have inconvenienced me, and for that, I am most annoyed."

"Oh," the Druid gasped as the energy around the wand gathered into a small ball of fire and launched towards her. "Shit."

Mimi's head exploded.

"Kill them," the wand wielder ordered as Mimi's body fell to the floor, the rest of the team too stunned to do anything for a moment.

It only lasted a moment, however. As the others put away their daggers and pulled small crossbows from beneath their cloaks, Rick felt a surge of rage wash over him. Mimi had only been trying to help everyone. There had been no good reason to kill her. None at all.

"Lancaster, Toddson, flanking position!" he roared, swinging his swords to the ready. "Emi, we need covering fire!"

Nothing happened. Seeing their foes readying their weapons, Rick glanced over his shoulder to find Emi paralyzed, eyes fixed on Mimi's still form, wide and tear-filled behind her glasses. To either side, Toddson and Lancaster hesitated, glancing about as panic began to set in.

The situation was already out of control.

"Shit," Rick snapped. "Toddson, get Emi out of here, now! We're falling back!"

They were in no condition to fight. He saw that. They were too shocked. Too hurt. Too angry. Trying to engage these people would only get more of them killed. The best he could do now was get them out alive. If he could even manage that.

"Mark," Toddson floundered.

"Get Emi out of here!" Rick shouted, snapping the Cleric out of his stupor.

With a nod, Toddson turned and scooped the fear-paralyzed Elf over his shoulder, running for the doors. Thankful for that, Rick hedged closer to Lancaster who was still glancing around, eyes wide and full of terror.

"Fall back," he urged, nudging the Rogue with his elbow. "Cover their escape. I'm right behind you."

"But..." Lancaster whimpered "We can't leave her like that."

"No choice," Rick snapped. "We're outnumbered and that guy has a wand. Our only choice is to run for it. Now move."

Gathering himself, Lancaster moved back, leaving Rick to cover him as the other men aimed and their leader shook the wand a few times, scowling. The first salvo was going to be the hardest, but Rick had been taught well. These guys had nothing on his mother.

At the first twang of the bowstring, Rick snapped the Whip Blades close, deflecting several of the bolts. Behind him he heard Lancaster cry out in pain, and as their opponents set about reloading, he darted back, catching the Rogue as he slumped against the wall, a bolt in his shoulder.

"Lancaster," Rick urged.

"Hurts like hell," the other man grated out. "But I'm okay. I can move."

"Go, I'll cover you."

"Rick."

"Go."

Pushing off the wall, Lancaster stumbled through the doors, Rick trailing behind him, swords at the ready. The others were slow, he realized, giving them just the few seconds they needed, and by the time the second salvo came, he was through and into the hall.

Spotting Lancaster waiting for him at the turn of the hall, Rick waved him to hurry, and with a nod, the Rogue vanished. Keeping an eye out behind them, Rick moved as quickly as he could, rounding the turn and planting himself against the wall. He had to buy the rest time.

It took only a heartbeat before he heard the swinging doors slam open and the sound of footsteps. A second heartbeat later, Rick swung out with his right hand, decapitating the first of their pursuers in a single, clean blow. Swinging around, he brought the second blade into play, slicing upward, catching another pursuer off guard and splitting him in half.

Gagging at the smell of blood, he pushed back as those following staggered away, shocked at how quickly he'd killed the first two. It gave him time, just enough he hoped, and he ran as fast as he could. They wouldn't hesitate long and their crossbows would give them range. His only hope now was that they would think twice and hesitate.

Spotting Lancaster ahead of him, Rick slowed slightly, not wanting to outpace the other man, but the whiz of a bolt past his ear made him rethink that choice. Skidding to a stop, he swung a blade up, deflecting a second bolt, and held his ground, the narrow hallway something he could use to his advantage for a moment.

They rushed forward, dropping their crossbows, daggers sparkling in the shafts of moonlight. That made the situation a lot worse, he realized, and slid back a step. The tight confines may have helped him against their range, but daggers against scimitars in that same situation put him at a disadvantage.

Part of him silently thanked Castor for his well-rounded training as he held his breath, waiting for them to get close. As soon as they were within his reach, Rick shoved forward, catching their daggers against the Whip Blades and holding them at bay. He only had seconds before they had backup and he knew it.

A dagger buried itself in the forehead of one, startling him and his other opponent. Rick recovered first however, and shifted his weight, allowing the man to stagger forward as he relaxed his grip on his own weapon, letting it spin. Flipping the other sword around along his forearm, he turned, letting his opponent overreach and stagger forward before dropping his forearm down, laying the man's back open.

Looking up, he saw Lancaster readying another dagger and nodded his thanks. Instead of getting an acknowledgment, the Rogue threw his blade and Rick heard a cry of pain from behind him. Jerking around, he watched another of their foes stagger and fall.

Farther down the hall, the last of their number, save their leader, who Rick didn't see anywhere, hesitated and then grasped at his crossbow, struggling to reload it. Deciding not to wait, Rick darted forward, Lancaster already on the move. If they could make it to the loading bay, they might be able to get out of this, losing their remaining pursuers in the maze of processing plants.

"That guy," Lancaster panted. "The one with the wand. I recognized it. It's a Karashev. I think it may be a type three. It's got a recharge time of about a minute, maybe two."

"You recognized his wand?" Rick stammered.

"Trained Rogue," the other man replied. "Point is, we don't have a lot of time. If he catches up with us, we've got no way to defend against that thing."

"Then we better hurry the hell up," Rick suggested.

Easier said than done, he admitted. Lancaster was bleeding heavily from the bolt sticking out of the back of his shoulder and already looked like he was about to drop. Not to mention there was one more guy with a crossbow behind them, and somehow Rick doubted he was going to risk getting close, which meant he had the advantage.

What had seemed an eternity earlier, however, seemed like only seconds as they burst through into the loading dock, clear of the hallway. Urging Lancaster on, Rick slowed, watching his back as he scrambled down the steps and hurried for the doors. Not spotting any pursuit, Rick began to turn to follow, when a sharp pain shot through his leg, sending him to his knees.

Crying out, he hit the ground and rolled, grasping his leg as pain ripped through him. Twisting himself, he spotted the bolt sticking through his calf and grimaced at his own stupidity. He only had a moment while the man reloaded, and he was a sitting duck laying there. Palming around for the sword he'd dropped, he felt his hand close around it and rolled away, tumbling down the steps and hitting the floor hard.

"Rick," Lancaster called from the doorway. "Hang on! I'm coming!"

"No," he snarled out pushing himself up. "Run! Go cover Todd and Emi!"

Gaining his feet, he saw the Rogue hesitating and waved at him to hurry. Emi was too stricken with fear and grief to defend herself, and Rick had no idea if Toddson would even be able to remember they were in danger. All he had now was Lancaster, and he wasn't in much better shape than Rick himself.

Finally, he saw the Rogue move away, grimacing in pain and grief as he disappeared beyond the bay doors. Relieved, Rick forced himself forward, his injured leg barely able to move, much less hold his weight. Getting out of this wasn't going to be easy, but he was Delilah Wonder's son and giving up was not something he could do.

"Impressive," the leader of the other men called. "You are far more skilled than I expected. You've taken out most of my men. It is almost a pity to kill you."

Stopping, Rick hobbled around, facing him as he reached the top of the stairs, the wand already beginning to glow again, his remaining team member leveling his crossbow. The doors were still several feet away. There was no way to reach them.

"You'll have to forgive me," Rick said, bringing the Whip Blades up. "I've got no intention of dying here. Gonna have to make you earn it. I'm sure you understand."

"I do," the other man smiled, raising the wand. "Actually, believe it or not, I rather respect you for that. You truly are your father's son, it seems."

Rick blinked. How could they possibly know who he was? Who the hell were these people? For that matter, how had they known Manascetti had hired him and his team? What was really going on here?

More questions tried to cloud his mind, but Rick stilled himself and pushed them away. None of that mattered now. He wasn't getting out of this alive. He could see that. Even if he could dodge the wand attack, the other man with the crossbow had him dead to rights. All he could take solace in now was that he'd gotten his team out. The others would survive.

Bracing himself, Rick glanced down at the swords in his hands. He had never mastered them. He wasn't his father. He never would be. Max Wonder would have cut through them like a whirlwind. All he had been able to do was run away, and he'd failed to even do that.

Rick cocked his head as a thought hit him out of nowhere. Cut through. The Whip Blades were enchanted. They could cut through pretty much anything. Maybe, he thought, even a magic attack.

Glancing back up, he saw the man with the wand smirk as the energy coalesced. There was no harm in trying. Flicking the blades together, he angled them, creating a wedge, and shoved them out before himself as the ball of fire launched forward.

At worst, he would die trying to defend himself, standing on his own two feet. There was little more he could ask for.

The magical ball of fire hit the Whip Blades and they sliced through it, splitting the assault in two, sending each half angling away to impact the walls on either side of the loading bay. For the briefest of moments, Rick was actually surprised that had worked.

"What the hell?" the man gasped. "Impossible!'

"Nah," Rick grinned, sweeping a blade out to deflect the bolt fired by the crossbowman. "It's a Wonder thing."

As the crossbowman struggled to reload, his superior shook the wand, getting nothing from it. It was brief, and he had only moments, but his strange luck had given him an opening. He could never mount the steps in time, but he'd gotten pretty good at throwing over the years, playing ball with Maari.

"Hurry up, you idiot," the wand wielder shouted.

A moment later, a scimitar was embedded in his chest.

The crossbowman gaped as his leader tumbled down the steps, dead. Jerking towards Rick, he saw only a flash of silver, then nothing more, his head tumbling away as his body sagged and fell off the dock onto the rusted rail line.

Slumping, Rick took a moment to gather his breath, feeling more exhausted than he ever had in his life. Somehow, he was still alive. He honestly hadn't expected the Whip Blades to deflect the magical attack, but he supposed what Castor had said was true. They really were pretty much indestructible.

Limping over, he gathered a sword from the dead wand wielder, as well as the wand, before dragging himself up the steps to retrieve his other sword. Pausing a minute to collect himself, he began the seemingly long walk to the doors. Every step was agony, the bolt in his calf shooting pain fresh and new with even the slightest movement.

Dazed, in pain, covered in blood, and nearly in shock, he staggered out into the yard and almost got a dagger to the face. That woke him quickly. Traced the blade down to Lancaster's hand, as the Rogue lowered it then let out a deep breath, Rick did the same.

"I almost killed you," he said.

"That would have really sucked," Rick told him.

"Yeah, it really would have," Lancaster agreed, sliding the dagger away and grabbing Rick as he staggered. "Easy, boss. I got you."

"Emi and Todd?" he asked.

Lancaster nodded across the yard. "Over there, hunkering down. Once I got them secure, I came back for you."

"Thanks," Rick said with a thin, tired smile.

"What about those guys?"

"Dead," Rick told him, tugging the wand out of his belt. "Better them than us."

Lancaster looked away. "Most of us."

Rick felt a knot in his gut. "Yeah, most of us."

Reaching the other two, Rick found Emi sobbing uncontrollably as Toddson tried to comfort her to no avail. Looking back at the plant, Rick wondered just what had actually happened. How everything could have gone so wrong so fast. Unable to find answers, he set it all aside and eased himself down next to Emi.

"We have to get out of here," he told Toddson. "They might not have been alone. Go see if you can find us a ride."

"To where?" the Cleric asked, eyeing the bolt in Rick's leg.

"I know a place we'll be safe," he assured him. "Just go. Worry about this after we're out of here. We get set upon right now, we really will be done."

Hesitant, Toddson nodded. "You got it, boss. Hang tight. I'll be back in a minute."

Nodding, Rick laid his head back. "Lancaster, keep watch, okay? I think I'm about to pass out."

"I got you covered, Rick," the Rogue replied, only to realize Rick didn't hear him, having already fallen unconscious.

He stood guard until Toddson returned, tears running down his cheeks to the sound of Emi's sobbing, daring anyone to get near them.

Chapter Seven: The Razor's Edge

THERE WERE ONLY TWO THINGS in the world Inspector Costanza truly hated, which many considered pretty remarkable for a Half-Orc. The first was bad coffee, a fact well known among the members of his precinct, due to his many tirades about the matter. The second was being called in to work early, though that was mostly due to his rather overzealous late-night activities.

Grimacing at the cup of truly terrible coffee in his hand in the just rising sunlight, Inspector Costanza couldn't help wonder just which of the many gods he had angered recently. If he was to guess, it was probably Imonya. With three divorces under his belt and a girlfriend who was half his age, he somehow doubted the patron deity of hearth, home, and family was overly fond of him these days.

"You look like shit."

Costanza threw his partner a dirty look. "Gee, thanks. So do you."

Inspector Guinell smirked at him. "I bet you say that to all the Elves."

"Nah, you're special," Costanza snorted. "Really. I mean it."

"Love you, too," Guinell chuckled, waving a hand at the abandoned processing yard before them, where dozens of police officials combed the area. "Any thoughts on this mess yet?"

Costanza shrugged. "Well, it's a mess, I can say that much for sure. Just what really went down, though, is gonna take a bit to figure out."

"We don't have a bit," his partner told him with a meaningful look. "You know who wants this to break a certain way."

"I take it he's done been in touch?" Costanza asked, already well aware of the answer.

Guinell nodded. "Of the two bodies we found in the packing facility, one was the girl he hired those kids to find."

"And the other?"

"Don't know yet," the Elf shrugged. "She's got no head, so identifying her is going to be hard. Odds are, she's one of those adventurers, though."

"Great," Costanza groaned. "Just what I need today."

Guinell said nothing for a moment, looking back over his shoulder at a commotion from the street. "Yeah, it just got a lot worse, pal."

Turning, Costanza saw it as well, and with a few choice curses, tossed the awful coffee he'd not been able to bring himself to even sip. "Fantastic. Like this mess wasn't already going to be a pain to deal with."

Moving through the crowd of onlookers and media were two men in sharp suits, one a human, the other Chthonian, both wearing sunglasses and carrying themselves with an air of superiority Costanza knew all too well. Whatever had actually gone on at the processing plant yard it had drawn bigger attention, and quickly.

He already knew who they were, too, their reputations preceding them. The human, with his shock of white hair, and the lavender-skinned Chthonian were both well-known in law enforcement circles for their skills as well as their persistence. If they'd been assigned, then this was not some run of the mill gang dustup. It was serious.

"Inspectors," the human said as they approached, flashing his badge. "I'm Percival St. Claire. This is Molly Tanabuar. Royal Inspectors Special Services Division. Tell us what you've found, please."

Exchanging a glance, Costanza took point, allowing Guinell to step back. "Sorry, but what the hell does the R.I. care about a gang squabble out here in this neck of the woods?"

"That's our business," St. Clair replied with a flat tone. "Just tell us what you've learned so far."

"What my dear colleague means to say, gentleman," Tanabuar offered with a toothy grin. "Is that we're here to help with the investigation, so the why isn't really relevant, yes?"

"Bullshit," Costanza spat. "Until we got some reason to believe this is anything other than some gang fight, you got no business stepping in. So either tell me what the hell is going on, or piss off my crime scene, assholes!"

"Inspector," St. Claire said slowly, removing his sunglasses in a way meant to intimidate. "We are not in the habit of explaining ourselves to our inferiors. Kindly do as you are told, or you will be not only be removed from this investigation, but from your job. Do I make myself understood?"

Costanza's jaw worked in impotent rage for a moment. "Buncha horseshit, you ask me."

"We didn't," Tanabuar pointed out with a smirk. "Still, if I may suggest we get on with it. My partner is using his nice manners and that rarely lasts for long. Once he stops, well, let's just not find out how that will go for you, hmm?"

"Fine," Guinell offered, resting a hand on Costanza's shoulder. "Forgive my partner, please. He's not a morning person and we aren't use to getting advisors from R.I. out here in Auberdeen."

"All's forgiven," Tanabuar replied, removing his own glasses and tucking them in the breast pocket of his jacket. "One day, I'm sure we'll all look back on this and laugh."

"I don't find murder a laughing matter," St. Clair drawled.

"You don't find anything a laughing matter," his partner returned with a snort.

St. Clair gave him a withering glare. "Sure I do. I look at you every day."

"I can feel the affection," the Chthonian deadpanned. "Distant, cold, and aloof though it is, I feel it."

"Let's get to work," the human groaned, rubbing his eyes.

"This way," Guinell motioned, waving Costanza to let him handle the rest. To his relief, the Half-Orc grunted and followed his lead. Things were already difficult enough, there was no sense making it worse.

"We've got blood pooled here, around these old crates. Not a lot, but enough we can pretty much assume someone was wounded," the Elf said, as the two Royal Inspectors followed him. "The trail leading back to the packing facility indicates they may have run from there and taken a moment to catch their breath."

"Obviously," St. Clair said in a bored tone. "I understand there were bodies recovered."

"Inside," Guinell agreed. "Come on. May as well let you see the fun stuff."

"Oh, fun stuff." Tanabuar grinned. "I love it when there's fun stuff."

"Something is very wrong with you," his partner muttered.

Trailing the Elf into the packing building, the Royal Inspectors paused at the steps as Guinell knelt down. "We've got a lot of blood here and more at the top and on the tracks over there. Too much for a single person to lose and not be dead."

"Two people," St. Clair intoned, mounting the steps. "First one fell down the steps. The other, off the side. Where are the bodies?"

"Good question," Costanza said. "You guys are the genius detectives. Maybe you can figure it out."

"Percy," Tanabuar called. "I've got a partial boot print over here, and what looks like drag marks."

St. Clair joined him, glancing about the dust. "Hard to tell. Crime scene is a mess."

"I'm sure," his partner insisted. "Better eyes, and all that."

"Fine," St. Clair accepted easily, before snapping his fingers at one of the officials loitering about. "We'll want pictures of all this."

"There's more, I take it," the Chthonian called to the Inspectors as his partner directed the evidence gathering for a moment.

"Down the hall, yes," Guinell confirmed, joining him on the dock. "More of this mostly, though. Lots of blood, no bodies. The interesting stuff is in the packing room."

"Show us," St. Clair stated, motioning the photographer to follow them.

They paused twice more, St. Clair wanting photos of the blood stains, especially outside the packing room, where a large swath of crimson told him a story. It wasn't one he cared for, however. Whatever had gone on the night before, it had been no mere gang fight. His trained eye told him a skilled swordsman had killed at least two people there, maybe more.

Stepping into the packing room, he had to admit, things did get more interesting. Enough so, even Tanabuar gave a low whistle. Two bodies, though neither showed the sort of massive blood loss they had seen coming down the hall, lay in the floor. One of them, he recognized.

"The first victim here," Guinell said, pausing over a woman in green leather armor who was surprisingly absent a head. "Cause of death is pretty obvious. We haven't been able to find her head, but charring around the neck and shoulders says we probably won't."

"Fireball?" Tanabuar speculated.

"No," St. Clair replied, crouching to get a better look. "No blast radius or scorching anywhere below her neck. I'd say this was a fireburst. Smaller, more localized version of the same spell. More difficult to cast and control, but pretty popular among military casters, at least when it's enchanted into a wand, which is pretty common."

"Military hardware?" the Chthonian grumbled with a shake of his head. "That's not something easy to come by."

"It's not," his partner agreed as he stood. "Which is not the most bothersome thing in this room, making it a bit more surprising."

"You mean the second victim," Costanza said, motioning them over to the pretty, young, and very dead Elf woman.

"Lucinia Avalinion, daughter of the head of the Scarlet Ring," St. Clair confirmed, joining him. "Looks like a single stab wound to the chest."

"Way I figure it," the Half-Orc offered, "bunch of wannabe heroes got wind of some kind of a deal and thought they'd make a name for themselves. Busted in here and things got ugly. The lady here got stabbed, and that one over there got her head popped. The uninvited guests panicked and ran for it, leading to the fight down the hall."

"Sounds plausible," Tanabuar commented, already knowing what his partner was going to say.

"If you're an idiot," St. Clair snapped. "The wound on Miss Avalinion is clearly self-inflicted. Just look at the angle of it. Which leaves me with only two questions."

"What's that, smart guy?" Costanza growled.

"Where's the weapon she stabbed herself with," the human replied, looking around the room. "And why didn't they take her body with them when they cleared out the others?"

Guinell and Costanza looked at each other, then frowned. Those were two very good questions, neither of which they had considered. They would have to figure out how to explain that in their report of course, in order to cover their other employer's ass. Without a word, both understood that they may not be able to keep this quiet the way they were expected. Especially with R.I. now involved.

"Anything else?" Tanabuar asked as St. Clair wandered around the room, taking in any detail he could find.

"Logs show there was a Puffer in the area last night," Guinell decided to admit, figuring it best to not hide anything at this point. "We've called for it. It should be here any time."

"We'll want to be there for that," St. Clair called. "There's a great deal about this that does not make sense."

"Ya think," Costanza muttered.

"I do," the human replied, pushing past the Half-Orc with a scowl. "It makes me wonder why you were so quick to write it off as gang activity."

Costanza blanched. "It was just a first impression!"

"Naturally," Tanabuar agreed, then shot him a strange look. "Though, I would think a seasoned Inspector like yourself would preface his comments as such."

Guinell grabbed his partner by the shoulder, stopping him from making an ass of himself. "Like I said, he's not a morning person."

"Let us hope that's all it is," St. Clair snarled as he headed out of the room, motioning the photographer to follow, Tanabuar on their heels. "It would be unfortunate if we were to investigate you, as well."

"Cocky piece of..." Costanza muttered.

"Settle down," Guinell hissed. "This is out of our hands. Best thing we can do is hand everything over to them and put some distance between ourselves and you know who. This comes down on him, I'd rather not get caught in the fallout."

The Half-Orc glanced around as the crime scene boys began wrapping up to make way for the coroner. "Yeah, I get it. R.I. came in and snaked it out from under us. Dunno about you, but I got some leave coming. Might be a good time to take it."

"Best time in the world," the Elf agreed, patting his shoulder and heading to trail the Royal Inspectors.

Tired and annoyingly coffee free, Costanza shoved his hands in his pockets and wondered for the millionth time this year alone how his life had gotten so damn messed up. Then he remembered he had three different alimony checks and two different sets of child support payments, as well a gambling problem and a drinking problem. Manascetti had made everything easier to deal with.

For the first time in a long time, he began to see at what cost that ease had come.

* * *

St. Clair stood a few yards away from the main bustle of activity, his gaze fixed on nothing in particular as his mind pieced together the events that had led to two confirmed dead, and likely many more. Across the way, Tanabuar was interviewing a couple of homeless Gnomes, but it was unlikely they had seen anything. They bedded down on the north end of the plants, too far from whatever had happened.

He did take a moment to watch as the coroner carried the two bodies out, and offered a silent prayer to Imonya that they find shelter with her now. There was nothing he could do for them, save that and bring whoever was responsible to justice. If anyone was.

While he doubted Costanza's ability as an Inspector, the gruff Half-Orc had been right about a few things. While Avalinion had stabbed herself, someone else had killed the woman in the green armor. It was likely that her allies had then fled, engaging others in battle down the hall and being injured as well.

Though he could think of a few other likely scenarios. His cursory examination of the woman in green had left the scent of marijuana in his nose. Coupled with Avalinion being the apparent head of the Scarlet Ring these days, he couldn't ignore that a drug deal had gone south.

That hardly explained everything, however, and left him wondering just what scenario would. Especially since the latest information had placed Avalinion out of the country. Then there was the matter of a fireburst, most likely from a wand, being used. It wasn't easy to get something like that, so he had to accept that it may not have been a wand at all. That placed a caster at the scene, but that he was aware, only a few of the local gangs had anyone capable of that particular spell.

"Hey, Percy," Tanabuar called, dragging him back from his musings. "The Puffer is here. Figured you'd want to see if it had anything useful."

"Of course," St. Clair said, digging out his regular glasses and putting them on. "Did you tell that photographer to send everything to our local office?"

"Naturally," his partner said, sounding slightly offended. "Hey, where are you? You got that look on your face that makes me worry."

"No idea what you mean."

Tanabuar rolled his eyes. "Yes, you do. That look that says you haven't already figured out exactly what went down, how, and why. What's up? We've been here a good twenty minutes already."

St. Clair slowed to a stop. "I'm missing something, Molly. I know I am. Some key piece of evidence that should be here, but isn't. It's vexing me greatly."

The Chthonian scratched at one of his horns. "This is new."

"And all the more bothersome for it," St. Clair agreed. "Someone went to great pains to remove only certain bodies and evidence. I feel as if perhaps we are only seeing what we are meant to see."

Tanabuar gestured to where Costanza and Guinell waited with the Puffer. "Maybe we'll catch a break here and you can go back to being your usual moody, instead of this pensive moody. I don't like your pensive moody. It makes me itchy."

"Something is very wrong with you," St. Clair groused.

"But only in the best ways, yes?" his partner asked with a bright smile.

"Sure," the human drawled. "Go with that."

Deciding to let the matter drop, Tanabuar followed his partner of ten years over to where the small, ball-shaped creature hovered. Similar to an Older, only much smaller, Puffers had taken up an integral role as city surveillance, utilizing both their ability to record and replay anything they saw, and their latent ability to become invisible to be an irreplaceable aspect of police work.

"Bout time you joined us," Costanza grumbled.

"Identity yourself," St. Clair said to the Puffer, drawing first its droopy central eye, then the ones at the end of the five stalks that ringed its body.

"M-me?" it stammered, quivering in the air.

"Obviously," the human snorted, showing the creature his badge.

"R-royal Inspectors?" the Puffer trembled, rolling in the air. "Oh... oh boy... oh, man... this is big... big league... too big... ahhh!"

St. Clair looked at Tanabuar, but got only a less than helpful shrug. "Please, identify yourself."

"Oh... um... okay..." the Puffer stammered as it wobbled about, doing a lazy circle before them. "Puffer three-five-nine-three-zero-five. My friends... um... my one friend... more of an acquaintance... calls me Quiver, though."

St, Clair rubbed his eyes behind his glasses. "Very well, Quiver. Were you in this area last night?"

"I dunno," the Puffer replied in a quavering voice as it sank towards the ground, eye stalks tucking against it. "Who's asking?"

"What is wrong with this thing?" the human asked anyone that might know.

"We don't get as much funding out here in Auberdeen since the plants shut down," Guinell told him. "So we tend to get the less useful people and things."

"That's great," St. Clair moaned. "Hey, Quiver, over here. Look at me."

"I'd r-rather not," the Puffer whimpered. "You're scary!"

"Only if you make me angry," St. Clair returned. "Now pay attention and answer my questions."

The Puffer screamed and thudded to the ground, where it tucked its stalks against its body, and proceeded to just sort of roll around while crying. For a moment, St. Clair had no idea what to do. Finally, he looked at Tanabuar and jabbed a finger at the sobbing creature.

"Make it work, Molly."

The Chthonian flipped his hair with a dramatic flick of his wrist and fell into a crouch before the whimpering thing. "Hey, Quiver. Buddy. If you help me out, I'll make the scary guy go away. How about it, me amigo?"

Slowly, the Puffer opened its main eye and gave him a weepy look. "Do you promise me t-that?"

"Cross my heart and hope to... well, not die, but yes, I promise," he assured.

"O-okay, I guess," the Puffer agreed, untucking itself and floating back into the air a few feet. "Just... make him look away. Those eyes are eating my soul!"

"Percy," Tanabuar smirked. "You're scaring small children again."

"Whatever," the human groused, turning so he wasn't facing the creature directly, but could still see whatever was going on.

"Better?" the Chthonian asked with a bright smile.

"A l-little, maybe," Quiver stammered, all of his eyes bouncing from St. Clair to Tanabuar. "What was it you wanted to know?"

"A crime happened here last night," Tanabuar told him, pushing to his feet. "Two people were murdered. We were hoping you might have spotted something unusual that could help us."

"Murder?" Quiver wailed, sinking towards the ground again. "Like, a s-serial killer that collects eyes as t-trophies?"

"Ah, no," Tanabuar replied, mystified by that reaction. "Just a regular murder. Nothing that interesting."

"And here they thought we were slacking," Costanza muttered, drawing a snicker from his partner.

The Puffer trembled in the air, rolling on his side again. "Well, I might have seen something weird I guess. I don't think it'll help any, though. It never does."

Tanabuar patted it on the head. "Why don't you show me and let me decide, hmm?"

Quiver went very still, his central eye going wide. "Physical contact? Oooohhhh.... I'm feeling kinda queasy now!"

"Seriously?" St. Clair groaned.

"Welcome to our world," Guinell chuckled. "He's not even the weirdest. You should meet our Older. He's got this thing about germs."

"Don't care," St. Clair growled. "Molly. Get on with it."

"Easy, easy," Tanabuar was saying in his most soothing voice. "Deep breaths. You've got this. Just show us what you saw and I'll make everyone go away, okay?"

Beside him, Quiver was gulping air. "I got this! I got this! I can play in the big leagues!"

"What the hell?" St. Clair groused.

"Never mind Captain Grumpy Pants over there," the Chthonian said. "Do this for me, Quiver. Because we're friends."

The Puffer bobbled about in the air for a moment, then steadied and furrowed what passed for its brow, projecting a nighttime image of the yard into the air. "T-that's it! I did it! I'm one of the b-big dogs now!"

"Yes, you are," Tanabuar crowed. "Now, fast-forward to the part where you saw something."

"Ooohh... this is too much excitement... I think I'm gonna hurl!" the Puffer cried as he did as the Inspector asked.

St. Clair shifted slightly, watching over Tanabuar's shoulder as a group of five, one a woman in green armor, headed towards the packing facility doors. Judging from their movements, they were being stealthy, which meant they anticipated trouble. After a few moments, they headed inside.

"Useful," the human commented.

"Did you see anything else?" Tanabuar urged.

"Ummm... yeah... a l-l-little later..." Quiver sobbed. "Oh, my breakfast wants outta me, man!"

"Show me, buddy," the Chthonian begged. "Show me and then you're almost done!"

"Ahhhh!" the creature cried, fast-forwarding again. "I don't think I can be a big dog!"

St. Clair resisted the urge to punt the annoying Puffer, and instead watched as the same group, minus the woman in green armor, exited the building. One of them was injured, a crossbow bolt in his shoulder, while another was limping badly. That wasn't what really caught his eye, however.

The limping man was carrying twin scimitars, both covered in blood.

"That's enough," he said.

"Good job, Quiver," Tanabuar whooped. "You're our eyewitness!"

Costanza and Guinell turned away, stifling laughter at the terrible joke as the Puffer ended the replay and turned green. "Will I have to t-t-testify?"

"No, don't worry about that," Tanabuar assured. "Just forward all of this to the local R.I. Older and then you can take it easy. You've earned it."

"Oh... okay... I I th-think..." Quiver stammered, then hurled everywhere.

"I hate this borough," St. Clair sighed.

* * *

Three hours later, St. Clair and Tanabuar returned to their workspace in the sub-levels of the local Royal Inspectors' office. While Tanabuar had at first hated the location, St. Clair had always prized it for the easy access to the building's Older, a maroon-hued behemoth with two missing eyestalks that went by Podest.

"You think those two idiots got copies of that surveillance?" Tanabuar asked as he slung his jacket over the back of his chair and perched on his desk.

"I know they did," St. Clair replied, settling in his own chair. "I'm fairly certain they will attempt to pin both murders on the people we saw coming out of the building. Odds are, they are trying to identify them as we speak for that very purpose."

Tanabuar groaned. "Dirty cops make it so much harder."

"That they do," his partner agreed, reclining back in his chair and swiveling around to face the other man. "What did you see that looked out of place, Molly?"

The Chthonian quirked an eyebrow. "Is this a test?"

"Everything in life is a test."

"I hate tests," Tanabuar groaned. "But, yes. I saw a few things that got my interest."

"Such as?" St. Clair asked, steepling his fingers and watching his partner closely.

"Two of them had crossbow bolts stuck in them, but we found no evidence of any crossbows at the scene. Which means they got cleaned out along with the extra bodies." Tanabuar paused, thinking for a moment. "I think you're right. Somebody wants us to see something that didn't happen, instead of what did."

"What about the man with the swords," St. Clair nudged. "What stood out about him?"

"Huh?" the Chthonian asked, genuinely puzzled. "Aside from being shot, you mean?"

"He's not gonna get it, Percy," Podest called as he floated up from the back. "He's too young, and no matter how smart you think he is, he's not that smart."

St. Clair gave a cynical smile. "I take it you got the surveillance footage?"

"Yup, sure did," the Older said, telekinetically moving a stack of papers onto St. Clair's desk. "Already ran a search on them, too. Didn't get much on most of them, but your boy with the swords had already been flagged in the Older network. Somebody did a search for him a couple days ago."

St. Clair was already rifling through the facial captures Podest had made. "Is that so? Tell me more."

"I hate when you guys ignore me, you know," Tanabuar huffed.

Podest threw him a very large eye roll before turning his attention back to St. Clair. "Richard William Wonder."

St. Clair looked up, eyes going wide for a moment. "No way."

"Gotta be a coincidence," Tanabuar offered, suddenly realizing the significance of the twin scimitars the man had been carrying. "I mean, come on. That's crazy."

Podest spun, projecting two images, one of them a close-up taken from Quiver's footage, the other a high school graduation picture. "I'd love nothing more than to say it was, but this is kind of solid evidence. I referenced his birth certificate, too. Delilah Wonder is listed as the mother, and last known residence is Townglen."

"A really big coincidence?" Tanabuar suggested.

St. Clair settled back in his seat, staring at the images for a moment. "No. It's no coincidence. Max Wonder's son is town, and it looks as if he's already taken up his father's line of work. Which just leaves the obvious question of who did that recent search for him?"

Dismissing his projected image, Podest spun back around, a wide, toothy grin on his face. "What do you take me for, Percy? An idiot? Of course I already cross-checked that with the Elder Older."

"I assumed as much," St. Clair smirked.

"It was done by the 12th Precinct Archive Older. Goes by Sensor, and get this, he's got a history with Max Wonder," Podest chuckled. "How do you like them apples?"

"Well, I guess we'll be having a chat with this Sensor fellow next, then," St. Clair replied, nodding as he pushed to his feet. "In the meantime, see what you can find out about the rest of these people. Odds are, they're adventurers, but I doubt they'll be League affiliated. Access whatever Puffer footage you need to, as well. See if you can locate and track down where they are now and where they've been."

"You got it, boss," Podest agreed, then jerked slightly. "Ah, hell. That's not good."

"What?" Tanabuar asked.

"An A.P.B. just went out naming these kids prime suspects in a double homicide," the Older replied, looking annoyed. "I think those goons in Auberdeen just jumped the gun on you."

St. Clair drummed his fingers on his desk for a moment. "Let it stand for now."

"Uh, you sure about that?" Tanabuar asked, more than a little surprised. "We know those guys work for Manascetti, Percy. Hell, that's the whole reason we went to that crime scene in the first place. Our actual assignment here is to bust those guys and get them to roll on their boss."

St. Clair shrugged. "This is a more interesting case."

"Oh, well, in that case, let's just do whatever we want," Tanabuar groused.

With a soft sigh, St. Clair shook his head and gave his partner a wan smile. "The heir to the Scarlet Ring, which has a violent history with Manascetti's Ironriggers, turns up dead in the Ring's old stomping grounds, and these would-be heroes, Wonder included, are right at the center of that. Not to mention, two cops on Manascetti's payroll just happen to catch the case. Perhaps, Molly, our best chance to catch those two in the act, is to use Wonder and his team as bait."

"Say that's true, and those two scumbags are trying to cover Manascetti's ass on this," Tanabuar replied, obviously bothered by St. Clair's attitude. "They get them in a cell, odds are, they're gonna kill all of them to keep them quiet."

"*If* they get them in a cell," St. Clair pointed out. "For now, let's let them do the leg work for us. As soon as they have any of them in custody, we'll snatch them up and get them to safety, so we can find out what really happened."

"That's risky," Podest commented.

"So would be our office releasing a conflicting report at this time," the human said. "Until we know for certain who the other players were in that packing building, our best bet is to keep our own cards close to the vest for now."

Tanabuar and Podest exchanged a concerned look, but didn't bother arguing the matter further. St. Clair was usually three steps ahead of them anyway, and they'd both learned it was best to follow his lead. While he was a gambler, Percival St. Claire wasn't one to risk others' lives, which just meant he was already forming some kind of a plan.

"Let's go talk to that Older, Molly."

* * *

Rick woke in his own bed at Charlotte's. That was the first surprising thing of the day. The second was the noon day sunlight coming in through the window. It didn't take him long to figure either of them out, but for a moment, it almost let him believe the previous night had been a bad dream.

Any lingering hope of that was dispelled as soon as he tried to sit up, the sharp pain running up his leg making him wince in agony. Taking a moment to let it pass, he examined the bandages around his calf and accepted the harshness of reality.

He couldn't help but feel he'd been doing too much of that lately. In this particular instance, however, he resented it more than he ever had.

Sitting on the edge of the bed, he let it wash over him, the grief and the self-recrimination. Mimi was dead and there was no one to blame but himself. They hadn't been ready for something like that, and because he'd pressed ahead, one of his team had died.

No, he thought. It was worse than that. Mimi had died trying to do the right thing. The thing she'd come to Riscadil to do. To heal the world and just be kind. That was no reason to die. He'd led her into that situation, and then failed to cover her back.

He spent a few minutes crying, wishing he'd stayed home after all. If he had, she'd still be alive. Mostly, though, he regretted leaving her like that, lying there in that place. She had deserved better. He'd owed her better.

Forcing himself up, Rick limped into the washroom and cleaned himself up. Pausing, he stared at himself in the mirror and found the reflection seemed somehow unfamiliar.

It was more haggard and carried an air of sorrow he had never seen on his own face. The why was plainly obvious, but it still made him feel worse to realize it was so easy to see.

Getting dressed, he hissed in pain as he pulled on his pants. That was nothing, he knew, compared to what it was going to be like facing Emi. He'd made her promises, ones he realized now he hadn't been able to keep. Somehow, he doubted she'd want to continue on after this, and he could hardly blame her.

Taking a steadying breath, he made himself leave the room to face the truth, and he was sure, the blame. None would be worse than what echoed in his own mind. He had brought them together and he alone shouldered the blame for their failures and their deaths.

Halfway down the stairs, he heard voices coming from the kitchen and paused, listening. Charlotte was easy to pick out, the heavy South Seas rumble distinctive. The other, he realized, was Lancaster, which left him disoriented. Why was he still here?

Moving forward, he reached the bottom of the steps and heard a soft laugh. After a moment, he realized it was Toddson, making him hesitate again. They were all here, waiting for him, to accuse him. To condemn him for Mimi's death.

For not being as good as his father.

Accepting it, Rick walked down the hall and into the kitchen to find the three of them sitting around the table, chuckling at something. Spotting him, Charlotte stood, the other two following a moment later, looking at him with sorrow and grief. Of Emi, there was no sign.

"I..." Rick started, then felt a hitch in his throat and tears began to burn his eyes.

Before he knew it, Charlotte was hugging him and holding him tight. He had wanted to be brave. To be strong. To face it all with resolve. In her arms, he collapsed and began to sob, begging their forgiveness.

Softly, in his ear, he heard the Ogre say, "There be nothing to forgive, me boy."

"No," he choked, pushing her back, but unable to break free of her completely. "It's my fault! She's dead, Charlotte, and it's my fault! Who can forgive that?"

"We can," Lancaster replied, stepping up and grasping his shoulder. "Because it wasn't your fault, Rick."

"It was," he insisted.

"No," the Rogue told him, a sad smile on his face. "I was right there with you. I agreed to storm the room without having any idea what we were up against. Unlike you, I froze. If it hadn't been for you, we all would have died."

Shaking his head, Rick tried to argue it. "But I'm the team leader. It was my call and on my shoulders. Not yours."

"That's not what a team is, though," Toddson argued, not having moved from where he'd been. "We all stand together and carry it all together, right? The only thing you are to blame for, Rick, is that you couldn't see the future. That's it. We knew what we were getting into, all of us."

"I..." Rick tried, then bowed his head. "I'm sorry."

"We know," Lancaster assured him. "Even Emi knows. She's blaming herself, same as you. Unlike you, though, she won't hear anything else."

Glancing back up the steps, Rick steadied himself. "I'll talk to her in a bit. For now, how are you two?"

The Rogue rotated his arm around. "Not bad. Toddson healed the worst of it, so I've just got a bit of stiffness left. How about you?"

"Tender," Rick admitted, before looking to Charlotte. "I'm sorry I put Emi in so much danger."

The Orc snorted and guided him to a chair. "Emi been trying to put herself in danger for months. You kept the fool girl from getting killed. Nothing for me to be mad about there."

"Thank you," he said, meaning it sincerely as he winced, pain shooting fresh as he sat.

"I got that," Toddson mumbled, before setting about casting a healing spell on Rick's injury. "I was tapped out last night or I'd have finished taking care of it before you woke up."

"Forget about it, Todd," Rick said as the pain eased. "All that matters is that we're all okay."

"Actually," Lancaster said slowly. "We're alive, but I don't think any of us are actually okay."

Rick lowered his gaze and nodded. "True enough. I didn't mean to imply Mimi meant so little to any of us."

"Not what I meant," the Rogue scowled. "There's been a development while you were out."

Looking back up, Rick admitted he didn't like the sound of that, but asked anyway, "Such as?"

The Rogue eased back down as Toddson took his seat again, Charlotte fetching Rick something to eat and a cup of coffee. "We heard it on the radio a little bit ago. The police are looking for four people, possibly adventurers, in connection with a double homicide in the Auberdeen processing yard last night."

It took him a moment to grasp just what the other man was saying. "Wait. You mean, us?"

"It be looking that way," Charlotte confirmed. "The descriptions match, at least. So far, they just be saying it be for questioning, but it be true the authorities are on the lookout for all of you now."

Rick slumped back in his chair. "Great. Okay. So this is not exactly the kind of fame I was looking for when I came to Riscadil."

"They aren't naming any of us, at least, not yet," Lancaster told him with a pained look. "So we have that going for us, anyway. It should give us a bit to plan our next move."

"Whatever that is," Toddson offered softly.

"Turning ourselves in, obviously," Rick snorted. "I mean, it's the police. They want us for questioning, then our best move here is to hand ourselves over and explain what happened."

Lancaster settled back in his chair, looking at Rick in annoyance. "Which is what, exactly? The report on the radio specifically stated a double homicide. Think about that for a second, will you?"

Rick started to contest the Rogue's attitude, then paused as it hit him. "What about those seven guys we fought?"

"My point exactly," Lancaster said with a snap of his fingers. "Somebody cleared those bodies out, and I'm betting any other evidence that would suggest they were there, or at the very least, that would point to who they were."

"So, the two bodies..." Rick said slowly.

"Two women, according to the news," Toddson confirmed. "Lucinia and Mimi."

"Crap," Rick muttered, slumping in his chair. "Okay, that makes it harder, I admit. Still, we can explain the scenario. There's plenty of people at the Slaughterhouse who saw Mimi with us, so we have something to back up our version of events."

"Hearsay," Lancaster countered. "Not to mention, you have already told an actual police officer that we were looking for the other dead woman found at the scene. That's going to go against us in a big way."

"A woman we can prove was already dead," Rick shot back. "I still have that medical examiner's report."

"Yes, and I'm sure, if they pressed him, that doctor would tell them the same story he sent our way," the Rogue agreed hesitantly. "But that's not going to clear us of suspicion of killing her a second time."

Rick kind of hated Lancaster again in that moment. "If we go to Anton and tell him what happened..."

"We have the world of a beat cop against Inspectors," Lancaster cut in. "Who are probably dirty cops, on Manascetti's payroll."

"Hold up," Rick struggled. "What difference does that make? He's our employer as well."

Lancaster ran a hand over his face and groaned. "Gods above and below, Rick. We were set up! Probably for this! He hired us to go around looking for her, even sent us to places she'd never been so there'd be plenty of people aware we were looking for her, all while he had other people looking for her, to kill her! And when they did, the blame gets shifted to us."

"No, I don't buy that," Rick argued.

"He's a mob boss, Rick!" Lancaster shouted, slamming the table. "You really think setting innocent people up to take the blame for his criminal activities is somehow beneath him? Get real, dammit!"

"Easy," Toddson said. "Fighting with each other isn't going to solve anything."

Both men cooled their tempers, with Rick being the first to speak. "Okay, you have a lot of good points. So, if turning ourselves in is a bad move in your mind, what do you suggest we do next?"

"Go see Manascetti and get some answers out of him," the Rogue suggested.

"Just like that?" Rick asked in bewilderment. "Seriously? You really think, if he's behind all this, he's going to let us just walk in to his house?"

"Hey, hello, Rogue here," Lancaster shot back. "Getting into and out of other people's homes unnoticed is what I do."

Rick scowled. "So, you want to clear our names of a fake criminal offense by committing a real criminal offense?"

"What I want," Lancaster said, shoving his temper down. "Is to find something that proves he was the one behind all of this. Something that clears us and puts the blame straight on him. Then we take that to the cops, maybe even your buddy, whatever his name is, or better yet, to the Royal Inspectors."

"His name is Anton," Rick replied, thinking Lancaster's suggestion over carefully.

Odds were, if Anton hadn't already taken the information he had to the Royal Inspectors, he would soon. By now he was probably aware Rick and the rest of Powerage were suspects in the murder of the very woman Anton himself had confirmed to have been, for a little while anyway, dead already. Which again just meant he was probably already telling the Royal Inspectors everything he knew.

Therefore, Rick begrudgingly admitted, having something that showed Manascetti to be the real villain in all this, if he even was, would only strengthen their own position when the time came. He hated it, and it went against everything he believed in, but Lancaster had a valid point. Turning themselves in now would only make their story harder to prove.

"Fine, okay," Rick finally accepted. "We'll do that. Now we just have to figure out how to pull it off, cause after last night, there's no way in hell I'm going to let you go alone."

"Not gonna lie, I'm kind of relieved," Lancaster laughed. "I really didn't want to go alone, either."

Charlotte pushed up from her seat, having listened to their entire conversation without a word. "I got just the thing you gonna be needing. I be right back."

"Uh... okay," Rick fumbled as she swept out of the room. "I guess all that leaves is what to do about Emi."

"Right now, nothing," Toddson offered. "Though, I think it best if I stay here with her while you guys deal with this other thing. I'm pretty sure I'd be a liability in this case, and if Emi does come down from her room, seeing me still here will let her known we didn't abandon her."

Rick blinked a few times. "Todd, from time to time, you are staggeringly insightful."

"Thanks, Gary," Toddson replied with a happy grin.

"Sometimes," Lancaster drawled.

Rick sighed softly, shaking his head. "I'm not wild about any of this, to be honest. We're already in pretty deep. If this goes wrong, we're going to be in way too deep to ever get ourselves out."

"I agree," Lancaster said, frowning. "But we owe it to Mimi to try. She deserves better than being a victim."

Rick had no argument for that.

* * *

Cato Manascetti had built his entire life around the concept that anyone, and really everyone, was predictable if you just knew enough about them. It didn't even take that much study. Just enough to get a sense of their character and what they wanted. With just that, he had long ago learned to organize his own actions to be one step ahead of everyone around him.

Over the years, he had used this concept to stay ahead of the police, the Royal Inspectors, other criminal organizations, his own allies, and even his own family. It had allowed him to rise to the top in the Ironriggers and stay there longer than almost anyone before him. In that time, he had grown confident in his abilities and barely even gave it any thought anymore. He just did what he did and everything stayed the way it was supposed to be.

With him in charge and everyone else doing what he wanted. He wasn't fool enough to think anything lasted forever, no more than he believed his way of doing things was perfect. People still surprised him on occasion, but it was rare, and he always took into account that they may act differently than he expected. So even when they did, he was ready and already had a plan in place to deal with it.

Which really just meant he was almost never actually surprised. It was something that had grown foreign to him. Far more than he knew. He realized just how much when one of his men arrived in his study to inform him that Lucinia Avalinion was standing outside the gate, asking to see him.

Despite his ability to predict the actions of the living, Cato Manascetti had never gotten the knack of guessing what the dead would do. Especially when they were dead twice over. In his experience the first time stuck, and when it didn't, the second certainly did.

After a moment of struggling for words, he got a grip on himself and ordered the man to admit her. Whatever the Elf was looking for, he could only assume it had some connection to her ability to get over being dead, and something like that was of value to him. All his usual tactics to extort the truth from her had failed, so he figured he may as well see what she wanted in exchange for it.

Provided it wasn't his head on a stick or anything. Some things really couldn't be bought.

Besides, he had a feeling knowing what she wanted might just help him with another problem he had.

Deciding to adopt a position of superiority, Manascetti settled into his overstuffed lounging chair, a cigar in one hand, a glass of whiskey in the other. Setting his features into a scowl, he waited, knowing well that how he presented himself would set the tone for the entire exchange. Whatever Lucinia was after, he couldn't appear to be giving it willingly.

Moments later she was shown in, and against the obvious, if silent, objection of the guard, Manascetti waved him to leave. It was best there be as few extra ears around as possible for this. Especially considering that he didn't actually plan to give her anything.

"So, you've proven pretty hard to kill, lady," he stated before taking a long pull on his cigar. "If you even are a lady in there."

"Funny," Lucinia said. "The guys who killed Mimi said the same thing."

Manascetti's scowl deepened, but quickly turned to shock as the Elf removed a ring from her finger and transformed before his very eyes into Rick Wonder, the leader of the adventuring party he'd hired to deal with the woman with whom he'd thought he was talking.

It took him a moment to find his voice, but when he did he could only be honest. "Now that, kiddo, was some pretty damn clever thinking."

"Thanks," Rick drawled, shoving the ring in his pocket and resting his hands on the hilts of his swords. "You'll forgive me if I'm not gushing right now at your praise."

Manascetti decided that sometimes, even his ability to predict people could be way off. Two surprises in a day could do that. "I suppose you expect me to beg for my life or something here?"

"What?" Rick balked. "Why would I expect that? I just came to talk."

"Oh," the Dwarf managed, surprised for the third time in only a few minutes. "I figured you'd be out for revenge or something."

"Not against you," Rick snorted. "At least, not yet. It depends on how our conversation goes, I suppose."

Manascetti laughed, waving him to sit. "You need to work on your intimidation routine, kid."

"Yeah, I know," Rick grumbled, falling onto the couch. "It was never one of my stronger skills."

"Staying ahead of the cops seems to be, though," the Dwarf smirked. "I gotta hand it to you. I didn't see this particular trick coming. You're more resourceful than I thought."

Rick frowned. "Is that why you set us up to take the fall for Lucinia's death?"

Heaving a sigh, Manascetti shook his head. "You got it all wrong, Rick."

"So you aren't the head of the Ironriggers, then?"

Surprise number four was enough, and Manascetti let the act drop. "Way more resourceful than I thought. I'd ask how you learned that, but I get the feeling you'll just say something clichéd, like you got your ways, or some shit."

"Something like that, yeah," Rick smirked. "So how about you tell me what the hell is actually going on here, and why you fed us that line of crap?"

Shoving to his feet, Manascetti wandered over to the bar, refilling his drink. "If you figured out who I am, then I'm guessing you know who Lucinia is, too. That about right?"

"Apparent head of the Scarlet Ring, an organization you had some bad dealings with years ago."

"Yeah," the Dwarf said, looking him over with a more appreciative gaze. "Much more resourceful than I figured. I'm impressed. Didn't take you long to sort out what was what, and who was who. You got a bright future ahead of you, Rick."

"If I stay out of jail for two murders I didn't commit, you mean," Rick replied, his smirk fading quickly.

Manascetti nodded at that, settling back in his chair again. "That is some unfortunate turn of events there, I agree.

Wasn't exactly what I had in mind when I hired you kids, though."

"What *did* you have in mind then?" Rick asked, not sure whether he could trust the Dwarf.

With a shrug, he said, "For you to bring her to me. That's all."

"Why?"

Manascetti considered that for a moment. "A bit back, I got word that she was in town. Made me think the Scarlet Ring was gearing up for another run at getting a slice of the Riscadil pie. Last time we tangled, it got pretty messy, and I was in no hurry for that to happen again."

"I can see that," Rick admitted, trying desperately not to glance up at the ceiling. Somewhere over his head, Lancaster would either be making his entrance, or already inside.

"Believe it or not, I like things quiet around here," the Dwarf told him. "Noisy is bad for business. So I sent some of my guys to have a chat with her. She didn't want to talk to them, and we spent a few days playing ring around the rosies. Finally caught up to her on the Bayonne Bridge, me and a few of my guys. I just wanted to talk, but things got out of hand, and she sort of fell into the Keening Straight."

"Fell?" Rick echoed, his doubt obvious.

"She may have had some help from an over-excitable employee of mine," Manascetti skirted. "Not that it matters. She fell, and a couple days later they pull her out of the Bay. Done is done, right?"

"Doesn't seem that way," Rick observed.

"Tell me about it," the Dwarf snorted. "Couple days later, one of my boys says he seen her. I didn't buy it of course, till a couple more say they did, too. So I sent some guys to find her and track her, thinking maybe she didn't die after all."

"She did," Rick told him. "I've got the medical examiner's photos to prove it."

"Seen that myself," Manascetti admitted. "Obviously this changes things, yeah? Somebody dies and comes back, that's not right. Making it stranger, she catches some of my boys trailing her and messed them up real good. Fought like she's had years of training. Even without a weapon, she took down five of my guys."

"I think I'm starting to see where this is going," Rick said.

Manascetti nodded. "I needed people she wouldn't see coming. Which brings me to you and yours. I thought if I hired some outside contractors, she wouldn't be so quick to put up a fight, and maybe you kids could drag her ass back to me so I could find out how she skipped over death, and what the hell she even wanted here in Riscadil in the first place."

"What makes you think she didn't come looking to carve her own place in the city?" Rick asked.

With a shrug, Manascetti replied, "She didn't have no guys with her on the bridge. Just her, all by her lone self. That ain't something she woulda done if she was looking to get established. Hell, I pretty much run this town, and I don't go nowhere without at least a dozen of my people with me."

Rick considered that for a moment. "So what was she doing here, then?"

"Kinda what I was hoping to know," Manascetti said. "Except now she's dead again, and somehow, I'm betting her little resurrection trick is a one-time thing."

"Maybe," Rick said slowly. "Unless she has a necromancer working with her."

Manascetti said nothing for a moment. "Ain't no necromancers no more."

"That we know of," Rick pointed out. "We, me and my team, have reason to believe that the Scarlet Ring had some in their employ, and that's how Lucinia came back the first time. Which means she might come back a second."

"Well ain't that the cat's tits," the Dwarf said, before downing the rest of his drink in one pull. "One of them Hazaminie dipshits might still be kicking around after all."

"Hazaminie?" Rick asked, not having heard that term before.

Manascetti nodded. "That's what the bunch of wizards what took up with Obedell called their little cult what worshiped him. The Hazaminie. Took it from his last name, back when he was still a breathing person, instead of a damn Lich."

"That's Elven," Rick pondered. "Which means we may well be right that they are still working with the Scarlet Ring."

"They was back in the day," Manascetti told him. "After Obedell went off to wherever he got banished to, the cops rounded up all they could find. Could be a few slipped away when the Ring pulled up stakes and headed home to lick their wounds."

"If that's the case, then the more time the police put into looking for me and my team, the more time that necromancer has to get away," Rick groaned. "Fantastic."

"Makes me wonder why you killed her in the first place," the Dwarf said. "She woulda been everybody's best chance to find the sneaky little bastard."

Rick shot him an annoyed look. "We didn't kill her. She stabbed herself."

"Must really not of wanted to talk to me," Manascetti grunted.

"That's not it," Rick told him, shaking his head. "We didn't even get a chance to mention you. She did it because of the other guys who were there trying to catch her."

"Other guys?" Manascetti asked, looking surprised. "What other guys?"

"I thought they might have been yours, but I'm guessing they weren't," Rick told him. "One of them had a wand, and they mentioned something about their master and her being a vessel."

Manascetti thought that over for a moment, then shrugged. "Beats me. Once I hired you kids, I kept my guys out of your way. I didn't want to tip her off you was working with me."

"Which just leaves me wondering one thing," Rick said, giving the Dwarf a doubtful look. "Why send us to Riscadil University if you knew she wasn't a student there?"

Manascetti laughed at that. "Oh, yeah. I guess that don't make much sense now, does it? Truth is, that's one of the places my guys trailed her to. She went and visited the political science professor there for a while. I thought there might be some clue as to what she was after you kids could sniff out that my boys couldn't. They ain't real tactful, you know."

Rick nodded. "Okay then. I suppose I can see that. Still, why not shake down the professor yourself? I mean, I doubt they would have put up much of a fight."

The Dwarf waved that off. "There's some things even I can't just go and do around here, Rick. This city, it's a delicate thing. Most of the time, the cops stay out of my way, so long as I don't make big waves. They know I got pull, from some of their own on my payroll, to politicians in my pocket. I start shaking the trees too much, they gotta shake mine, and the whole thing starts getting ugly."

"Kidnapping a professor would be shaking the trees too hard, then?" Rick asked, not sure if he could believe anything the other man said.

"Something like that, yeah," Manascetti admitted. "Look, I got my reasons, okay? Some things you just don't do in this town, no matter who you are. Messing with certain people is just not a good idea. That's all there is to it."

Frowning, Rick accepted that the crime boss wasn't going to give him anything more on that. "Fair enough. So you know, my team and I are looking to clear our name, so as far as we're concerned, we're still on the case. Are you good with that?"

Manascetti blinked, surprised yet again. "I'm good with that, though I don't see what you plan to do."

"Find that necromancer," Rick told him as he stood. "I'm guessing the guys who were trying to grab Lucinia last night are connected with them. Maybe she had a falling out, or for all we know, they've seized power and want to use her as a pawn in the Scarlet Ring. There's too much we don't know yet, but I believe that finding those answers will prove our innocence."

"Innocence is overrated," Manascetti snorted. "But still, I gotta admit, I respect your gusto, kid. If Lucinia does come back from the dead again, then as far as I'm concerned, our deal still stands. Bring her to me, and you'll get paid."

"Fair enough. Though, I won't lie. That's not our top priority anymore."

"Can't blame you for that," the Dwarf admitted. "But I figure you still wanna get something out of this, and money goes a long way to making a man feel better about the shit he's gotta walk through in this life."

"Good to know we're on the same page," Rick replied. "But, if I find out you did double-cross us, then as far as I'm concerned, our next priority will be to take you down."

Manascetti smiled at that. "You can always try, kid."

"You might want to remember how resourceful I can be before getting too cocky, sir," Rick warned.

Manascetti's smile faded slightly. "Tell you want, kid. I'll have some of the cops on my payroll divert their attention away from you. Maybe that'll help you and me both. How does that sound?"

"I won't turn it down," Rick admitted. "But it doesn't change anything."

"I like you, Rick," the Dwarf smirked. "I really do."

"Have a nice day, sir."

As he walked out, slipping the Chameleon Ring Charlotte had given him back on his finger, Rick just hoped he'd bought Lancaster enough time to find something. Whatever Manascetti may claim, Rick felt certain that trusting him was a very bad idea.

Chapter Eight: Highway To Hell

AS RICK WAS LEAVING MANASCETTI'S HOME, St. Clair and Tanabuar were returning to their office, their conversation with Sensor yielding little in the way of helpful information. Where Tanabuar was relieved, hoping to get back on track with their actual investigation, his partner had grown only moodier.

While Tanabuar couldn't really think of a time St. Clair's instincts had ever been wrong, the Wonder angle was looking pretty much like a dead end. The Older hadn't been able to give them anything except the name of a patrol officer who had requested the search a few days ago, and even then, it had appeared to mostly be out of curiosity.

The Chthonian was well aware that St. Clair craved a challenge to his towering intellect and deductive reasoning skills, but for once he was glad to see the man disappointed. Their charge as part of the Special Services Division was in rooting out corruption, not chasing down murder suspects with ties to legendary heroes.

Granted, it was doubtful this younger Wonder had anything to do with the two dead women currently laying in the morgue over in Auberdeen, but at the very least, he was a material witness. While Tanabuar could see pursuing that lead on the grounds that the kid might have seen something they could use in their case against Costanza and Guinell, he found even that a long shot. It was far more likely that he and his team of adventurers had simply been in the wrong place at the wrong time.

As they headed down the stairs to the office, though, Tanabuar could take it no more. "Are you going to sulk the whole time?"

St. Clair paused, looking at him in confusion. "What's that mean?"

"The Older lead went nowhere, Percy," the Chthonian said, giving him a meaningful look his partner ignored. "You can't stand being wrong, and now you're sulking. It's annoying."

"I'm not sulking," St. Clair snorted, continuing down the steps. "I'm thinking."

"Face like yours, it's hard to tell the difference," Tanabuar muttered.

"I heard that," St. Clair grumbled. "Leave my face out of it, will you? We need to find that officer and confirm what the Older told us."

"Uh, why?" Tanabuar asked, exasperated beyond words. "It's a dead end, Percy. Let it go. You were wrong. It happens to us all."

St. Clair paused again, giving his partner an irritated glare. "Officer Strakinsy may know where Mr. Wonder and his people went to ground. This is a rare opportunity, Molly. Rather than waiting for Costanza and Guinell to make their move, we can beat them to the punch, get those kids to safety, and find out what they know. We just need to locate Officer Strakinsy first."

Tanabuar stood on the steps, his mind reeling. "Okay. I hadn't thought of all that."

"Obviously," St. Clair groused, heading away again. "It may be a long shot, but anything they can tell us about what happened in that packing facility could help us figure out how to prove Costanza and Guinell are on Manascetti's payroll. If we're really lucky, those two will flip on their boss, and we can put the Ironriggers out of business. We have very few leads, and this is the only one that I think might actually get us somewhere."

"Yeah, but only if Manascetti is involved in what happened in the packing facility," Tanabuar pointed out, hopping a few steps to catch up. "We don't know for sure that he is."

"No, we don't," St. Clair admitted. "All the more reason to have a long chat with Mr. Wonder and his crew. They may know something we need to know and not even be aware of it themselves."

Tanabuar sighed, hanging his head. "Figures you'd be a couple steps ahead of me."

"How's that?" St. Clair smirked, pausing outside their office door.

Giving him a look of annoyance, the Chthonian scratched at a horn, saying, "You think this Wonder kid and his people are innocent bystanders in a Manascetti-ordered hit. The reason for that is because Costanza and Guinell are handling the case, even though both were off duty when the call came in. This makes Wonder and company either material witnesses or accomplices, and you want to get to them before those two knuckleheads can shut them up for good."

"Very good," St. Clair said with a slight nod. "There may be hope for you yet, Molly."

"But," Tanabuar stated, pulling himself up into a dramatic pose, one finger in the air, stopping his partner before he could step through the door. "You have missed one possibility, my dear Percy."

"I doubt that strongly, but by all means, amuse me with your insight," St. Clair drawled.

"What if Officer Strakinsy is also on Manascetti's payroll?"

St. Clair nodded slowly. "The thought crossed my mind. That's why I left word with his Captain that we wanted to speak with him. If he bolts, then we know."

"Ah," Tanabuar managed, dropping his hand. "That gets us no closer to Mr. Wonder and his team, however."

St. Clair shrugged. "But it does give us Strakinsy, and I suspect getting him in custody will yield just as much useful information if he is dirty. Either way, we stand to gain ground on this."

"I hate you," Tanabuar groaned.

St. Clair smirked at that. "Still, good thinking. Maybe one day you'll actually be able to engage me in a meaningful conversation."

"Just, so much, I hate you," the Chthonian growled, jogging down the last few steps to catch up with the human. "Now and again, you could give me praise that isn't also an insult."

"When you earn it, my friend," St. Clair teased, pushing the door open. "You still have to learn not to be so surprised by every little thing first."

They'd no more stepped through, then both paused at the sight of Podest hovering near a Half-Elf in a patrol uniform, and an elderly Halfling. Try as he might, St. Clair could not make sense of that gathering.

"Hey guys," Podest rumbled with a chuckle. "You're gonna love this."

"Inspectors," the officer said, stepping forward. "I'm Anton Strakinsy, with the 12th. I know you're both busy, but I think you really want to hear what I have to say."

"I tend to agree," St. Clair managed.

Next to him, Tanabuar leaned around, grinning at him. "This expression. It fills me with joy. This look of complete surprise. My soul knows happiness right now."

"Shut up, Molly," St. Clair snorted, shoving the other man away. "Officer, I see you got our message."

Anton frowned, shaking his head in confusion. "What message?"

Tanabuar burst into laughter, drawing a glare from his partner, which he completely ignored, leaving the human to turn back to the Half-Elf, saying, "We left word with your Captain, just a short time ago, that we wanted to ask you a few questions."

"I've been here, waiting to speak with you, for almost an hour," Anton told him, looking completely baffled.

"He has, too," Podest confirmed. "Showed up not long after you two left."

"I love it," Tanabuar howled.

"Molly, please, shut up," St. Clair snarled.

"Wait... why are you guys looking for me?' Anton fumbled, unable to get a grasp on anything that was happening.

Taking a deep breath, St. Clair tugged his glasses free and produced a cloth to clean them with, saying, "You recently requested a search from the Archive Older Sensor on a man named Richard Wonder. We would like to know why."

Anton cocked an eyebrow. "What's that got to do with anything?"

"I assure you, Officer, it is quite important," St. Clair stated, recovering from the rather surprising turn of events.

Anton frowned. "I think what I want to talk to you about is a lot more important, since it involves a possible necromancer operating in the city."

Tanabuar stopped laughing, for which St. Clair was deeply thankful, though the officer's statement did cause him to pause, startled all over again. Slowly he put his glasses back on, trying to figure out what the two things had to do with each other, and after a moment, hitting on an idea.

"Very well, you go first," he said.

"Uh, Percy," Tanabuar started, but fell silent as his partner raised a hand.

"Right, then," Anton agreed, before gesturing to the elderly Halfling who had, until now, simply stood, looking confused. "This is Jonas Burke, who was, until recently, the Chief Medical Examiner for the city."

"Hello," Burke said, offering them all a very baffled wave.

"Dr. Burke," St. Clair returned. "Please, go on."

In short order, Anton and Burke related the events of the woman who got up and walked out of the morgue, leaving both Inspectors more than a little surprised. Thankfully, Tanabuar saw fit not to burst into laughter again, for which his partner was grateful. Before he could even ask either of the men a question about their story, Burke offered him a file folder, which St. Clair took, flipped open, stared at for a moment, and then handed to Tanabuar with a heavy sigh.

"Holy shit on a cracker," the Chthonian gasped.

"Can I assume you have seen this woman, then?" Burke asked.

"Lucinia Avalinion," St. Clair confirmed.

"Wait," Anton gaped. "You don't mean the Scarlet Ring Avalinions, do you?"

"I do," St. Clair confirmed, pushing past both the officer and the Halfling to settle at his desk. "She was found, early this morning, in an abandoned packing facility in Auberdeen where the Ring once held power. She is very dead, though it appears to be suicide at the moment."

"Don't count on her staying that way," Burke snorted.

"Percy," Tanabuar said, holding the folder out so Podest could take it. "This can't be a coincidence."

"I agree," his partner replied with a nod, motioning for their two guests to have a seat. "Puffer footage shows Mr. Wonder and members of his team leaving the scene, and we believe a second body found there was one of his people."

"Second body?" Anton asked. "Can you tell me more about that?"

"Female, wearing green leather armor," St. Clair replied. "Her head is gone, apparently from a fireburst. We have yet to confirm her identity."

"Mimi," Anton told him. "I don't know her last name. She's a Half-Elf, Druid I think. She was getting high when I met her."

"Marijuana?" St. Clair inquired.

"Yeah," Anton replied. "Why?"

"Recreational user," Tanabuar said. "We weren't sure if this was a drug deal gone bad or not."

Anton shook his head quickly. "I doubt that. Last time I saw Richard, he was looking for Avalinion for a client he met through the Shy Market."

"Did he say who?"

"No," Anton admitted with a note of frustration... "He's trying to be professional, so he kept those details confidential."

"You don't think?" Tanabuar asked.

"I wouldn't be surprised," St. Clair said, leaning back in his chair. "If his client was Manascetti, it would answer a lot of questions."

"Cato Manascetti?" Anton asked in shock. "The crime boss?"

"Yeah, that one," Tanabuar confirmed. "Him being the client would put a lot of things in perspective, like Percy said. However, it also puts Mr. Wonder in a bad spot."

"He becomes an accomplice, yes," St. Clair agreed. "What's your take on him, officer?"

"Richard?" Anton paused to give the question serious thought, then shook his head. "I have a hard time seeing him getting mixed up with a crime boss knowingly. He's too focused on trying to follow in his dad's footsteps. From what he told me, they only took this job because they thought it was a missing person case, so I don't think he even knows who Avalinion is, much less Manascetti."

"Frame job, then," Tanabuar said, a look of disgust on his face. "That's gonna be hard to prove. Manascetti's smart, so he'll have made sure Wonder and his team are the obvious suspects."

"And have had time to make sure his dirty cops build a solid enough case they can't prove their innocence," St. Clair agreed. "Okay, then, this has been informative."

"What about the necromancer?" Anton pressed.

"For now, a ghost," St. Clair replied with a casual shrug. "We'd need to talk with Avalinion to get more information about that, and I'm afraid she's dead."

"For now," Burke pointed out again. "I saw plenty of necromancy cases back in the day, son. Trust me, if that's what this is, then she won't be staying dead long."

"Then when she revives, we can have words with her," St. Clair told him. "Until then, all we can do is track down Wonder, and hopefully, if he really is innocent, protect him."

"Well, if he reaches out to me, I'll be sure to let you know," Anton said, standing. "He's a good kid, so anything I can do to help him, I will."

"Good to know," St. Clair agreed, pushing to his feet and shaking hands with both the officer and the former medical examiner. "Otherwise, I'd ask you to stay out of our way. It's not personal, of course, but..."

"He means we'll call you if we need you," Tanabuar cut in, too familiar with his partner's lack of polite manners.

Anton gave them both a smile. "I got it. This isn't my first time around R.I. I know the drill."

"There is one other thing," Burke said, putting a hand on Anton's arm to stop him from leaving.

St. Clair nodded, and waved him to go ahead.

"After she got up and left, I reported it, like I'm supposed to," the Halfling told him with a weary look. "All the old protocols from back when are still in place, just in case. All I got back was that I must have misplaced the body, and to shut my mouth."

St. Clair frowned slightly. "If you followed protocol, then..."

"I submitted a report to the Royal Inspectors Arcana Task Force, yeah," Burke agreed. "Shortly after that, I was politely asked to retire, to save myself the embarrassment of being fired."

"Now that is interesting," St. Clair said softly.

"He means disturbing," Tanabuar offered. "Percy always gets those two mixed up."

"Not my business," Burke told him with a shrug. "I just wanted you to know my house might not be the only one what's gotten a bit dirty."

"Not to worry," Tanabuar chimed in. "We're very good at tidying up."

St. Clair threw his partner a glare, but just got a smile in return as the other two men excused themselves. Once they were gone, he settled back in his chair, pondering the various pieces of the puzzle they had given him.

"Molly, I think perhaps you should go pay a visit to the Shy Market," he said after several minutes. "See if you can use that abundant charm of yours to get the name of Mr. Wonder's client out of them."

"Sure thing," Tanabuar agreed. "What are you going to be doing?"

"I'm heading over to Auberdeen to check up on Ms. Avalinion. I want to make sure she's still there. If what Dr. Burke said is true, then perhaps I can catch her in the act of defying death, and get some fresh perspective from her."

"Sounds like a plan," Tanabuar said, heading for the door.

He'd almost reached it when Podest yelped, his central eye wide in surprise. "Too late, Percy. I just got word through the network. Avalinion's body has gone missing from the morgue."

"Dammit," St. Clair snapped, jumping up. "Podest, contact every Puffer in the network and give them all her image. I want her found, as quickly as possible. Whatever the hell is going on, she's right in the middle of it."

"On it," the Older jumped, settling into the network trace without another word.

"Still going to Auberdeen?" Tanabuar asked.

"Damn straight," St. Clair growled. "We'll meet up tonight. Watch your back, Molly."

"You, too."

* * *

By the time Rick returned to Charlotte's, his concern over Manascetti had turned to full-blown fear. The Dwarf had been evasive, and much like his original story, this new one had too many holes in it. Lucinia conveniently falling from the bridge, mysteriously visiting a university professor, and his claim that he just wanted to talk to her. It all felt wrong, but with the way things stood, Rick couldn't see refusing his help in clearing their names.

Pausing in the entry way, he pushed all his fears aside and decided it was best to just focus on what he could do at the moment. With luck, Lancaster had gotten in and out of Manascetti's home unnoticed, and with useful information. Otherwise, all they had left was turning themselves in, and after his conversation with the crime boss, Rick somehow doubted that would end well for them.

Looking up, he found himself staring into Emi's wide, shocked eyes. Letting out a sigh of relief that she had, at last, come down from her room, it didn't hit him until she dropped the plate in her hand, along with the sandwich on it, and ran away screaming.

Rickwit was still wearing the Chameleon Ring, like a Rickwit would.

"Emi, wait," he cried, but she was already gone, running down the hall for the kitchen, screaming bloody murder.

Groaning, he chased after her, rounding the door, to get smacked in the chest with a platter as Charlotte and Toddson gaped at the Elf's sudden panic. Staggered, Rick fell back, hitting the wall of the hall, as Emi came at him again, hurling gibberish and swinging the platter blindly.

"Emi, stop," he begged.

It took a few hits, but Charlotte managed to shake off her daze and grab the Elf, pulling her back into the kitchen. Rick slumped, then threw a glare to Toddson, who was still standing by the dining table, marveling at it all.

Yanking off the ring, Rick let the illusion drop and held up his hands. "Emi, it's me! Calm down!"

Blinking several times behind her glasses, the Elf went through several emotions very quickly, from terror to shock to relief to tears. That last one Rick could have done without. As usual, the universe didn't care what he could do without.

Hurling herself at him again, Emi beat her fists against his chest. "Stupid Rick! I thought you were a ghost! Or a zombie! Or something worse! I don't know what's worse than a zombie, but I thought you were it! You scared me to death!"

Grabbing her hands, he offered her a smile. "Sorry. My head was somewhere else. I didn't even pay attention when I walked in. I didn't mean to scare you."

"Okay," Emi sniffled. "I'm sorry I hit you."

"Forget about it," he said, patting her head. "At least I know you can take care of yourself."

"I wish," she muttered, before dragging herself back into the kitchen. "I dropped my sandwich."

Charlotte groaned, and with a shake of her head, assured the Elf she would take care of it. Moving past Rick, she grumbled something in Orc that sounded rather unpleasant, leaving him to walk over and slap Toddson upside the head.

"Ow," the Cleric yelped. "What'd I do?"

"You could have warned her," Rick said. "Or stopped her from beating me with a serving platter."

"Oh, yeah," Toddson grimaced. "Sorry. I forgot it was you."

"Of course you did," Rick groaned, falling into a chair. "Is Lancaster back yet?"

Toddson shook his head. "Not that I noticed or remember, but that doesn't mean anything."

"I hope he's okay," Emi sobbed. "He probably is, since I'm not there to get him killed."

Rick wanted to go to his happy place, but Emi was already in it, so instead he just rubbed his eyes and faced what had to be done. "Emi, you didn't get anybody killed."

"I got Mimi killed," she sniffled. "She was my friend. I don't have many friends. I get them killed, so that's probably why."

"You didn't get Mimi killed, Emi," Rick insisted, not sure how to deal with this new, morose version of the already difficult to manage Elf. "If it's anyone's fault, it's mine."

"I don't think it's your fault, Stu," Toddson said as he sat down, petting Emi on the head.

"Even Toddson thinks it's my fault," Emi wailed.

Rick slumped, then shot the Cleric another glare. Getting a sheepish grin in return, he decided to try a new tactic. "Mimi died doing what she believed was right, Emi. That isn't anyone's fault except the guy who killed her, and I already killed him. She wouldn't want you to cry over this, either. You know how Mimi was, she liked it when everyone was happy."

"I guess," Emi mumbled, face down on the table. "I should have stopped the wand from going off. I know the right incantations. I think. I might know the right incantations. It doesn't matter. I froze, and Toddson had to carry me out. I was useless. I am useless. Everybody was right about me."

"None of us could've saved Mimi," Rick said. "We all froze up. We all ran away. If you want to blame yourself, I can't stop you, but you have to blame the rest of us, too, cause if it's your fault, then it's all of our faults."

Emi moaned, long and low. "I can't blame you guys. I should have known I really was useless. Everyone told me I was."

"You aren't useless," Rick snapped. "You got scared. You panicked. That's normal. Even Lancaster and Toddson froze up. Hell, Emi, I froze up. Do you think we're all useless because of that?"

"No," she whined. "Just me."

"Well, I don't think it, and Toddson doesn't think it, so you don't get to think it, either," he told her. "You are part of this team, and we need you. So you can't be useless, cause of that. Got it?"

Emi said nothing for a long time, but finally lifted her head enough to look at Rick, a slight smile on her tear-stained face. "Got it... boss."

Rick smiled and nodded, ruffling her unruly hair again. "Good. Now. We're gonna find out what's really going on and make sure Mimi gets the justice she deserves. Right?"

"Okay," she managed, setting her glasses aside to wipe her eyes. "I'll try harder. I promise."

"And you'll be awesome," he said, giving her a warm smile. "If you get scared again, that's okay. Just do what I tell you and you'll be fine. Can you do that?"

"I think," she sniffled.

"Good," Rick said, feeling slightly better now that he had gotten past that hurdle. "We're still Powerage, so we're still in this fight. Now we just wait for Lancaster to get back, and hopefully, he'll have found something we can use to clear our names."

Emi cocked her head to the side. "Clear our names of what?"

Rick blinked several times, then gave Toddson yet one more glare. "Oh, I'll explain it later. Hey, look, Charlotte's back! Hi, Charlotte!"

"Don't be using me as no shield, boy," the Orc warned. "Oh, and I found your other lost lamb in the entryway."

As she moved over to dump the remains of Emi's sandwich and the plate in the trash, Lancaster made his entrance, posing in the doorway and taking a moment to run a comb through his pompadour.

"Be amazed," he smiled, throwing Emi a wink.

"I was starting to get worried," Rick told him.

The Rogue frowned. "The least you can do is go 'oh.' I mean, that was a great entrance."

"Oh," Rick deadpanned.

"You are no fun," Lancaster pouted. "But at least I see our lovely Wizard is back among us, and ready to face the thrills and danger once more."

"Uh... mostly... I think..." Emi stammered.

"Worry not, my precious flower," Lancaster cooed, leaning in to blow her a kiss from an inch away. "Before you know it, we'll have cleared all charges against us, and instead of hunting us, the police will be throwing us a parade."

"Gods damn it," Rick groaned as he face-palmed.

"We're... we're.... we're wanted... by the police?" Emi screamed.

Lancaster's face fell. "Guess you didn't get to that part, huh?"

"Was working up to it," Rick grumbled.

"Hey, we're criminals," Toddson said, smiling at Emi. "Ain't that awesome?"

"I don't wanna be a criminal!" Emi wailed.

"Gods damn it," Rick muttered again, going to his happy place, face down on the table.

* * *

After nearly an hour of getting Emi calmed down, and more fully explaining the situation to her, Rick was almost ready to throw himself to the mercy of a probably corrupt police force. It couldn't be any more painful than dealing with a hysterical Elf. Maybe. He wasn't sure anymore.

Finally, however, they did get her calm, and after a bit more time, understanding of the situation they were in. Somehow she came to terms with it, though Rick was pretty sure Charlotte was spiking her tea with something. He decided he'd rather not know, and chose to forge ahead as if everything was fine.

"Okay, now that we've got that sorted, Lancaster, please tell me things went well for you?" Rick all but begged.

"I was going to ask you that," the Rogue countered. "After all, I so enjoy letting you go first."

Rick rubbed his eyes and counted to ten. "Can you please be serious?"

With a sigh, Lancaster nodded. "Fine, fine. We'll do it the less fun way. I did find something, but I'm not sure just what it means yet. I was hoping I might understand it better after you fill us in on your conversation with Manascetti."

Accepting that, Rick told them everything that had happened between him and the Dwarf, and as he had expected, Lancaster showered him with looks of doubt. It was enough to confirm his suspicions as well that yet again, their client had been less than honest with them. Which just left them with a new batch of lies to muddle through.

"I hate to say it, but I was kind of expecting that," Lancaster grumbled, settling back in his chair at the dining table. "I had hoped he might let something slip, but I guess you don't get to be the boss of a crime syndicate by being careless."

"No, I don't think so," Rick agreed. "Though he did at least tell me a few things, whether he meant to or not."

"Such as?' the Rogue asked, puzzled.

"Well," Rick said slowly. "He was pretty reluctant to talk about that university professor, and in my opinion, acted like she was someone who should be left alone. She has some connection to Lucinia, though, so we might be wise to check that out and see what we can learn about her."

"Damn," Lancaster muttered. "Mimi might could have helped us out there. She's already met her."

"Yeah," Rick said, feeling that same pain. "Besides that, he seemed to think that it isn't Lucinia in Lucinia's body, but someone else. Same as those guys at the packing facility did. So, he knows a lot more about all this than he's letting on."

"Good point," Lancaster agreed, considering that for a moment. "You said he claimed those guys weren't working for him, though?"

"He did, but I'm not sure I believe that either," Rick admitted. "Again, they wanted to take her somewhere, and he claims he wanted us to bring her to him. If they aren't working for him, then that's one hell of a coincidence."

"Probably best to assume they are working either for or with Manascetti then," the Rogue said, obviously troubled by that. "Which means we may have tipped our hand too much already."

Rick shook his head. "When I left, he seemed to think we were still working towards his goal."

"You aren't that good of a liar, Rick," the Rogue snorted.

"Yeah, that's fair," he sighed.

"Still," Lancaster said, rubbing his eyes. "You raised a good point that she will likely come back from the dead again. We found her before, and even with all his resources, we did it as quickly, or quicker, than his own people. He probably won't overlook the asset we may provide at the moment."

"At least enough to stay out of our way until we find her, if she does come back," Rick replied, glad to see that he and the Rogue were still on the same page.

"Say she does and we do find her, then what?"

Rick shrugged. "We take her to the Royal Inspectors and spill everything we know. Like it or not, she's the only person who can clear our names right now. We need to find her before anybody else does."

"Can't find much argument for that," Lancaster said, digging in his pocket. "I don't know if this is going to be helpful, but it was about the only thing I found in Manascetti's office that looked even remotely like a clue."

With that, he placed a heavily scribbled on piece of paper on the table. Rick stared at it for a moment before picking out the white lines, and that they spelled out something. What, though, he couldn't tell.

"This is?" he asked.

"He had a notepad on his desk," Lancaster explained. "I could tell that he'd written something on it very recently by the indentations it left behind on the piece of paper below the one he wrote on. I tried to bring it out, but as near as I can tell, it's just an address, which may mean nothing."

"Four, something, something, one, something street," Rick read, then shook his head. "Yeah, I can't pick it out."

Toddson picked it up, glancing over it, then muttered something to himself as Emi tried to get a peek.

Lancaster gave a half-hearted shrug. "I've heard that trick works, but this is the first time I've tried it. Either I messed it up, or it's a total load of crap to start with."

"Forty-six eighty-one Gasnerry Street," Toddson said.

Everyone turned to stare at him in surprise. Rick had started wondering why they always did that.

"You can read that?" Lancaster asked, his sense of bewilderment at the Cleric's odd abilities much less than it used to be, but still present.

"Oh, no, not at all," Toddson laughed. "I cast a spell that made the traces of what had been written appear."

"Good to know you can do that," Rick said with a grin.

"Do what?" Toddson asked, looking confused.

"Forget about it," Lancaster sighed.

"Sure," the Cleric nodded, then looked at him in confusion again. "What were we talking about?"

Grabbing the note away from the befuddled Cleric, Charlotte filled in the address, and slid it back to Lancaster. "That be the old Hawthorne Theater. It's some six blocks southwest of here. Use to be where all the rich and powerful would meet to watch the burlesque and talk about business without being interrupted."

"Now that's interesting," Lancaster said softly. "How long has it been abandoned?"

"Some twenty years or more now," the Orc replied. "Long enough that nobody really remembers when it was the center of culture in Riscadil, or the old women who use to be the stars of the show."

"Good place to do business out of sight still, though," the Rogue commented.

"Could be," Rick agreed. "Or it could be a dead end."

"Only one way to find out."

"Very true."

"Are we going to the theater?" Emi asked.

"Yes," Rick said with a wicked smile. "We most certainly are."

* * *

St. Clair slammed through the door of the office he shared with his partner, muttering curses in several languages. Across the room, Tanabuar glanced up in surprise, and then settled into accepting as the human stormed to his desk and all but threw himself into his chair.

"Went that good, huh?" he asked with a toothy grin.

"Not a single person, Molly," St. Clair snapped. "Not one damn person saw anything. Nobody. None of the medical examiners, none of the staff, none of the Inspectors who were there, not even the damn janitors! Nobody saw a blessed thing!"

Tanabuar nodded along. "That is passing odd, yes."

"I honestly cannot fathom how any of those people found work in any branch of law enforcement. They are beyond incompetent. All anyone knew was that she had been laid out for autopsy, and between then and when the examiner arrived, she just vanished into thin air."

"Wow," the Chthonian drawled. "Almost like she up and walked away, huh?"

"If you are trying to be funny, you aren't succeeding," St. Clair warned. "I'm in no mood for your jokes."

"Fine, fine," Tanabuar waved, pouting. "It's just, I was in such a great mood because I got information."

St. Clair's head snapped up. "You did? What is it?"

Holding up a stack of papers, he gave a devilish grin, saying, "Everything."

"You got their names from the Shy Market?" St. Clair exclaimed, grabbing for the papers and missing when Tanabuar snatched them away.

"Well, no," he admitted, sighing softly, waiting for St. Clair's face to fall. "Those I got from the Slaughterhouse, which I visited after my stop at the Shy Market."

"You are a complete and total asshole," St. Clair smiled.

"Nice of you to notice."

Taking a deep breath, the human relaxed back in his chair. "So share."

"Right," Tanabuar said, dropping the stack back on his desk. "So, starting at the top, this little team of would-be heroes goes by the name Powerage, which is pretty darn catchy if you ask me."

"A little over the top, but whatever," St. Clair dismissed.

"However," the Chthonian continued with a snide tone, "The door guard at the Shy Market, a lovely Hobgoblin by the name of Tunya, did finally give in and confirm that they accepted a request to locate a missing person, posted by one Cato Manascetti."

St. Clair spun in his chair. "That tracks with what Strakinsy said."

"Yup," Tanabuar agreed. "Now, as for the fine details, I snagged a set of the Puffer photos and hit up the Slaughterhouse bartender and some of the regulars. They were able to give me a lot of information about these people."

"Okay," St. Clair urged, waving the Chthonian on before he could indulge in his penchant for drama.

"You really are no fun when you're grouchy, you know that?"

"Molly, it's late, can you get on with it?"

"Fine, Captain Crabby," Tanabuar pouted, standing to join St. Clair at his desk. "First one is human male, goes by the name Toddson Oscar, and claims to be a Cleric of the Forgotten One. According to people who talked to him, he suffers from severe short term memory loss, and apparently is looking to be an adventurer because his god told him to."

"That's new," St. Clair commented, glancing over the photo and accompanying notes in Tanabuar's scrawled handwriting.

"Next up, Lancaster White," his partner continued, dropping the related material on the desk. "Claims to be a Rogue from the Night Brand, and is in it for money, fame and women."

"The Night Brand?" St. Clair snorted. "Didn't they disband years ago?"

"Last I heard, yeah," Tanabuar said, then shrugged. "Maybe they still have a chapter house operating somewhere."

"Might be something to look into after we deal with this."

"Sure, why not," his partner drawled. "Moving on to Emeri Landari, a Wizard from Gulinlan. According to the bartender, she came to Riscadil seeking to be an adventurer to prove herself to her teachers at the Solarium that she wasn't a total failure."

"Long way to go to show up some stuck-up magic instructors," St. Clair said, setting that one aside with barely a look.

"Next, our mysterious headless woman, one Mimi Avaman," Tanabuar continued. "A Druid of the Knot Hill Clan. From what I learned, she's here on a mission to heal the world of evil with love and peace."

"Guess that didn't work out so well for her," St. Clair murmured, taking a moment to feel bad for the poor woman. "She probably would've done better to start anywhere but this rotten damn city."

"Probably," Tanabuar agreed. "That just leaves us with Richard Wonder, who we already know about."

St. Clair spread the images and their paperclip attached notes across his desk, considering them. "I'm not seeing anything in this that would indicate people ready to commit cold-blooded murder."

"Me either," his partner agreed. "To me, it looks like a bunch of kids who wanted to be heroes bit off more than they could chew. One's already dead, and based on what I've learned about the rest, I wouldn't be surprised if they are in a shallow grave somewhere already."

"Let's not count them out just yet," St. Clair chided. "They may still surprise us. We know they got out of the packing facility and the processing yards alive. My guess is they've gone to ground."

Tanabuar smirked at that, flipping one last piece of paper up as if it were a playing card. "Someplace like cute little Miss Landari's home address?"

Settling back, St. Clair crossed his arms and smiled, giving the other man a nod of approval. "Well done, Molly. I'm impressed."

The Chthonian blinked. "Seriously? No insult? Oh, wow, I'm not sure my heart can take this."

"Now if only you had checked deeper into their backgrounds for any link to either Manascetti, Avalinion, or either of their organizations, I'd call it a solid victory."

"There it is," Tanabuar wilted, then pulled himself up. "Actually, that's what I was getting ready to do. Now that I've got their names, I can pull more complete files on them as soon as Podest is free."

"You guys talking about me?" the Older asked he floated up from the storage room. "If so, I hope none of it is good."

"Molly was just succeeding in impressing me," St. Clair replied.

"Be in awe of me," the Chthonian gushed, snapping into a pose and giving a bow. "Receiver of the St. Clair nod of approval."

"Yeah, awesome," the Older drawled. "How about I lay some actual police work on you, kid?"

"Come on," Tanabuar whined.

"I take it you found something?" St. Clair asked, waving his partner to calm down.

"Sure did," Podest smirked. "Found several somethings, actually. What you in the mood for, Percy? Good news, bad news, or confusing news?"

"Hey, three flavors of news," Tanabuar snickered. "My favorite!"

St. Clair threw a stapler at him. "Would you calm down, please? I'm trying to concentrate."

Tanabuar sulked as he retrieved the stapler from the floor. "My pride is mortally wounded, but my body will survive."

"You two should take this comedy act on the road," Podest deadpanned as Tanabuar put the stapler on the desk then slid it away from St. Clair's reach. "Dive bars across the world are dying to heckle you."

Giving his partner a dour look, St. Clair waved a hand at the Older. "Please, from the top, if you don't mind?"

Turning, Podest projected an image into the air, saying, "Sure. A Puffer in the area caught a few seconds of footage showing Avalinion leaving the medical examiner's office under her own power. So we can safely say she's back from the dead."

"Again," Tanabuar put in.

"Basically, yeah," the Older agreed. "That's the good news. Bad news is that after the Puffer lost sight of her, she hasn't shown up again anywhere on city surveillance, so we've got no idea where she went or how she got there. Basically, she's ghosted right out from under us."

"Hardly surprising for someone who has now cheated death twice," St. Clair said with a frown.

"So, what was the weird news?" Tanabuar asked.

"Molly, I'm glad you asked," Podest smirked, dismissing the image.

"Glad to ask, thank you," the Chthonian grinned.

"Somebody, kill me," St. Clair growled. "It's a fate far kinder than either of you trying to be funny."

"Someone is grumpy tonight," the Older snorted, turning to project another image. "A Puffer here in Aven caught this image of Avalinion leaving the residence of one, wait for it, Cato Manascetti. How ya like them apples, pal?"

Both men stared at the image in confusion, but it was St. Clair who managed to ask first, "Wait, what?"

"You said she didn't show up on city surveillance after she left the medical examiner's officer," Tanabuar fumbled.

"And she didn't," Podest chuckled, putting the Auberdeen footage up again. "Check the time stamps. This image of her leaving Manascetti's is from before we even got word that she had vanished from the medical examiner's office, and before the other footage of her leaving said office."

"What the hell?" St. Clair stumbled.

"She got a twin or something?" Tanabuar asked, looking from one to the other and back in utter confusion.

"No," St. Clair intoned. "Podest, run an arcane spectrum analysis of the Aven footage."

The Older laughed at that. "I knew you'd catch it, Percy. I was getting ready to do just that when I heard you two yammering in here, and decided to show ya what I had."

"What, what are we doing?" Tanabuar asked, more lost by the minute.

Neither answered as the Older dismissed the Auberdeen image, and focused on the one from the Aven Puffer, scanning it for residual arcane energy. After a few moments, during which Tanabuar sulked as loudly as he could, the image changed to show swirls of color surrounding Avalinion.

"Bingo," St. Clair smirked. "A Chameleon Ring."

"I get it now," Tanabuar said.

"Gimme a second, Percy," Podest said. "I think I can filter out the illusion magic, so we can get a look at the real person's face."

St. Clair nodded, leaning forward to rest his chin on his hands, watching intently. This could be the thing he had been looking for, the clue that made it all make sense. Whoever was disguising themselves as Avalinion may well be behind the murder of Mimi Avaman, and whatever force kept bringing the real Lucinia back from the dead.

Or not.

"Well, that's unexpected," Podest grunted as the image cleared, revealing the face of Richard Wonder behind the illusion.

"What the actual hell?" Tanabuar gaped.

"I honestly don't know," St. Clair sighed, rubbing his eyes behind his glasses. "However, this does answer two questions. First, that Mr. Wonder, at least, is still alive and capable of hiding himself from surveillance. Second, that he is knowingly working for Manascetti."

"Shit," Tanabuar groaned. "I was all ready to ride in to the kids' rescue, too."

"Podest, alert every Puffer in the city to be on the lookout for these people," St. Clair said as he stood, offering the Older the images and information Tanabuar had handed him earlier. "Names, faces, and even this bit of information, that they may be using Chameleon Rings. I want the whole city on the lookout for them, and I want them arrested on sight."

"You got it, boss," the Older said, floating the paperwork to him. "You sure, though? I mean, this kid, he's Max Wonder's son."

"Apples sometimes fall far from the tree, my friend," St. Clair replied. "For now, we follow the evidence, and it has not taken us somewhere that supports Mr. Wonder's innocence, I'm afraid."

"Still, Percy," Tanabuar started to say, then fell silent, shaking his head. "This is gonna not gonna play well to the media."

"The truth rarely does, Molly," his partner admitted. "For now, let's get some sleep. We'll go check that address you got first thing in the morning, okay?"

"Sure," Tanabuar said, looking glum. "Tell your wife I said hi."

"If she's still awake," St. Clair snorted.

"Please," Podest chuckled. "She's probably sitting on the couch with her bow, ready to shoot you for missing dinner again."

"Probably," the human smirked. "Maybe I should let her loose to track these guys down."

"Nah," the Older laughed as he floated away. "We want them alive to answer questions."

"True enough," St. Clair chuckled. "Goodnight, gentlemen."

Pausing as he reached the door, St. Clair looked back. "Molly, it's been a while since you've been over for dinner. Why don't you join me?"

A frown flickered over Tanabuar's face, followed by an understanding nod. "Sure, Percy. I'd love to."

"Excellent. I think we have much to talk about."

* * *

Once night had fallen, Powerage slipped from Charlotte's brownstone through the rear door, stealing out into the back alleys and side streets of Riscadil, hoping to be ghosts. They weren't very good at it for the most part, but they managed as best they could.

Toddson had left his armor behind, wearing only the padding that was usually under the heavy pieces, so as to make things easier. Past that, there was little they could really do to improve their chances of reaching the theater unnoticed. The only real hope Rick had was that the local patrol officers weren't keeping too keen an eye out.

Against his better judgment, Rick let Lancaster take point. During their exploration of the packing facility, he had displayed some skill with stealth, so despite his tendency towards gaudy outfits, he at least seemed to know how to get around unnoticed. He'd also gotten into and out of Manascetti's home without being seen, which was enough for Rick to show him trust.

During the trip, he began to miss Mimi all the more. Her keener eyesight would have been welcome each time they had to cross a main street. Emi had quickly proven useless on that front, both by being too nervous, and as Rick had learned, from being terribly near-sighted by Elf standards. Without her glasses, she couldn't see more than ten feet clearly.

To his surprise, they not only made it the scant few blocks to the theater, but apparently did so unnoticed. He wasn't sure if should chalk it up to luck or Lancaster's skill, but in the end decided to let it be an even split of the two. However capable the Rogue had shown himself to be, Rick simply couldn't get past his outlandish style and behavior.

Before leaving, Charlotte had told them what she knew of the old theater, providing them a point of access. How she knew so much, Rick hadn't asked, any more than he had about the Chameleon Ring she'd allowed him to borrow. Sometimes, he thought, it was better to not know.

Slipping down the alley, the team came to the fire escape she told them about. After a few false starts, Lancaster even managed to get the ladder down, making more than enough noise in the process to give them all pause. When no one came looking, they scrambled up it quickly and ascended towards the roof, watchful of the large, dark windows they passed along the way.

Near the top floor, Lancaster paused, finding the window Charlotte told him had a broken lock. Good to her word, it opened easily, allowing them inside. Once there, Rick stopped to take a deep breath, feeling as if he'd been holding it in all the way there.

Looking around, Rick found there was little to see, whatever purpose the room had once served long lost to time and decay. Plaster had broken away from the walls, leaving most of them little more than boards with holes that showed through to the hallway outside. The ceiling was little better, the floor littered with debris as it had slowly crumbled. Even the floor creaked uncertainly under his foot, making him more wary than he'd been outside.

Across from him, Lancaster was peeking out the door into the hall. Behind him, Emi and Todd tried to pick their way across the room, making as little noise as possible. However unsure he'd been on the trip over, it really had been nothing compared to this.

"Rick," Lancaster hissed, waving him over.

Joining him, he peeked out, spotting a flicker of light coming from somewhere further on down. "We're not alone here."

"Nope," the Rogue said, then grinned. "Let's go check it out."

"After you, sneaky man," Rick urged.

Lancaster shot him a surprised look, before his grin widened. "Sneaky man. I like that."

"You would," Rick muttered, waving him on.

Picking their steps carefully, the team trailed Lancaster as he hedged his way forward, watching for anything that might make a noise. After what felt like an eternity, they reached an intersection, the light coming from somewhere ahead. Waving Todd and Emi to hold up, Rick joined Lancaster in taking a look.

A dozen feet or so ahead, the offshoot corridor ended in a balcony that overlooked the main stage area of the theater. Beyond it, the entire interior was lit up, stage lights and house lights alike bathing the massive chamber. Voices from below drifted up to them, telling them more than enough.

"The manager's office is farther down," Lancaster whispered. "Should have a view that will keep us from being spotted too easily. I say we check that out."

"Sounds good to me."

Powerage continued on, each of them wondering just what they'd actually gotten themselves into. For himself, Rick set it aside and focused on what was in front of him, mindful that this wasn't the time to let his mind wander. Every step was a potential alarm to whoever was down there, and if it was what he suspected, he definitely didn't want to get their attention.

Finally, they rounded a turn, coming to the front of the theater, and reached the manager's office. Testing it, Lancaster found the knob turned easily, and slid the door open, watching for any sign of movement. Seeing no one, he hunkered down and snuck forward, aiming for the wide windows on the far side of the room, half covered by curtains.

Following him, Rick allowed a moment for his eyes to adjust to the half-light coming from the auditorium below, spotting a desk that looked far too new to have always been here, as well as several chairs and a small bar sporting several types of alcohol. Glancing down, he found the layer of dust that had coated everything else they'd passed wasn't present here, meaning this was a place frequently visited.

"You might wanna see this," Lancaster said.

Ignoring the room for a moment, Rick moved to join him, dropping low and peeking out into the auditorium below. Emi slid up beside him, Toddson moving to the far side of Lancaster, allowing them all a clear view.

Several floors below, dozens of men and women of various races moved about, apparently repairing the stage and audience seating. While Rick would have first though them to be construction workers, this was quickly betrayed by the all black garb they wore. Clothing identical to that worn by the men who Powerage had fought in the packing facility.

"That is not good," Toddson said.

"Nope," Lancaster agreed. "That is very, very bad."

"Okay," Rick said. "Looks like we found their base of operations. Whoever they are."

"The bad guys, I know that," Lancaster snorted.

Emi eased away from Rick's side. He watched her go for a moment, then turned his attention back to the Rogue.

"Yeah, and they outnumber us by way too many. There's no way we can take them on. We need a new plan."

"I forget now, what was the old plan?" Lancaster asked.

"Find out if this place has any connection to Manascetti," Rick told him with an annoyed look.

"Rick," Emi called, keeping her voice low. "You need to see this."

Giving the Rogue one last glare, Rick backed away from the window, and moved to join Emi by the desk. Blinking a few times, he tried to get his eyes to adjust back to the deeper gloom of the office as she held something up. Shaking his head, he turned so the light coming from the auditorium would help.

"Are you ready for eternal life," he read softly, looking over the brochure Emi handed him. "What the hell?"

"Inside," she urged.

Folding it open, Rick felt his breath catch as his stomach dropped and his whole world turned sideways.

"Guys, I think we may be in over heads way more than we knew," he said.

Glancing back, Lancaster saw the look on his face and slipped over to join him. "Why? What is it?"

Rick held out the brochure. Not liking how pale Rick had turned, the Rogue took it, glanced at the front, and then flipped it open. He instantly regretted that decision.

"Join us in our praise for Obedell the Eternal, who we will return to this world, and in exchange, be blessed with immortality."

Looking up at Rick, Lancaster struggled for something, anything to say. In the end, he could think of nothing, as Rick leaned against the desk, trying to grasp it all.

"Hey, um, what were we doing here again?" Toddson asked in a hushed tone.

"Looking for something on Manascetti," Lancaster told him, grabbing Rick by the shoulder to steady him.

Toddson looked back out the window for a moment. "I think we just found it."

Shaking his head, Rick pulled himself together and gave Lancaster a thankful nod. Together, they headed over to join the Cleric, but Lancaster kept a worried eye on Rick all the same. This was beyond any of the bad things they had imagined. Way beyond.

Reaching the window, they both glanced at Toddson, who just pointed down at the stage. Following his finger, they spotted it as well, and both men began to wish they hadn't come to the theater after all. They had been happier in their ignorant bliss.

On the stage, Manascetti himself stood, shaking hands with a tall, gaunt Elf in the black clothing of the cult of Obedell, the Hazaminie.

"We need to get the hell out of here," Rick said. "Now."

Chapter Nine: Dog Eat Dog

HALFWAY ACROSS THE OFFICE, Emi grabbed Rick's arm, bringing the whole party to a stop, her eyes wide and fearful. Before he got a chance to ask her what was wrong, Lancaster tensed, backing up a step. It only took a moment more for Rick himself to hear it.

Voices, soft still, but approaching.

"New plan," the Rogue hissed, shooing everyone back as he glanced about quickly. "Over here."

Moving as quickly as he could while keeping silent, Lancaster reached a second door in the room and eased it open. After a brief look, he motioned for everyone to move, and thankfully, nobody took their time, quickly stepping into the chamber beyond.

As soon as the door closed, they were plunged into complete darkness, Lancaster at the door, gripping the handle tightly. Rick felt around until he found the man's shoulder and gave it a gentle squeeze. To his left, he heard Toddson fumbling, and after a moment, Emi whispering to him as she moved deeper into the room.

They both fell silent a heartbeat before Rick heard the office door open and two people, talking softly, entered. Light flared around the door, allowing him to make out Lancaster's silhouette as the Rogue hunkered, watching through the keyhole. While he couldn't make out what they were saying, Rick held his breath and hoped they would be quick about leaving.

Seconds stretched on seemingly forever, before two new voices arrived, one clearly the deep baritone of Manascetti, the other a weedy rasp that instantly made Rick think of the gaunt Elf the crime boss had been standing with on the stage. Shuffling followed, and the office door closed.

Bracing on Lancaster, Rick leaned closer, listening intently.

"You try my patience, Manascetti," the Elf said as he crossed the room, the floor creaking under his feet. "I charged you with but a single task, and you have failed in that most miserably. Yet, you have the nerve to come and stand before me, still expecting to be rewarded. It is beyond impertinent."

"Cry me a river," the Dwarf snorted. "This mess ain't my fault."

"The vessel that was once Lucinia Avalinion found the vaults of my forbearer, and destroyed the sacred tomes," the Elf snapped. "How is that not your fault, when her death was the single goal you needed to accomplish in order to receive the blessing of immortality from the great and powerful Obedell upon his return from the beyond?"

"Man, you like to talk," Manascetti grumbled. "Look, pal, I threw the dame off a bridge. That usually takes. How was I to know she was going to bounce back from being dead? That seems like the kinda thing you should have told me might happen."

The Elf was silent for a moment. "Indeed, that was unexpected. I am quite vexed as to how the soul residing within her earthly form was able to accomplish this. It does not change, however, that she did a great deal of damage to our cause."

"She burned a few old books," Manascetti replied dismissively. "So what?"

Rage rippled from the Elf's harsh retort. "Those old books were the spell books of Obedell, himself. Hundreds of years' worth of knowledge. Invaluable resources in returning him from the place of beyond. Without them, we must resort to far less efficient means of breaching the dimensional barriers."

"Sounds like a whole lot of your problem," the Dwarf said. "And none at all of mine."

The Elf paced the room for a moment. "So you say, but without having fulfilled your end of the bargain, there will be no reward in this for you."

Manascetti laughed at that. "Well, she'd be a pile of ash right now if you hadn't screwed everything up by not telling me that your own people were roaming around looking for her, too."

"What choice did I have?" the Elf yelled. "Your idea of dealing with the problem was to hire adventurers! It was obvious that dealing with the situation was beyond your ability."

"It's called outside contracting," Manascetti shot back. "Word of advice, my overly dramatic friend. The best way to get caught doing something illegal is to have your fingerprints all over a murder. Especially when it's somebody what you done murdered once before. Keeping me and mine out of sight was the best way to deal with her."

"And look how well that went," the Elf sneered. "Not only was she able to discern the location of the sacred tomes before we could, but she managed to destroy them, while all you accomplished was bringing the son of our master's arch rival into the mix!"

"That wasn't exactly the plan, I admit," Manascetti said, slightly chastised. "The gods, they got a sense of humor to them. I was as surprised as you when it was Wonder's brat that turned up on my door."

"I can assure you, Obedell does not share in their mirth," the Elf growled. "He will not find any of this humorous upon his return."

Manascetti laughed again. "Well, be sure to tell him it's your fault. If you'd filled me in on them spell books sooner, we'd have them right now."

"As if I would allow them to fall into your hands," the Elf replied, wandering closer to the door Rick and Lancaster hovered behind. "No, I had to insure their safe recovery."

"That went great, too," the Dwarf told him with a chuckle. "I had a fine time cleaning up the pieces of your boys from that packing facility. If they hadn't been there, we wouldn't be having this conversation, because the whole place would have suffered a mysterious fire, leaving a bunch of unidentified remains."

The Elf walked away from the door. "And the spell books would still be lost to us."

"Not if I knew you was looking for them," Manascetti replied with a trace of humor. "See, this is what's called a lack of communication. You can't expect me to help you if you won't trust me."

"As if I could trust a greed-soaked brigand such as you," the other man growled.

"Now, that hurts my feelings," Manascetti said. "Here, I let you come into my town to do your little ritual and even offered to help, and you act like I'm the bad guy."

The Elf let out a bitter laugh. "The bad guy? Oh, no, Manascetti. You are more like the buffoon I am saddled with. In fact, I do not think I can any longer tolerate your incompetence. After all, while you brag about dealing with my fallen brethren, you left Lucinia's body for the police to recover."

"She was dead," Manascetti answered, sounding bored. "Figured the second time would do the trick."

"I suppose so," the Elf sighed.

"It didn't, by the way," the Dwarf added. "That's what brought me here. One of my boys on the inside said she walked out of the morgue. Again."

The Elf was silent for a long moment, before saying with great exasperation, "Incredible. Now, not only is she still a problem, you've thrown coal on the proverbial fire by putting a Wonder in the mix. Could you be more idiotic?"

"Watch it, buddy boy," Manascetti snapped.

"No, I think not," the Elf snarled. "It is time you serve Obedell, and your free will is not required for that."

"Might want to think twice before you go using your dark mojo on me, pal," the Dwarf said. "I tipped Wonder to you boys being in town."

Rick could hear the Elf fall back a step. "You did what?"

"Right now, if he gets to talking to the wrong cops, your whole operation could be exposed. Which means you need me, with all my facilities intact, if you want to keep doing what you're doing without the Royal Inspectors coming down on your head like a bag of hammers."

"I do not need..." the Elf started.

"You do," Manascetti cut in. "My guys, they'd know if I was being controlled. I got my own Wizards, you know. Which means you and me, we're still equals in this little venture. You feel me, pal?"

"Your nerve exceeds your capabilities," the Elf replied in outrage.

"Always keep your friends by the short and curlies," the Dwarf laughed. "That's how you stay breathing in this town. So, if you're done threatening me, I got a girl to find, and a bunch of wannabe heroes to put out of their misery."

The Elf said nothing for a moment, though when he did, it was with venom in his voice. "Do not fail again, Manascetti, or I assure you, when Obedell returns, and that will be very soon now, you will be rewarded only with death."

"Yeah, like I ain't heard that before," the Dwarf told him. "Keep your people out of my way this time, pal. Got that?"

"Indeed."

Manascetti departed, the heavy sound of his footfalls fading quickly. The Elf lingered for a time, irate beyond words, before leaving as well, the room beyond darkening. Rick leaned back as it did, the full scope of just how screwed they were settling on him.

* * *

After waiting a short time to ensure no one else entered the office, Rick and Lancaster felt their way along the wall, trying to find Emi and Toddson. When that proved fruitless, the complete lack of light rendering them both effectively blind, Rick decided to chance it and hissed out a soft call to them.

Getting one in return, he reached out in that direction, Lancaster's hand on his shoulder, and groped through the pitch until his hand fell on Emi's oversized hat. Feeling downward, he caught her shoulder, and felt her small, trembling hand grip his wrist.

"Okay guys," he whispered. "We may be in a lot more trouble here than we thought."

"Emi, do you know any spells for light?" Lancaster asked.

"Um... no," the Wizard timidly replied.

"I do," Toddson put in. "I think. Maybe. I don't remember."

"Probably not wise, anyway," Rick told them. "We don't want to attract any attention."

"Hang on," Toddson replied. "I got something."

A few whispered words later, a tiny light flared in the tip of the Cleric's finger. Slightly more than a book of matches would provide, it still allowed them to at least see each other, and Rick admitted it was better than the complete darkness. Motioning everyone to gather around, he hoped to block any chance of it being spotted, and settled in to the conversation he knew they needed to have.

"So, looks like we've stumbled into a cult that worships Obedell and wants to bring him back," he said slowly. "That's pretty bad."

Lancaster shot him a look. "Pretty bad? Rick, the way those two were talking in their very clichéd conversation, it sounded like they actually can pull that off. I'd say that's world-ending bad."

"That would be bad for the world, yeah," Toddson sighed.

Rick sighed heavily, then nodded. "Okay, yes, I undersold it. I get it. I don't really think that's the big point we should be focusing on right now."

"I kind of can't stop focusing on that," Emi said, her voice quivering. "I mean, it's Obedell, Rick. He's really evil."

"Yeah, got that, thanks," Rick told her. "I kind of have a history with the guy, remember?"

"That's fair," Toddson allowed, nodding.

"Thank you. Now, we know for a fact that Manascetti is working with them, and as Lancaster speculated, they're using us to keep the cops from noticing what these guys are up to. It's best to assume that means they are very close to making their move. Which means we are in way too far over our heads here. We need a plan, and a good one, fast."

"I suggest we start by getting the hell out of this theater," Lancaster said. "But I appreciate you acknowledging that I was right. That's means a lot. Thank you."

"Seriously," Rick sighed. "Right now?"

The Rogue shrugged. Rick decided to drop it, mostly because he had a really good point. The first order of business was for all of them to get out without being spotted. There were far too many cultists for them take on, and no doubt Manascetti had some men of his own mixed in.

"Okay, let's take a second here," he said. "Getting out obviously comes first. The next question, and I think we need to address this right now, is where are we going?"

The other three looked at each other in surprise, with Emi being the one to ask, "Aren't we going back to Charlotte's?"

"Crap," Lancaster sighed, picking up on where Rick was going.

"Manascetti has cops on his payroll, and I'm betting they aren't going to take us in," Rick told her. "I think going back to Charlotte's would be putting her in danger, and I can't do that, not after all she's done for us. We need someplace else to hide out while we plan our next move."

"Someplace people won't think to look for us," Lancaster added.

"And we aren't putting other people in danger by harboring us," Toddson pondered, drawing another look of surprise, though at this point, it was brief and far less amazed than it once had been.

Silence fell for a minute as everyone considered their options, but came up empty. For his own part, Rick simply knew nowhere else to go, still far too new to the city to be aware of good locations. Toddson probably didn't remember any, while Emi was unlikely to be any more aware of good hideouts than Rick was.

Finally, rolling his eyes, Lancaster sighed and said, "Okay, fine. I know a place. It's a ways away, though. I can't promise we'll get there without getting caught. Even if we do, you guys have got to mind your manners."

"What's that mean?" Rick asked.

"It's kind of complicated," the Rogue replied. "Just... trust me, okay?"

Staring at him curiously for a moment, Rick nodded. "I can do that."

"Let's get moving then," the other man grimaced. "If we're lucky, we can get there before sun up. Provided we get out of here unnoticed, and don't get caught by cops on the way."

"Good cops, or bad cops?" Toddson asked.

"At this point, I don't think it matters," Rick told him. "Either way, I don't think any of us will live long if we get busted."

With that sobering thought, Powerage made ready to escape the theater lair of the cult of Obedell.

* * *

The sun was peeking over the horizon when Lancaster finally brought them to a stop in a dank alley on the outer east end of the Weeds District. Letting them know he was going to check to make sure the coast was clear, the rest of the team took the moment to catch their collective breaths and try to ease their rattled nerves.

The trip across the city had been far more harrowing than Rick liked, even worse than slipping out of the theater.

More than once, they'd only narrowly avoided patrolling officers, and even other citizens who may have recognized them. It had taken them the entire night, but at last, he hoped, they could maybe find a measure of safety.

At least the others could. The trip had cemented in Rick's mind just how far into the deep end of trouble they actually were. With no way of knowing whether every police officer they saw was going to arrest them or just try to kill them, no allies to speak of, the largest crime syndicate in the city out for their blood, and a cult of necromancers looking to bring the most powerful Lich the world had ever seen back from where ever Max Wonder had banished him, they had few options before them.

Save one. Rick hated it, but at this point he didn't see any other choice. As soon as the others were secure and safe, it was time to keep his promise to his mother and throw himself at Aunt Neba's feet, hoping she could save him and his friends. If she even remembered who he was, of course.

Lancaster reappeared from the back entrance to a shop and waved them on. Pulling himself up, Rick fingered the Chameleon Ring in his pocket and committed himself to his course of action. All he could hope for now was that he made it there.

"Okay, guys," Lancaster was saying as they slid through the door he held for them. "Like I said, mind your manners. We can probably hole up here for a while, as long as you don't piss him off."

"Piss who off?" Rick asked, making one last check of the alley before closing the door.

"Me, kid," a voice heavy with age answered.

Pausing, Rick took a moment to study the old man who hobbled up from the gloom of the interior. Taller than Rick by a bit, he leaned heavily on a cane, his thick head of hair bone-white and tumbling down past his shoulders. Easily in his eighties, the man paused, looking them over, or at least, that was what he seemed to do. The thick, white cataracts over his eyes said he saw nothing.

"These the losers what got you in trouble, dumbass?" he asked, jabbing his cane into Lancaster's chest.

"Uh... yeah, Grandpa," the Rogue grimaced. "This is my adventuring team. Toddson, Emi, and Rick. We had a fourth, but..."

"Got herself killed," Lancaster's grandfather snorted. "I told ya that would happen. But, no, what's an old man like me know?"

"I don't think this is really the time," Lancaster urged quietly, before throwing the rest of the group a nervous smile. "Guys, this is my Grandpa, Larry Garmine."

Rick's jaw dropped. "Lavish Larry?"

The old man chortled at that. "Rick Wonder, wasn't it? That takes me back. I knew your folks, and that uncle of yours. Real buncha nutjobs they were."

"Sir, this is a real honor," Rick started, holding out his hand.

Larry snorted at that, turning away. "Might have been back in the day, kid. Not anymore."

Rick's hand dropped, watching the stooped figure shuffle away. Lavish Larry Garmine had been, back in his day, one of the most famous Rogues in the world. Enough so he had once trained a woman named Delilah Rumble in his secret, advanced techniques. More than that, he had, for a time, run his own Thieves Guild, dedicated to fighting corruption in the city and across the country. Larry himself had brought down everything from dirty cops to a Prime Minister embezzling taxpayer money to a member of the Royal family.

"Lancaster," Rick said quietly. "What was the name of his guild back in the day?"

The usually flamboyant Rogue gave Rick a pained smile, saying only, "The Night Brand."

"How could I have forgotten that," Rick chastised himself. "They were famous."

"Everybody's forgotten them, kid," Larry called from deeper in the shop. "World went and changed. Don't want heroes no more. Makes you all pretty damn stupid, if you ask me."

"He doesn't like to talk about it," Lancaster told Rick. "Try not to bring it up. There was some bad stuff that went down back in the day. I had to hide his prune juice to get him to train me."

"So, your contact," Rick realized, pausing as the full weight of what Lancaster was saying hit him. "Whoa. This explains so much."

"Yeah," the other man said. "Come on. We can use the upstairs area to plan our next move. Just, you know, don't bother Grandpa or anything, okay? He doesn't really like people these days."

"Sure," Rick agreed, waving the other two to follow the Rogue as he ducked into the back of the shop and headed up a set of stairs. Taking the rear, Rick paused again to look around, finding himself in a locksmith's, keys hanging everywhere. At the counter, Larry had settled on a stool, staring towards the windows as the sky brightened.

For the first time, Rick seriously considered his future and wondered if being an adventurer was really what he wanted.

Joining the rest upstairs, he found a comfortable sitting area awaiting them, beyond which a curtain sectioned off a small kitchen. Another curtain blocked his view any further, but he got the picture clear enough. Lavish Larry, one of the most skilled Rogues in the history of adventurers, lived here, in this tiny upstairs apartment.

Something about that just felt wrong.

"Make yourselves at home," Lancaster said. "We should be okay here for a while. Nobody knows he's my Grandpa, so it's not likely they'll look for us here."

"How's that work?" Emi asked as she eased down into a chair.

Lancaster gave her a smirk. "Dad wasn't really a one woman man."

"That makes sense," Toddson snickered.

"Hey, now," the Rogue grumbled.

"It does make sense," Rick said, patting him on the shoulder.

"Yeah, okay," Lancaster sighed, then shrugged. "What can I say? It's in my blood."

Rick laughed at that. "Welcome to the club."

"Why didn't you tell us sooner about this?" Toddson asked. "Or, did you? I might have forgotten if you did."

"I didn't," Lancaster said. "Grandpa is kind of against the whole adventure thing. Besides, you don't join a team led by Rick Wonder and brag about your own heritage. That's kind of like spitting into the wind, you know?"

Rick grimaced at that. "I'm not sure I'd go that far."

"Is being a Wonder a big deal?" Toddson asked, tugging his boots off.

Rick and Lancaster both sighed at that, the Rogue saying, "Not to everybody."

"I think you're both cool," Emi offered. "I don't have any famous relatives. Well, I do, but they were all famous for being bad people."

"You'll have to tell us about that some time," Lancaster said, giving her a bright smile.

Emi sank into the chair. "I'd rather not. It's kind of embarrassing."

"It's fine, Emi," Rick assured her. "It's not like my mom and uncle are actually awesome when you meet them. I get not wanting to talk about it."

Emi smiled a little, but Lancaster gave him a doubting look. "I'd think meeting your mother would be pretty awe-inspiring."

"You go with that," Rick encouraged, nodding.

Flashing a dazzling smile, Lancaster slid out into a pose, pointing at Rick with both hands. "Maybe I'll just do that."

Not meaning to, Rick started laughing. A moment later, Emi joined him, with Toddson falling in after that. Lancaster winked, and joined in, all four of them laughing hysterically. Shaking his head, Rick suddenly knew he'd go to the ends of the earth for these people, and no matter what it cost him personally, he'd see to it they walked away from this safe, alive and free.

"What are we laughing about?" Toddson asked, still snickering.

"Forget it, man," Rick chuckled.

"That I can do," the Cleric grinned.

"Probably already did," Emi giggled.

"Yup," Toddson affirmed with a nod.

Looking them over, Rick smiled. Yeah. The ends of the earth at the very least.

"Okay, guys, I know it looks pretty bleak right now, but I've got a plan," he said.

"Knew you would," Lancaster said, slapping him on the back. "Let's hear it, so I can poke it full of holes, and give you a better plan."

"You got one, I'll be happy to hear it," Rick snorted. "Cause my plan, it's about the only thing I got left."

"So, make with amazing me," the Rogue shrugged before falling onto the couch next to Toddson.

Nodding, Rick took a deep breath, and said, "I'm going to go beg for help from my Aunt Neba."

Toddson and Lancaster exchanged a brief look, then shrugged, both saying, "Who?"

"Neba Valsail," Emi said. "She was the Wizard in his parent's party back when. Even back home, she's really famous."

"More importantly, she's still pretty influential around here," Rick added. "After my dad died, she stayed in Riscadil, working with the League in the early days. She's got connections and, as much as I hate to say it, I don't think we can get out of this mess on our own."

"I agree," Emi said quietly.

Toddson tried to think about it for a minute, then just shook his head, saying, "Whatever you think is best, Jimmy."

Lancaster continued mulling it for a bit longer, before giving Rick a suspicious look. "And just how do you plan to get to see her? I mean, every cop in the city and all out for our heads won't make that easy."

"I've still got the Chameleon Ring Charlotte loaned me," Rick replied, holding it up. "If Emi's still got a little money for a cab, then I should be able to stay out of sight and disguised well enough to make to her place. After that, it's just a case of whether or not she'll help us out."

"So, this plan, it involves you going alone?" Lancaster pressed.

"Yeah, it does," Rick said slowly. "I want you guys to stay here, where you're safe. If this goes well, you won't have to be in any more danger."

The Rogue sulked instantly. "I didn't sign up to avoid danger, you know."

"No, none of us did," Rick agreed. "But this, it's way more than we expected, and way more than we can handle. There's no sense in exposing ourselves to any more, at least, not until we can get the police on our side."

"He's got a point," Toddson said, elbowing Lancaster.

"I know," the Rogue grumbled. "I just don't like the idea of him being the only one to take the risk of getting caught."

"If all of us get caught, then it really is over," Rick stated flatly.

Emi sighed, slumping. "He's not wrong."

Throwing his hands in the air, Lancaster spewed several curses. "Fine! I get it. I just don't like you being out there without us to watch your back."

"Not wild about that myself," Rick admitted. "But I got nothing else, so about now would be a great time for your brilliant plan."

Lancaster fell into a pout. "I don't have one."

"Then, this is the plan," Rick told him with a helpless shrug. "You guys hang tight here while I go see Aunt Neba and try to get us out of this mess. I'll come get you as soon as we're in the clear."

"Sucks that all we got is the one shitty plan," Lancaster groused, then gave Rick a glare. "But, okay. Just be careful out there, will you? I've gotten kind of attached to you."

"Same here," Rick told him with a grin.

"Me, too, Don," Toddson said, then smacked himself in the face. "I mean, Rick. Sorry."

Chuckling at that, Rick gave him a salute. "I'm used to it, so no worries."

Easing to her feet, Emi moved to look up at him, her face a mask of worry and dread. "Promise me you'll come back."

"Emi..." Rick started.

The Elf stomped her foot, shouting, "Promise me!"

Resting a hand on her shoulder, Rick smiled at her and nodded, saying, "I promise. I'll be back."

Returning his nod, she sniffed back tears and put on the bravest face she could manage. His smile widening, Rick mussed her hair, and gave them all another look. Yeah. To the very gates of hell. He could go that far for them. Easily.

"Be back before you know it."

* * *

A few hours later, Rick exited a cab outside the brownstone home of Neba Valsail. Situated in the posh Canal District, he couldn't help but notice it was only about half an hour's walk from Manascetti's own residence, which only served to remind him of how much danger he was actually in just standing there.

Glancing around, he eased open the wrought iron gate that separated the sidewalk from the front of the house and hurried up the steps. Taking a second to steady himself, he knocked on the door and removed the ring, dropping the illusion of Melvin, the barkeep from the Slaughterhouse.

The few seconds that passed felt like forever before the door swung open, revealing the middle-aged Elf he hadn't seen since childhood, who gave him a curious look before asking, "Yes?"

"Aunty Neba?" Rick returned, giving her an awkward smile.

Recognition filled her eyes as quickly as a smile found her face. "Ricky? Oh my gods, is that really you?"

"Yeah," he said, suddenly feeling like a child again in her presence.

"What are you doing here?" She laughed, wrapping him in a hug. "Come in. You should have sent me word you were coming."

Stepping into her home, he felt slightly more at ease once the door swung shut. "I would have, but you know how it is. Come to Riscadil, and make it on my own."

Crossing her arms, Neba gave him a smirk, settling into a stance he remembered well, one that spoke of authority. It was strange how different it seemed to him now that he was grown. Back then, she'd seemed aloof. Now, she just seemed capable, confident and relaxed.

Maybe it was just because she was still in her pajamas wrapped in a silk bathrobe. It was probably that.

"How's that going for you? Everything you hoped it would be?"

Giving her a nervous laugh, Rick admitted, "Not really. Truth is, I probably should have listened to mom and stayed home.

"I'm surprised she let you leave at all," Neba snorted, waving him to follow her into the living room. "Last time I visited, she would barely let you out of the house without sending Castor to play bodyguard."

"Things have changed a bit," he told her.

Neba cast a look over her shoulder, eyes landing on the Whip Blades at his hips, and assessing the armor he wore. "Obviously. Finally decided to try and live up to your dad?"

"I wouldn't say that," Rick muttered, easing down on a loveseat as Neba settled on the wide couch opposite the coffee table. "I was more trying to make a name for myself and maybe honor who he was than live up to him."

"Uh-huh," Neba drawled, crossing her legs, elbow hitting her knee and chin in her palm, giving him a look that told her she wasn't buying a bit of that. Classic Neba.

"Okay, maybe it was a bit trying to live up to him," Rick muttered.

Neba smiled. "So tell me the truth, Ricky. Being an adventurer. Not so fun, is it?"

"Not at the moment, no," he said, rubbing at the back of his head nervously. "That's actually part of why I'm here."

"Dee-Dee made you promise to come to me if you got in over your head," Neba said, a smirk playing around her lips as she dared him to deny it.

Rick scowled. "Yeah, that's exactly it."

"I had a feeling," she said with a grin. "Even as a little boy, you weren't one to do things the easy way. I guess you've been in town for a bit then, and already found out that this whole career path you've chosen isn't as simple as you thought."

"Well, in my defense, I was a really little kid," he pointed out. "And, uh... no. It's a lot harder than I thought."

She shrugged. "Could've told you that, if you'd bothered to come here and ask before diving in the deep end."

"That's how you guys did it back when," he reminded her.

"Yeah, it is," she sighed, eyes getting a bit wistful. "That was a different time, though, Ricky. The whole world was different back then. Now a days, that's not the smart way to go about it."

"I did try to join the League," he told her. "That went poorly."

"I can guess," she said, her tone telling him her entire opinion of the League. "Well, first things first, let's get you some coffee and something to eat, then you can tell me what sort of trouble you're in."

Rick stood as she did. "If you don't want to help, I'll understand."

Neba paused, looking at him as if he was an idiot. "Of course I'll help you, Ricky. That's not even a question. But you look like crap, and before you get into it, I want to make sure you've had a decent meal in you. Your mother would kill me if I didn't."

"Pretty sure you could take her," Rick replied with a tired smile.

"Yeah," Neba retorted, laughing as she walked to the door leading to the kitchen. "I'm not, and trust me, I know what she's capable of way better than you. Now sit down, shut up, and give me a minute. Last thing I need is to get stabbed to death in my sleep cause I didn't feed Delilah Wonder's baby boy."

"Yes, ma'am," Rick said with a smile, and immediately sat back down, feeling for the first time in a while that everything was going to be okay.

* * *

As Rick was knocking on Neba's door, a knock came to Charlotte's door as well. Sitting in her kitchen, her first cup of coffee of the day barely touched, she gave the sound a wary look. Across from her, June stopped trying to keep her own coffee hot long enough to glare. Emi and the others hadn't come back from the theater, and somehow, she doubted they would use the front door if it was them.

Rising, she made her way to answer it, waving at the ice pixie to stay put. Pausing at the peephole, she saw two uniformed officers standing on her stoop, glancing around the street. Frowning, she shook her head, knowing this was bound to happen sooner or later. Unlocking the door, she opened it, glaring down at the police officers.

"Excuse us, ma'am," one of them said. "We're looking for a woman by the name of Emeri Landari. We understand that she lives here. Would she be home?"

Charlotte's glare deepened as she took the two in, a human and a Half-Orc, neither of which she had seen in the area before, and she knew every patrol officer in the neighborhood by name.

"There be no one by that name here," she grumbled.

The human who had spoken gave her a smile. "Do you mind if we come in and have a look around? Just to be sure."

"I do be minding, yes," she huffed. "I still have me rights, you know."

The human's smile never wavered. "We won't be a minute, ma'am. Better this way than with a warrant, wouldn't you agree?"

Snorting at that, Charlotte pulled the door wider. "Fine, then. But you best no be making a mess of me house, or I'll be having words with your Captain."

"Of course, ma'am," the human said, stepping in as she backed away.

Moving to put her back to the small living room, Charlotte allowed them in, noting that neither removed their cap. Turning her back, she stepped away, eye falling on the mirror above her fireplace mantel, catching the look the two exchanged.

So it was to be like that, was it? Fine, then.

As soon as she was through the door, Charlotte slid to the side and spun around. Hearing the human yelp at her sudden disappearance, she braced herself. He didn't disappoint her, appearing a moment later, a wand in his hand.

Pulling back, she swung forward, her massive hand catching him around the throat, and swinging him off his feet. Behind him, the Half-Orc cried out in surprise as his partner suddenly came flying back, a literal human shield against the now raging Orc.

Charlotte didn't hesitate to slam the flailing human into the Half-Orc, pinning them both to the wall. Leaning in, she held them easily, neither a match for her superior strength. The human did try to get the wand up, but she clasped his wrist, and with a twist, heard bone snap.

"Now then, I think you be telling me who sent you, if either of you want to be drawing breath again."

The human gurgled something, unable to speak around her hand on his throat. Behind him, the Half-Orc struggled to reach a wand as well, only to have a dozen shards of ice pepper his arm. The wand fumbled away as June fluttered up, magic swirling around her hands.

"Manascetti," the Half-Orc finally yelled. "Cato Manascetti!"

"Now that damn fool gone and done it," she muttered. "Made me mad, and messed up me home. Guess it be time I got personally involved in this all. That be bad news for him. You boys be sure to tell him that, too. You let that fool Dwarf know, he got on the angry side of Charlotte Goodkin."

The Half-Orc tried to press back, grunting out, "You think he cares about some old lady? You're as good as dead already!"

"You be caring about this old lady right now," she growled, pulling back suddenly, and slamming the now limp human into his partner, sending them both into a nice long nap.

"Ain't even finished me coffee yet," she harrumphed before giving them both a solid kick to the temple to keep them out a while. "Done gone and ruined me whole day."

With that, Charlotte swung her front door shut, and went to get dressed. She had work to do.

* * *

Unbeknownst to either Rick or Charlotte, St. Clair and Tanabuar were arriving at their office, pushing through the door at the same moment fateful knocking was occurring elsewhere. While Tanabuar was in his usual high spirits, St. Clair appeared even moodier than usual, signaling to the Chthonian that it was going to be a long day.

"Are you gonna be pensive all day?" Tanabuar asked as they approached their respective desks. "Cause, I don't like being itchy, and the pharmacy was all out of that cream I use."

St. Clair paused, giving him a baffled look before shaking his head. "Sometimes, I think you say things like that just to confuse me."

"I do," the other smirked. "I enjoy seeing the look in your eyes. Plus, it makes you a bit more bearable for a few minutes."

"Part of me wants to be touched."

"Which part?"

St. Clair took a moment. He needed more, but there was work to be done. "Grab what you need, and stop being so annoying. We have an address to check, and I want to go over the crime scene photos one more time. I still feel like I'm missing something."

Tanabuar leaned on his desk, his mirth fading. "You know, I was thinking about that last night."

"Were you, now?" St. Clair asked with a trace of humor.

"I keep going back to what Strakinsy said, about there being a necromancer in the city," the Chthonian replied, ignoring his usually dour companion's brief flirtation with humor. It hadn't gone well, but he was a nice person and decided not to point it out.

"If there is one," St. Clair added.

"It adds up, though," Tanabuar insisted. "There was a lot of blood at the scene, but we know Wonder's team, except Avaman, made it out alive. We also know that Avalinion's body was left there, which suggests it wasn't her people who cleaned the area."

St. Clair paused, listening.

"If we approach it logically, then we have to assume a third party was at work, or rather, a fourth. It doesn't make sense for Manascetti to hire Wonder's team then leave the very thing he wanted them to find. Namely, Avalinion."

"Unless all he wanted was for her to be dead," St. Clair stated.

Tanabuar shook his head, looking doubtful. "That's kind of what hit me, though. She already died once and came back. I'm willing to bet my paycheck that it was Manascetti who was behind her ending up in the Bay in the first place."

St. Clair leaned back, considering that. "You think, then, that he would know about her ability to return from the dead?"

"Most likely," the Chthonian replied. "Evidence suggests she killed herself, so it stands to reason she did that knowing she would come back and just needed a way out of whatever situation was going down at the moment."

A frown settled on St. Clair's face. "Still, if Manascetti knew..."

"Unless he didn't know she could do it more than once," Tanabuar cut in.

"Okay, let's say that's true," St. Clair humored him. "That she killed herself would suggest it."

"Which brings me back to the fourth group in play," Tanabuar said, wagging a finger at him. "Even if they suspected, odds are, in order to get out alive the way they did, Wonder's crew probably killed all of them. Which means..."

"The only people who would know for sure she killed herself was Wonder and his team," St. Clair finished, getting where he was going.

"Thus, do we come to the conclusion," the Chthonian stated with a bow. "What if the necromancer that Strakinsy was talking about has allies, and that's who Powerage fought."

"Well, now," St. Clair said slowly, actually impressed. "If that's the case, then either Manascetti's people cleaned up the bodies, suggesting they are in league with the necromancers, or they have other allies in the city."

"Exactly," Tanabuar grinned. "And who were the necromancers we know had an alliance with the Scarlet Ring in their turf war against the Ironriggers?"

"The Hazaminie," St. Clair replied, eyebrow arching in concern. "Which ties all the evidence we have together, but doesn't give us anything we can easily follow. It is, at best, speculation, Molly."

"Maybe so," the other man allowed. "But say the Hazaminie seized control of the Ring and Lucinia was a loose end. That would explain why they would be working with the Ironriggers."

St. Clair started to object, then really thought about it. Slowly, his eyes widened. "Now that is a solid piece of reasoning. Molly, I think you may be right."

"I am?" Tanabuar asked, genuinely surprised.

"I'm not willing to say it was the Hazaminie themselves, but there must be a fourth group at play," the human considered aloud. "Perhaps in a fragile allegiance with Manascetti, or trying to use him for their own goals. It does add up."

Tanabuar leaned forward. "Can we go back to the part where I was right, and figured out something you didn't?"

With a sigh, St. Clair turned, giving him a smile. "Yes, of course. Forgive me. I got caught up in the case. I obviously should have made time to praise you for not being woefully wrong."

"When you say it like that," Tanabuar sulked.

"The point here is," his partner urged, wanting him to see the bigger picture for once. "This does explain why the crime scene was altered. Any group of necromancers wouldn't want to be found out, and the Ironriggers certainly wouldn't want to be caught associating with such a group. You've done well. Thank you."

"That's what makes us a good team, isn't it?" the other man suggested, suddenly feeling awkward with the praise.

"Indeed, it is," St. Clair agreed. "When we get back from checking Miss Landari's home address, I want to go over everything again from this fresh perspective. See if we can figure out who might be involved."

"Might wanna hold up on that," Podest called as he hovered into the room. "I've got a hot tip for you. Richard Wonder has been reported at a private residence. Two thirty-five Cobalt Road. Records say it's the home of one Neba Valsail."

St. Clair went wide-eyed, as Tanabuar glanced over at the Older, saying, "That name seems familiar."

"Should," the creature told him with a chuckle. "Valsail use to be part of Max Wonder's crew back in the day. She's a pretty capable Wizard, and these days, holds a lot of political influence."

Tanabuar groaned. "He's trying to get out of the city."

"Probably," the Older agreed. "Valsail could make it happen, too."

As they talked, St. Clair's hand had gone to his vest pocket, pulling out a small gold key. He stared at it for a long moment, before asking, "How solid is this tip, Podest?"

The Older looked back at him, his smirk fading at the sight of the key. "Very solid. I'd say there's at least a ninety percent chance Wonder is there right now."

St. Clair nodded before crouching, unlocking the bottom drawer of his desk with the key. "Very well. For the record, I, Percival St. Clair, Royal Inspector with the Special Services Division, am enacting Emergency Protocol Seven."

Podest recoiled slightly as St. Clair retrieved the only two items in the drawer, a small box, and an oilcloth wrapped object. "Um... okay... the record is noted, against my better judgment."

"And mine," Tanabuar added, looking at the oil cloth in disgust. "You know I hate those things, Percy."

"I do," St. Clair agreed. "However, let us assume that you are correct about who the fourth player involved in the packing facility incident was. You saw for yourself what young Mr. Wonder is capable of with those swords of his. We have to be able to defend ourselves."

Tanabuar scowled. "I don't disagree, I just..."

"Consider it an order," St. Clair interrupted. "Now, Molly."

Shaking his head, Tanabuar went to his desk, following St. Clair's lead, and retrieving his own items. "I want the record noted that I objected to this course of action. Emergency Protocol Seven is not to be taken lightly, and at the moment, we have no reason to believe the lives of law enforcement are in imminent danger. Mr. Wonder may not resist arrest at all."

Podest hesitated a moment, shooting St. Clair a pained look, before saying, "The record has been noted. As a reminder, an Older's memory is admissible in a court of law."

"Yes, I know," St. Clair replied, giving Tanabuar a soft smile. "I would expect no less from you, Molly. Thank you for always holding to your principles. It's what I respect most about you."

"Let's just make sure we don't have to use these, okay?" Tanabuar said, looking at the thing on his desk with open hate.

"I hope we won't, either," his partner agreed, before looking to Podest again. "Assemble a team of officers. Have them equipped properly, and ready to go immediately. It's time Mr. Wonder answered a few questions."

"Already on it," Podest told him, not liking where this was going.

St. Clair took a deep breath, reached down, unfolded the oilcloth, and lifted the heavy revolver. However much Tanabuar hated them, he hated them even more. The great equalizer, requiring not the years of study and mental discipline Wizards had to undergo, firearms had changed the world, and eventually, become heavily regulated, available only to the military. Even law enforcement operated under restrictions as to their use, limited to times of extreme emergency, when fear of danger was great enough to warrant it.

Accepting things were moving faster than he had anticipated, St. Clair began loading the gun.

* * *

Blissfully ignorant of what was coming his way, Rick sat in Neba's living room, halfway glancing at the pictures, commendations and awards that decorated her wall and mantle. Too many thoughts and fears crowded his mind as he twitched and fiddled his thumbs, waiting for her to return.

When she finally did, a hearty breakfast in hand, he found himself relaxing slightly, grateful for her soothing presence. Whatever it took, even if she asked him to give up being an adventurer and go home, he knew he would do it to get his team, his friends, clear of the trouble they had fallen into.

As he ate, he explained everything to her, from how his mother had agreed to let him try this, to the League, all the way up to coming to her door, and why. Neba listened, never interrupting, taking it all in with a kind, if attentive eye, allowing him to spill it all out. As soon as he finished, Rick had to admit he felt better. There was just something about telling it to someone with more experience that made it all feel easier to carry.

"Well," she said at length. "That is certainly a tale."

"It's all true, I promise," he said quickly.

She waved him down with a laugh. "I wasn't doubting a word of it, Ricky. I apologize if it sounded that way. It's just... wow... that takes me back. Your parents, Castor, me, and the rest, getting ourselves in trouble like this. Gods, some things really don't ever change."

"So, you believe me?" he asked nervously.

Neba gave him a pained look. "Of course I believe you, Ricky! Come on! I've been there, and trust me when I say this, I've been in worse messes than this. I'm not so old that I've forgotten what it's like to be in over your head."

Rick relaxed, heaving a sigh of relief. "You have no idea what that means to me. I mean, we tried dealing with this, we really did, but every time we turned around, somehow it just got worse."

"Yeah, that's kind of how it works," she laughed. "And why Dee-Dee never wanted you to get into this life. She knew, same as I do, that it can go from bad to catastrophic in the blink of an eye."

"She tried to tell me," Rick admitted. "I just didn't want to hear it."

"We were no different, back then," she told him with a soft smile. "Diving in head first, never looking, and finding ourselves in so far over our heads, we thought we'd never see daylight again. Everyone tried to tell us, but we just knew we were going to be different."

Rick slumped slightly. "How did you get through it all?"

"The skin of our teeth," she snorted, lifting her mug to have a sip of coffee. "And luck, mostly. A lot of luck. More than a few fights. More than a few lost friends. More than a few scars. Eventually, you just kind of get the knack for not panicking when the proverbial shit hits the fan."

Rick shook his head. "I don't think I'm going to get that far. If this has taught me anything, it's that mom was right. I'm not ready for this."

"Nobody ever is, Ricky," Neba told him with a warm smile. "Don't give up on yourself just yet. At least, not until we deal with this situation."

"Yeah," he said, giving her a tired smile in return. "First things first."

Neba nodded. "And on that note, we need to get your friends rounded up so we can work the problem together."

"Of course," Rick replied, relieved. "I can take you to them, or bring them here. Whatever you want."

A knock came at the door before she could answer, bringing a look of irritation to her face. Rick missed it, however, as he tensed, hands going to the hilts of his swords. He half rose from the loveseat, before Neba stood, groaning.

"Easy, killer," she said with a laugh. "Don't tell me you've already forgotten who I am, much less what I'm capable of."

Rick relaxed somewhat. "No, of course not. It's just..."

"I get it," she said, walking towards the hall. "I was expecting someone though, so it's fine. I'll just take care of this, and then we can get back to it, okay?"

"Sure," he said, letting out a deep breath, forcing himself to relax as he eased back down onto the loveseat. As Neba turned into the hall, he chastised himself for being so paranoid. Of course he was safe. Of course everything was okay. He was with Aunt Neba. It wasn't like any cultists, or even Manascetti, was going to actually mess with a Wizard of her caliber.

Wiping his eyes, he slumped forward, staring down at the coffee table, feeling more like a Rickwit than he had in a while. The last few days had been pretty stressful, so he figured it was to be expected, but still. For a moment there, he'd actually been afraid, with Neba sitting right across from him.

Right there. Drinking her coffee. From her Riscadil University mug.

It took a moment for that to sink in.

When it did, Rick turned his head, looking at the awards and commendations on her wall much more closely. Slowly he stood, his mind reeling, his entire world turning on the side.

"Ricky," Neba said.

Everything was moving so slow. He couldn't quite grasp reality. He'd had his problems with that in the past, yes, but nothing like this. His entire body felt as if he was trying to move through molasses. As if he were in a dream. A really awful dream.

Neba stood in the doorway to the hall. Two men flanked her, a human with a shock of white hair, and a Chthonian with lavender skin. Both of them were holding guns. Actual guns. Aimed right at him.

"Richard Wonder," St. Clair said. "Hands on your head. Now."

"Neba," Rick managed. "I don't understand. You... you knew... all along, you knew."

"Now," St. Clair shouted, pulling back the hammer on his revolver.

"Percy," Tanabuar hissed.

"Molly," St. Clair warned.

"Ricky, calm down," Neba urged.

"Stay back, professor," St. Clair said, putting a hand out in front of her.

"It was you," Rick stammered, feeling as if he was falling into a long, dark pit. Tears stung his eyes as his heart ached and his stomach tied itself in a knot. "You were... Neba... why?"

Tanabuar holstered his weapon, easing towards Rick. "Percy, that's enough. The kid's not resisting. Just, back down a little, okay?"

St. Clair said nothing, the gun in his hand so heavy, but not wavering even slightly. Seeing the look on his partner's face, Tanabuar moved to Rick's side, touching his shoulder lightly.

"Richard, I need you to take your hands off those swords, okay?"

Looking to the Chthonian for a moment, then down, Rick saw he was gripping the hilts and had them slightly pulled. Shocked, he let go, not even sure what was happening.

"I didn't... no... this isn't right..."

"It's okay," Tanabuar urged calmly. "I just need you to help me here. Come on, man. We're Royal Inspectors, okay? We're the good guys, yeah?"

Rick blinked several times, lost and dazed. "I don't... I mean... yeah... I know, but..."

His heart pounding, Tanabuar took Rick by the elbow and nudged his arm up. "Please, Richard. I know you don't want to hurt anyone and neither do we. Let's just figure this out. Come on, buddy."

Nodding, Rick did as he asked, raising his hands and putting them on the back of his head. He felt Tanabuar release his sword belt, heard it hit the floor, and for a moment, it sounded almost like a death knell. Then he was being handcuffed.

"Percy," Tanabuar said. "I've got him."

St. Clair's hand trembled for the first time, before he pulled the gun up then lowered it. "Good. Well done, Molly."

"Okay, good," the Chthonian breathed a sigh of relief. "Good job, Richard. We're okay now. Everything is okay now."

"It isn't," Rick whispered, staring at Neba in anguish.

"Good job tipping us he was here, professor," St. Clair said, holstering his weapon.

"I'm glad you came, Percival," Neba replied, patting his shoulder. "It's a relief to know you haven't forgotten your old teacher."

"Never," he assured.

"Neba, why," Rick stammered as Tanabuar guided him towards the door.

"The world has changed, Ricky," she said, reaching out to stroke his cheek. "I did this to protect you. I'm sorry."

"No," he cried. "Why did you lie to me? You knew. You knew Mimi. You knew Lucinia. You knew everything. Neba, you must know, they're trying to bring Obedell back. What are you doing?"

"He's not a threat, Percival," Neba said looking at St. Clair. "He's just confused."

"Neba, why?" Rick shouted as Tanabuar pulled him away.

"Because the world has changed, Ricky," she said.

"We'll take care of him from here, professor," St. Clair told her. "Don't worry. We're just after the facts."

"I know. It's just that he's so confused," Neba replied, a slow smile crawling over her face as Rick was dragged from her home. "It breaks my heart."

Chapter Ten: Jailbreak

"BREAKING NEWS AT THIS HOUR. Royal Inspectors arrested a suspect in connection with the recent Auberdeen double homicide in the abandoned processing yards. Richard Wonder, rumored to be the son of legendary hero Max Wonder, was taken into custody at the home of Neba Valsail. Valsail, once a member of Max Wonder's team of heroes, reportedly contacted authorities herself after Richard Wonder broke into her home. Royal Inspectors have yet to release an official statement, but it is believed they will be charging Richard Wonder within the next few hours. And now, back to the Earl Gilmore Band, on today's New Jazz Radio."

Lancaster turned the radio off, staring at it morosely. He'd known letting Rick go alone was a bad idea. His gut instinct had screamed at him not to do it. Yet he had, and now Rick was in custody, and who could know how long he would live, defenseless and with no backup.

Behind him, he heard Emi crying and clenched his fists. It was just the three of them now, and they had little to work with. No allies, no real skills, no resources, nothing that could help Rick or stop their enemies. Never in his life had he felt so helpless or powerless.

"Okay, that's bad news," Toddson said softly. "Now what?"

"Now nothing," Lancaster growled. "That's it. We're finished. The only thing left is to try and figure out how to get out of town."

"And abandon Rick?" Emi all but yelled, glaring at Lancaster past tears.

The Rogue tried to look at her, but found he couldn't meet her eyes. "I don't know what else to do."

"We could start by coming up with a plan that doesn't involve running away," Toddson offered. "Or have I forgotten something?"

"Probably, yeah," Lancaster snorted. "I don't like it, either, but it isn't like we're running ¦and hiding. There is one last place we can go. One last thing we can try."

"Which is?" the Cleric asked.

Lancaster turned, facing them. "We go to Townglen. We get Delilah Wonder and Castor Rumble. Maybe, with their help, we can still get out from under this, save Rick and not get killed, in jail, or both."

"Or we could..." Emi started, rubbing her eyes on her sleeve.

"That's two weeks just to get there," Toddson shouted. "A month before we're back! Rick doesn't have that long, Lanny! Hell, the world probably doesn't have that long before those crazy necromancers bring Obedell back!"

"Guys, I think..." Emi tried again.

"It's all I've got," Lancaster yelled back at him. "I get that it's a risk, that we'll probably fail, but I don't know what else to do here, okay?"

"Wait, I had an idea..." Emi begged.

Toddson shoved to his feet. "We don't run. If we do, then we fail. I think my god set us on this path to stop this, which means we still have a chance. We just have to figure out what it is."

"Please, listen..." Emi fumbled.

Lancaster threw his hands up. "Well, maybe a little divine intervention to give us a clue would be helpful at the moment, you think? Cause short of that, I don't see any way to rescue Rick from the freaking Royal Inspectors' office, much less stop the damned Hazaminie, and that's not even mentioning the Ironriggers, who are also out for our heads."

Emi rolled her eyes and wondered why boys were so dumb.

"Okay, yeah, it's a challenge," Toddson admitted. "But I've got faith. We just gotta dig deep, find our way, and trust that everything is going to work out."

Lancaster gaped at him. "That's it? That's your plan? Have faith? Are you serious right now? Cause we need a lot more than a plucky attitude if we're gonna get out of this, and this is me saying that, so you know, maybe take that into consideration, yeah?"

"Okay, that's a fair point," Toddson said, waving a hand at him. "But still, we can't just leave Rick. He wouldn't leave one of us."

"He left Mimi," Lancaster countered.

"That was low," Toddson told him after a long pause. "He had no choice. None of us did. Besides, Mimi was dead. Rick isn't."

"Yet," Lancaster shot back.

"The longer we leave him where Manascetti's guys can get to him, the worse his chances of staying alive get," Toddson said, trying to recover his calm. "Until we've explored every option, I say we stay."

Lancaster bowed his head, taking a moment to settle himself. "It's not like I disagree, Todd. I don't. I want to save him, too. I just don't see how. It's the three of us against damn near the whole city, and I don't see any other way. So, unless one of you has an idea, I think we need to find a way to get to Townglen, as fast as possible."

"I've got an idea," Emi said, thankful they had both stopped talking long enough to hear her.

Both men turned to look at her in surprise, with Lancaster asking, "You have an idea?"

"Um... yes," Emi mumbled, suddenly uncomfortable under their doubtful gaze. "Just the one, and it's probably terrible."

"Well, by all means, let's hear it," Lancaster exclaimed.

Toddson slapped him upside the head. "Hey, be nice. At least she has an idea."

Giving Emi a chagrined look, Lancaster waved her to go ahead. She shuffled her feet a moment, afraid to say it out loud, until Toddson offered her a kind smile. She closed her eyes, thought of Rick and nodded to herself.

"The other day, when Rick and I went to look into Lucinia, I met some of Rick's friends," she told them. "I think they may be able to help us. We just need to get to them and see if they can."

"Rick has friends other than us?" Lancaster asked, honestly surprised by that.

Toddson slapped him again before asking, "Who were these friends, and can we trust them? Cause Rick thought he could trust that Neba lady, and that didn't work out so well for him."

"I think we can, yes," she replied, forcing herself to be as brave as possible. "And I know which one to start with."

The door to the downstairs part of the shop creaked open as Larry pushed his way through. "Now that, young lady, is an adventurer's spirit. Sure, you're probably gonna get caught and killed, but at least you're thinking, utilizing resources and making a grab at victory instead of running away."

"Grandpa," Lancaster stated, only to fall silent as the old man held up a hand.

"I didn't want this life for you, boy, but here it is," he said slowly. "You're in the thicket now. Takes me back. All you can do when it gets dark and scary like this, is keep pushing ahead, using anything you can to get through. The girl's got the right idea. So where's your spine, huh?"

Slumping, Lancaster stared at his feet. "I didn't expect it to be this hard, Grandpa. I thought I could just bullshit my way through, and with the right people, everything would work out. Now though, we have to be realistic. We have to think things through logically. If we go out there, we won't last long enough to do anything."

"Probably not," Larry agreed with a shrug. "But better to fail at trying than to run away, do nothing and fail anyway."

"That wasn't exactly inspiring, sir," Toddson grumbled.

"Eh, I was never good at that part," Larry told him, waving it off. "Never mind that, though. Go to my bedroom, Lancaster, you big dumb ass, and get into my chest. The one I keep locked. You'll find something there that can help you."

"Seriously?" Lancaster asked in disbelief. "You're gonna help us?"

"Nope," Larry said as he turned to go, throwing a wink in Emi's direction. "You weren't even here. Never met the lot of you. Don't know a damn thing."

Glancing at each other as he left, the three remaining members of Powerage shrugged. What did they really have left to lose at this point? For better or worse, they could at least try and spring Rick and stop the return of Obedell.

* * *

St. Clair stared at Rick through a two-way mirror, going over his story, taking it apart, looking at every detail, examining it for any flaw. He somewhat hated that he couldn't find one. It would've been easier if he could.

"He's telling the truth," Tanabuar commented.

"Obviously," St. Clair replied distantly.

"So, what's up with the pensive face, then?" his partner nudged.

St. Clair shook his head. "It all fits too well. Too neatly."

Tanabuar gaped at that, then threw his hands up. "Give me a break, will you? Usually you love it when that happens!"

"I love it when I do it," the human retorted. "When someone else does it, it's kind of annoying."

"Welcome to my world," the Chthonian grumbled. "Point is, now we know. He's not the bad guy in this."

St. Clair tugged his glasses off, rubbing his eyes with the back of his hand. "Yes, I get it, Molly. We're too far into it now, though. We have a chance here, and we have to take it."

"Percy, I need you to back up, and get some perspective," Tanabuar replied, his voice heavy with fear. "This is not what we talked about. All of it rested on Rick in there being in the know."

"And I remain unconvinced he isn't," St. Clair stated. "While his story does add up, and certainly explains everything, he could easily be leaving out his own guilt."

"Are you serious right now?" Tanabuar groaned. "You know he's innocent. You just said so!"

"He's a suspect, Molly," his partner pointed out. "We have to take everything he says with a grain of salt."

"Yeah, okay, fine," Tanabuar argued, waving all of that away. "But still, if he *is* innocent, like *I* think he is, then what we're about to do could cost us both our badges."

St. Clair snorted at that. "You're letting his family name influence you."

Tanabuar all but screamed at the ceiling in frustration. "Percy, when you recruited me, you said it was because you needed my gut instinct. That is literally the entire reason I am standing here right now. Am I wrong?"

Giving him a pained look, St. Clair twisted his glasses in his hand a moment, then put them back on. "No. You are not wrong. I do need that. I am aware of my own shortcomings. You are, and have been for many years, the best partner I've ever had."

"Then listen to what I'm saying, please," Tanabuar pleaded. "You are trying to justify what we're doing, and ignoring the evidence in front of you to do it. Talk to him. Give him the option to work with us. *He's* not the bad guy. *He's* innocent, and maybe, just maybe, he can help us."

Shaking his head slowly, St. Clair sighed. "I'll consider it. Let me talk to him one more time, and I'll decide after that. Fair?"

"No," his partner snorted. "But from you, that's a huge concession, so I'll take it."

St. Clair laughed at that. "Thanks. I feel deeply loved right now."

"You're lucky you don't feel me slapping you in the head right now," Tanabuar retorted.

"Fair enough," the human agreed. "Go get a team to check out the Hawthorne. I'm going to start preparing the train like we discussed. It's an easy enough thing to stop, but a difficult thing to start. Best we cover our bases. Then, I promise, I'll talk to him again."

His dislike of this clear on his face, Tanabuar nodded anyway. "Fine. This goes bad, Percy..."

"Your objection was noted on the record," St. Clair said, holding up a hand. "I told you, I wouldn't let this fall on your head."

"Your head is the one I'm worried about right now," the Chthonian muttered with a grimace before grabbing his jacket and leaving to do as his partner asked.

Alone in the room, St. Clair admitted to himself his own doubts. He had taken many gambles in his career and they'd always paid off. This one, however, felt different. There were more variables in play than he'd anticipated. Factors that he had failed to predict. As Tanabuar had said, this could all go wrong, far too easily.

Accepting it, St. Clair headed out to set things in motion.

* * *

Emi sat on a bench not far from Rumble Park and waited, huddled in the cloak Lancaster's grandfather had provided. While it was no Chameleon Ring, it did have a mild enchantment on it that caused a perception distortion around her, making the eye travel over her as if she weren't there. Not as good as invisibility, but it didn't trip a Puffer's arcane detection senses the way true invisibility would.

She almost would have preferred actual invisibility. She was more nervous than she'd ever been in her entire life. It felt as if her vision was funneling to a point, like she might faint at any moment. Not to mention, there was the chance that she could sit there all day and Enzo wouldn't notice her any more than anyone else would.

Glancing to her right, she saw Lancaster loitering half a block away. To her left Toddson did the same. Feeling slightly reassured by that, she sighed and waited, hoping that the Goblin would be able to help them. He and Rick seemed to have a friendship, but she'd never really been good at judging people, so this may all be for nothing.

Without Enzo, her whole plan went up in smoke, too.

"What we got here?" a voice whispered in her ear. "Little girl trying to post up, and not get noticed. That be extra coin, or get bled."

Turning her head, she looked in Enzo's eyes, and struggled to make any noise that wasn't squeaking. She failed completely, but she tried, and for her, that was something.

"Emi?" Enzo asked, startled as her face came into focus. "Hey, it is you! The racist Elf girl! What are you doing here?"

"I'm... um..." Emi stammered, then started crying. She didn't want to. She hated herself for it. Always so weak. Always so quick to get weepy at any little thing. She was pathetic and always had been.

"Hey, whoa," Enzo said as he climbed over the back of the bench. "I'm sorry. I was just joking. I didn't mean that. You okay?"

"Rick's been arrested," Emi wailed, grabbing him and hugging him.

Enzo patted her shoulder lightly, unsure what to do. "Yeah, I heard. Bunch of crap if you ask me."

Pulling herself together, Emi pushed him back, staring at him intently. "I need your help to get him out."

Enzo felt certain mental whiplash was a thing a person could get, and that he just had. "What? Back up. You wanna what?"

"Bust him out. Spring him. Stop the coppers from making him cool his heels in the slammer," Emi blathered.

"Slow down," the Goblin begged, shaking her slightly. "Emi, that's really... crazy of you. This is the Royal Inspectors we're talking about here, not the local police station. It'd take an army to get him out of there."

"That's why I need your help," she said, sniffling again. "I can't do this without you, Enzo! You're my only hope!"

"Oh, for crying out loud," he groaned. "Look, I'd love to help you out, and Rick too, of course, but man, there's no way to spring him from a place like that."

"If we don't, Manascetti's bad cops will kill him," Emi pleaded. "And those Hazaminie guys are about to bring Obedell back from the beyond, and we can't do this without Rick, so we just gotta get him out, and I don't know anybody else who can help us, so it's gotta be you!"

Enzo blinked several times. "The who the what now?"

Near to hyperventilating, Emi took several gulping breaths to calm herself, and explained the entire situation to him. Enzo listened, nodding along, getting most of it. Enough, at least, to know he should be incredibly terrified right now. Like, immediately and very.

"Okay, I get it," he said, shaking her to get her to stop talking. "Still, what you're asking, it may not be possible, okay? I can poke around and ask a few questions of the right people, but I can't promise anything, yeah?"

"I know," Emi whimpered. "I just don't know who else to go to. Everyone else has it in for us, and you seemed like you wouldn't betray him, or us, so, I thought, maybe, you might could help."

"That's a big maybe," the Goblin admitted, then looked into her frightened, sad eyes again, and sighed heavily. "But I can try. Okay?"

Emi nodded. "Okay. Thank you."

Wondering why he always had such a soft spot for hard luck cases, Enzo dug out his notepad and scribbled an address for her. "Meet me here later on. If I'm not there, wait for me. You'll be safe. Deal?"

"Deal," Emi agreed as she took the offered note and stuck it in her pocket. "I've got one other thing to do, then I'll head there."

"Okay, but be careful, will you?" Enzo said, feeling genuinely bad for the Elf. "Sounds like you guys got yourselves into one hell of a mess."

"We did," she sighed. "But right now, I just want to help Rick."

"Same goes for me, doll," he told her, offering her a smile. Getting one in return, he patted her shoulder and hopped up. "Wait for me, got that?"

Emi nodded vigorously, feeling relived. At least they had one ally, after all.

* * *

St. Clair stepped into the interrogation room, having already made arrangements for Rick to be transferred to the Sentry Island facility. Located on the outer edge of Copper's Bay and accessible only by train rail, the former fort, once the city's bastion of defense, had some years ago been rebuilt into a state of the art housing site for suspects and a central operations hub for the Royal Inspectors across the west coast of Liaob.

Tanabuar had a point he couldn't ignore, however. Rick was obviously innocent. Which meant that if things went the way he planned for them to, he was risking the young man's life without his consent, and that went against everything his badge, and the oath he'd sworn, stood for.

He wasn't just gambling his career. He was gambling Rick's life. He had to be certain.

"Mr. Wonder," he said as he sat across the table.

"If you want me to go over it all again," Rick groaned, "I'm sorry to tell you this, but it's gonna be the same story I've already told you three times."

St. Clair gave a slow nod. "No, I don't think there's any need to go over it again. At the very least, you've convinced my partner enough that we're sending officers to investigate the theater."

"I hope you're telling them to be careful," Rick replied, a slight note of panic in his voice. "The ones we tangled with had this wand..."

"A fireburst wand, yes," St. Clair cut in. "They are being properly equipped and briefed. We'll know soon enough if your story is true or not. That isn't what I wanted to talk to you about though."

"Really," Rick said in disbelief. "Cause that kind of seems like the bigger issue at the moment."

"Perhaps," St. Clair said slowly, folding his hands in front of him. "Tonight, you will be transferred to a secure facility, where you will likely be a guest for some time. How long depends entirely on how that investigation goes and how you answer the next few questions I have for you."

"Fantastic," Rick sighed, slumping over the table.

"There's a few things I don't understand, and I want you to explain them to me," he said, then hesitated a moment. "It doesn't make logical sense to me, and I am trying to understand these things, but I just can't."

"So, ask away," Rick groaned, sitting back up. Even his happy place offered him no comfort anymore.

"Why did you leave Miss Avaman in the packing facility?"

Rick shrugged. "I told you already, she died very suddenly, and we were all shocked. Most of us froze up in that moment. The Hazaminie, they had that wand and crossbows. There was no way we could cover the distance, not without more of us dying. I made the decision to run in order to save the lives of my team members. That's all there was to it."

"Yes, but, you have the Whip Blades, do you not?" St. Clair pressed. "Surely, with those..."

"I can't make them work," Rick bit out, glaring at him. "I'm not my dad. I never was. I never will be. For a while, I thought maybe I could be, but I see now that I was wrong. I can't use them the way he could, 'cause I'm not good enough, and Mimi died because of that, okay?"

St. Clair leaned back, considering that for a moment. "Very well. I can understand your desire to protect the rest of your team. However, I must also ask how you came into possession of a Chameleon Ring."

"That, I'm not going to tell you," Rick stated.

"Mr. Wonder, at this point..."

"I was given it, and that's all I'm saying," Rick interrupted. "There's no point, and no good, in dragging anyone else into this."

St. Clair nodded. "If you are trying to protect Charlotte Goodkin, I should tell you, I already suspect you got it from her. Miss Landari's home address is Ms. Goodkin's residence, and after a brief look into her background, I can surmise you acquired it from her."

"Wow," Rick snorted. "You already know everything. Makes me wonder why you're talking to me at all."

"I'll take that as a yes," St. Clair said. "Last question, Mr. Wonder. You told me about your visit to the theater. Why didn't you come straight to us after that? I can understand your fear of Manascetti's dirty cops, but surely you could have turned yourself in to Anton Strakinsy, and he would've brought you to my partner and me. So, why didn't you do that? Why bring Professor Valsail into this?"

Rick looked at him in surprise. "Bring her into it? Aunty Neba was already involved in this. Man, you can't see the forest for the trees, can you?"

"What's that mean?"

"I didn't come to you, or Anton, because I didn't know who to trust," Rick told him, leaning forward, the anger in his voice thick. "I thought I could trust Aunt Neba, but look how that turned out. It's because she was already in on it all along."

"How so?" St. Clair asked, a tickle in the back of his mind keeping him hanging on Rick's every word.

"She's the professor of political science at Riscadil University," Rick told him, as if that explained it all. When St. Clair shook his head, Rick sighed, and laid it out for him. "Manascetti sent us there, claiming Lucinia was his ward and that she had changed after getting involved with the other political science kids. Mimi learned that was a lie after talking to the professor."

"Yes, but..."

"When I went back and confronted him about it, Manascetti admitted that he only sent us on that hunt because some of his men had seen Lucinia visiting the professor of political science," Rick continued. "And when I went to her and told her everything I've told you, she sat there and didn't say a word. She already knew, because she was already involved."

"I don't..."

Rick slammed his hands on the table. "You aren't listening! Neba knows Lucinia Avalinion, knows she came back from the dead, knew me and my team were looking for her, and knows all about Manascetti and the Hazaminie. I don't know what she's after, or whose side she's on, but she's been in on this from the start."

St. Clair sat for several moments, then nodded and stood. "Thank you, Mr. Wonder. That will be all. My partner and I will be back for your transfer later on this evening."

"Hey," Rick yelled as St. Clair left the room. "Are you even listening? She's in on it! Neba is on in it all!"

Out in the hall, St. Clair paused, pushing aside his personal feelings and everything else until he was left with nothing but cold, unattached logic. Examining it from that angle, he could not so easily dismiss Rick's claims.

"Hey," Tanabuar called as he came down the hall. "I got five officers heading out to check that theater. They'll be leaving in about an hour or so. What's up with you? You look paler than usual."

"Molly," St. Clair said slowly. "I think perhaps your gut instinct was right. I'm going to finish making preparations for Mr. Wonder's transfer. We'll go ahead with the plan, though there has been a wrinkle, and it does give me pause."

Tanabuar said nothing for a moment. "Percy, we can still back out of this. If that train leaves, we can't."

"I am aware, yes," he agreed, nodding. "We went over the risks. I still believe they may be worth the reward. I also believe our guest in there is as innocent as you think. Not that it matters. I don't think we have any choice but to use him, with or without his consent..."

"What happened?"

"I'll explain it later," his partner assured him. "Once this is done, you and I need to bring in Neba Valsail for questioning."

"Why?" Tanabuar asked, completely lost.

"Because, I suspect she knows the truth behind why Lucinia Avalinion doesn't seem to want to stay dead, and if I am right, she may well have had a hand in creating that phenomenon."

"Oh," Tanabuar replied. "Shit."

* * *

Across town, Emi was stepping into the lobby of the Cantasol, feeling braver than she had in her entire life. Things had gone well with Enzo, and while she wasn't ready to call herself a newer, braver Emi, she did at least feel some measure of confidence in herself for once.

Mastoval was already approaching as she flipped the hood of the cloak back, Lancaster and Toddson joining her. The Half-Elf paused as his face registered recognition and surprise. It lasted only a moment, however, before his soft smile returned and he joined them.

"Miss, it's good to see you again," he said. "Though, I think perhaps this is not the best place for you to be at this time."

"It isn't, and we won't be staying long," Emi replied, hanging on to that bit of courage she'd found. "I'm just here to ask you to deliver a message."

"To whom?" Mastoval inquired, meeting her gaze with one that was calm, steady and somehow, she found, reassuring.

"Lucinia Avalinion," she told him. "I know she didn't stay dead after what happened in the packing facility over in Auberdeen. I also know she's staying here, and you are aware of who she is, and probably, what she's doing. So, I want you tell her something for me."

Mastoval's smile faded slightly. "I see. I can't say that I understand, but I will of course hear this message, and if my path happens to cross with the lady in question, I'll be sure to deliver it."

Emi's jaw worked slightly, not in anger, but in doubt. Steeling herself, she forged ahead. "Rick's been arrested for her murder. That's wrong, because she stabbed herself. We plan to bust him out from the Royal Inspectors' office, and stop the Hazaminie from summoning Obedell back. I think she may be trying to do the same. If she is, tell her what we're doing. Tell her we're on the same side and it'd be nice if we could work together to get what we all want."

Mastoval nodded slightly. "I will deliver this message, should I ever have the fortune to meet Miss Avalinion."

"She's upstairs, in the penthouse," Emi shot back. "Don't give me the act, Mr. Mastoval. I don't have time for it."

Wondering just what had changed the nervous young woman he'd last seen into this, Mastoval considered her for a moment, then nodded again. "It will be done, Miss."

"On your Scouts' Honor," she pressed.

"On my Scouts' Honor," Mastoval agreed after a moment's hesitation.

Nodding, Emi flipped the hood back up, and led the other two back outside. Turning into the first alley she saw, she paused, grabbing the wall to hold herself up as her nerves threatened to betray her. Feeling Lancaster and Toddson grab her by the elbows, she offered them a wan smile and steadied herself.

"Emi, I don't know what's come over you, but I like it," Lancaster said once she seemed to be okay.

"Same here," Toddson said with a grin. "You're a good leader in Rick's absence."

"Thanks," she said with a nervous laugh. "I don't think I could do that again, though. I almost fainted."

"You're tougher than you give yourself credit for," Lancaster said, patting her back. "Though I'm wondering, what was that about the Scouts' Honor?"

"He said it before, when Rick and I were here," she told him. "He was a Wonder Scout back when. It was Max Wonder's fan club for young people. Giving your word, on your Scouts' Honor, was the same as a promise you couldn't break."

"How about that," Lancaster marveled. "Learn something new every day."

"It's how I knew I could trust him," Emi agreed. "Hopefully, Lucinia will help us rescue Rick. Otherwise, I don't know what we're going to do."

"Figure it out," Toddson said, shrugging. "That's all we can do."

"Yeah," Lancaster grinned. "What he said."

Smiling, Emi nodded. "Yeah. Of course. Let's go. It's best if we aren't on the streets too much right now."

With that, Powerage headed out, hoping against hope to save Rick, and the day.

* * *

The address Enzo had provided turned out to be an abandoned shop front, not far from Wonder Plaza. Everyone decided it was best not to ponder on that too much as they made their way as deep into the place as they could. Long empty, judging from the graffiti on the walls and faint stench of urine that permeated the air, they all agreed it was unlikely any of their assorted enemies would find them there.

Settling in to await Enzo, they all soon realized just how long they had been awake, as sleep claimed them for several hours. The events of the previous day and night, as well as the new day, had taken a toll, leaving Emi to wonder if her burst of assertiveness had been little more than sleep deprivation.

She was snoring before she could consider that any further.

The sun was low on the horizon when Enzo woke Emi, shaking her gently. Coming to and realizing she'd fallen asleep, she almost panicked. Backing up a step, the Goblin assured her she was safe and gave her a moment to calm herself.

"So, who are these guys?" he asked as she stood, shaking her head to clear the cobwebs.

"Lancaster and Toddson," she said. "The rest of our team. They're okay."

Nodding, he stood back, letting her rouse them. While he doubted Emi could've hurt him seriously, aside from poking him in the eye while she flailed, the other two looked much more capable.

Once they were all awake, Enzo offered them some food he had collected on the way. Little more than sandwiches and pie, it was still more than they'd had since morning. A thermos of tea finished it off, and with that done, they looked to each other, ready to hear what the Goblin had learned.

"Well, it ain't good news, I can tell you that," Enzo said, perching on an old barrel. "The Royal Inspectors, according to my source, are preparing to transfer Rick to the Sentry Island building. It's their base of operations for the west coast, so once he's in there, any hope we have of getting him out is gone."

"Nobody said it would be easy," Emi offered, hoping she sounded braver than she felt.

"How are they moving him?" Lancaster asked.

"By train," the Goblin said. "Only way to and from the island is a trestle bridge, and maybe about twenty blocks of track in town. It's a one-way line that goes from the R. I. office to Sentry Island, used only to move supplies, personnel and prisoners. So, odds are, it'll be pretty heavily guarded.

"This is not looking good," Toddson grumbled.

"Not really, no," Lancaster agreed. "But, we've got twenty blocks to pick a spot to try and get on the train, get Rick, and get off. That's something, at least."

"So, where is this line?" Emi asked.

"Beats me," Enzo shrugged. "Most of the lines around here are underground now. I don't know about any aboveground ones, either. It may run below the streets until it hits the trestle for all I know. That twenty block part is just a maybe, like I said. Which, I might point out, throws this rescue plan out the window."

"Right, so we need to find that out," Lancaster said, waving the matter off. "Anybody know anything about local train lines?"

"Actually," Emi said. "I know just the person to ask."

Toddson and Lancaster exchanged a look of surprise, with the Rogue asking, "Okay, so, let's say we find a point where we can do this. What then? It's not like we can just lay siege to a moving train."

Reaching into her satchel, Emi pulled out the wand Rick had taken from the Hazaminie leader in the packing facility. "How about this?"

"Where the hell you get that?" Enzo yelped.

"Long story," Lancaster told him. "But this gives me an idea, and maybe a plan. First, we need to know if there's a point we can hit the train. If so, we might have a chance here."

"Okay, then," Enzo offered doubtfully. "Let's go see this person you know."

"You don't have to come with us," Emi told him, passing the wand over to Lancaster. "This is going to be dangerous. You've done more than enough already, so it's fine if you want to sit the rest out."

"I probably will," Enzo told her with a laugh. "For now, though, I'm kind of curious, so I figure I'll hang with you guys a bit."

"Even that's pretty risky," Toddson told him. "Especially as I'm without even my armor right now."

"Where'd you leave it?" the Goblin asked.

"Charlotte Goodkin's," the Cleric replied. "You know her?"

"Can't say I do, but if you give me an address, I can go pick it up and meet you guys back here."

Nodding, Toddson dug out his notebook, and then stared at it for a minute, before offering it to Emi. Smiling slightly, she jotted it down and pulled out the page, saying, "It might be being watched, so be careful, okay?"

"Guy like me always has to be careful," he chuckled. "You guys do the same, and just know, if you die or get busted before you get back here, I'm gonna pawn that armor."

"Nice to know," Lancaster scowled.

"Nah, it's cool, I get it," Toddson said, giving the Goblin a thumbs-up.

"Whatever," the Rogue sighed.

* * *

"Okay," Lancaster mused as he looked around. "I guess the train station is the place to find a guy who knows about trains."

"Hang on," Emi said, ignoring the Rogue. "Over there. That's the guy. Leo, I think is his name. He seemed to know a good bit, or at least, can point us to someone who does."

"Let's go see a man about a train, then," Toddson said before walking away.

"You sure about this, Emi?" Lancaster asked, holding her back a moment. "I mean, we're trusting an awful lot of people here."

"I know, and believe me, it makes me nervous, too," she told him. "But at this point, I don't think we really have much to lose."

Accepting that she wasn't wrong about that, Lancaster waved her on and trailed behind, keeping an eye out for anyone who looked fishy. Of course, they were in the center of the main station for the whole of Riscadil, so fishy quickly became subjective.

A moment later, the trio closed around Leo as he finished loading some bags onto a cart. It took him a moment to notice them in their cloaks, but as he did, he put on a nervous smile, tipping his hat their way, saying, "Just be a moment, lads."

Emi pulled back her hood. "Leo, isn't it? We met the other day. I was with Rick Wonder."

Recognition lit his eyes after a moment as a more relaxed smile settled in. "Ah, right. I remember you, Miss. I'm guessing you come around on account of what they're saying on the radio. Right bit of nonsense, Ricky being some kind of criminal and all."

"Actually, yes, that's exactly why we're here," Lancaster put in, flipping his own hood back. "We need to ask you a rather odd question. Hopefully, you can help us out."

Leo gave him a curious look, but nodded anyway, waving another porter over to handle the luggage cart. "If I can help, then I will, of course. Any friend of Rick's and all."

Motioning him to join them someplace less crowded, they quickly explained the situation to him, as well as what there was of their plan. Leo's smile faded quickly the more they talked, replaced by a growing look of horror at what they were suggesting. Shaking his head, he backed away a step.

"I'm all for helping Rick, don't get me wrong, but this, now. I don't know. This is proper criminal activity and all. You'll have to excuse me, but I don't think I want to be getting involved in all that."

"You won't be," Emi assured him. "We just need to know where the R. I. line runs. That's all."

"Even if I tell you," he hesitated, "I don't think this is such a bright idea, to be honest. I mean, you're talking about assaulting a Royal Inspector vehicle. That's right bonkers."

"He's not wrong," Lancaster intoned.

"What choice do we have?" Emi asked, waving at the Rogue to hush.

"She's not wrong," Toddson said with a grin.

"You hush, too," Lancaster grumbled.

"Please, Leo," Emi begged. "If for no other reason than to satisfy your Scouts' Honor."

Sagging at that, Leo grumbled to himself a moment, then nodded. "Fine. I can mark it on a map for you. Just don't be telling nobody that I was involved, right? Much as I want to help Rick out, I'm in no hurry to be an accessory to a crime."

"Count on it," Emi pledged. "No one will ever know you were involved."

"Fine," he sighed. "Give me a couple minutes. I'll be right back."

As he walked away, Lancaster nudged Emi gently. "Him, too, huh?"

"Yeah," she said with a shy smile. "I hate putting him in this position, but what choice do we have?"

"We keep saying that a lot," Lancaster pointed out. "Enough so, it's making me uneasy."

"Me too," Emi admitted. "I guess this is where we find out if we're really cut out to be adventurers or not, though."

"Having no other choice will do that," Toddson added sagely with a nod.

Emi and Lancaster gave him a curious look, but got only his casual grin in return. Long past being surprised by his odd statements, they looked at each other, shrugged, and admitted he was right. They really did have no choice now but to find out if they actually had what it took to do this all the time.

So far, the outcome did not look promising.

* * *

After joining back up with Enzo, Powerage set about organizing their plan. Half the Royal Inspector private line traveled underground, but it reached the surface on the north side of town, where it passed through an abandoned rail yard before looping back near the edge of Copper's Bay to the bridge, and finally, the island. That gave them exactly one opportunity to catch it, just a mile before it and Rick would be out of their reach forever.

As Toddson donned his armor, Enzo let them know that Charlotte's home had been standing unlocked and it appeared as if a struggle had taken place. Concerned for her, the trio still decided to focus on helping Rick first. Whatever had happened at Charlotte's, Emi felt certain the hulking Orc could handle herself.

With their makeshift plan in place, Enzo offered to join them, knowing a shortcut to where they wanted to go. With a little luck, they could even beat the train and have time to set up their ambush. Unless, of course, Rick had already been transferred, in which case they would find out soon enough, when no train appeared.

Night had fallen by the time they arrived, and after exploring the area a little, they picked a spot where a natural hill on the north end of Old Town gave them their best advantage. Settling in, they began their wait, hoping against hope they weren't already too late.

"Mind if I ask you something?" Enzo nudged Emi after a bit.

"I don't guess so."

"Why you going so far out of your way for Rick?" the Goblin inquired, giving her a curious look. "I mean, he's a nice guy and all, but still, this is pretty heavy stuff you're doing. You sweet on him or something?"

Emi flushed brightly at that. "No! Nothing like that! It's just... I mean... he's part of our team... and our leader... and stuff. He'd do it for us, I think. That's all."

"That was almost convincing," Enzo smirked.

"Almost," Lancaster chuckled from a few feet away.

"Not really," Toddson snickered to Emi's other side.

"Hey," she whimpered. "I mean, he's good-looking and all, but he's got a girlfriend already, so it wouldn't do me any good anyway."

"Well, when this is over, if you want a boyfriend, I'm available," Lancaster suggested with a wink.

Emi made a face that left him feeling less happy than he'd have liked. "I think I'd be better off with Enzo."

"That almost made me feel good," the Goblin muttered.

"Not me," Lancaster pouted.

"I'm feeling pretty good," Toddson offered.

Lancaster threw a rock at him.

"How about we don't talk about my lack of a love life," Emi suggested. "Odds are, we're all going to be dead soon anyway, so it's not like it matters."

"She's got a point," Enzo admitted. "You guys are all probably gonna die here pretty quick."

"You're here, too," Lancaster pointed out.

"Yeah, which just makes me as dumb as the rest of you," the Goblin chuckled. "Just had to go and get a soft spot for the big, dumb hucko."

"Light, in the distance," Toddson hissed. "I think it's the train."

"Showtime," Lancaster said, pushing to his feet, wand in hand. "Here goes nothing."

* * *

Rick glared at the floor, wondering if it had actually been necessary to chain him hand and foot. Of course, it was probably just standard procedure, but still. Also, he had to pee kind of bad. That wasn't a really important thing, he knew, but along with everything else, it was pretty annoying.

"You've been awfully quiet," St. Clair said.

"Not much left to say, is there?" Rick replied. "It's pretty obvious you aren't going to believe me anyway."

"I dunno about that," Tanabuar grinned. "But try looking at it this way, buddy. At least you'll be out of Manascetti's reach on Sentry Island. That's good news, isn't it?"

"If you say so," Rick groused, leaning back against the wall. "I'd rather be out there stopping the Hazaminie from calling Obedell back, though. At least that way, I'd be doing some good."

St. Clair smiled at that. "You still don't get it, do you? The world has changed, Richard. The work of protecting it falls to men like us now. I'm afraid you were just born to the wrong time for what you're looking for."

"If that's true," Rick said, throwing him a snide look. "Then why are there so many adventurers still around?"

"The past is a hard thing to let go of," Tanabuar answered. "Lots of people want those times to go on so they can be like the people they read about in history books. Sad truth is, the Abomination Wars and all the stuff that came after, it brought the world together in a way nothing else could, as well as getting rid of all the big threats guys like you use to go after. There's just nothing left for you guys to do."

"Except it was a guy like me who stumbled onto a plot to bring Obedell back," Rick said with a smirk. "Guys like you didn't even see it coming."

"If it's coming at all," St. Clair replied.

The door to the next car slid open, revealing Anton who gave Rick a pained look before saying, "Inspector Tanabuar, there's a call for you on the radio. Something about those guys you sent to look into a theater."

"Ah, answers come calling," the Chthonian grinned as he stood. "You be okay alone with our friend here while I get that, Percy?"

"There are ten armed guards in the cars on either side of us, and I've got my gun," St. Clair drawled. "I think I'll be fine with a prisoner who's bound hand and foot, Molly."

"Just checking," Tanabuar replied in a mock hurt tone. "No need to get snippy with me."

"I swear," St. Clair sighed as his partner left with Anton. "Sometimes, I think he believes he's my mother."

Rick gave him a soft smile. "If you really want to know, that's what we're all actually looking for. That kind of trust, like you two have. That's why we form into teams and chase down the most dangerous stuff we can find. We all want to have a bond with others where we know they'd die for us, and we'd die for them."

St. Clair considered that for a moment. "That's not such a bad thing, really. I just think there's better ways to go about it."

"If you pitch me the police work speech, I'll barf," Rick groaned. "I mean, you guys are aware of how many dirty cops there on the force, right?"

"All too aware, yes," St. Clair admitted. "But still, you have to..."

He never got to finish. An explosion ripped through the train before he could, sending the car airborne. St. Clair hit the wall, before being thrown into the ceiling, as Rick tried his best to brace himself. A split second later, they were rolling, the entire car separated from the rest of the train.

Over almost as quickly as it started, the car rocked slightly and went still, the lights having gone dark almost immediately, leaving them in the gloom. From outside, Rick could distantly hear the sounds of people shouting and gunfire.

Shaking his head, he tried to get his bearings and found the car had landed on its side. Reaching up to slap his own face, hoping to clear the stars he was seeing, he paused, realizing he was loose from the floor clamps. Shoving himself over, he pushed to his knees and spotted St. Clair a few feet away, lying face down.

A light flared outside, filling the car with brilliance before dimming slightly and seeming to hover. Shaking, Rick scrambled forward on his hands and knees, rolling St. Clair over. A gash on his head was bleeding badly, but otherwise he seemed okay, or at least Rick hoped he was.

"Sorry about this," he whispered, searching the Inspector's pockets quickly and turning up the keys to his manacles, as well as the man's gun. Ignoring that for a moment, he freed himself and glanced around, trying to decide what to do.

Heavy scrapping drew his attention as the door that had led to the next car was forced open. Breathing fast, his heart racing, Rick put a hand on St. Clair's gun, hoping like hell it was Tanabuar. A moment later, the door squealed open and a uniformed officer levered himself up, looking over both Rick and St. Clair.

"You guys hurt?"

Rick tightened his grip on the firearm as the officer climbed into the car. "I'm okay. St. Clair is hurt. Not bad, I don't think, but he's bleeding.

"Shame you shot him escaping," the officer grinned, pulling his sidearm and aiming it at Rick. "Manascetti sends his regards."

Rick yanked the revolver free, falling back and firing blind. It was heavy, more than his swords, and kicked, harder than he'd ever heard. It was loud, so incredibly loud. His back hit the wall of the car as he swung the gun back down, ready to fire again.

The officer was down, groping at his chest as blood poured from a wound. Gaining his feet quickly, Rick eased over, kicking the man's gun away, then backing up. A second later, the officer went limp.

"Hell of a thing, isn't it?" St. Clair asked.

Spinning, Rick found him awake and dragging himself back into a sitting position. Not meaning to, he pointed the gun at him.

"Technology," St. Clair coughed. "It gives us so much. Radio. Trains. But then it gives us that. The means to kill more efficiently than any Wizard. At least they have to incant. This, though. You just have to squeeze."

"I... I had to..." Rick stammered.

St. Clair gaze him a dazed look. "There's a reason people still carry swords, you know. You have to mean it with those. It has to be on purpose. A gun, on the other hand. It's too easy. Too impersonal. Accidents can happen. Too much can go wrong."

Rick lowered the weapon. "That's what your partner was afraid of at Neba's wasn't it? An accident?"

"Yeah," St. Clair said quietly. "Another one."

"Rick!"

Spinning towards the sound, he saw Emi's hat bob across the open door. Not sure what the hell was going on, he simply stared at it as it passed, trying to wrap his head around her being here, amidst all of this.

Unless...

"Emi!"

The hat bobbed back, hesitated, then turned into an Elf as she jumped, grabbing the door. "Rick! I found you! Are you okay?"

"I think so," he said. "What are you doing here? Did you do this?"

"Um... no," she said, slumping back down. "I mean, we were going to do something like this, but not this. Before we could, the locomotive exploded."

"Manascetti," St. Clair said. "He must really want you dead."

"You have no idea," Rick told him. "Emi, where are Lancaster and Toddson?"

She glanced around a moment. "Lancaster is getting your stuff, and Toddson is trying to help some people who are hurt. What do you want us to do?"

"Stay right there, I'm coming," Rick told her. "I just have to... um..."

He looked back down at St. Clair, then at the gun in his own hand. St. Clair sighed softly, already understanding the dilemma Rick faced. In his position, the Inspector knew what he would do.

He wasn't Rick Wonder, though.

Taking the gun in his other hand, Rick held it up butt out, and lowered himself into a crouch. "I'm not your enemy here, Inspector. I don't want to hurt anybody. You're gonna be tied up with this for a while, though, I think, and somebody has to stop the Hazaminie. I hope when we see each other next, you won't feel the need to have this with you."

With that, Rick placed the gun down and stood, going to join Emi. St. Clair watched him go, and with a smile, accepted he had been wrong about Rick Wonder. More than that, though, he saw Rick was wrong about himself.

He was just like his father.

Sliding out of the door, Rick hit the ground as the light, a flare he saw, faded. Grabbing Emi by the hand, he eased his way forward, glancing about as police officers wandered in a daze or lay on the ground, some screaming, others not.

Spotting Toddson a few yards off tending to a wounded man, Rick fell into a couch and went towards him.

From behind, he heard Tanabuar yelling for his partner, but didn't stop. St. Clair was most likely fine. Tanabuar would find him quickly enough. For now, Rick had to focus on getting him and his team out of there.

"Todd," Rick called, dropping to a knee as he reached the Cleric. "We gotta go, man. Come on."

"One second," Toddson said. "If I stop now, he'll die."

Looking down, Rick took in the officer stained in blood and gripping Toddson's hand tight as the Cleric poured healing magic into him. The faint hope in his eyes, the desperation, all of it was more than Rick could ignore.

"As soon as you got him, okay?"

"Yeah."

"Emi, Manascetti had at least one guy here, and somehow, I doubt that was all he had," Rick told her quickly. "Todd and I are out of this fight. Can you cover us?"

She went wide-eyed for a moment, then settled into a grim look. "I can."

"Richard," Tanabuar yelled, drawing Rick's eye back towards the derailed train to find the Chthonian stalking towards them, his weapon drawn.

"Inspector, wait," Rick called, holding up his hands. "Please. St. Clair is in the car. He's hurt, but I think he'll be okay."

Tanabuar hesitated. "Richard, I need you all to stop this. Please. Come on, man. Nobody else has to get hurt."

"This wasn't us," Rick yelled. "Look at us! He's saving this guy's life. She's not even armed. Neither am I. It was Manascetti, dammit!'

A pained look crossed the Inspector's face as he grappled with the obvious and his training. "I want to believe you, Richard. I do. But, come on! They were here!"

"So was one of Manascetti's dirty cops, Molly," Rick told him. "He came after me and St. Clair. I shot him. He's got to have more. We do not have time to argue about this!"

"Let's say I believe you," Tanabuar replied a moment before a gunshot sounded and his shoulder blew blood.

Stunned, Rick watched him collapse, bleeding heavily, as a man stood upon the overturned train car behind them, lining up Rick.

"Shit," Rick gasped.

"Firebolt!" Emi screamed.

Arcane energy swirled around her outstretched hand for a moment, before launching itself toward the man. Brilliant red, it arced almost too fast to follow, striking him in the face, sending him toppling back. Another shot sounded as his dying reflex pulled the trigger.

"Shit, Molly," Rick panted, scrambling over to roll the Chthonian on his back.

"Fuck me," Tanabuar wheezed. "That really fucking hurts!"

"Thank the gods," Rick whimpered, dropping his head on the man's chest. "I thought you were dead."

"Am I not?" he asked, seemingly surprised by that. "I feel like I am."

More gunshots rang out as Toddson pulled free of the officer he had been tending, shouting that he was done. Glancing back, Rick saw the man grasping the Cleric's hand, thanking him, as Toddson pulled away, grabbing Rick by the shoulder.

"Wait, this guy, he's hurt pretty bad," Rick said.

Toddson shook his head. "I'm tapped, Rick. I got nothing left. I'm sorry."

"Dammit," he yelled.

"Go, Richard," Tanabuar told him, pushing him away. "Go stop them. You gotta go stop them."

"I can't leave you like this," Rick insisted.

"There's nothing we can do now," the Chthonian pressed. "You're all we have left.

That message I got earlier. They told me the team we sent to the theater hadn't checked in. We're gonna be here with this mess for hours. You have to go, now."

Struggling with it, Rick finally nodded. "Do not die, okay?"

Tanabuar gave him a wry grin. "Well, I'm not real sure I can do much about that, either, but I'll give it my best shot."

Grasping his hand, Rick stood, waving to the other two. "Let's go."

Darting across the field towards the rise of the hill, Rick was blinded for a moment as another flare shot up from the far side. Slowing, he shielded his eyes. He wasn't sure who was firing those off, considering Emi and Toddson were with him, and Lancaster had to either be near the train or on his way back as well. Friend or foe, he figured he'd find out soon enough.

"Rick, down!"

He didn't even think. Wrapping an arm around each of his friends, he went to the ground at the sound of Enzo's voice. He didn't know what he was doing there, either, but as two shots sounded, he was sure glad he was. The flare had left him open, visible, and blind. An easy target.

* * *

St. Clair fell out of the car door as the second flare went up and shoving the pain aside, rolled to his feet as Rick and the others hit the ground.

Two men, one wearing a police uniform, fired on them, and then he saw Tanabuar down.

"Hey, hold fire," he yelled, limping forward. "Hold fire, dammit!"

The one in uniform spun, squeezing off a shot at him. St. Clair felt a searing pain in his leg as he was pitched forward, hitting the ground hard. So it was like that, huh? Fine, then. Lifting his head, he swung his gun up, braced in both hands, and shot one, then the other.

Ahead of him, he saw Rick and his allies get up and race towards the top of the hill. Trying to gain his feet, he accepted he wasn't going to be running them down, the bullet wound in his thigh stopping him from doing much more than crawling.

"Well, hell," he muttered, making his way towards Tanabuar.

Reaching his partner, he collapsed and checked his pulse quickly, finding it still strong. Breathing a sigh of relief, he gave the man a slap to the face.

"Ow, what the hell, Percy?" Tanabuar whined.

"Sorry, thought you were unconscious," he told him.

The Chthonian gave him a dark look. "I was resting. I've been shot."

"Yeah, me too."

"Bad?"

"Not really."

"Damn."

St. Clair gave him an incredulous look at that. "What's that mean?"

"Figured we could have matching manly scars," Tanabuar grinned.

"There is something so very wrong with you," St. Clair retorted with a smile.

Two gunshots rang nearby, drawing both of their weapons up, to see Anton lowering his gun. Glancing back, they saw two more armed men go down. Tanabuar dropped his weapon at that, muttering several foul things in his native language.

"Strakinsy," St. Clair called. "Wonder and his people went that way. Go stop them from making their lives harder, won't you?"

"Wait, Percy, don't," Tanabuar started.

"You guys okay?" Anton asked, looking towards the hill, and hesitating.

"We're fine, go!"

"No, don't," Tanabuar begged, but Anton was already running, leaving him adding several new things in another language.

"What?" St. Clair asked. "Don't tell me you want them to be fugitives?"

Tanabuar reached up and slapped him, then told him what he'd told Rick.

St. Clair blinked a few times, then hung his head, getting what his partner was trying to do, and why.

"You could have said something," he chided.

"I was trying," Tanabuar shot back, then grimaced.

"Settle down," his partner said. "You've been shot."

"I hate you."

"No, you don't."

"No, I don't. I'm sorry I said that."

"It's okay."

"Hey, Percy?"

"Yeah?"

"You know those little lemon cookies your wife makes at her bakery?"

"Yeah?"

"I want some of those. Like, a lot of those."

"Sure, Molly," St. Clair laughed. "All you can eat, for life."

"And Percy?"

"Yes, Molly?"

"Raspberry donuts."

"Don't push it."

* * *

The moment things went still, Rick was shoving Emi and Toddson, yelling, "Go! Go now!"

Scrambling up the hill, Rick glanced back to see St. Clair falling to his knees by Tanabuar, and offered a silent prayer of thanks to any gods that were listening. While they didn't see eye-to-eye, Rick couldn't help but respect both of them. As much as he wanted to be a hero, even he had to admit they already were, and greatly unappreciated ones at that.

Cresting the top, Rick almost bowled Emi over. Steadying them both, he began to bark at her to hurry, when his eyes fell on what had brought her to a stop. His whole body went numb at the sight of Enzo clutching his chest, his shirt stained in blood.

"Rick," the Goblin whimpered before collapsing.

"Go," Rick snapped, shoving Emi to run. "Toddson, get her out of here!"

"Rick, please," the Cleric begged. "Not again."

Dropping to a knee, Rick scooped Enzo up. "Never again. Now go. Get Emi away from here. I'm right behind you."

Grimacing, Toddson nodded, taking Emi by the hand and running. Cradling his friend, Rick jogged after him. At the base of the hill, he saw Lancaster waiting, daggers in hand and Rick's gear in a pile by his side. Waving Emi and Toddson on, the Rogue spotted Rick and even from a few yards off, Rick could easily make out the look of shock on his face.

Toddson and Emi paused by Lancaster, waiting as Rick hurried to reach them. Behind him, he heard more gunshots, but couldn't spare anything to hope the two Inspectors were safe. Everything he had was wrapped up in the small form he carried.

Passing the others, Rick ran without even seeing, tears burning his eyes as Enzo struggled just to breathe. Dashing past a small cluster of abandoned buildings, Rick staggered and fell to his knees, the rest of his team catching up as he cradled Enzo close, begging the gods to show mercy.

Just this once. Just a little.

"Rick," the Goblin gurgled, groping at his face.

"Easy, buddy," he whispered. "Just hang on. It's gonna be okay. I got you."

Behind him, he heard Emi sobbing but couldn't look. He heard Toddson trying to invoke a healing spell, to no avail. After a moment, he fell silent.

The whole world seemed to fall silent.

"Rick," Lancaster said, kneeling by him, a hand on his shoulder. "He's gone, Rick."

"No," Rick choked, shaking his head. "No. He's okay. He's gonna be okay. I can't... I can't again..."

Glancing to the others, Lancaster struggled with what to do.

"Rick, we can't stay here. We have to go. I'm sorry. Gods, I'm so sorry."

"I'm not leaving someone behind again," Rick whimpered, his voice cracking as his grief overflowed, pouring out of him. He could say nothing more. All there was left was to scream, to sob, to wail at the injustice, the cruel unfairness of the world.

Lancaster could only watch. He tried to think of something, anything, he could say that would help, but nothing came. All he could do was hold Rick as he cried, rocking Enzo's still form against his chest.

His first real friend in the city. The first person who had believed in him. The one who had shown him the way. Without him, Rick would have given up and returned home, defeated. He never would have met the people who stood around him now, who had fought by him, sacrificed with him and gone so far to get him back after the person he should have been able to trust more than any of them had betrayed him.

Slowly, Rick stilled and pushed to his feet. Gasping for breath, he looked towards the lights of mid-town. Out there, the people responsible were still plotting something unspeakable. First Mimi and now Enzo had died because of them.

"We're going to kill all of them," Rick snarled.

"Richard, stop."

Turning his head, he saw Anton standing a few feet away, his gun leveled on them.

Choking down both his grief and his blooming anger, Rick turned, letting him see. Anton's eyes went wide, his gun drooping then falling from his hand.

"I'm going after the people who did this," Rick said, walking towards him, holding Enzo. "Do not get in my way. Don't any of you get in my way. Understand?"

Shaken, Anton took the still Goblin, looking at Rick in anguish. "I don't..."

He stopped, words lost at the look of rage on Rick's face. Slowly he nodded and backed away.

"Make them pay."

"We will," Rick vowed, dropping a hand to close Enzo's eyes. "Don't let him be a part of this. He deserves better."

Anton said nothing as Rick turned, gathering his gear and looking to his comrades. Emi huddled against Toddson, crying, as the Cleric tried to comfort her. Again. Lancaster just stood, looking dazed.

"Let's go rain hell down on these bastards," Rick bit out.

"You're gonna need some help for that."

Dropping everything but his swords, Rick swung, ready to attack. Even his grief was dulled for a moment by the sight of Lucinia Avalinion standing a few feet away, watching him sadly. Shooting Lancaster a questioning look, he saw the Rogue was as surprised as he was.

"What..." Rick tried.

"Not here," she said moving to join them. "I'm sorry about your friend, Rick. I really am. I wish we had time to do more, but Manascetti's men are regrouping. Charlotte's waiting a few blocks over with a carriage. We have to go now."

Unsure what was happening, trapped in a surreal world that no longer made sense to him, Rick just nodded.

Giving Anton one last look, hoping that wherever Enzo was now, he could forgive him, Rick waved his team to move out.

In the city, the Hazaminie began to gather.

Chapter Eleven: Thunderstruck

LUCINIA HAD BEEN AS GOOD as her word. A few blocks away, through the abandoned area of the city on the north bank of Copper's Bay, Charlotte awaited them with a carriage. Distantly, as they walked, Rick realized they were in Old Town, the very place Enzo had told him Goblins were almost forced into, until Max Wonder had stood up for their rights.

As they approached, and he grappled with that, Charlotte sent another flare into the sky from a wand she was holding, then tucked it away, watching them approach. Lucinia had spoken to her quietly for a moment before leaving them, claiming she would meet up with them again later. Rick hadn't really believed that, but felt too numb to do anything about it as the Elf departed.

The trip had been long and winding, Charlotte taking care to make certain they weren't being followed. Emi had eventually cried herself to sleep, wrapped in Toddson's arms as the Cleric stared out the window at nothing, his usually easy-going nature replaced with a deep melancholy. Even Lancaster had been silent, sitting by Rick and staring at the floor, idly twisting one of his daggers in his hands.

Somewhere in the wee hours of the night, they finally stopped and Charlotte ushered them into the back door of a building. Rick hadn't been paying much attention, too lost in his own thoughts. It wasn't until they were in an old freight elevator that he started to look around, wondering just where they were.

At the end of the ride, they passed through an opulent hallway and to another elevator, this one manned by a Kobold who kept to himself. They changed elevators again soon after, and in his daze, Rick stopped paying attention again.

He didn't even really think about the fact that Charlotte and Lucinia seemed to know each other, or at least, were working together. He'd seen it, but not really processed it. He felt like he should, but he was so tired. All he really wanted was to go to sleep, and hopefully, wake up from this terrible nightmare.

Next thing he really knew, Charlotte was setting him down in an overstuffed chair. He blinked a few times, taking in his surroundings, and slowly began to grasp what he should have noticed much sooner. The furnishings were more than opulent. They were grand.

It still didn't really hit him until Mastoval leaned into his view, watching him with concern. He was at the Cantasol.

"If I may say, he doesn't look well," Mastoval said.

"He done had a bad night," Charlotte rumbled from nearby. "Leave him be for a bit."

The Half-Elf frowned very slightly. "He's getting blood on the Uberhausen."

"It just be a chair, boy," Charlotte grumbled.

"A chair worth a very considerable sum of money," he fretted.

Charlotte sighed and grabbed him by the collar. "So, get it cleaned later. We got more worries than that to be dealing with."

"Yes, of course," Mastoval sighed. "I'll need to come up with a way to explain it, as usual."

Charlotte said something else, but Rick didn't really hear it. He sat there for a long time, how long he wasn't sure, drifting in and out of sleep. It'd been so long since he'd slept. He wasn't sure just how long. Too long. Trying to figure it out was too much effort.

At some point, he woke and really grasped what was going on. Enough so he came to his feet, looking around for the rest of his team in a panic. All he saw was Charlotte, sitting on a couch, reading a book. Noticing him, she set it aside and pushed to her feet, watching him with concern.

"Ricky, me boy," she said softly. "You be okay?"

"Are we where I think we are?" he blurted, then felt stupid for asking that.

"We are," she confirmed with a nod. "Take it easy now. We be safe here."

"The others," he yelped, looking around frantically.

"Resting," Charlotte said, stepping over to him and taking him by the arm gently. "They all be bone tired, same as you. Be needing some sleep."

Soothed by her voice, Rick nodded, forcing himself to slow his breathing. "You sure we're safe?"

"Sure as a soul can be," she smiled, though it was tinged with sadness. "Come, you need to clean yourself up. We got much to do and almost no time to do it. Enough, maybe, you can rest a bit more, but we got to be quick about things here very soon."

"Lucinia," he said as Charlotte guided him from the parlor towards a washroom. "Is she really coming back?"

Charlotte paused, thinking of how to answer that, before nodding slowly. "I believe so, yes. Sooner or later, she be turning up here. Seems to me, anyway, she be knowing you need answers, the kind only she can provide. That, and me be thinking she's going to be needing your help for what comes next."

Accepting that, Rick followed her and nodded his thanks before stepping into the washroom. At this point, Charlotte was about the only person he knew he could trust so, if she said so, then he figured he may as well believe her.

By the time he emerged, he found the old Orc wasn't wrong. It had taken him a while to wash Enzo's blood off his hands, and even after a shower, he still felt as if it was all over him. Eventually, he'd given up on it and when he found his way back to the parlor, Lucinia was sitting on a loveseat opposite Charlotte, the two talking quietly.

"He lives," the Elf said, waving at Rick as he entered.

"Such as it be," Charlotte muttered.

Lucinia gave her an annoyed look. "No need to be dramatic. He's up and mobile. Looks like he's got his head together, too. All things considered, I'm gonna call that a good start."

Charlotte made a sound that spoke volumes of how much she disagreed, and left it at that. Rising, Lucinia gave her another annoyed look, but didn't argue the matter any further, either. Instead, she turned her attention to Rick, staring at him curiously.

"You do have your head together, right, Rick?"

"Depends on what you mean by together," he retorted, walking over to flop down next to Charlotte.

Lucinia considered that a moment, then shrugged. "I guess sarcasm is as good an answer as any. At least I know you're thinking, which is more than you were doing earlier."

"I watched a friend of mine die," Rick snapped. "How did you want me to be doing?"

"You chose to be an adventurer, kid," the Elf said with a scathing look. "If you plan to keep at it, you had best get used to watching a lot of your friends die. Otherwise, pack your shit and run home to your mommy."

"Screw you," Rick muttered.

"Now there was a pithy comeback," Lucinia laughed.

Charlotte rubbed her eyes, and shot the Elf a dark glare. "How about you leave him be. There be more important things going on."

"Fair enough," Lucinia said, backing down. "I'm going to make some coffee. Why don't you two get the others up? We need to start getting a plan together here, and frankly, I need to know what I've got to work with. Cause, if this is the best shot we've got, we're all fucked."

"Go on with you, then," Charlotte snapped.

At a wave of the Orc's hand, Lucinia scrambled away, obviously not wanting to anger the woman any further. Already not liking her, Rick ignored her, missing the look she gave him and the sadness it carried. He wouldn't have understood what it meant anyway.

Once she was gone, Rick gave Charlotte a curious look, asking, "Do you know her?"

"In a manner of speaking," Charlotte told him. "I do, yes, but also, no I do not. It be kind of a strange situation."

Rick had no idea how to respond to that.

* * *

With dawn only a couple of hours away, Rick and Charlotte woke the others, and found themselves joined by Mastoval, who had apparently disapproved of Lucinia's attempts to make coffee. Once they were gathered, the Half-Elf set about serving them with a practiced ease before retiring to a corner. Why, Rick wasn't sure, but considering how the concierge had behaved when Rick had first mentioned Lucinia, he figured Mastoval knew more than he did at this point.

Nodding her thanks to him, Lucinia turned to Rick and his team and sighed. "Well, I guess we best get this party started. I imagine that before we get into what needs to be done, you lot want to ask a lot of unimportant questions, so why don't we get all that out of the way first."

Glancing to the others and getting soft nods from them, Rick turned back to the mysterious Elf, saying, "I guess the first thing to get out of the way then is the obvious. You are not Lucinia Avalinion."

"No, I'm not," she grinned. "Though, I gotta admit, her body comes with some fun perks I never would have imagined."

Charlotte gave a disapproving cough at that.

"Not that that's important, of course," the Elf added quickly.

"Okay, then, who are you?" Rick continued, ignoring the obvious implications of what she'd said. There were some things, he had learned, he didn't really want to know.

Lucinia shrugged. "Doesn't really matter."

"Kind of does," Rick replied in considerable disbelief.

The Elf chewed her lip a moment, then gave a look of nonchalance. "Not really. My soul, it doesn't belong here. Sooner or later, this body is going to kick me out. Might be tonight, might be twenty years from now. There's no way to know. The point, however, is that who I am, or rather, use to be, doesn't matter much in light of that."

Rick thought about that for a minute, then nodded his acceptance of it. "So, you want us to just call you Lucinia, or what?"

"Nah," she chuckled. "That's a bit too much for my taste. Shorter is better, though only in this case, and trust me, I get that in all kinds of new ways now. Call me Lucy."

"Must you be crass?" Charlotte grumbled.

"Figure this is the only chance I'm gonna get to make those kinds of jokes, so why not?" Lucy grinned.

"I think she use to be a dude," Toddson whispered, very loudly.

Rick buried his face in his hand. "Thanks, Todd. Got that."

"Oh," the Cleric mouthed, then settled back, waving them to continue.

"Wow," Lucy said slowly. "This is the best you could find?"

"Talk about them like that again, and I'll feed you your teeth," Rick snapped. "Now, bigger question. Is Lucinia dead?"

Holding her hands up to let him know she got it, Lucy thought about his question a moment, then gave a half-hearted nod. "I think so. I'm not really sure. I don't sense her in here, anyway. Not that I'm sure I would, what with this being my first time driving around in a body that isn't mine, but I'm pretty sure she's dead, yeah."

"What happened?"

Lucy shrugged. "Don't really know for sure. I mean, I was someplace else when it happened. Then, kind of suddenly, I was in her. That was pretty confusing already, you know? Though, from what I've been able to piece together since then, I think Fergum Tashitia expelled her soul to make room for someone else."

"Who's that?" Lancaster asked.

"Fergum Tashitia?" she asked in surprise. "Sorry. Figured you guys already knew. He's the current head of the Hazaminie. Tall Elf, looks like he needs to eat something solid, like, very regularly and for several months."

"That guy," Rick said, scowling. "Okay, yeah, we know who that is. We just didn't know his name."

"Okay, good, we're getting somewhere," Lucy said with a wide grin. "Anyway, like I said, this is mostly stuff I've figured out along the way, but I think Tashitia was trying to call his predecessor back from the lands of the dead and stick him in Lucinia here. Something obviously went wrong, and he got me instead."

"But, why?" Rick asked. "I mean, why her?"

"That's a long story," Lucy told him. "Short version is, the Scarlet Ring and the Hazaminie use to be tight. They had a falling out, I guess, a while back. Lucinia's dad died soon after, under rather mysterious circumstances, and the Hazaminie tried to seize control of the Ring. That went badly, so they figured they could pop Tashitia's old boss into Lucinia's body, and rule through a figurehead."

Rick frowned at that. "What's that got to do with bringing Obedell back?"

"Okay, too short a version," Lucy muttered. "Basically, the Hazaminie wants to use the Ring as Obedell's new base of power when he returns. They have their fingers in a lot of pies, after all. More importantly, Tashitia's predecessor knew the location of some of Obedell's hidden labs, where the old Lich kept copies of all his spell books, and other fun toys."

"Like the ones you burned in the processing yards," Lancaster cut in.

Lucy shot him a look of approval. "I take it back, you got a good one there."

"Thank you," Lancaster smirked. "I'm good at lots of things. If you want to know my really special skills, just let me know later."

"Spell books they need to bring Obedell back," Rick said, steering the conversation back on track.

"Spoil sport," Lancaster pouted.

"Well, no, not exactly," Lucy admitted, giving the Rogue a knowing wink. "I mean, they can do it without them, but it would be a hell of a lot easier with them. Trying to breach the dimensional barrier without those books comes with a chance of failure. Tashitia has already lost a lot by failing to gain control of the Ring, and loosing this body. He can't afford for the ritual to fail."

Rick shook his head slowly. "So he figures out, probably from a higher ranking member of the Ring, that Obedell stashed copies of his spell books here in Riscadil, back when the Ring was fighting the Ironriggers. He comes here, hoping to get them, but ends up clashing with Manascetti and has to cut a deal with him just to operate in the city at all."

Lucy snapped her fingers. "A deal he has no intention of honoring. Very good, Rick."

"Okay, so here's what I don't understand," Rick said, ignoring the compliment entirely. "If they can try without the spell books, why even bother coming to Riscadil at all, much less dealing with Manascetti? I get this Tashitia guy needs a win, but I'd think considering all he's risking, doing this literally anywhere else would have been in his better interest."

Lucy laughed at that, throwing Mastoval a look. "You said he was quick. He is."

"Indeed, so," the Half-Elf replied, giving Rick a soft smile. "He found you here when no one else had, after all."

"Yeah, that's great," Rick scowled. "But, seriously."

Lucy's smile faded. "Cause, there was already a breach in the barrier here. At the exact right place. Riscadil is the only place they can try this with any hope of succeeding. Tashitia hedged his bets. If they had the right spell books, maybe they could pull it off somewhere else and get a portal open. If they were incredibly lucky, it would even be to the right dimension and not one of the countless billion other ones out there. Without them, this is their only shot. He knew that, and he was prepared for the possibility those books might not be here."

"Or were long since destroyed," Rick said, getting the picture. "Okay, so that explains all that."

"Almost," Lucy said. "There's one other thing they needed. Something nobody was ever able to find. Not over hundreds of years. I don't know how they found it, but they did."

"What?"

"Obedell's apocryphanal," Lucy said, a dark expression crossing her face.

Everybody looked at Emi, who just shrugged. Everybody looked back at Lucy.

"Right, so, an apocryphanal is an object that a Lich stores their soul in," Lucy explained, rubbing her eyes. "So long as that exists, they can't be killed. Just delayed. You can destroy their body all you want, and they will reform from their apocryphanal and come at you again."

"Wait, so, you're saying that if Obedell's apocryphanal is destroyed, he'll die? Like, for good?" Rick boggled.

"Yup, exactly," Lucy replied with a grin. "Thing is, Liches are weird. They tend to make their apocryphanal out of things that look so innocuous, so commonplace, nobody gives them a second thought, or look. Then they hide them someplace, sometimes not even in the same dimension, making it all but impossible to locate them. They're also heavily warded, so destroying one is no easy task, even if you find it."

"Yeah, yeah," Rick said, waving all that aside. "I get it. But still, Obedell isn't unkillable. Just nigh unkillable. And from what you're saying, the Hazaminie has his apocryphanal thingy right now, here in town at the Hawthorne."

A slow smile spread across Lucy's face. "Now he gets it."

"They want to bring Obedell back," Lancaster said slowly.

"But they gave us a shot at killing him for good," Toddson added.

"Bingo, kids, you get a gold star," Lucy laughed. "Put it someplace nice."

Rick settled back on the couch, marveling. They had something. It was slim, but they had a shot. Not just to stop the Hazaminie, but Obedell himself. It wasn't impossible. Close, but not quite.

"Okay then," he said at length. "Without the spell books, they have to go to plan B. What's that involve?"

"Human sacrifice," Lucy replied casually.

"Oh," Rick staggered.

"Well, I say human, but I guess any sentient will do, really," she added, looking a bit perplexed. "Sorry to all the non-humans in the room. Didn't mean to make you feel unimportant."

"Perish the thought," Mastoval muttered.

"Don't be caring," Charlotte grumbled.

"Thank you," Emi squeaked.

Lucy pointed at her as if that meant something. Everyone else just let the matter pass. Emi seemed a bit proud of herself, for some reason.

"All right," Rick finally said. "I guess all that's really left is to ask what his apocryphanal is?"

Lucy gave him a nervous smile at that. "I have no idea."

"Seriously," Rick groaned, slumping. "How can you not know that, when you know all this other stuff?"

"Hey, it isn't like I didn't try to find out," Lucy balked. "But come on, kid, it could be anything. A ring. A goldfish bowl. A petrified turd! I have no idea, okay? Besides, I've spent the last few months running from the Hazaminie, trying to screw with their plans, never knowing when I was gonna get kicked out of this body, so it wasn't exactly the top priority, you know?"

"Fine, fine," Rick groused, waving her down. "Are they going to put it in some kind of prominent place, or something? Do you know that?"

Lucy shrugged. "Beats me. They aren't real sharing people."

"Great," Rick shouted. "So, what are we supposed to do, huh? Bust in there and just smash everything we see?"

"That's an option," the Elf replied hesitantly. "But probably not a good one, since like I said, it could be anything. There's no way to know for sure."

"Detect magic?" Toddson asked, looking hopeful.

"Nah," Lucy told him sadly. "The warding spells on it hide it from stuff like that. The whole point is to make it so hard to find, nobody ever does."

"Nuts," the Cleric pouted.

"Well, fine then," Rick fumed. "What was your plan?"

Lucy shot him a pained look. "I was kind of making it up as I went."

"Gimme a break here," Rick muttered, burying his face in his hands, and counting to ten. When he finished, he did it again, just for good measure.

"There's one other problem," Lucy offered with a conciliatory tone. "Turns out, I can't get near the theater. I tried last night after we got you guys away from that train wreck. Soon as I stepped up to the place, I felt my soul being tugged out of this body. Whatever you're going to do, I can't help."

"For fuck's sake," Rick muttered. "Why? Do you have any idea why?"

Lucy shrugged, giving him a baffled look. "I know pretty much nothing about magic, kid. Wasn't my forte back when I had my own body. Punching stuff. That was what I was good at. Hell, I don't even know why I keep coming back from being dead! Which, thank you for asking, is a damn unpleasant thing."

"Is that why you went to see Neba?" Rick asked.

Lucy instantly frowned. "That's... not important."

"She sold me out to the cops, so I kind of think it is," Rick snarled.

Lucy *hmmed* a moment, then shook her head. "I don't know why she did that. I don't know why she does anything she does. I'm not even sure me going to see her was wise. But, to answer your question, yeah, I needed her arcane expertise. She was less than helpful, by the way, so don't feel special. Neba looks out for Neba, it seems."

Rick stared at her for a long moment. "You knew her before, didn't you?"

"Kind of," Lucy hedged. "Look, it doesn't matter. For real. Whatever she's doing, it doesn't change what we need to do. Stop the Hazaminie and try to figure out what that apocryphanal is so we can destroy it, if that's even possible."

Rick leaned back, glaring at the Elf in near hate. "I need to think about all this."

"Think fast, cause I'm pretty sure they are gonna make their move tonight," Lucy replied. "We have very little time to figure out how to deal with this."

"Yeah, I get that," Rick snapped, pushing to his feet. "But before I risk the lives of my team, I need to think about this."

Lucy rolled her eyes. "Rick, listen. I get it. Trust me, I get it. This is bigger than them or you or me. Even if we all die, so long as we stop them, it'll be worth it."

"Then call the damn Royal Inspectors," Rick yelled. "Let them handle it!"

"Can't," Lucy countered. "By now, they'll have erected warding barriers, which is probably what I ran into, I would guess. Nobody is getting in that theater."

"Then what are we supposed to do?" Rick shouted.

"That's kind of why we need a plan here," Lucy replied sarcastically.

Throwing his hands up, Rick stormed away. "Let me think, dammit!"

Once he was gone, the rest of them remained, sorting through it all. The risk, great though it was, was worth the reward. That much was obvious. As Lucy had said, even if it meant all of them lost their lives, none of them could say that success was not worth that. None of them would, either.

"Well," Lucy said after a few moments. "That went well."

"You be one huge pain in me ass," Charlotte grumbled as she stood.

"That's what makes me lovable," the Elf offered in a false hurt tone.

Nobody wanted any part of that.

* * *

Nothing made sense anymore.

Rick stood on the balcony atop the Cantasol, staring out over the predawn city, trying to wrap his head around everything he'd learned, and just couldn't. It was like some kind of a cruel joke no matter how he looked at it. One played by the gods and fate and his own hubris.

Just a week ago, it had all seemed so clear. At that very moment, seven days ago, he'd been only hours away from arriving in Riscadil and starting his new life of adventure. All his goals and dreams laid out before him, and all he had to do was grab them to make them his own.

It was almost laughable how naive he'd been. To think he could just show up in a city like Riscadil and walk the same path his father had. That was all he'd really wanted. No matter what he'd told Maari, or his mother, or anyone else, he couldn't lie to himself anymore. He'd wanted to follow in his father's footsteps and be just like him.

He wasn't. He never could be. All those stories he'd heard growing up had made him too big. Beyond larger than life. There was no way he was ever going to live up to that. There was no way anyone could. Max Wonder had been an impossible goal to reach from the start.

He'd known that, somewhere deep down. He just hadn't wanted to face it. If he'd done that, then he'd have had no choice but to admit that his father was someone he could never understand. Past being like him, that was what he'd really wanted. To know him in a way the stories could never allow. To walk in his shoes and understand how he thought, how he saw the world and what he'd felt, that had always been his real dream.

What little boy didn't want that, really?

Of course, Rick had never expected that the very first job he took would bring him into conflict with a cult of necromancers bent on bringing Obedell the Arch Lich back from the beyond, either. The very monster that even Max Wonder hadn't been able to beat without sacrificing his own life was all but staring him in the face.

Therein, he saw, lay the joke that gods and fate played on an arrogant boy named Rick Wonder. He'd wanted to be like his dad and they had obliged. Faced with it, his nerve buckled and his dream, which just a week ago had been something he could touch, faded into the illusion it always had been.

He wasn't Max Wonder. He never could be. There was no way he could do this. No way could he ask Lancaster, Toddson, and Emi to do this. Max had been backed by some of the greatest adventurers alive, and it had still cost him his life. Rick and his team, they were nothing like them. Success wasn't just an illusion, it was an absurdity.

The horizon glowed with the coming of the sun as Charlotte joined him, leaning on the railing by his side, watching Riscadil as it greeted a new day. She never really slept, that city, but she did doze, and as Rick faced the impossible task laid out by gods who laughed at his comical pride, that great city prepared to wake fully.

It had no idea what stirred at its very heart. It couldn't. Obedell was coming and there was no Max Wonder to stop him this time. There wasn't even a pale imitation.

"About your age, I was, when first I come to this city," Charlotte said. "All of nineteen years old, I watched her rise up before me on the horizon as the ship sailed into the Bay. Thought I was gonna drown in all this back then."

"That sums up how I feel about now, yeah," Rick replied morosely.

"Things was bad in the Fursha Islands back then," she continued. "Lots of things roaming about the seas making tidal waves and earthquakes. My momma and daddy, they sent me here to be with my Aunty Grace in the hopes I be safe from what felt like the end of the world."

"Was it?"

She shrugged slightly. "For many. My parents, they lived, and I got to see them again when they come to visit. They never let me go back, though, and I have not to this day. This city, it come to be my home somewhere along the way."

Rick nodded slowly.

"Aunty Grace ran a boarding house in Old Town back then," Charlotte told him with a faint smile. "Big old four-story thing, long since gone now. Was near to, then, mind you. The whole thing was held together by prayers and roach shit, I swear."

"Don't oversell it," Rick replied with a faint grin.

"That ain't something nobody could do," she snorted. "Even then, Old Town was falling apart. Only people what stayed in the firetrap was dumb kids what come to this city hoping to be adventurers, like you. Hearts all caught up in it, and eyes full of the piles of gold they was gonna be rolling in."

Rick shook his head and started to say something, but Charlotte held a hand up, stopping him.

"Made things harder on Aunty Grace, they did," she said, her smile fading to a look of sorrow. "Most never come back from chasing that call to adventurer. Can't get rent from a corpse what nobody found, and all that. Just the way it was back then. Wouldn't none of them in there, or you probably, survived long the way the world was then."

"Well, I feel better, thanks," he snorted.

Charlotte cuffed him across the head. "Shut up and listen, boy. Age and wisdom all I got left to hand out, and I be doing that now."

Rubbing his head, Rick gave her an apologetic smile. "Yes, ma'am."

She huffed, giving him a stern glare, before continuing. "I be there about a month when this boy show up. Like all the rest, he was. Full of himself. Think he was gonna save the world. Had nothing to his name but some ratty old armor and a rusty sword he was always trying to polish. Aunty Grace told me, take a good look. That's one what won't live to pay his rent."

She shot him a look, making sure he was listening. "Seen a hundred like him, she had. Still, she gave him a bed and fed him, 'cause that's the way she was, Aunty Grace. Good woman, gods rest her. I carry on her ways even now, which is why you been having a bed to sleep in and food in your belly, so you best be thanking her, boy."

"Thank you, Aunty Grace," Rick said to the brightening sky.

"Good," Charlotte praised, nodding. "Cause of all them what never come back and the old place falling down round our heads, I got work at the Hawthorne, dancing in the burlesque. Never had an Orc before, of course. They all thought it was funny. Laughed themselves half to death at me, but I took it all and danced anyway cause the money was good. Aunty Grace never liked it, but never said a word, neither."

"If I may," Rick replied, looking up at her. "I bet you were a hell of a dancer."

"Still am," she laughed, giving him a bit of a twirl. "That boy, though. The one what Aunty Grace told me would never live long enough to pay rent, he didn't care for the way they laughed at me. While he was looking for a team, he'd come to walk me home, saying it wasn't right for a lady like me to be unescorted, with ridicule all about me the way I was."

She paused, staring out at the first peek of the sun. "I wanted him to never find a team, I did. Wanted him to never go off and not came back. He did, though. Rounded up eight others in the house and took work from the city. One morning, they all walked out the door and into the sewers, looking for whatever down there was making noise and eating on some maintenance workers."

"Holy crap," Rick started.

Charlotte shrugged. "World be different back them. That kinda thing, it happened."

"Yeah, but still," Rick said slowly, shaking his head.

"Off they went, as I was saying," she told him pointedly. "After three days gone by, Aunty Grace told me not to be expecting them back. That I should get me up to their rooms and clean out their things. I did for all but that boy what walked me home each night. Just couldn't do it. I wanted still for him to come back."

"Did he?" Rick asked.

She nodded. "After five days gone by, he did, with two of the others. Nine went out, only them three come back. What they saw down there, none of them ever said a word about far as I know. That boy, when they come back, he stayed in his room for another three days. Kept the light on all the night, barely slept and barely ate. Just lay there, staring at the wall."

Rick said nothing as she paused, her heartbreak at recalling it obvious.

"Took him food and drink. Sat with him. Did all I could. Walked home each night from dancing, alone. Aunty Grace said to me, he done been broken of his dreams. He be running home soon. Thought for sure he would, too. Made me heart ache. Aunty Grace, she thought I done gone sweet on some human boy, but that wasn't it. I respected that boy, 'cause he respected me."

Rick nodded, getting that. He didn't even know the man and he respected him.

"After three days, as I was going to work, I stopped and told him thank you. Just that. Thank you. For always being so kind to me. For treating me with dignity in a city what hadn't shown me much. That night when I left the burlesque, he was waiting for me and walked me home. Few days later, he got another bunch together and went out again."

Rick straightened up, his own worries gone, too captivated by the story she was telling.

"He come back sometimes with all of them he left with. Most times not. Always come back, though," she said with a sad laugh. "Time passed and he did well. Got him a better place to live. Even then, long as he wasn't off working, he come and walk me home. When he met him a woman, he bring her and they both walk me home. That just be the kind of man he was, you see."

"I do see," Rick said with a soft smile. "He was a good man."

Charlotte nodded, looking at him with a mixture of sadness and love. "Yes, your daddy was a good man, Rick. A damn good man, despite himself. He had his flaws for sure, and his demons besides, but even after Aunty Grace passed on and that old boarding house fell to ruin, he would come and walk me home."

Rick stared at her, stunned beyond words.

"I moved up, became a stage manager there at the Hawthorne," Charlotte told him. "Built me a reputation and moved on, doing more in this town. Was a time, and still is I think, me word alone could start or end anything in the theater community around here. Even then, when I was producing, directing and even writing, Max would come and walk me home. Him, Delilah, and even that damn fool uncle of yours."

Shaking his head, Rick struggled for words. "Mom... she never said..."

Charlotte shrugged. "They ate at my table, as I ate at theirs, but when Max went into that hole in the world they made for Obedell, your momma, all she wanted was to be away from this place and all the ways it reminded her of him. That included me. I don't blame her for that, and anyone what says a bad word about your momma to me, they find out how precious she be to me even now by way of the back of me hand."

"Still," Rick crumpled. "I didn't know. Charlotte, I didn't know."

"I no be telling you for that," she replied. "Not so you feel you owe me anything. You don't. I be telling you all this, Rick, so you know the things about your daddy what nobody ever be telling. All anybody want to hear is the stories from later on, when he was done somebody. Don't nobody want to tell the ones from when he was a kid and hide in his bed for days, terrified out of his mind by what he done seen."

He got it, of course. He understood what she was saying. It was impossible to miss. "I'm not him, though."

"He wasn't always him," she stated. "Max became the man he was. He walked through blood and death and nightmares to get there, too. Same as you do now. Doubted, same as you do now, too. He just did what he thought was right, as best he could. You don't gotta be him, boy. You just gotta do that, same as he did. What you think is right, as best you can."

"What if we fail?" Rick asked her, his meaning plain as the brightening day.

"If you stay here and do nothing, what difference would there be?" she asked.

"None," he admitted.

"Then what you gonna do?" she asked. "You gonna let it be, or you gonna stand up, fight back, bleed and yes, maybe even die, trying to stop it? Cause I think I know what you gonna do. You just want someone to tell you that it's okay to go and do it."

Rick gave her a tired look. "You really think that's what I want?"

"I do," she smiled, patting his cheek. "Same as your daddy did back then. He just wanted someone to tell him that all he been through, it mattered, and even if he died the very next day, his suffering was a gift to at least one other soul. He wanted to hear that thank you, 'cause it made it all okay."

Rick looked out over the city. "So, what you're saying is..."

"Thank you, Rick," Charlotte told him with a smile full of love, appreciation, and sorrow.

"How about that," he marveled as all his fears distilled down to a single focus. Obedell was coming. He could try and stop him and maybe die. That was better than hiding, though. Not because it was what Max Wonder would do. Because it's what he wanted to do.

"Ready?" Charlotte asked.

"I am," Rick said. "If I die today, I want you to know, I'm glad I met you, Charlotte Goodkin. You have made my world a better place to live in."

"And you done the same for me," she replied.

"Time to do something really stupid."

"Done too late for that," she huffed. "You done something stupid the moment you come looking for adventure."

Rick slumped. "Kinda killed the mood right now."

"Don't be caring," she replied with a sniff. "Go on, then. Do your stupid thing. I be waiting here for you to come walk me home."

Rick reached out and hugged her as tight as he could. "Count on it."

* * *

Lucy stood back, watching Rick and Charlotte talk on the balcony, wondering what they were saying, but knowing better than to butt in. Charlotte would knock her head clean off if she tried. That much, she could be damn sure of.

"I take it the eavesdropping is not going well?" Mastoval asked, making her jump half out of her skin.

"Will you not do that?" she hissed, shoving him back and out of sight before Charlotte could spot either of them.

"I would think you would have gotten use to your Elven senses at this point," the concierge drawled. "Silly me."

Lucy glared at him for a moment, getting only his soft smile in return. "You're still a pain in the ass, you know that?"

"I've no idea what you mean," the Half-Elf replied.

Waving it off, Lucy fell against the wall, trying to peek around the corner to see what they were doing on the balcony. "You think she can get his head straight?"

Mastoval rolled his eyes slightly. "I think, perhaps, if you were to go out there and be honest with him, it would do more than anything Miss Charlotte could manage."

"Not gonna happen," Lucy growled.

"Max," Mastoval said in a hard tone. "He's your son."

"All the more reason for him to never know," she replied, sadness creeping into her voice. "He can't know that I'm alive."

"By all the gods above and below," Mastoval muttered. "Why not?"

Lucy shook her head slowly. "He needs to become his own man. If he knew, he'd chase after me, try to get me back. He'd give up his whole life for that and I won't have it."

"He has already given up his whole life to chase after you," the Half-Elf retorted. "Or have you completely missed the point of what brought him here in the first place?"

Lucy shot him a scathing look. "Oh, gee, thanks for stating the obvious there. I meant, he *can* still choose to walk away from this life. From being an adventurer. He can go home and pick any life he wants. If he knows I'm alive out there, in that place that will limit his options in his own mind to one."

"You can't know that," Mastoval retorted.

"Oh, yes I can," she shot back.

"How?"

"He's my son," she grinned. "And that's what I'd do."

Shaking his head, Mastoval gave up. "I would think, all things considered, that you would want to take advantage of this... whatever this is, to spend at least a little time with him. To get to know him."

"I would," she admitted. "But I've already seen enough to know what kind of man he's grown up to be."

"Have you?"

Lucy slapped him on the shoulder. "Yup. I couldn't be prouder."

Lucy walked away, leaving Mastoval to accept a decision he vehemently disagreed with. There really was no arguing that, however.

* * *

"Rick!" Lancaster yelled, waving at him frantically as he returned from the balcony. "Rick! Come here! Hurry! Toddson had an idea!"

This should be good, he thought.

"I did," Toddson called, joining Lancaster in the hallway. "I had an idea! A good idea! I think. I think I had an idea. What was my idea?"

Rick started looking for a cabinet to bang his head against. None looked conveniently located.

Lancaster turned to the Cleric, exasperated beyond words. Grabbing him by the shoulders, he finally said, "Toddson, you are a beautiful, wonderful man, and I love you. But I kind of want to strangle you right now."

Toddson grinned at that. "Aw, thanks man. Except for that last part, that was really sweet."

"Guys," Rick begged.

"Right," Lancaster all but shouted, then shook Toddson. "This guy, he had an idea about how to get into the theater without being noticed."

Rick stopped in front of them looking at Lancaster then Toddson. "He's right. You are beautiful. What was the idea?"

"I don't remember," Toddson said with a wide smile.

Rick turned to the Rogue. "Lancaster. What was Toddson's idea?"

"Dispel Magic," Lancaster squeed.

Rick didn't ever want to hear him do that again.

"Yeah," Lucy called from behind Rick. "That's a great idea, but there's no way he's powerful enough to dispel a barrier that size."

"I wouldn't have to," Toddson said, snapping his fingers as it came back to him. "I just need to find a weak point in the barrier, and dispel that."

"I have no idea what you're talking about," Rick said, rubbing his eyes.

Lancaster grabbed him by the shoulder. "That's why we need Emi to explain it. Come on!"

Sighing heavily, Rick allowed the Rogue to drag him back to the parlor where Emi sat in a chair looking mildly terrified as all eyes turned to her. He really wanted to be bothered by that, but at this point, it had just become normal.

"Emi," Lancaster demanded. "Explain Toddson's idea to Rick."

Emi made a strange noise.

"Makes perfect sense now," Lucy drawled.

Rick shot her a glare over his shoulder before walking over and dropping a hand to Emi's head, saying, "You got this. You busted me out of a moving train swarming with dirty cops and Royal Inspectors. This is nothing."

Slowly she nodded, setting her face to brave, or something close to it. "Okay... um... depending on what kind of barrier it is, then it may be possible – if we can find a small enough spot – to break it, without them knowing."

"What kind of small spot you be thinking?" Charlotte asked, joining them.

"Like, a window, maybe?" Emi said, shrinking into the chair.

"Can that work?" Lucy asked no one in particular. Which was good, since no one except Emi had any idea.

"Well," she whimpered. "It depends on the spell, like I said. If it's a bubble, then no."

Lucy shook her head. "It wasn't. I got right up to the front doors before I had to back off. That mean anything?"

Emi chewed her lip, thinking. "Maybe. Yes. I think that means it's the shielding kind, where the barrier clings to the building like a second skin. So if we can find a small entrance, something that could be removed, then the spell should be weak there. We could, maybe, dispel that effect on that point, open it and get in."

"Like a sewer entrance?" Charlotte asked.

"Yeah, that would do," Emi agreed.

"I know just the thing," the Orc grinned. "In the basement, there be an old manhole cover. I remember that from my dancing days. The new girls, we had our dressing room down there and it always stunk terrible."

Rick nodded as it he thought it over. "Okay, so, Toddson?"

"I can do it," the Cleric assured them with a nod.

"Okay, then, that's our way in," Rick said firmly, patting the Cleric on the shoulder. "Good job, Toddson and Emi, both. We all get to go die now."

"Hey," Lancaster said, jabbing at Rick. "Now's no time for you to get all negative. We're gonna go save the day and be heroes."

"Or we could just try to stay alive long enough that the whole city doesn't get wiped out by an angry Lich," Rick replied, giving him a thin smile.

Lancaster shrugged. "Sure, I mean, I guess we can do that, too."

"How about that?" Lucy chuckled. "You guys actually came up with a plan."

"Now we just have to get into the sewer without being spotted," Rick pointed out.

"Not a problem," Mastoval put in. "There's an access way in the basement here. This building was constructed around the same time as the Hawthorne. It may take you some time to navigate the tunnels, but I see no reason you can't get from one to the other without being spotted."

"That's how I've been getting around the city," Lucy admitted, shrugging.

"Is it now?" Charlotte asked.

"Bite me," Lucy deadpanned.

"Okay, good," Rick deflected. "First, though, I have to say this. You three, you don't have to come with me. You've done enough. You've sacrificed enough. I won't hold it against you if you want to stay out of this fight, 'cause it is going to be a fight. Maybe one that'll kill us all."

"Don't be stupid," Lancaster snorted. "Of course I'm going with you. We're a team, right?"

"Yeah," Toddson added. "We all go in together, and if we're gonna die, we do that together, too."

Emi pushed to her feet, all but yelling, "'Cause we're brave and we're adventurers and this is what we do!"

Everybody stared at her for a moment. She turned a violent shade of red.

"Emi, you're right," Rick said with a smile. "This is what we do. Let's go kick some ass and either save the day, or die trying."

"After we get some sleep, though, right?" Toddson asked. "Cause, I haven't had enough to recover much in the way of magic. Just throwing that out there."

Rick hung his head. "First, we take a nap, then we'll save the day, or die trying."

"That feels kinda anti-climactic," Lancaster mused.

"Yeah," Rick sighed. "It really does."

Chapter Twelve: Back In Black

LATE THAT AFTERNOON, as Powerage was rising from their pre-apocalypse nap, Royal Inspectors St. Clair and Tanabuar were finally returning to their office. The aftermath of the train derailment, as well as the ensuing debacle, had kept them for some time. As both uniformed officers and gunman suspected of being in the employ of the Ironriggers were identified and either arrested or covered with sheets, they had given their account. Several times.

Even when that was more or less dealt with, the emergency field treatment they'd both received had given way to more extensive healing and care. Both had refused full healing magic, preferring it be used on the good cops who had suffered the stark betrayal of their brethren. Many had been near to gone, and were in the care of more skilled spell casters at a nearby clinic.

It had, very frankly, been a complete shit show. Both men were aware of how deeply Manascetti had gotten his claws into the police force, but the revelation of the lengths he would go to or the level of damage he was willing to inflict to kill one person was still staggering. There would be many questions, for a very long time, about just how the hell things had managed to spiral so wildly out of control.

St. Clair, more than his partner, was aware that eventually the Royal Inspectors would need a scapegoat. He had authorized the use of firearms and Manascetti had used that to his advantage. Normally, even the Ironriggers were smart enough not brandish such weapons. St. Clair had armed the police and the Ironriggers had responded in kind. He knew that eventually, the blame would fall on him.

In other words, everything had gone exactly as he had planned. It almost made him want to smile.

Leaning heavily on a cane, he made his way towards his desk at a slow limp, while by his side Tanabuar had an arm in a sling, his injury improved but far from properly healed. St. Clair would have preferred he accept more extensive treatment, but the Chthonian wouldn't hear it. It would look good in the papers, or so he claimed.

He wasn't entirely wrong. Even now St. Clair knew, the gears would be turning. The higher-ups would be already looking for who to blame. He was already several steps ahead of them and before this day was done, he was going to expose every single corrupt one of them.

All that was left was to wait.

As the two reached their desks, Podest hovered up from the archive, his large central eye going wide at the sight of them. "Holy hell, you two look like shit."

They paused, staring at him in exhausted annoyance.

"I mean, I'm not one to talk," the Older fumbled, aware of how lopsided his missing eye stalks made him look. "I'm just saying, for you, you kinda look terrible."

They continued to stare at him.

"Yeah, I'm just gonna stop talking now," he grumbled, turning to float away, then spinning back. "You sure you shouldn't be at, like, a clinic or something? Cause I've seen things on the side of the road that looked healthier than you guys."

Tanabuar moved to fall into his chair. St. Clair rubbed his eyes.

"Okay, I get it," Podest mumbled. "Shut up and go away. Sorry for expressing a modicum of concern. I'll leave you to wallow in your self-pity."

Tanabuar did a lazy circle in his swivel chair. St. Clair leaned on his desk, watching the Older in boredom.

"I'm just saying, you probably shouldn't be here," the creature tried again, for some reason. "At the very least, you know, maybe go home, take a shower, and freshen up a little. Something. Cause, honestly, I've seen zombies that had more going for them."

Tanabuar stopped spinning. St. Clair didn't change his expression.

"You know, back when zombies were a thing, anyway," the Older offered. "I should stop, huh?"

"Could you," Tanabuar begged. "Please?"

"Right," the Older sighed. "You guys need anything? Want anything?"

"Lemon cookies," the Chthonian said.

"Huh," Podest managed after a moment of confusion. "Not what I was thinking, but, whatever."

"Could you, perhaps, manage to give us an update, please," St. Clair finally asked. "Before I die of old age."

Grimacing, the Older floated back. "Sure. Why not? Not like you two haven't already been through the wringer. Why not dive back in for another round?"

"Podest," St. Clair pleaded. "Today."

"Yeah, yeah, I got it," he grumbled. "Well, the train mess is all over the news, obviously. No official statements being made yet, but that probably won't last long."

St. Clair nodded slowly. "About the Hawthorne situation. I'm already aware of what's going on with the train issue. I was there."

"Getting shot," Tanabuar added.

Podest scowled. "You know, Percy, every now and then, even you need to take a break. Go bang your wife. Something."

"I still have my gun," St. Clair pointed out.

"Infernal gods," the Older groaned. "Fine! Riscadil Police Department has sealed off the whole area. Late last night, while you guys were getting kicked around and Wonder was escaping, a barrier spell went up around the whole damn building. The cops who went in never came out and nobody has been able to breach it, as yet. Whatever is going on in there, we got no idea."

"Just like you said," Tanabuar chuckled.

"Indeed," St. Clair agreed.

"Wait, what?" Podest blinked. "Percy? What the hell you gone and done now? And why didn't you include me! I hate it when you do crap like this and don't include me!"

"Your memory is admissible in a court of law," St. Clair reminded him. "Not to mention, you are required by the terms of your visa to share everything you know with the Older Network."

Podest frowned. "Okay, those are some good reason, but still. I thought we were a team, man."

"We are," St. Clair said. "You're just the distraction."

Podest fell into a sulk. "You're a dick, Percy. By the way, Chief Inspector Shade is on her way down."

"How long do we have?" Tanabuar asked.

Their office door slammed open, followed by the sharp tick of heels across the floor.

"About now," the Older grinned.

St. Clair gave him a point for that one. "Chief Inspector Shade. Nice to see you."

Topping out at three feet, the middle-aged Gnome in the sharp suit stopped a few feet from him, glaring fiercely. "Inspector St. Clair, I can promise you, that will be a very fleeting experience."

Tanabuar leaned around his desk. "Hi, Chief. Is that a new skirt? It's nice."

Shade's angry look faded into mild confusion for a moment. St. Clair managed not to grin at how easily she'd been disarmed.

"Ignore him," he offered. "He's on some heavy painkillers right now."

"Cause I was shot," Tanabuar added, pointing at his shoulder. "Percy owes me lemon cookies for it."

"I don't give a damn!" Shade roared.

"And here I complimented her skirt," Tanabuar sulked.

Turning back to St. Clair, she eased forward a few steps, a move that intimidated the hell out of younger Inspectors. "St. Clair, I've got dead cops scattered around a field north of Old Town. I've got a million lita train laying in pieces. I've got the Chief of Police trying to take up residence in my ass. I've got the media eating us alive. All because of you. Care to try explaining any of this?"

"I can, if you like," St. Clair replied, his expression carefully neutral. He wasn't sure yet if she had been compromised. He hated the very idea of it. He'd known Shade a long time.

"By all means," she sneered. "But be advised, if I don't like it, the next thing I'll be asking you for is your badge."

"The Hazaminie are working with the Ironriggers to summon Obedell back from the beyond at the Hawthorne Theater and both are trying to kill Max Wonder's son out of fear he can stop them."

Shade's jaw worked for a moment. "Okay, you get to keep your badge. Fill me in."

Starting from when he and Tanabuar had arrived in the Auberdeen processing yards, St. Clair told her everything, leaving nothing out, including his carefully laid plan to insure Manascetti exposed himself. That part had been the easiest to manage, really. It'd only taken a couple hours after dinner for him and Tanabuar to figure out how to do it.

"So, let me get this straight," Shade said, pacing the room slowly. "You and Tanabuar decided to invoke

Emergency Protocol Seven as soon as you had a chance to grab this Wonder kid, hoping Manascetti would bust out his illegal stash of firearms in response, then used Wonder as bait by moving him on our train, thus giving the Ironriggers a chance to come at him."

"Exposing the depth of corruption in the Riscadil Police Department, yes," St. Clair said with a nod. "Both Tanabuar and I can confirm that most of the suspects firing on us were uniformed officers working in coordination with Ironrigger members, who were already on the scene. It's why I requested we use only local police, rather than Royal Inspectors. I needed them to leak the information, and to take the bait."

"They blew up the train," Tanabuar added. "A Royal Inspector train."

"He really on painkillers?" Shade asked.

St. Clair nodded. "Actually, yes."

"I was shot," Tanabuar told her. "Percy was, too, but not as bad. My scar will be way sexier."

Rolling her eyes, she turned back to St. Clair. "Of all the dumb stunts you've pulled in your time, Percy, this has got to take the cake."

"Sorry, Gwen," he replied, offering her a tired smile. "I wasn't sure how high this went. When I learned that Jonas Burke had been forced into retirement after revealing a possible case of necromancy to the Royal Inspectors, I had to assume it possible that even you may have been compromised."

"Thanks for the trust," Shade growled.

Settling on the edge of his desk, St. Clair shook his head. "It has nothing to do with trust. After all, a dead woman walking out of the morgue should have raised a big red flag with Riscadil Police Department and with us. Instead, it was all hushed up."

"Who did Burke report this to?" Shade asked, concern clouding her face.

"The head of the Arcana Task Force," Percy answered. "Who, if I'm not mistaken, you've already dispatched to the Hawthorne in an attempt to breach the barrier spell. How's that going, by the way?"

"It's not," she replied slowly. "You think he's in Manascetti's pocket?"

"I think it's a possibility," St. Clair admitted. "One of two, as I see it. First, we've been compromised. That's a disconcerting thought to say the least. Not as much as the second option, however."

"Which is?"

"The Arcana Task Force hasn't had a case of necromancy in twenty years, yet they still draw funds for experts in that field, which we currently do not have on staff," St. Clair explained. "I checked. The last one retired ten years ago."

Shade crossed her arms, frowning. "They've been padding their budget."

"Which will look just as bad to the public should it come to light, as one corrupt Inspector," St. Clair added. "Either way, they are currently attempting to bypass a barrier spell, raised by actual necromancers, with no active expert on that class of magic on hand. Be it deliberate misdirection, or simple stupidity, both at the moment are just as bad."

"And you have a plan to deal with this, as well, I take it?" she asked, already knowing the answer.

"Of course," he confirmed with a smile. "I'm just waiting for Mr. Wonder to make his move. I think it should be coming just about nightfall."

"You mean the suspect you allowed to escape." It was a statement rather than a question.

St. Clair gave a slight nod, looking bemused. "That wasn't exactly part of the plan, but I did make a contingency for it, yes. I had hoped to secure all of his people as well as the corrupt officers and members of the Ironriggers in one fell swoop. Even my plans don't always go as planned."

Shaking her head, Shade accepted that, as usual, St. Clair was ten steps ahead of everyone else. "How much in the know was Wonder on all this?'

St. Clair shook his head. "Not at all. I wasn't certain how much he could be trusted, and I'm still not. However, I do believe he will try to stop this."

"Okay, explain it to me," she sighed. "You know I can't keep up with all your little machinations."

Pausing to clean his glasses, St. Clair gave her a smug look that he knew she hated. "Wonder's crew will, I am sure, have already figured out a way into the Hawthorne. Likely something that will allow them to keep out of sight. They've proven rather resourceful already, and odds are, we wouldn't even know about the Hazaminie gathering at the Hawthorne had it not been for them. Once they're inside, they will create a considerable amount of chaos for the Hazaminie. As they do that, we breach the front doors and catch them all, leaving neither the necromancers nor the Ironriggers any path of escape."

"And how, exactly, do you plan to breach the front doors?" Shade drawled.

"This is the good part," Tanabuar snickered.

"Podest, of course," St. Clair replied, gesturing to the Older, who looked as shocked as Shade did.

"Uh, what?" Podest managed.

"Olders have the ability to project an anti-magic field from their main eye," St. Clair explained. "Certainly powerful enough to bypass a barrier spell."

"Oh, yeah, that," Podest said slowly. "That thing I am bound by law to never do, under threat of having my visa instantly revoked and being deported to my home plane of existence immediately."

"Yes, that," St. Clair agreed.

"I hate this plan," Podest stated.

Shade chewed her lip as she considered it, then nodded. "Okay. Podest, you are temporarily promoted to Acting Inspector, with all rights and privileges, including the use of your anti-magic generating abilities."

"You can't be serious?" the Older squawked.

"I am," she replied sternly. "Percy, you dodged the bullet, again. Try to keep your manipulations to a minimum in the future. I can't cover your ass with the guys in the home office forever, you know."

"I am aware," he said with a slight bow. "As always, I'm grateful for your tolerance, Gwen."

"I'll get some Inspectors rounded up to enact this plan of yours. You two, get some rest," she ordered as she turned to go.

"Actually, I would prefer to head up this operation myself," St. Clair called after her.

She paused, then slowly turned, scowling. "Percy."

"Then I will happily take a week of leave, as punishment."

Throwing her hands up, she nodded. "Fine. A week without you two blowing something up will be like a vacation for me, anyway. Get your battering ram over there ready, as well as anything else you need. I want this done. And before you go on your little sabbatical, you better believe I want a full report on all this. With a flowchart explaining how you pulled it all off, so I can explain it to my own superiors."

"With pleasure, Chief," St. Clair agreed.

"I've been shot," Tanabuar called after her.

"She knows, Molly," his partner said.

"I think the painkillers are wearing off."

"Oh?"

"Yeah," Tanabuar said. "Because I'm starting to realize that I'm in a lot of pain over here."

"Too much?"

He thought about it for a moment, then smiled. "Nah."

"Excellent."

"I hate you, so much," Podest sulked.

* * *

As St. Clair expected, night had fallen by the time Rick and his team managed to navigate the sewers and reach the manhole Charlotte told them about. The rough map Lucy had drawn helped, while the heavy stench did not. Emi had had to stop to hurl on the way, followed by Toddson a few minutes later. Lancaster held it together somehow, while Rick had spent enough time cleaning out chicken coops back home to not be overly bothered by it.

Not to say it was enjoyable, but all thing considered, he was just glad nobody had fallen in the slow moving river of crap that had kept them company all the way there. He figured they would've dealt with it, but he doubted it would be a story anyone would be telling their children.

If any of them lived to have any.

Scouting the area ahead with a flashlight in hand, Rick waved the rest to move into the small alcove beneath the access point. Once they were in, he scanned the sewer tunnel one more time. He'd almost felt as if they were being watched as they'd made their way along, but aside from the ever-present sound of water dripping and the occasional rat, he'd neither seen nor heard anything.

Regardless, he felt more cautious than usual and clicked the light off, waiting in the darkness. After a minute, he shook his head and turned back to the others. The past few days would've rattled anyone, he supposed.

"Toddson, you're up," he said in a hushed tone, waving a hand at the cover a few feet above them.

"I am?" the Cleric asked in confusion. "For what?"

"The Dispel Magic attempt," Lancaster urged.

After a moment, Toddson grinned. "Oh, yeah. Sorry. Forgot what we were doing down here."

"Shocking," Rick sighed.

"Totally," Lancaster deadpanned.

"You guys have kind of gotten used to it, huh?" Toddson asked with a smile. "That's so cool. I love you guys. And girl. You're cool, too. Wasn't trying to leave you out."

"I wasn't feeling left out," Emi fumbled. "But, thank you."

"No worries," the Cleric assured her. "Anyone else feeling like a group hug would fit here?"

"Nope," Rick groaned.

"No," Lancaster slumped.

"Kinda... but... no... maybe... not really... I guess," Emi floundered.

"Cool," Toddson accepted. "What was I doing again?"

Rick turned to the wall, as Lancaster pointed up. Looking up, Toddson laughed and gave a thumbs up. Then stood there for a moment. Rick wondered how bad the wall would hurt his head. Lancaster pointed up again.

"Right," Toddson finally said as it really settled in his brain. "On it. Just, let me check it real quick."

"Please," Lancaster begged. "This sewer air is bad for my hair, you know."

"Is it?" Emi asked, looking worried as she tugged at her own mane.

"For me, yeah," the Rogue told her. "I figure you're fine. It'll probably just make your hair curl a bit more, which might look hot."

Emi made a strange noise and turned bright red. Rick thudded his head against the wall. It hurt. Not too much, though, so he did it again.

Above them, Toddson reached the top of the short ladder and touched a finger to the manhole, setting off an amber-colored ripple. Watching it for a moment, he grunted and climbed back down, dusting his hands off on each other and considering the heavy metal plate for a bit.

"So?" Lancaster asked.

"Definitely a barrier spell," Toddson replied. "I've got an idea, though."

"Todd, I swear to Imonya," Rick snapped.

The Cleric shot him a wide grin. "I'm just messing with you. I think I can dispel the area around the cover. Gimme a minute. Gotta get the boss to put it in my head."

"Did he just say he was messing with us?" Lancaster gasped.

"He did," Rick noted, just as stunned.

"It was pretty funny," Emi giggled.

Both men looked at her in surprise. She flushed again and looked at anything but them. Glancing at each other, the two shrugged. At this point, it really shouldn't have been that surprising.

"Divine one, I beseech thee," Toddson began, a soft golden light gathering around his fingers. "Cast aside this shadow that holds before mine eyes. Pass thy grace on to thine faithful servant, that thy will be done. Wash away this darkness, that thine eyes not be made to suffer it."

As soon as he finished, the light from his fingers danced away, striking the manhole cover, setting off a shower of sparks that went on for several seconds. Save Toddson, everyone ducked, covering their eyes, until the spell effect ended.

"Wow," Toddson said softly. "I was not expecting that. It was kinda cool, though."

"Did it work?" Rick asked.

"Dunno," the Cleric replied. "Guess I should go check that, huh?"

Rick stared at him a moment, still occasionally unsure how to take the man. "Yeah."

Climbing back up, Toddson reached out, touching the cover. Nothing happened. Giving the rest a shrug, he shoved on it, forcing it up. Grinning broadly, he called down, "Hey! It worked! We can get in... wherever this is. Pretty cool, huh?"

"I'll be damned," Rick muttered.

"Whatever else he is," Lancaster chuckled. "He sure does come through when it counts, huh?"

"That he does," Rick agreed. "Okay, Powerage. Let's do this."

"Hang on a sec," Lancaster said, waving Toddson back down. Once he had joined them, the Rogue held a hand out. "No matter how this goes, we do this for Mimi."

Nodding, Rick dropped a hand on his. "And Enzo."

Toddson joined them, saying, "And all the good officers who died last night."

Emi hesitantly added her own hand. "And for ourselves, because we're adventurers and we're brave."

Lancaster smiled at her. "Damn straight."

"Time to go," Rick declared. "No matter what happens, you guys are the best team anyone could ever have. Thank you for being here."

"No place else I'd rather be," Lancaster announced, slapping him on the back.

"Same goes for me," Toddson grinned.

"And me," Emi agreed. "Even if we die, I'm glad it's with you guys."

Patting her shoulder, Rick smiled at her. "Let's rock."

* * *

As Powerage was approaching the manhole above their heads, St. Clair and Tanabuar were arriving outside the Hawthorne, Podest in tow. They had spent their last few hours well, leaving nothing but allowing the final pieces to fall into place. Once that was done, St. Clair knew the outcome of his gambit was up to the gods and the determination of mortals.

"Inspector Mosai," Tanabuar called, waving to the head of the Arcana Task Force.

The Elf glanced their way, and then wandered over to them, shaking his head. "You two should be in a clinic, not here. You had your chance to deal with this. It's my turf now, so take off."

"I understand," St. Clair replied, stepping forward. "However, before we do, I was hoping you could tell me how things are going here. We've put a lot of time into this, after all."

"It's not going," Mosai sorted. "That barrier is tough to break. They must have a dozen casters inside keeping it up.

We'll get through it eventually of course, but it's gonna take time."

"Of course." St. Clair cast a critical eye over the amber glow that rippled around from the points where the Task Force members were trying to counter it. "Out of curiosity, if you'll indulge me, when does Mr. Manascetti plan on it coming down?"

"Excuse me?" Mosai snapped. "You're way out of line, St. Clair!"

"Your financials disagree," Tanabuar snickered, waving a stack of papers. "Unless you're just embezzling money, of course, which would still be terrible. Though that new pool looks nice, I admit."

Mosai stared at him in shock, trying to mouth something, likely an excuse. After a moment, resignation took over, leaving the Elf sagging slightly. Seeing that, St. Clair wiggled a finger, bringing forward several Inspectors he was sure were clean.

"I wouldn't worry too much, Mosai," he said as the Inspector was handcuffed. "Where you're going, you'll have lots of company. Feel free to curse my name on the way out, though it will do you little good."

"You think this is going to do anything?" Mosai asked with a sneer. "You have no idea how deep this goes, St. Clair."

"You are correct," he replied, turning to face Mosai. "But I'm certain you will tell me. These sorts of things are tough to break, of course. It'll take time. We'll get there, though."

With a nod from the human, Mosai was escorted away as several more Royal Inspectors moved in, arresting more members of the Arcana Task Force and a scattering of police officers standing a few yards off. When all eyes turned to him, St. Clair beckoned Podest forward.

"I've got a dozen Puffers already surrounding the building," the Older reported. "They're almost in position. Gimme a second and we should be able to get some idea of how many targets are inside."

"That was fun," Tanabuar beamed, waving to the people being taken away to a waiting police wagon. "We should do this more often."

"We do this all the time," St. Clair snorted.

"Well, yeah, but not with such a big audience," his partner replied with a wicked smile. "I wonder how many people are gonna be calling in sick tomorrow?"

Podest gave a laugh at that. "Hey, Percy, that reminds me. Costanza and Guinell just got arrested at the Auberdeen station. Looks like they were heading out for vacation."

"Solstice came early this year," the human said wryly. "How wonderful."

"Puffers are up," Podest announced, turning slightly to project a three-dimensional image of the theater. After a moment, small dots of red began to appear. At first, it wasn't many. Very quickly, that changed.

"Aw, shit," Tanabuar wilted.

"Indeed," St. Clair agreed.

"Okay, this is bad," Podest snarled. "We've got more than fifty hot bodies in there. Most of them are in the main auditorium area, but it looks like we've got a few patrolling the hallways, too."

"Any way to tell which ones are Wonder's team?" St. Clair asked, studying the map intently.

"Nope," the Older admitted, turning the image slightly. "The barrier is putting up some interference. The Puffers can't get anything but heat signatures. No way to tell who's who in there."

"This is not good, Percy," Tanabuar pointed out.

"It isn't, no," his partner sighed, his whole plan starting to come apart.

"Hold up," Podest said. "Four new signatures just popped up in the basement. Dunno how they got there."

"Think it's them?" Tanabuar asked.

St. Clair looked down at the manhole cover a half a step away from him, a slow smile beginning to spread across his face. So very resourceful, indeed. For a moment, he was actually surprised, a sensation he wasn't overly familiar with. Or at least, he hadn't been before Rick Wonder came into his life. It seemed to be happening a lot since then.

"Get ready," he told the other two. "It'll be our turn to take center stage soon enough."

"Pretty sure he means that's them," Tanabuar offered.

"It's good you've learned to speak Percy," Podest drawled. "Dark gods know, I wouldn't have figured that out on my own."

"Be nice," the Chthonian protested. "I've been shot."

"Stop milking it, Molly," St. Clair deadpanned. "Podest, get in position. As soon as they breach the auditorium, we go. It's time to end this."

"So dramatic," Tanabuar breathed. "So sexy."

St. Clair felt it best to ignore him for once.

* * *

Rick went first, slipping into the basement of the decaying theater with barely a whisper, his eyes scanning the dark for any sign of movement. He held there on one knee for what felt like several minutes, barely allowing himself to breath. Finally he eased forward allowing Lancaster to join him.

As soon as he was clear, the Rogue darted across the room, putting his back to the wall by the door, listening. Rick held position over the open manhole, covering the other two as they climbed up. Toddson first, who all but tiptoed across the room, easing his mace out to the ready.

Last was Emi. Rick knew she was a ball of nerves at this point, probably more terrified than she'd ever been. She barely showed it, though. As she entered the wide, empty room, she steadied herself, pulling the fireburst wand free of her belt and nodding that she was good to go.

In that moment, he found her beautiful and brave.

Casting a wary glance to Lancaster and getting an all clear sign, Rick rounded them up, keeping his voice barely above a whisper as he said, "I'll take point. Lancaster, you cover our rear. Toddson, you get my back and give Emi some cover. Got it?"

They nodded, each of them as ready as they could be for what they knew was sure to be a slow march to a brutal death. None of them hesitated, though. Rick felt he should say something, tell them how proud he was, how glad he was to have them there, to know them. In their eyes, he saw it wasn't necessary. They felt the same.

Moving to the door, Rick paused, listening, pulling one of the Whip Blades free. Turning the handle slowly and getting a soft click as it opened, he palmed it the rest of the way and stepped out into the hall. To his right, the passageway went to a dead end, while to his left, a flight of steps headed up a few feet away.

Giving a hold sign, he slid forward, pulling his other sword. Mounting the steps one at a time, he watched the door at the top draw closer by inches, barely allowing himself to breathe. After a brief eternity, he stood before it and put his ear to the old wood. Hearing nothing, he felt tenser and waved the others up.

When they had joined him, he put Lancaster to the hinge side of the door as he moved to the handle, twisting it lightly. The creaking sounded deafening in the silence, making him wince. Getting the faint click that let him know it was free, he pushed on it, sending it open an inch. Across from him, Lancaster squinted, scanning the hallway beyond.

Again, time stretched out impossibly until the Rogue gave a nod. Spending a half second to breathe, Rick pushed the door wider and swung out, facing the direction Lancaster hadn't been able to see. Dark, empty corridor greeted him. Turning back, he saw the same in the other direction and allowed himself to let go of the breath he'd been holding.

Peeling, moldy wallpaper decorated the hall dotted with old wall sconces, many of which drooped, long broken. Pushing forward, he felt Lancaster swing out, covering his back, allowing Toddson and Emi to take up position between them. Glancing back, Rick nodded and headed deeper into the theater.

He knew they were somewhere near the rear of the building. Charlotte had told him that much. Backstage would be accessible somewhere ahead, as would a way into the lobby and the central auditorium. All he had to do was keep moving forward and sooner or later, he'd find them.

A few yards along, he spotted a branching hallway to his right and pulled up short at a flicker of light along the wall. Holding up his fist, he brought them all to a stop and crept closer, stopped at the corner and waited. Soft voices reached him, little more than murmurs that steadily drew closer. Made sense there would be patrols.

How many was too hard to pick out. At least two, for sure. Sliding back a step, he readied himself, swords low and pulled back. The flickering of light grew brighter as the patrol drew closer, their voices becoming clearer as they complained about having to wander the halls while the big shots in the auditorium breached the dimensional barrier.

Three, Rick realized, as they drew close. There were three. He could pick out their voices clearly. There was no time left to warn the others. He had to hope for the best. If they blew it here, they'd never get close to the auditorium. Every guard in the place would come down on them, pen them in and likely kill them. At best, hold them up until the ritual was done and over.

As soon as they cleared the corner, two in the lead, one trailing two steps behind, Rick lunged forward. The two in front, a Half-Elf and a human, gaped in shock as he sprang at them, impaling both, lifting them off their feet and slamming them down as he went to a knee. The third jerked back, then hesitated. A dagger found his throat before he could do anything else, sending him toppling to the floor.

Pushing up, pulling the Whip Blades free as he did, Rick nodded to Lancaster and got one in return. As the Rogue searched their pockets, Rick scanned the passage they had come down, but could see little. Glancing back the way they had been going, he struggled with it for a moment. Either way would likely get them where they wanted to go, but which way reduced their chances of running into another patrol?

Lancaster stood up, shaking his head. Besides a couple of short swords, they'd had nothing of use on them. Rick had kind of hoped to get another of those fireburst wands, but it didn't really matter. All they could do now was work with what they had and hope for the best.

Deciding to push on in the direction they'd been going, they soon reached a set of double doors, which Rick realized would be the backstage access Charlotte mentioned. Beyond would be another long hall that would take them to the lobby and likely, past at least one access point to the auditorium. From here, things were only going to get more dangerous.

Shaking that away, Rick waved Lancaster up and allowed him to spend a moment listening at the door. When his face clouded with concern, Rick leaned in, hearing something but unable to make out what. It was soft, distant and rhythmic, whatever it was.

To hell with it, he thought and nodded to the Rogue to be ready. Each grasped a doorknob, and after a brief three count, threw the doors wide, revealing the expected passage and a trio of guards a few feet ahead.

Shit.

Rick darted ahead, hoping to catch them before they recovered, and felt a dagger whistle past his ear. Before he'd covered half the distance, one went down, Lancaster's shot finding his eye. A step later, a bolt of energy shot past him, striking the second in the head and immolating it into nothing. Two steps later, almost to the third, Rick saw him jerk and run into a passage on the right he hadn't been able to see.

Rounding it, Rick came to a fast stop as the guard yelled at another trio positioned deeper into the passage, which let out into the auditorium. Back lit by blazing lights, the guards all looked to him as the sound he and Lancaster had heard came into focus. Chanting, at least a dozen voices, all in perfect unison.

"Aw, hell," Rick muttered as the guards pulled their weapons and came running, joined by six more from within the auditorium itself.

"Run!" he snapped, rushing down the hallway towards the lobby, hoping he could get in the auditorium from another passage.

Toddson huffed at his heels, his armor clanking heavily as he tried to keep up. A few steps behind him, Emi gave a squeal and ran as hard as she could, while Lancaster covered her back, throwing another dagger and dropping one of their pursuers.

Seeing a second entry to the auditorium, Rick skidded around the corner and kept going, hoping to catch the chanters unaware while their guards gave chase. Spotting another guard ahead, Rick groaned and sped at him, knowing the others were right on his heels.

Seeing him, the guard jerked a wand up and backpedaled away as Rick broke into the auditorium. Red-orange energy coalesced and sparked off a ball of arcane energy, one Rick had seen before. A fireburst. If it hit him, he was finished.

Jabbing one sword ahead of him, he twisted the other down and swung at the ball as it closed on him. He'd managed to cut through it before. Too late, he realized he had gotten the angle of his blade wrong, as he caught the fireburst with the flat of the scimitar and batted it away, changing the angle to up.

Startled by that, Rick slowed to a stop, the guard having fled at his approach. Two things hit him in that exact moment. The first was that the Whip Blades could do way more than he'd been told. The second was the almost forty people in the auditorium who were coming to their feet, suddenly aware of the intrusion and looking right at him.

Then he noticed the third thing. He felt he should have noticed it first, but a lot was happening, so he wasn't going to be too hard on himself. After all, he was about to die, staring at a mass of swirling black energy ripping the fabric of space open above the stage. Surrounded by the chanters he'd heard chanting, Rick stared into a breach of the dimensional barrier and the place beyond where Obedell had been banished by his father.

"Aw, come on," he heard Lancaster say from behind him.

The auditorium burst into action as the fireburst Rick had deflected hit the ceiling and exploded, showering them all with debris.

* * *

"Looks like they dealt with that," Podest chuckled as Rick's team dispatched the first patrol they encountered. "If they hang that right, they should be able to reach the main stage from the back."

"I doubt that," St. Clair commented, studying the theater layout. "The Hazaminie probably sealed it off. They tend to be cautious."

"Looks like they thought of that, too," Tanabuar agreed as Rick's team moved on. "Though they're gonna hit that bunch in the hall ahead now."

"Should we do something?" Podest asked.

"Not yet," St. Clair replied. "We want chaos, remember?"

"We also want Rick and his people to survive," Tanabuar argued.

St. Clair hesitated, then shook his head. "Give them a bit. Let's see what they do."

The Chthonian and Older exchanged a look, but offered nothing more. St. Clair was in charge and knew, if anything went wrong, it would fall on him. A moment later, they watched as Rick's team tackled the next batch of guards and saw the one escape.

"That's gonna make some chaos," Podest said. "Never thought I'd be against the idea."

"They're on the move," Tanabuar added. "I think they have the Hazaminie's attention now."

St. Clair nodded at that. "Agreed. It's about time for us to make our big entrance then."

"Oh, shit," Podest gaped as he saw Powerage round the turn, heading into the auditorium. "Not a smart move there, kids."

"Percy," Tanabuar snapped.

"Right," the human said, turning towards the assembled Royal Inspectors. "Everyone..."

A small explosion ripped through the roof of the Hawthorne, sending even St. Clair back a step. Recovering quickly, he pressed ahead. "All assault teams, in position, now!"

Twenty Royal Inspectors, outfitted with arcane resistance vests and helmets, rushed towards the doors. Most carried firearms, but several were sporting stun wands as well. They would need to capture as many as possible alive if they hoped to root out how deeply the corruption had gone.

"Podest, it's time," St. Clair called, waving the Older forward.

"I got it from here," he chuckled, dismissing the projection of the interior. "Check it out."

Concentrating on the building before him, Podest's central eye went wide, rippling with blackish-green energy. The barrier around the Hawthorne reacted vibrantly for a moment before shattering, raining amber sparks down on the assault teams.

"That felt good," the Older sighed in delight.

"Go!" St. Clair bellowed.

* * *

Rick ran for the central aisle of the auditorium, not wanting to get caught up in the narrow spaces between the seating or one of the small side aisles. Behind him, he heard Emi go screaming in the same direction, their pursuers catching up with them. He couldn't tell where Toddson and Lancaster where as a wave of Hazaminie came rushing at them.

Barely reaching the central aisle, Rick caught a short sword against a scimitar and jabbed forward with the other, sending a necromancer screaming to the floor. Spinning on his heel, he spotted Toddson caught up in the small aisle along the edge of the auditorium, swinging at enemies with his mace and doing a fair job of holding them off.

Another bolt of arcane energy shot from behind him, telling him where Emi was, or at least, he hoped so. He didn't have time to check on Lancaster, as three more Hazaminie came at him, two with short swords, and the third with a dagger. Backing up a step, he caught the two short blades against his own and felt the dagger dig past his armor and into his stomach.

Biting down the pain, Rick relaxed his grip on the swords, allowing his foes to overbalance, while he spun the scimitars around and caught them in the shoulders. As they fell, he pushed between them, catching the shocked dagger thrower with both blades in the chest.

Behind him, Emi was casting, throwing firebolts as fast as she could, but Rick could tell she was winded and half her attempts ended in her stammering and gasping. He had to get back and cover her. Glancing around, he knew he'd never make it.

Across from him, Toddson forced the knot forming around him back, giving himself enough time to chant a quick spell. Brilliant energy formed around the head of his mace as he swung it, knocking one Hazaminie's jaw off before the spell released, sending a bolt of golden white radiance tearing through the seating. Necromancers were scattered in the wake of it, giving him a moment to smile.

It lasted only that moment, as one of the pursuing guards saw a chance and pushed forward, sliding his short sword between the plate armor's seams, burying it deep. Toddson cried out and staggered, before driving an elbow back, sending the guard reeling. Spinning, he finished him with a blow from his mace.

In that brief blink, he saw Emi take a crossbow bolt to the shoulder, flopping back into a seat as she screamed. Further back, Lancaster was in a slow retreat, fending off enemies with daggers alone. Across from him, Rick was bleeding and facing the main bulk of the Hazaminie.

"This is not good," he muttered, looking down at the sword sticking out of him. "Really not good."

Rick heard Emi's scream as well, but couldn't spare a look back as enemies rushed him. Crossbow shots whipped past him, forcing him to dodge to the side, unable to block that many. Arcs of arcane energy came as well, sending him scrambling and allowing Hazaminie to close on him with swords and daggers.

The first two he deflected, but they left his own weapons too high, giving another dagger free purchase in his stomach. Grimacing, he slapped it away along with the first and waded into the thick of them, swinging wildly.

He'd known. Of course he'd known. This had been a one-way ticket from the start. There had never been any chance. Still, in the distance, as the gaping hole in reality grew wider, he couldn't help but feel as if he had failed. Not just his team, but his father.

Obedell was right there and Rick Wonder couldn't get any closer.

A sword slashed his bicep, cutting through armor and flesh alike, leaving his entire arm numb. The Whip Blade slipped away as a crossbow bolt found his leg, sending him to his knee. The Hazaminie with the sword stood over him, grinning as he swung. Just smiling away at killing a man.

Rick got his other sword up, sending the short sword sliding along it, but the force of the blow shoved his arm down too far. The Hazaminie jerked back, clocking Rick across the face with the pommel, making him see stars.

This was it.

Behind him, Emi was trying to stand, yanking out crossbow bolts as she did. Across from him, Toddson was being ganged, daggers and sword jabbing at the weak points in his armor. Somewhere, Lancaster fought a losing battle to stem the tide and reach his allies.

The Hazaminie short sword went up and Rick stared death in the face.

A gunshot echoed through the din, as the Hazaminie pitched backward, his killing blow aborted. Blinking, Rick turned his head and watched as two teams of Royal Inspectors rushed in from the lobby.

Even ten more with firearms wasn't going to be enough, he realized. The Hazaminie with wands were already regrouping near the stage, preparing an assault of their own as something in the portal stirred, reaching out for them all.

* * *

Further back in the auditorium, Lancaster felt panic setting in. From where he stood, he saw Rick go down. He saw Emi go down. He saw Toddson being swamped. He saw it all and could do nothing. His once pristine white clothes were soaked in blood, much of it his own. There were too many, and with his team scattered and dying, he knew he couldn't hold them off for long.

The gunshot was deafening as the assault teams stormed the chamber. Stunned for a moment, Lancaster could only stare as they took up positions, clearing the ones closest, which included the press closing on him. As the Hazaminie realized what was happening, they began to fall back, racing for the stage.

"Thanks, guys," he muttered as he ran back down the aisle, trying to reach Toddson.

The Cleric lay slumped over a seat, trying to stand and failing, as he bled heavily. Near panic bloomed fully in the Rogue as he saw just how bad Toddson's wounds were. He needed help fast, if he was going to survive.

"Hey, Todd, hang on," he called, slipping to a stop and grabbing the Cleric by the shoulders.

"Hey, yeah," Toddson murmured with a smile. "That'd be great right now."

"What?" Lancaster panted. "Todd?"

Looking up, Toddson chanted softly, holding out a trembling hand. Greenish energy swirled for a moment, then went dark as Toddson collapsed. Unsure what he'd been trying to do, Lancaster pulled him up and around, settling him in a seat.

"Hang tight, buddy," he said, glancing back to the armed and armored assault team as they picked shots across the auditorium. "I think the cavalry just arrived."

Toddson didn't hear him. Slowly, Lancaster realized it. Toddson slumped in the seat, smiling, his eyes seeing nothing.

Sagging, Lancaster choked out a sob and with a trembling hand, closed the Cleric's eyes. Then, grief turned to rage.

"You sons of bitches!"

* * *

Healing magic swirled around Emi as she tied to stand, gasping for breath. She felt her wounds close, at least mostly, as her struggle to get air into her lungs eased. Staggering for a moment, the pain fading to a dull ache, she glanced around, spotting the Royal Inspectors as they lay siege to the auditorium.

Then she saw Lancaster, as he bowed his head over Toddson's still form. The act of breathing, so hard a moment ago, then made easier by Toddson's dying act, suddenly became impossible.

Her chest tightened as her vision funneled down to a point, focused on Lancaster as he screamed and charged the Hazaminie that were falling back to the stage. Even the dull ache went away, replaced by a numbness that filled her and left her unable to move.

If only it had remained.

Anger exploded through her. Red hot, like a wild fire, it raged out from her heart, where she had long buried it. All her anger at the world, at her family, at her teachers and everything burst forth, boiling through her, setting her on fire.

She'd been a good girl. All her life. Just like they wanted. A good girl. She'd done as she was told. No matter what it was, she'd done her best. A good girl. It hadn't been enough. Never enough. Always those looks of disapproval hovered. In her parents' eyes. In her siblings' smirks. In her teachers' disdain.

Emi was sick of being a good girl. She just hadn't known it.

The fire inside her knew, though. She could never be good enough. Not for them. They didn't want her to be. They wanted her to fail. In her failure, they felt taller, better, superior.

Everyone wanted to look down on her. Everyone but her friends. Everyone but Powerage. Mimi hadn't looked down on her. Toddson hadn't, either. Lancaster didn't. No, not even Rick, the son of Max Wonder, looked down on her.

To them, she was good enough.

It burned so hot, the fire billowing up from her heart, where she had locked away her rage for so long. It burned and it wanted out.

Reddish energy swirled around her hands as she raised them, her face twisting into hate.

"FIREBOLT!"

* * *

Rick clenched his fist as the healing energy washed over him. Not sure what had just happened, he grabbed the sword he'd dropped and rose to his feet as he looked around. He saw Lancaster and Toddson and understood instantly what the Cleric had done, what he'd sacrificed. Lancaster's scream echoed the one he felt building in himself.

He saw the Hazaminie retreating to hold the stage, crossbows and wands firing back at the Royal Inspector assault teams. It felt distant, though. Like something he was watching from far away, unable to process the crossfire he was standing in.

Red energy flashed past him as he heard Emi screaming. Turning his head, he saw the hate and rage on her face as she advanced into the central aisle, marching towards the Hazaminie, blasting them with quick, single word incantations. The tears on her face and the rage in her eyes left him lost.

Lancaster was running. Rick saw that. He was running for the stage. Rick felt himself move, but he had no idea what he was doing. Not until the first bolts struck the Rogue in the chest. Lancaster didn't even slow down. Rick realized, as the world drifted back into focus, that he was running, too.

He was screaming.

Before him, above the stage, clawed hands of black smoke grasped the edges of the portal, pulling a shadowed figure forward. It roared out, but it was low, like a moan. Obedell was coming.

Deflecting crossbow shots and wand strikes, Rick gave Emi cover, allowing her to lay waste to the Hazaminie with her rage-soaked casting. Gunshots fell silent, but he couldn't care. All he could think of, all that mattered, was stopping them. Stopping him.

Bringing the scimitars up, Rick dropped to his knees, slashing out, disemboweling four necromancers in a single move. Springing up, he took two steps and jumped, rolling across the stage. No matter what, Obedell wasn't getting through. Not after all it had cost. For Mimi. For Enzo. For Toddson.

For Max.

No more death.

The casters knelt in a semi-circle on the far side of the portal Obedell's shadowed form struggled to get through, the homeless innocents they had sacrificed for it laying before them in pools of blood. Wrapped in a shroud of otherworldly smoke, the Lich clawed at that gash in reality, desperate to break free. To be free.

"You cannot stop this, boy!"

Rick snapped around to find Tashitia smirking at him. Behind him, Manascetti was scowling, glancing from Rick to Obedell. He didn't care about either of them. It was the semi-circle of casters he had to take out.

"I think, perhaps, you should feel pain as he returns," Tashitia gloated, raising a hand, angry purple energy gathering around it. "Writhe in agony as my master undoes your fool of a father's legacy, impudent child!"

Torn between going for the casters, and defending himself against the Elf's assault, Rick hesitated. Raising the scimitars, he braced himself. If he was fast enough, he could cut through the magic, dive across the stage, and kill at least a couple of the necromancers holding the portal open. If he was really lucky, maybe it would be enough.

Tashitia began to chant, then simply exploded into green ash.

Rick didn't know what to do with that.

"Hey, assholes," a voice boomed across the chamber. "I think that's enough of your shit!"

Stunned, Rick turned towards that voice and saw Tanabuar and St. Clair standing at the main entrance from the lobby, guns raised. Between them floated an Older, one of his eye stalks still wreathed in arcane energy.

"Nighty-night," Podest smirked, his central eye flaring.

The portal collapsed instantly, severing the half-formed body of Obedell. Rick jumped back a step as the Lich fell in pieces and crumbled to dust. Around him, the casters gaped in horror as their master not only failed to return, but lost several major pieces of himself in the attempt.

"Damn you, Ricky," Manascetti snarled, pulling a revolver as he advanced. "Immortality was in my hands! All you had to do was fucking die! Why won't you just gods damned die!"

Stunned, Rick barely got a sword up as the Dwarf fired on him. He felt the bullet hit the scimitar and staggered back, falling off the stage. Rolling, he gained his feet, surprised to be alive, as Manascetti glared down at him.

"All you fucking morons had to do was die so I could live forever," he snarled. "But none of you are even worth that!"

Rick snapped an arm back without thinking and swung. The Whip Blade segmented, lashing out and wrapped around Manascetti's throat. The Dwarf gurgled in surprise.

He didn't think about it. He didn't hesitate. He just yanked his arm back, pulling the Whip Blade to him. As it reformed into a sword, Manascetti's head rolled across the floor.

Rick stood for a moment staring down at it, as the Dwarf's body slumped and fell back across the stage. It was over.

"I guess," Lancaster said, staggering towards him, a smirk on his face. "You really *are* Max Wonder's son."

Rick tried to say something. Words wouldn't come. Slowly, Lancaster reached out for him, over a dozen bolts in his chest and stomach. Dropping the swords, Rick grabbed him as he fell.

"We did it, Rick," Lancaster whimpered in his ear.

"We did, yeah," Rick choked out, holding him.

"We're heroes, yeah?"

"Damn right we are," Rick cried.

Lancaster went limp in his arms.

Across the chamber, St. Clair lowered his revolver. He didn't feel the need for it anymore.

* * *

Rick sat on the curb wrapped in a blanket, staring at nothing. Emi sat beside him, huddled in a blanket of her own. She'd cried for a while, but eventually stopped. Rick kind of wished she would've continued. The dull look of pain on her face was worse.

"Rick, there you are," Tanabuar called, moving through the crowd of Royal Inspectors, police and more who filled the street outside the theater.

Giving him a glance, Rick went back to staring at the cobblestones.

Tanabuar paused, for once in his life not sure what to say. After a moment, he simply sat next to Rick, watching as people worked around them. There really wasn't anything to say, he supposed. Not after that.

"You guys been treated by a healer yet?" he finally managed, though it felt dumb and awkward.

Rick stirred slightly and nodded. "Yeah. The worst of the injuries anyway."

"The worst, yeah," the Chthonian replied, nodding as if any healer could tend the worst of the injuries Rick and Emi had suffered. "You need anything?"

"I have no idea," Rick admitted.

"Yeah, I get that," Tanabuar said, voice tinged with sorrow. "Give us a bit, okay? We'll get you guys home here shortly."

"Home?" Rick asked, giving him a curious look.

"You know, Charlotte's place," Tanabuar offered, trying to smile a little. "I mean, that's where you guys were staying, right?"

"Yeah," Rick faltered, turning back to Emi. "Home. Of course."

The Chthonian slumped slightly, feeling awful. He knew there wasn't anything that could be said to make it easier. He knew that personally. He'd been in Rick's position himself. Before he'd joined the Royal Inspectors, he'd lost partners and good friends in the line of duty. There really wasn't anything anyone could say. It didn't make it any easier, though. It always felt as if there should be something, even when there wasn't.

"I know it won't help," he finally offered, his voice low. "Nothing will. I get that. Still, I thought you might want to know. We're collecting everything. If Obedell's apocryphanal really is here, we'll find it and destroy it. Not that it matters. Pretty sure getting torn in half by the dimensional barrier will kill even a Lich."

Rick said nothing. Tanabuar hadn't really expected him to.

"Like I said, it won't help, but I thought you'd want to know, they didn't die for nothing."

"Thanks," Rick replied after a long pause. "I mean, I get what you're trying to say, and I appreciate it. Thank you, Molly."

"Yeah, sure," Tanabuar answered. "Percy says we can wait to get your statements. Probably a day or two, if you guys want. Right now, he just wants to get you two out of here, you know?"

"Tell him I said thanks," Rick replied at length. "He's an okay guy, isn't he?"

"Percy?" Tanabuar asked with surprise. "He's kind of a narcissist, a little condescending, terrible with people, rude, arrogant and he has no sense of humor."

"Other than that, though," Rick agreed with a tired, thin smile.

Tanabuar returned it, grabbing Rick's shoulder and giving it a gentle squeeze. "Other than that, yeah, he's the best."

"Thanks for coming," Rick told him. "We'd have died in there too, if it wasn't for you guys."

"It's what we do," the Chthonian grinned.

"Yeah. This city needs guys like you."

"And you," he pointed out.

Rick shook his head. "Nah. The world doesn't need adventurers anymore. St. Clair was right about that."

Tanabuar wasn't sure what to say to that. All he could do was sit, feeling a profound sense of sadness as Rick stood and took Emi by the hand. All he could do was watch as Rick told her they were going home and led her away.

The world has lost something, he thought. *Something precious.*

He sat on the curb, his shoulder aching, as Anton Strakinsy found Rick and Emi, struggled with what to say, then finally nodded, agreeing to take them back to Charlotte's.

"Take care, Rick," Tanabuar murmured. "To hell with the world. You're a hero in my eyes."

St. Clair found him sitting there a few minutes later, and after a moment, eased himself down to join his partner. Together they watched Rick Wonder leave. The media didn't notice. The other Inspectors, officers and officials didn't notice. Only they did.

"He'll be okay, Molly," St. Clair said after a bit as he tugged his glasses off and cleaned them. "He's just in shock right now. Give it a month and he'll be causing us all kinds of new problems."

"You think?"

"I do," St. Clair lied.

Heaving a sigh, Tanabuar looked back at the Hawthorne. "Well, at least this mess didn't get worse."

"It did not," his partner agreed. "Though, I think it might still."

"Why do you have to go and say stuff like, Percy?" the Chthonian whined. "I mean, come on!"

St. Clair gave him a tired smile. "Well, Valsail is in the wind, along with whatever she knew. We still don't have a bead on Avalinion, much less what part she played in all this, or what her agenda even was."

"Okay, fine," Tanabuar grumbled. "But Manascetti is dead and we have probable cause to search his home, and probably dismantle the entire Ironrigger operation. Not to mention, we got a lot of corrupt cops and Royal Inspectors in cells."

St. Clair shrugged. "Tip of the iceberg, Molly. Corruption spreads downward, you know."

"Oh, one other thing," Tanabuar griped. "Obedell appears to be dead for good. We got that."

"'Appears' being the operative word," St. Clair replied.

Tanabuar scowled at him, then very deliberately, slapped him upside the back of the head.

"The hell, Molly?" the human yelped.

"Just for five minutes, Percy," Tanabuar begged. "Five minutes. That's all I'm asking. Five minutes of you not being you. We got a win. Be happy."

"Molly," St. Clair started, only to get a hand slapped over his mouth.

"Five minutes," Tanabuar ordered. "Be happy, Percy. It's the least we can do for those two. They lost a hell of a lot tonight so we could have this win. Okay?"

To Tanabuar's surprise, as he removed his hand, St. Clair gave a slow nod and smiled warmly. "Yeah. Okay, partner. We got a win, and it's a damn good one."

"Thank you," the Chthonian huffed. "Now go get me my damn lemon cookies!"

"Yes, sir," St. Clair smirked, giving him a sloppy salute. "Here in about five minutes."

"Dick."

* * *

It took a few days to fully assess everything. Crime scene specialists went over every inch of the Hawthorne. Anything that might remotely be a possible apocryphanal was taken, cataloged and stored under constant guard. Prisoners were interrogated, yielding new leads on more corrupt officials higher in the police force and the city government.

Rick and Emi gave their statements, after which all charges against them were dropped. St. Clair and Tanabuar went on their vacation after a full report, complete with a flowchart, had been handed in to Chief Inspector Shade. Other Inspectors were assigned the plethora of new cases that night had created, keeping them busy for more days to come.

The search for Lucinia continued for a while, but eventually even that was dropped, the Elf having apparently vanished into thin air if she had ever been there, which most of the Royal Inspectors doubted. Necromancers, sure, but what St. Clair's report said about her was a bit hard to swallow. The same went for Neba Valsail. Much like Lucinia, she had simply disappeared without a trace, and eventually, people stopped looking very hard. Even after a search of her home had revealed a hidden room and a considerable library of books on necromancy.

Manascetti's autopsy revealed he had late-stage cancer. Even had Rick not killed him, the Dwarf wouldn't have lasted another month. A search of his house turned up medical information, which led to a healer who confessed he'd been keeping Manascetti alive for almost three years as the cancer spread, slowed by his spellcasting, but impossible to cure.

Friends were buried in simple, small ceremonies, attended by only a few who knew what part they had played in the events of that night. Slowly, time passed, days turning to weeks, as all that had happened began to fade into the background of more important news and needs.

Two full weeks passed. The Hawthorne returned to being an abandoned building, slowly collapsing as investors tried to figure out what to do with it. Already a relic of the past, the Hazaminie had made the former heart of culture and arts in Riscadil a pariah.

Nobody went near it, much less into it. For the city at large, the matter was settled and more pressing issues pulled their attention away. It took only two weeks for the grand old theater to fall silent and forgotten once more.

That night, exactly two weeks after Rick and his team fought for their lives, two of them in vain, something stirred. On the stage, directly below where the portal had opened, a single board rattled. Not heavily, but lightly, as if the wind had caught it for a moment.

Smoke drifted from it, slowly at first, wispy tendrils of thick darkness. Quickly, it grew into a billowing fog that swirled into a small cyclone, growing tighter and faster as the seconds passed. Parts of it broke off, splitting out, growing denser, thicker and more solid.

The cyclone became a humanoid form, not overly tall, just under six feet as it settled, constricting into bone, muscle and rotting flesh. When it was done, the remains of that thick, dark smoke, drifted down into a tattered old robe that closed around the figure left standing on the stage.

"Hello, Riscadil," Obedell the Arch Lich called out in triumph. "I'm back!"

Silence fell as he stood, arms flung wide. He stayed that way for a moment. Somewhere, a rat skittered away. Realizing that it was really quiet, Obedell looked around, his arms dropping to his sides. Turning a slow circle, he really took in the empty, dark, still theater.

"Well, that's just... rude," he grumbled, flopping his arms in agitation. "Big, grand entrance here! Been planning it for years! Hello?"

Silence answered him.

"Man," the Lich fumed. "You go through all the trouble and this is what you get. I've heard of tough crowds, but this is pretty ridiculous."

The silence didn't seem to care.

"I see you haven't changed at all, Riscadil," he pouted. "Bet I could go walking down the street looking like this and you wouldn't even notice. Kinda hurts my feelings a little, to be honest. I thought we had a thing."

Slow clapping broke the silence. Obedell turned, feeling somehow more offended than he already had. It was that kind of slow clapping that managed to be sarcastic. He'd always hated that kind of clapping. It was what people did when they wanted you to know they didn't mean it.

"Look at you," Neba chuckled as she walked out onto the stage. "All dressed up and nobody cares."

Obedell's fingers twitched, but he felt no arcane energy. Naturally. He'd been trapped in that other realm for a long time. It would take a while for his powers to return. Which just meant five minutes after getting back, he was already in deep shit. He wanted to be surprised, but when he thought about, couldn't be. That's sort of how things worked, really.

"Neba, you look... older," he finally offered.

"Gee, thanks," she snorted, waving a hand at him. "You look more decayed than usual yourself."

"Twenty years away from my source of power," he replied with a nonchalant shrug. "It's rough on the complexion, you know."

"No, yeah, I get that," she said, walking around him, a bemused look on her face. "Couldn't find a decent tailor, either, I see."

"You're lucky I've got this on," he retorted. "However bad my face looks, down there looks worse."

Neba coughed a laugh at that. "Think I'll pass on checking it out."

Obedell smiled, watching her wander her way around him. "So, nice as it is to catch up, last I saw you, you were holding open a portal for Max to banish me. Leaves a guy wondering, what's up with the friendly chit-chat?"

Neba shrugged, finally stopping to give him a humorous grin. "World's changed, Obedell. Things aren't how they use to be."

He wasn't sure how to take that. "I swear, if you've got Delilah, Caster, and that other guy... what was his name?"

"Garvin," she offered.

"Yeah, him," Obedell laughed, snapping his fingers. "Can't ever remember his name. Anyway, if you've got them backstage ready to play 'This is Your Life,' I'm gonna pass. At least until I've had a chance for a shower, some new threads, and maybe a few souls to suck on so I look less like a zombie. I'm sure you understand."

"I do, yeah," Neba agreed. "They aren't here, though. It's just us. I figured you'd be popping up about now, and considering how things went when they tried to pull you through, I thought you might could use some help."

Obedell really didn't know what to do with that. "Help? You? Helping me? Am I in the right dimension, 'cause this feels a little mirror universe-ry for me."

"Like I said, the world's changed," Neba told him with a shrug. "I thought, if I helped you, then maybe you could help me with a few things."

"Like?" he asked slowly, not sensing any other living beings around, but still very wary.

She bobbed her head around a little. "Oh, you know. A few wrinkles on the face. Things that didn't use to sag, sagging. That sort of stuff."

Obedell blinked in surprise. "Hold up. Seriously? You are betraying everything and everyone you once held dear because you're getting older?"

Neba shrugged. "Turns out, I'm kind of vain. Didn't see that coming, but the young never do until their good looks start fading. Weird how that works, isn't it?"

"Wow," the Lich managed. "I'm sorry, I'm just having a hard time with this. I mean, Neba, come on. There's shallow, then there's this. I feel ashamed just talking to you. I can't imagine what your friends would say."

"What friends?" she asked, turning serious. "Max threw himself through that portal. Delilah bailed on me and took Castor with her. Garvin went... wherever it is he went. My friends all walked out on me and left me to deal with the mess they'd made of this city. Not just in that fight, but after, as the whole damn world readjusted to a new reality without monsters like you rampaging around all the time."

"Ask for my help, then call me a monster," he sulked. "That's hurtful, you know."

"You eat people's souls," she drawled.

"Only the tasty-looking ones," he replied with a look of innocence that did not go well with his desiccated face.

Neba rubbed her eyes, having forgotten just how big a pain in the ass he was. "Okay, look, here's the deal. I'll help you get someplace you can recover your power and your appearance. In return, I want access to one of your labs so I can undo this whole getting old thing that I'm not enjoying. You in, or am I calling the Royal Inspectors to come toss you in an anti-magic cell, someplace very deep and very dark?"

"When you put it that way," he huffed. "Fine. Deal. Just let me grab my apocryphanal. It isn't the sort of thing you leave laying around in an abandoned theater, you know?"

Neba shook her head, watching as he knelt down, and pried up the board that had issued him forth. It took her moment to really get it.

"Your apocryphanal is an old board?" she asked, incredulous beyond anything she'd ever experienced, and she'd known Max Wonder.

Obedell held it up as he stood. "Well, yeah. It's from my room, when I was a kid."

"What?" she managed.

"I have a lot of fond memories of my childhood and playing in that room with my dad," he told her, seemingly genuinely hurt by her disbelief. "Don't judge me."

Neba held her hands up. "No, hey, whatever you say. I just, I dunno, thought it would be something a little more... fancy."

Obedell looked at the board, then back at her. "It came from a fancy house."

"Yeah, I'm done," she groaned. "Come on. I got a cab waiting."

"May I ask where we're going?" he pressed, not moving.

She looked back over her shoulder. "Someplace you'll be comfortable, nobody will think to look for you and you'll be protected by the best security in the city."

He considered that moment. "Is it posh? I like posh."

"Yeah, I remember," she sighed. "It's posh."

"Sweet," the Lich grinned. "Best of all, there's no Max Wonder around to mess it up."

"Yeah," Neba said as she guided him through the theater, a dark smile on her face. "No Wonders around here."

Acknowledgements

Many thanks to Chicky, Jim, and Wendy, without whom this book never would have happened.

Chicky and Jim, thanks for letting me bounce (sometimes literally) ideas off of you during the planning stage and occasionally during the writing process. You guys rock!

Wendy, Editor Extraordinaire and Queen of the Turtle People (inside joke), thank you for taking this goofy idea that I was going to toss at Kindle to see if it stuck, and making it into something real. So, yeah, thank you.

My deepest thanks to AC/DC, for being the band that rocked my youth, inspired me as a writer, shaped my voice, and continues to influence me every day of my life. Shoot to Thrill!

9 780960 050529